Food for thought —
Sue & Charles

The
OUTDOOR
Guide to
BRITAIN

National Parks · Nature Reserves · Zoos · Safari Parks

JOHN GOODERS

MICHAEL JOSEPH

Published in this revised and illustrated edition in 1989 by
Webb & Bower (Publishers) Limited
9 Colleton Crescent, Exeter, Devon EX2 4BY
in association with Michael Joseph Limited
27 Wright's Lane, London W8 5TZ

First published in Great Britain 1979 as
A Day in the Country by André Deutsch Limited
105 Great Russell Street, London WC1B 3LJ

Penguin Books Ltd, Registered Offices: Harmondsworth, Middlesex, England
Viking Penguin Inc, 40 West 23rd Street, New York, New York 10010, USA
Penguin Books Australia Ltd, Ringwood, Victoria, Australia
Penguin Books Canada Ltd, 2801 John Street, Markham, Ontario, Canada L3R 1DA
Penguin Books (NZ) Ltd, 182-190 Wairau Road, Auckland 10, New Zealand

Designed by Ron Pickless

Production by Nick Facer/Rob Kendrew

Picture Research by Anne-Marie Ehrlich/Hugh Olliss

Maps by Malcolm Couch

Text Copyright © 1979, 1988 John Gooders

British Library Cataloguing in Publication Data
Gooders, John, 1937–
    The outdoor guide to Britain.——Rev. ed.
    1. Great Britain. Organisms. Observation.
    Sites — Directories
    I. Title II. Gooders, John, 1937– Day
    in the country
ISBN 0–86350–202–4

Typeset in Great Britain by
J&L Composition Ltd, Filey, North Yorkshire

Printed and bound in Hong Kong

CONTENTS

INTRODUCTION

The function of *The Outdoor Guide to Britain* is simple – to pick out those areas where people who wish to can enjoy our countryside and the natural life that lives there, and to make their visits as straightforward and as pleasurable as possible. Such a task is not without its problems. Masses of people can damage fragile plant communities, disturb birds and mammals and destroy what they came to see. Many 'delicate' natural history sites have been omitted on this score, but I have worked on the assumption that visitors (and plenty of them) should be allowed unless a good reason could be found for not doing so. This is a guide to places where you can get a breath of fresh air and see wildlife in its many forms. Of course you can see wildlife anywhere – in city centres, sewage farms, on municipal rubbish dumps and so on. But this is a guide to wildlife, where the enjoyment of the surroundings is as important as the animals and plants themselves.

Wildlife is not confined to the countryside. Many animals live in zoos and parks in captive conditions that are far from their normal homes. Yet they are wildlife, are worth seeing, and give us just a taste of the unattainable wild country that we shall never be able to visit.

So this guide is a mixture, but hopefully one that will enable those with an interest in wild animals and plants to find somewhere handy to visit, and give those with no interest whatsoever the opportunity to expose themselves to the risk of being fascinated. There are nature trails through forest and marsh; safari parks where, with a little imagination, you could be on safari in deepest Africa; zoos with rare and strange animals from around the world; bird reserves with Britain's rarest wild animals; sea cliffs teeming with birds that are the envy of the rest of Europe; and quiet country walks where you may see much or little depending on your skill as an observer.

In Part One there are all of the reserves of the major national bodies, whether or not they can be visited, together with notes on conservation and the Country Code. In Part Two those places and areas able to cope with visitors and where there is something positive for

the visitor to see are detailed. The choice of such places is entirely personal, as indeed is the choice of places throughout this guide. As the boom in conservation effort and interest in our countryside develops, more and more prime wildlife areas are brought into the nature reserve system. Many such reserves are small, unwardened and unable to provide the necessary supervision and facilities for visitors, but progressively more are being opened up so that people can enjoy them.

The wildlife areas that are described at length can all be visited fairly easily – they vary from the open-to-all-for-free to the book-ahead-permit-only system. Details of access and what to look for are provided for each, with a checklist of species of main interest.

The major specialities of each reserve are indicated by symbols. Thus a sandpiper, a daisy, a deer and a butterfly signify the particular attractions of birds, flowers, mammals and insects respectively in each reserve or area. The absence of a symbol does not indicate a total absence of the life form, simply that there is no subject of special attraction. Anthony Chapman of the Royal Society for the Protection of Birds has kindly advised me on access to nature reserves by the physically disabled. In areas where access by wheelchair is practical, a symbol is given next to the place name. This does not mean that the disabled cannot enjoy other areas – from the windows of a car, for instance. The symbols are as follows:

The Law of trespass is remarkably ancient and remarkably vague. By and large, access to the countryside is restricted, and all users of this guide would be well advised to check access before entering any area. In all cases visitors should respect the Country Code detailed in Part One. Nothing is more likely to restrict our enjoyment of the British countryside than the misuse of privilege where it has been granted. Read the Country Code, obey it to the letter, and then perhaps we can all go on enjoying ourselves in the country.

JOHN GOODERS

PART ONE:
NATIONWIDE

PART ONE
CONTENTS

NATIONAL PARKS

The National Parks were established in the 1960s by what has since become the Countryside Commission. There are ten Parks in all, covering over 5000 square miles of some of the most splendid countryside in Britain. Yet the land itself remains in private hands, and visitors have no more right of access than they do elsewhere in the countryside. This apparent contradiction may lead some to question the validity of the National Park system, while others may simply wonder what is the point. However the Countryside Commission has the function of maintaining and improving the landscape of the Parks and encouraging visitors by supplying information and improving access. This it has successfully achieved by negotiating considerably improved access in many areas. The fact that an area is a National Park may facilitate its defence against intrusive development, but it is doubtful whether any regulations or agreements would, in the long term, prevent economic exploration and production of oil, copper, coal or what have you.

To the visitor from overseas the National Park system is particularly strange. He is used to such Parks being lonely wilderness areas devoid of permanent human habitation and often full of wildlife. The United Nations have laid down a set of rules that govern the declaration of an area as a National Park. Not surprisingly no British Parks are included in their official list. No, we British have once more defined the terms in our own way and for our own purposes. Who is to say that we are wrong to do so?

For convenience a list follows:

	area in square miles
Brecon Beacons	524
Dartmoor	365
Exmoor	265
Lake District	866
Northumberland	398
Peak District	542
Pembrokeshire Coast	225
Snowdonia	838
North York Moors	553
Yorkshire Dales	680

Postbridge on the East Dart River in Dartmoor National Park

NATIONAL PARKS AND LONG DISTANCE ROUTES

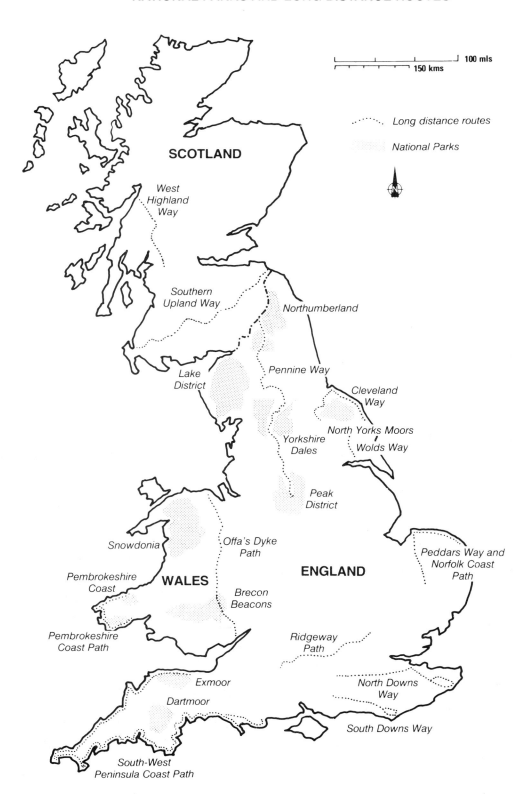

100 mls
150 kms

.... Long distance routes

National Parks

SCOTLAND

West Highland Way

Southern Upland Way

Northumberland

Lake District

Pennine Way

Cleveland Way

North Yorks Moors

Yorkshire Dales

Wolds Way

Peak District

Snowdonia

Offa's Dyke Path

Pembrokeshire Coast

WALES

ENGLAND

Peddars Way and Norfolk Coast Path

Pembrokeshire Coast Path

Brecon Beacons

Ridgeway Path

Exmoor

North Downs Way

Dartmoor

South Downs Way

South-West Peninsula Coast Path

NATIONAL LONG DISTANCE ROUTES

Several of the Long Distance Routes are included in the main body of this book, not because visitors are recommended to walk their entire length but because of the splendid countryside through which they pass and the access they give to many areas of wildlife interest. The idea of such routes is excellent, and the Countryside Commission is performing a valuable function in their establishment. Unfortunately many other footpaths and rights of way are disappearing from our countryside, mainly it must be said from lack of use, which is partly the result of automobilization. A footpath kept open by country people for generations soon disappears when the car makes the short-cut redundant. Yet as more and more people seek relaxation in the countryside they are progressively hard put to

locate the very walks that they could legally use. Local people know (or knew) where the footpaths were. The visitor not only lacks this local knowledge but finds it almost impossible to locate rights of way where they do exist. There are few signposts or marks, and even where such signs are found the paths themselves often disappear. In contrast the Long Distance Routes are in the main well marked, and publicity ensures that continued usage keeps them open. A full list follows:

1 *Pennine Way* (250 miles). A hill walk from Edale in Derbyshire along the Pennines and over the Cheviots to the Scottish Border.

Walkers are rewarded by the sight of choughs and Atlantic grey seals which breed at Pwllderi on the Pembrokeshire coast

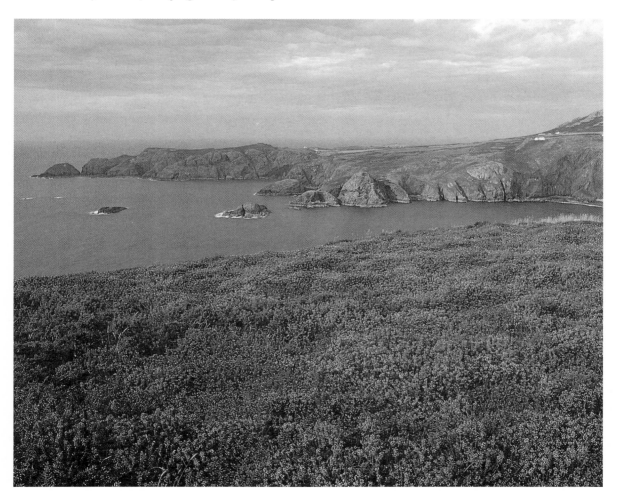

11

2 *Cleveland Way* (93 miles). Over the North York Moors and the Cleveland Hills from Helmsley to Saltburn and thence along the coast to Filey.

3 *Wolds Way* (79 miles). From Hull to join the Cleveland Way at Filey through pretty lowland dales.

4 *Pembrokeshire Coast Path* (180 miles). From Amroth to St Dogmaels, almost entirely within the Pembrokeshire Coast National Park.

5 *Offa's Dyke Path* (168 miles). From the Severn to Prestatyn, running through the borders of England and Wales.

6 *South Downs Way* (80 miles). From Beachy Head to the Hampshire boundary. The first long distance bridleway to be created it caters for riders and cyclists as well as walkers.

7 *South-West Peninsula Coast Path* (515 miles). Extends along the coast from Minehead in Somerset to Studland in Dorset. This is the longest of all the routes.

8 *Ridgeway Path* (85 miles). From Ivinghoe Beacon in Buckinghamshire to Overton Hill, near Avebury in Wiltshire, within the Chilterns and North Wessex Downs Areas of Outstanding Natural Beauty. The western section is open to riders and cyclists as well as walkers.

9 *North Downs Way* (141 miles). From Farnham in Surrey to Dover in Kent it follows or runs parallel to the Pilgrims' Way over part of its length.

10 *Peddars Way* and *Norfolk Coastal Path* (93 miles). From the Suffolk border to Holme at the corner of The Wash, then eastwards to Cromer along the coast.

11 *Southern Upland Way* (212 miles). Extends from Portpatrick in the west to Cockburnspath in the East, that is from the Atlantic to the North Sea via some of the most remote country in Britain.

12 *West Highland Way* (95 miles). From Milngavie, just north of Glasgow, to Fort William and Ben Nevis via Loch Lomond.

The British Tourist Authority publish a handy little leaflet called *Walking in Britain* that details these and other long walking routes. This is a useful source of local addresses from which details of accommodation along the way can be obtained. Write to: BTA, Thames Tower, Black's Road, London W6 9EL.

HERITAGE COASTS

The despoilation and development of our coastlines was completely out of hand soon after the last war. A rash of bungalow development threatened huge areas of coastline, while caravan parks sprang up willy-nilly everywhere. Clearly something had to be done and the Countryside Commission, aided by various public and private bodies, has declared some of the most spectacular coastal scenery to be Heritage Coasts. Such declaration has severely restricted development and, in some cases, led to enforced closure of caravan sites and even building destruction. Heritage Coasts are shown on the map opposite.

AREAS OF OUTSTANDING NATURAL BEAUTY

Thirty-two areas of Britain have been declared to be Areas of Outstanding Natural Beauty (AONB). They vary in size from the tiny Dedham Vale (22 square miles), on the Essex-Suffolk border, to the North Wessex Downs (676 square miles). Such a declaration makes little difference to the would-be visitor, who is as free to visit as he would be anywhere else in the countryside, i.e., not at all apart from rights of way. So two significant questions arise. First, what is the point? Second, how do such areas differ from National Parks? Taking the second first: the difference seems to be that National Parks are administered centrally by the government and aim to encourage recreation and access, whereas AONBs are locally administered to no public advantage. What then is the point? Here the answer seems to be that being declared an AONB confers a certain amount of protection to an area when it comes to planning development. A list follows.

	area in square miles
Anglesey	83
Arnside and Silverdale	29

Cannock Chase	26
Chichester Harbour	29
Chilterns	309
Clwydian Range	60
Cornwall and Camel Estuary	360
Cotswolds	582
Cranborne Chase and West Wiltshire Downs	371
Dedham Vale	22
Dorset	400
East Devon	103
East Hampshire	151
Forest of Bowland	310
Gower	73
High Weald	560
Isles of Scilly	6
Isle of Wight	73
Kent Downs	326
Lincolnshire Wolds	216
Lleyn	60
Malvern Hills	40
Mendip Hills	78
Norfolk Coast	174
North Devon	66
Northumberland Coast	50
North Wessex Downs	676
Quantock Hills	38
Shropshire Hills	300
Solway Coast	41
South Devon	128
South Hampshire Coast	30
Suffolk Coast and Heaths	151
Surrey Hills	160
Sussex Downs	379
Wye Valley	125

HERITAGE COASTS AND AREAS OF OUTSTANDING NATURAL BEAUTY

Heritage Coasts

Areas of Outstanding Natural Beauty

*   To become South Cornwall when completely defined.

30 mls
50 kms

COUNTRY PARKS

Country Parks are areas where people may relax and enjoy themselves, study natural history, walk and explore and generally be at home in the countryside. There are about two hundred recognized by the Countryside Commission, often located near large towns, and in general they are open throughout the year and offer parking, toilet and other facilities. Some have nature trails, wardens and information centres, though there is much variation. Entry to some is subject to a charge and some charge a parking fee. The vast majority are administered by the local authority, though some belong to the National Trust and others still are in private hands. A list follows:

LOCAL AUTHORITY PROJECTS

1 The Wirral
2 Elvaston Castle
3 Barton Farm
4 Beacon Fell
5 Normanby Hall
6 Emberton Park
7 Keynes Park, Cotswold Water Park
8 Pow Hill
9 Sherwood Forest
10 Bradgate Park and Swithland Woods
11 Bayhurst Wood
12 Berry Head
13 Yateley Common
14 Worsbrough Mill
15 Upper Hamble
16 Farley Mount
17 Padarn
18 Burton Dassett Hills
19 Etherow
20 Camer Park
21 Tandle Hill Park
22 Waseley Hills
23 Holme Pierrepont
24 Clare Castle
25 Kingsford
26 Seven Sisters
27 Eastham Woods
28 Black Park
29 Coombe Abbey
30 Robinswood Hill
31 Fort Victoria
32 Aldenham Reservoir
33 Frensham Common
34 Weald Park
35 Tredegar House
36 Llys-y-fran Reservoir
37 Talkin Tarn
38 Highgate Common

39 Parc Cefn Onn
40 Cannon Hall Park
41 Great Wood
42 Thorndon Park
43 Langley Park
44 Hainault Forest
45 Lickey Hills
46 Bolam Lake
47 Penistone Hill
48 Irchester
49 Porthkerry Park
50 Stockgrove Park
51 Hastings
52 Snelsmore Common
53 Trent Park
54 Lyme Park
55 Afan Argoed
56 Curworth Park
57 Derwent Walk
58 Shipley
59 Cannock Chase
60 Rufford
61 Waun-y-llyn
62 Tatton Park
63 Bardsea
64 Hardwick Hall, Durham
65 Danbury Park
66 Queen Elizabeth
67 Plessey Woods
68 Greenway Bank
69 Jumbles Reservoir
70 Barbury Castle
71 Durlston
72 Kingsbury
73 Brandon Park
74 Manor Park
75 Battlefield of Bosworth
76 Lightwater

77 Dare Valley
78 Westley Heights
79 One Tree Hill
80 Burntstump
81 Lepe & Calshot Foreshores
82 Tegg's Nose
83 Crickley Hill
84 Moel Famau
85 Loggerheads
86 Craig-y-nos
87 Colemere
88 Witton Park
89 Ditchling Common
90 Ham Hill
91 Mount Edgcumbe
92 Horton
93 Cosmeston Lakes
94 Caldicot Castle
95 Little Budworth Common
96 Marbury Park
97 Wycoller
98 Park Hall
99 Waldridge Fell
100 Pen-y-fan Pond
101 Marsh Farm
102 Forest Way
103 Newmillerdam
104 Trosley
105 Clent Hills
106 Hadleigh Castle
107 Wansbeck
108 Hollingworth Lake
109 Hartshill Hayes
110 Norsey Wood
111 Margam Park
112 Scolton Manor
113 Haigh Hall
114 Cudmore Grove

115 Eastcourt Meadows
116 Croxteth Park
117 Daisy Nook
118 Upton Park
119 Colwick
120 Hartsholme
121 Barnwell
122 Pembrey
123 Ferry Meadows
124 Daventry
125 Gelli Aur
126 West Stow
127 Queenswood
128 Knettishall Heath

129 Havering	139 Beacon Park	149 Baggeridge
130 Holt Woodlands	140 Buchan Park	150 Oakwell Hall
131 Bretton	141 East Carlton	153 Clyne Valley
132 Sandwell Valley	142 Priory Park Marina	152 Great Orme
133 Royal Victoria	143 Belhus Woods	153 Clyne Valley
134 Shotover	144 Tyne Green	154 Tilgate Forest Park
135 Dinton Pastures	145 Thrybergh	155 Chevin Forest Park
136 California	146 Rother Valley	156 Lotherton Hall
136 Werneth Low	147 Deep Hayes	157 Temple Newsam
138 Pennington Flash	148 Consall Nature Park°	158 Hunsbury Hill

159 Sywell Reservoir
160 Harrold-Odell
161 Capstone*
162 Nunnery Woods⅓*
163 Wanlip*
164 Woodgate Valley*
165 Brynbach⅓*
166 Bestwood*
167 Draycote Water*
168 Castle Hill*
169 Brigstock*
170 Tehidy Woods*
171 Grassmoor*
* New Sites
⅓ Not yet open to the public

EXISTING NON-PUBLIC PARK RECOGNIZED
BY THE COMMISSION (No grant aid)
  1 Suffolk Wildlife & Country Park

PROJECTS BY NON-PUBLIC BODIES
  1 Sandringham
  2 Knebworth
  3 Burton Constable
  4 Goodwood
  5 Fell Foot
  6 Weald & Downland Open Air Museum
  7 Box Hill
  8 Farway
  9 Cragside
10 Hardwick Hall, Derbyshire
11 Hatfield Forest
12 Robin Hill
13 Styal
14 Longshaw
15 Easton Farm Park
16 Clumber Park
17 Ilam
18 Broadway Tower
19 Wellington
20 Fritton Lake
21 Brimham Rocks
22 River Dart, Ashburton
23 Buxton and Poole's Cavern
24 Erddig Park
25 Dalemain
26 Lonely Farm Leisure Park
27 Mapledurham
28 Fountains Abbey, Studley Royal
29 Heights of Abraham*

NATIONAL NATURE RESERVES

The Nature Conservancy Council is responsible for the administration of National Nature Reserves. It is not, except in an unofficial consultancy capacity, concerned with private nature reserves, of which there are a considerable number owned and/or administered by a variety of conservation bodies in the UK. National Nature Reserves have been established throughout the country for a variety of purposes and for many differing reasons. In each, protection and conservation are of prime importance together, in some cases, with the opportunities provided for research. Though called 'National' Nature Reserves, this does not mean that the public have right of access.

The NCC has separate headquarters for England, Scotland and Wales, and within each country a network of regional offices responsible for the National Nature Reserves. The addresses follow, together with a complete list of National Nature Reserves. Details are given of the more interesting sites. Numbers refer to the map.

ENGLAND
Headquarters for England:
Northminster House
Peterborough PE1 IUA
0733 40345

EAST ANGLIA (Essex, Norfolk, Suffolk)
The Regional Officer for East Anglia, Nature Conservancy Council, 60 Bracondale, Norwich, Norfolk NR1 2BE
Tel. 0603 620558

Bure Marshes, Norfolk, consists mainly of unreclaimed fenland and includes four broads. The waterways contain fresh water and are noted for their abundance of plant, animal and bird life. The Hoveton Great Broad Nature Trail is open from the first Monday in May until mid-September and accessible by boat only. Admission includes a descriptive leaflet. A permit is required to visit other parts of the reserve. (1)
Hickling Broad, Norfolk, is a large shallow lake, surrounded by extensive reedswamp. The reserve is of outstanding importance for its populations of marsh birds, several of which are rare in Great Britain. The Norfolk Naturalists' Trust manage the reserve which is

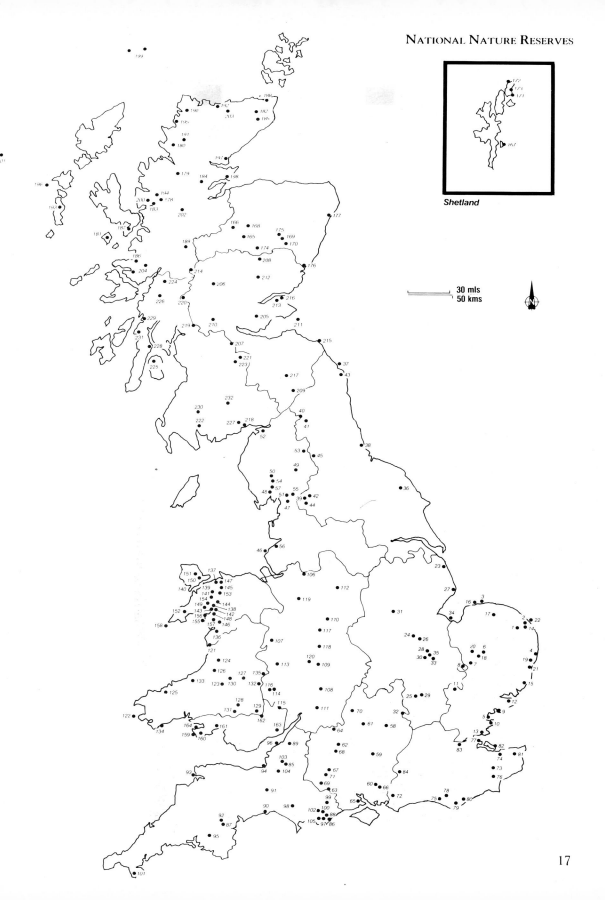

NATIONAL NATURE RESERVES

Shetland

30 mls
50 kms

N

17

open daily (April to November) to holders of permits obtained from the Warden's office, Stubb Road, Hickling, Norwich NR12 OBW. Tel. 069 261 276. Information about nature and water trails can also be obtained from the Warden. (2)

Holkham, Norfolk, covers fifteen square miles of the Norfolk coast between Overy Staithe and Blakeney. West of Wells, it consists mainly of sand dunes and reclaimed saltmarsh now used for agriculture, while to the east it includes one of the largest saltmarshes in England. There are also extensive intertidal sand- and mud-flats. It is managed by the Nature Conservancy Council in co-operation with the Holkham Estate, and is the largest coastal nature reserve in England. Access is open except for farmland. (3)

Other NNR in the region are:
Benacre, Suffolk, restricted access (4)
Blackwater Estuary, Essex, partially open (5)
Brettenham Heath, Norfolk, restricted access (6)
Cavenham Heath, Suffolk, restricted access except for nature trail (7)
Chippenham Fen, Cambridgeshire (partially open) (8)
Colne Estuary, Essex, partially open (9)
Dengie, Essex, partially open (10)
Hales Wood, Essex, restricted access (11)
Hamford Water, Essex, partially open (12)
Leigh, Essex, open access (13)
Ludham Marshes, Norfolk, partially open (14)
Orfordness-Havergate, Suffolk, open access except for Havergate Island, managed by the Royal Society for the Protection of Birds, which requires a RSPB permit (15)
Scolt Head Island, Norfolk, open access but some restrictions during bird breeding season (16)
Swanton Novers Woods, Norfolk, not open to the public (17)
Thetford Heath, Suffolk, restricted access (18)
Walberswick, Suffolk, partially open (19)
Weeting Heath, Norfolk, restricted access (20)
Westleton Heath, Suffolk, partially open (21)
Winterton Dunes, Norfolk, open access (22)

EAST MIDLANDS(Bedfordshire, Cambridgeshire, Hertfordshire, Leicestershire, Lincolnshire, Northamptonshire, Nottinghamshire)
The Regional Officer for the East Midlands, Nature Conservancy Council, Northminster House, Peterborough PE1 1UA
Tel.0733 40345

Saltfleetby-Theddlethorpe Dunes, Lincolnshire, have been formed by seven centuries of accumulation of material from the sea. A long depression between two prominent lines of dunes is poorly drained and forms a freshwater marsh. The Saltfleet Haven area at the northern end of the reserve is more sheltered, and here silt deposited by the tide has collected to form muddy saltings. This process and colonization by plants is continuing today and will change the appearance of the coastline in the future. There is open access to the reserve, but a large area of it lies within the danger zone of firing ranges. Visitors are therefore asked to comply with Royal Air Force Safety regulations as displayed at entrances to the reserve. Cars may be parked in a number of locations on the landward side of the reserve at Sea View Farm, Rimac, Coastguard Cottages, Old Brickworks, Crook Bank and Saltfleet Haven. (23)

Other NNR in the region are:
Barnack Hills and Holes, Cambridgeshire, open access (24)
Barton Hills, Bedfordshire, open access (25)
Castor Hanglands, Cambridgeshire, partially open (26)
Chippenham Fen, Cambridgeshire (see East Anglia Region) (8)
Gibraltar Point, Lincolnshire, open access (27)
Holme Fen, Cambridgeshire, restricted access (28)
Knocking Hoe, Bedfordshire, access for research workers only (29)
Monks Wood, Cambridgeshire, restricted access (30)
Muston Meadows, Leicestershire, restricted access (31)
Tring Reservoirs, Hertfordshire, open access (32)
Upwood Meadows, Cambridgeshire, access for research workers only (33)
The Wash, Lincolnshire, restricted access (34)
Woodwalton Fen, Cambridgeshire, restricted access (35)

NORTH-EAST (Cleveland, Durham, Humberside, North Yorkshire, Northumberland, Tyne and Wear)
The Regional Officer for North-East England, Nature Conservancy Council, Archbold House, Archbold Terrace, Newcastle-upon-Tyne NE2 1EG
Tel. 091 2816316

Forge Valley Woods, North Yorkshire, despite human interference, retains many of the features which characterised the prehistoric forests of the area. An iron industry was established here in the thirteenth century which led to the felling of native trees and the introduction of sycamore to supply timber for the smelting process. A woodland walk has been established to show the various features of this semi-natural woodland. (36)

Lindisfarne, Northumberland, comprises some of the best examples of dune saltmarsh and mudflat habitats in Britain whilst the flocks of ducks, geese, swans and waders which frequent the area, particularly in winter, make it a site of international importance. No permit is required to visit the reserve but visitors should check the time when the island is accessible. (37)

Other NNR in the region are:
Castle Eden Dene, Durham, open access (38)
Colt Park Wood, North Yorkshire, restricted access (39)
Coom Rigg Moss, Northumberland, restricted access (40)
Grain Heads Moss, Northumberland, restricted access (41)
Ling Gill, North Yorkshire, open access (42)
Newham Bog, Northumberland, restricted access (43)
Scar Close, North Yorkshire, restricted access (44)
Upper Teesdale, Durham, partially open (45)

NORTH-WEST (Cumbria, Greater Manchester, Lancashire, Merseyside, South Yorkshire, West Yorkshire)
The Regional Officer for North-West England, Nature Conservancy Council, Blackwell, Bowness on Windermere, Windermere, Cumbria LA23 3JR
Tel. 096 62 5286

Ainsdale Sand Dunes, Merseyside, is the finest example of a sand dune system on the north-west coast. It consists of two square miles of foreshore, dunes, slacks and woodland. Since the end of the eighteenth century this diverse area has been famous for its variety of plants and animals. The pinewood, planted earlier in the century to stabilize mobile sand, is managed to improve the wildlife habitat. A series of descriptive leaflets is available. A system of concessionary pathways together with rights of way are open to the public. (46)

Gait Barrows, North Lancashire, contains the most important single example in Great Britain of low level limestone pavement. The pavements are surrounded by a woodland of mixed native trees and shrubs, yew being the dominant species. The reserve also includes the small tarn of Little Haweswater. It was declared on 31st May 1977 to commemorate the Silver Jubilee of

Her Majesty Queen Elizabeth II. A permit is required away from the public right of way. (47)

Roudsea Woods and Mosses, South Cumbria, lying on the eastern flank of the Leven Estuary, this low level woodland and surrounding raised sphagnum bogs contain a number of diverse habitats. Limestone and slate outcrops support rich and characteristic native woodland, flora and fauna. The reserve has been subject to intense management for over twenty years converting coppice back to high forest. A permit is required. (48)

Other NNR in the region are:
Asby Scar, Cumbria, partially open (49)
Blelham Bog, Cumbria, restricted access (50)
Clawthorpe Fell, Cumbria, restricted access (51)
Glasson Moss, Cumbria, restricted access (52)
Moor House, Cumbria, partially open (53)
North Fen, Cumbria, restricted access (54)
Park Wood, Cumbria, partially open (55)
Ribble Marshes, Lancashire/Merseyside, restricted access (56)
Rusland Moss, Cumbria, restricted access (57)

SOUTH (Berkshire, Buckinghamshire, Hampshire, Isle of Wight, Oxfordshire, Wiltshire)
The Regional Officer for South England, Nature Conservancy Council, Foxhold House, Thornford Road, Crookham Common, Newbury, Berkshire RG15 8EL
Tel. 063523 8881

Aston Rowant, Oxfordshire, comprises an attractive stretch of the Chiltern escarpment. The 321 acres encompass fine examples of the semi-natural habitats characteristic of the Chiltern Hills, particularly beech woodland, mixed and juniper scrub and grazed chalk grassland. There is an unmanned display and a nature trail. (58)

Other NNR in the region are:
Ashford Hill, Hampshire, restricted access (59)
Beacon Hill, Hampshire, restricted access (60)
Cothill, Oxfordshire, restricted access (61)
Fyfield Down, Wiltshire, partially open (62)
Martin Down, Hampshire, partially open (63)
North Meadow, Cricklade, Wiltshire, partially open (64)
North Solent, Hampshire, partially open (65)
Old Winchester Hill, Hampshire, partially open (66)

Parsonage Down, Wiltshire, restricted access (67)
Pewsey Downs, Wiltshire, partially open (68)
Prescombe Down, Wiltshire, restricted access (69)
Wychwood, Oxfordshire, permit required but access for research only (70)
Wylye Down, Wiltshire, restricted access (71)

SOUTH-EAST (East Sussex, Greater London, Kent, Surrey, West Sussex)

The Regional Officer for South-East England, Nature Conservancy Council, 'Zealds', Church Street, Wye, Ashford, Kent TN25 5BW
Tel. 0233 812525

Kingley Vale, West Sussex, was established principally to maintain what has been described as the finest natural yew forest in Europe. It also includes a wide variety of other plants and animal communities. During the summer there is a manned display/information centre open on Sundays and a nature trail. (72)

Wye, Kent, was established primarily to maintain one of the best remaining examples of Kent chalk downland rich in wild flowers and insects – a habitat which is declining rapidly as a result of modern farming methods. During the summer there is a manned display/information centre open on Sundays and a nature trail. (73)

Other NNR in the region are:

Blean Woods, Kent, partially open (74)
Castle Hill, East Sussex, partially open (75)
Ham Street Woods, Kent, partially open (76)
High Halstow, Kent, partially open (77)
Lewes Downs, East Sussex, partially open (78)
Lullington Heath, East Sussex, partially open (79)
Pevensey Levels, East Sussex, restricted access (80)
Stodmarsh, Kent, partially open (81)
The Swale, Kent, partially open (82)
Swanscombe Skull Site, Kent, restricted access (83)
Thursley, Surrey, open access (84)

SOUTH-WEST (Avon, Cornwall, Devon, Dorset, Somerset)

The Regional Officer for South-West England, Nature Conservancy Council, Roughmoor, Bishops Hull, Taunton, Somerset TA1 5AA
Tel. 0823 283211

Ebbor Gorge, Somerset, includes a fine example of a Mendip Valley carved out of the limestone by an ancient river. There are marked walks, an unmanned display and a general leaflet. Also, a short nature trail is particularly designed for the wheelchair disabled (leaflet available). (85)

Studland Heath, Dorset, contains a wide variety of habitats including sand-dunes, heathland, woods, boggy ground and a lake. There are two nature trails and an observation hut open at weekends. There is unrestricted access on foot and on public bridleway. (86)

Yarner Wood, Devon, is managed to conserve examples of Dartmoor woodland habitats. There is a nature trail and a woodland walk, also an unmanned display. (87)

Other NNR in the region are:

Arne, Dorset, restricted access (88)
Avon Gorge, Avon, open access (89)
Axmouth–Lyme Regis Undercliffs, Devon, partially open (90)
Barrington Hill, Somerset, restricted access (91)
Bovey Valley Woodlands, Devon, partially open (92)
Braunton Burrows, Devon, open access (93)
Bridgewater Bay, Somerset, partially open (94)
Dendles Wood, Devon, restricted access (95)
Gordano Valley, Avon, partially open (96)
Hartland Moor, Dorset, partially open (97)
Hog Cliff, Dorset, permit required (98)
Holt Heath, Dorset, partially open (99)
Holton Heath, Dorset, restricted access (100)
The Lizard, Cornwall, partially open (101)
Morden Bog, Dorset, restricted access (102)
Rodney Stoke, Somerset, partially open (103)
Shapwick Heath, Somerset, restricted access (104)
Stoborough Heath, Dorset, restricted access (105)

WEST MIDLANDS (Cheshire, Derbyshire, Gloucestershire, Hereford & Worcester, Peak District National Park, Shropshire, Staffordshire, Warwickshire, West Midlands)

The Regional Officer for the West Midlands, Nature Conservancy Council, Attingham Park, Shrewsbury, Shropshire SY4 4TW
Tel. 074377 611

Rostherne Mere, Cheshire, is a deep lowland lake of outstanding importance for wildfowl and is used for research in fresh-water ecology. The main purpose of the reserve is to provide an undisturbed refuge for waterfowl so public access is not possible. However, a bird observatory provides a wide view of the Mere. (Permits from the Manchester Ornithological Society, 13 Kingston Drive, Sale, Cheshire M33 2FS.) (106)

The Stiperstones, Shropshire, is the most important of the Shropshire Hills for wildlife with upland birds such as merlin, raven and red grouse. Geologically, the Stiperstones is important for its extensive exposures of Mytton Flags, Tankerville Flags and Stiperstones Quartzite. The latter forms the ridge itself and the impressive tors. The Mytton and Tankerville Flags are the source of the vein minerals, mainly lead and barytes, on which the local mining industry was based. Access on foot is possible by several routes, and there is a car park at the southern end of the site. (107)

Other NNR in the region are:
Bredon Hill, Hereford and Worcester, restricted access (108)
Chaddesley Woods, Hereford and Worcester, partially open (109)
Chartley Moss, Staffordshire, permit required (110)
Cotswold Commons and Beechwoods, Gloucestershire, part formerly Workmans Wood: partially open (111)
Derbyshire Dales, Derbyshire, partially open (112)
Downton Gorge, Hereford and Worcester, permit required (113)
The Flits, Hereford and Worcester, restricted access (114)
Lady Park Wood, Gloucestershire/Gwent, partially open (115)
Moccas Park, Hereford and Worcester, permit required (116)
Mottey Meadows, Staffordshire, permit required (117)
Wren's Nest, West Midlands, open access (118)
Wybunbury Moss, Cheshire, permit required (119)
Wyre Forest, Hereford and Worcester, open access (120)

WALES

DYFED/POWYS
The Regional Officer for Dyfed/Powys, Nature Conservancy Council, Plas Gogerddan, Aberystwyth, Dyfed SY23 3EB
Tel. 0970 828551

Dyfi, Dyfed (Ceredigion), has three main components – a river estuary, a dune system and a raised bog. The estuary is the most important station for wildfowl and migrant waders in Cardigan Bay. The dunes form an important part of the estuarine complex and have great botanic interest. The raised bog, Cors Fochno, although subjected to extensive reclamation around its margins, is one of the most extensive tracts of unmodified raised bog vegetation in Great Britain. There is unrestricted public access on foot into the Ynyslas section, but a charge is made for parking cars on the edge of the dunes in the spring and summer. The Reserve Warden may be contacted at the Aberystwyth Office, or at his home address, Llwyn Awel, Talybont, Aberystwyth. Tel. 097 086 485. (121)

Skomer, Dyfed (Preseli), is the home of many birds which include Manx shearwater (the most numerous), storm petrel, fulmar, puffin, razorbill, kittiwake and guillemot. Grey seals are present around Skomer at all times of the year and it is the second most important breeding site in the south-west. There is a landing fee for visitors. (122)

Other NNR in the region are:
Allt Rhyd y Groes, Dyfed (Carmarthen), partially open (123)
Coed Rheidol, Dyfed (Ceredigion), partially open (124)
Coed Ty Canol, Dyfed (Preseli), partially open (125)
Cors Caron, Dyfed (Ceredigion), partially open (126)
Cors y Llyn, Powys (Radnor) (127)
Craig Cerrig-gleisiad, Powys (Brecknock), partially open (128)
Craig y Cilau, Powys (Brecknock), partially open (129)
Nant Irfon, Powys (Brecknock), restricted access (130)
Ogof Ffynnon Ddu, Powys (Brecknock), partially open (131)
Rhos Goch, Powys (Radnor), (132)
Rhos Llawr Cwrt, Dyfed (Preseli), restricted access (133)
Stackpole, Dyfed (South Pembrokeshire), partially open (134)
Stanner Rocks, Powys (Radnor), partially open (135)

NORTH WALES (Clwyd, Gwynedd)
The Regional Officer for North Wales, Nature Conservancy Council, Plas Penrhos, Ffordd Penrhos, Bangor, Gwynedd LL57, 2LQ
Tel. 0248 370444

Cadair Idris, Gwynedd (Meirionnydd), is situated about two miles south of Dolgellau. This reserve is of great interest to geologists for its Ordovician lavas and ashes in which there is a band of igneous rocks

Skomer Island, a haven for many seabirds including Manx shearwater, puffin and guillemot

together with fossil-bearing mudstones and slates. Cadair Idris is one of the most southern areas in Britain for Arctic-Alpine plants. (136)

Coedydd Aber, Gwynedd (Arfon), is four miles east of Bangor. The reserve includes the wooded valley from Aber village to the falls (Rhaeadr Fawr). There is a wide variety of woodland and open habitats in the valley, and consequently it is rich in birds. It has a good bryophyte (moss or liverwort) flora. There is a display/information centre. (137)

Coedydd Maentwrog, Gwynedd (Meirionnydd), is on the northern slopes of the Vale of Ffestiniog near Maentwrog. This reserve of oak woodland has a ground cover of bracken and thus contrasts strongly with the north-facing Coed Camlyn on the other side of the valley which is carpeted with bilberry. There is a nature trail. (138)

Cwm Idwal, Gwynedd (Aberconwy and Arfon), situated five miles west of Capel Curig. It is a natural amphitheatre of Ordovician rocks, both volcanic and sedimentary, rising to above 3,200 feet. Llyn Idwal lies in the bowl at 1,223 feet above sea level. There is an outstanding Arctic-Alpine flora, a remnant of the period immediately after the last Ice Age. There is a nature trail. (139)

Newborough Warren/Ynys Llanddwyn, Gwynedd (Ynys Mon), is located on the southern extremity of Anglesey, and is one of the largest and biologically richest expanses of sand-dunes in western Britain and the finest of its type in Wales. All stages of plant colonization and succession from beach zone to fixed dune grassland are well represented and there is a great variety of ecological zones and habitats around the edge. The reserve includes parts of two estuaries and the peninsula of Ynys Llanddwyn. This has a varied flora and, like the rest of the reserve, is of considerable interest to ornithologists. The main features of the reserve are visible from the public rights of way but a permit is necessary away from these. (140)

Y Wyddfa – Snowdon, Gwynedd (Dwyfor), nine miles south of Bangor, is the largest reserve in Wales, ranging from the oak woods near Llyn Dinas at 176 feet above sea level to the main Arctic-Alpine plant communities on the calcareous cliffs and the windswept sub-Arctic heath of the exposed summits at over 3,000 feet. There are two nature trails. (141)

Other NNR in the region are:
Ceunant Llennyrch, Gwynedd, partially open (142)
Coed Camlyn, Gwynedd (Meirionnydd), restricted access (143)
Coed Cymerau, Gwynedd (Meirionnydd), partially open (144)
Coed Dolgarrog, Gwynedd (Aberconwy), partially open (145)
Coed Ganllwyd, Gwynedd (Meirionnydd), partially open (146)
Coed Gorswen, Gwynedd (Aberconwy), partially open (147)
Coed y Rhygen, Gwynedd (Meirionnydd), restricted access (148)
Coed Tremadoc, Gwynedd (Dwyfor), completely closed (149)
Cors Bodeilio, Gwynedd (Ynys Mon), restricted access (150)
Cors Erddreiniog, Gwynedd (Ynys Mon), restricted access (151)

Cors Geirch, Gwynedd (Dwyfor), restricted access (152)
Cwm Glas Crafnant, Gwynedd (Aberconwy), restricted access (153)
Haffod Garnegog, Gwynedd, restricted access (154)
Morfa Dyffryn, Gwynedd (Meirionnydd), partially open (155)
Morfa Harlech, Gwynedd (Meirionnydd), restricted access (156)
Rhinog, Gwynedd (Meirionnydd), open access (157)
Ynys Enlli/Bardsey Island, Gwynedd (Dwyfor) partially open (158)

SOUTH WALES (Gwent, Mid-Glamorgan, South Glamorgan, West Glamorgan)

The Regional Officer for South Wales, Nature Conservancy Council, 44 The Parade, Roath, Cardiff CF2 3AB
Tel. 0222 485111

The *Gower Peninsula* is rich in plant and animal life, and with many important geological features. A number of reserves have been established in South Gower to safeguard these special qualities. These reserves consist of rocky shores and limestone cliffs stretching for almost six miles from Rhossili to Port-Eynon in the south-west corner of Gower. The tidal island of Worms Head and two parts of the mainland cliffs comprise the Gower Coast National Nature Reserve. A leaflet *South Gower Coast Nature Reserves* gives details of access. (159)

Oxwich, West Glamorgan (Swansea), is an unspoilt piece of Gower countryside with a great variety of different habitats. The two-mile long sandy beach of Oxwich Bay ends in a rocky shore around the exposed headland of Oxwich Point. A small saltmarsh lies behind the northern end of the dunes, which together enclose a large freshwater marsh with several fresh-water pools. There is a manned display and information centre. The reserve has a general leaflet and two nature trail leaflets. (160)

Other NNR in the region are:
Crymlyn Bog, West Glamorgan, restricted access (161)
Cwm Clydach, Gwent (Blaenau), partially open (162)
Penhow Wood, Gwent (Newport), restricted access (163)
Whiteford, West Glamorgan (Swansea), partially open (164)

SCOTLAND

NORTH-EAST SCOTLAND

The Regional Officer for the North-East, Nature Conservancy Council, Wynne-Edwards House, 17 Rubislaw Terrace, Aberdeen, AB1 1XE
Tel. 0224 572863

Cairngorms, Highland and Grampian Regions, is the largest NNR in Britain (100 square miles). Glacial action has carved out many high corries, some of which contain arctic-alpine lochs, and has left extensive sand and gravel deposits on the lower slopes. The summit represents the largest area of high ground in Britain; the Arctic-Alpine communities of plateau, cliff and scree lead down into extensive moorland, bog and mire at lower levels. The flora is characteristic of acid soils. The fauna includes a wide range of species typical of the Scottish Highlands; red deer is the largest mammal and ptarmigan one of the commonest birds of the high tops. Access to the reserve is unrestricted, but visitors are asked to co-operate with the Nature Conservancy Council and estates during August, September and October when deer culling may be taking place. A visitor centre and nature trail are located at Loch-an-Eilein. (165)

Craigellachie, Highland Region (Badenoch and Strathspey District), situated immediately to the west of Aviemore, contains one of the largest birchwoods in the Spey Valley and open moorlands rising to 1,700 feet. Ornithological and entomological interest is considerable. (166)

Noss, Shetland. This island reserve is situated four miles east of Lerwick and with its great sandstone cliffs is one of the most spectacular seabird colonies. Guillemot, kittiwake and gannet breed as well as a wide variety of other seabirds. A ferry service to the island, where there is a visitor centre, is operated across Noss Sound by the NCC during the summer. (167)

Other NNR in the region are:

Abernethy Forest, Highland Region (Badenoch and Strathspey District), partially open (168)

Dinnet Oakwood, Grampian Region (Kincardine & Deeside District), restricted access (169)

Glen Tanar, Grampian Region (Kincardine & Deeside District), partially open (170)

Haaf Gruney, Shetland Islands, open access (171)

Hermaness, Shetland Islands, open access (172)

Keen of Hamar, Shetland Islands, restricted access (173)

Morrone Birkwoods, Grampian Region (Kincardine & Deeside District), partially open (174)

Muir of Dinnet, Grampian Region (Kincardine & Deeside District), open access (175)

St Cyrus, Grampian Region (Kincardine & Deeside District), open access (176)

Sands of Forvie and Ythan Estuary, Grampian Region (Gordon District), partially open (177)

NORTH-WEST SCOTLAND

The Regional Officer for the North-West, Nature Conservancy Council, Fraser Darling House, 9 Culduthel Road, Inverness IV2 4AG
Tel. 0463 239431

Beinn Eighe, Highland Region (Ross and Cromarty District), is located twenty-four miles north east of Kyle of Lochalsh. The mountain slopes of Beinn Eighe are of great geological, physiographical and floristic interest. Visitors are recommended to contact the Warden for further information. There is a summer-manned display/information centre and two nature trails. A general reserve leaflet and two trail leaflets are available. (178)

Corrieshalloch Gorge, Highland Region (Ross and Cromarty District), adjoins the south side of the Garve-Ullapool Road just west of the road to Dundonnell at Braemore. About a mile long, the reserve is a magnificent example of a box-canyon, formed by the cutting back of a river (Abhainn Droma) through hard, horizontal rocks. The tree growth in the gorge walls is generally scanty and dwarfed, except for the upper levels. The plant communities are of much interest. (179)

Inverpolly, Highland Region (Ross and Cromarty District), is a wild, remote, almost uninhabited area on the north-west coast near the Sutherland border, which includes three summits over 2,000 feet and the whole of Loch Sionascaig. There is a great diversity of habitats: lochs, streams, bogs, moorland, woodland, screes, cliffs and summits. On the east boundary is the classic geological locality of Knockan Cliff. The reserve contains relatively untouched relics of primitive birch-hazel woodland and the fauna of the reserve is typical of the West Highlands. There is a summer-manned display/information centre and both a nature and a geological trail. (180)

Rhum, Highland Region (Lochaber District) is seven

miles south of Skye. Rhum is an outstanding area for geological and botanical research and for studying red deer. The reserve leaflet is also available in French, German and Spanish. There is a nature trail and leaflet. Permission is required to visit parts of the Reserve away from the Loch Scresort area. (181)

Other NNR in the region are:

Achanarras Quarry, Highland Region (Caithness District), open access but collecting by permit only, obtained from NCC, Golspie House, Bank Road, Golspie. Tel. 040 83 602 (182)

Allt Nan Carnan, Highland Region (Ross & Cromarty District), open access (183)

Ben Wyvis, Highland Region (Ross & Cromarty District), restricted access (184)

*Blarnam Faoileag, Highland Region (Caithness District), restricted access (185)

*Claish Moss, Highland Region (Lochaber District), restricted access (186)

Coille Thocabhaig, Highland Region (Skye & Lochalsh District), partially open (187)

Dunnet Links, Highland Region (Caithness District), restricted access (188)

Glen Roy, Highland Region (Lochaber District), open access (189)

Gualin, Highland Region (Sutherland District), restricted access (190)

Inchnadamph, Highland Region (Sutherland District), seasonal permit (191)

Invernaver, Highland Region (Sutherland District), open access (192)

Loch Druidibeg, Western Isles Islands Area (South Uist), partially open (193)

*Loch Maree Islands, Highland Region (Ross & Cromarty District), restricted access (194)

Loch a'Mhuillin Wood, Highland Region (Sutherland District), open access (195)

Red deer stags on the shore at Rhum

Monach Isles, Western Isles Islands Area, restricted access (196)

Mound Alderwoods, Highland Region (Sutherland District), partially open (197)

Nigg and Udale Bays, Highland Region (Ross & Cromarty District), open access (198)

*North Rona and Sula Sgeir, Western Isles Islands Area, restricted access (199)

Rassal Ashwood, Highland Region (Ross & Cromarty District), open access (200)

*St Kilda, Western Isles Islands Area, restricted access (201)

Strathfarrar, Highland Region (Inverness District), open access (202)

*Strathy Bogs, Highland Region (Sutherland District), open access (203)

*Sunart Woodlands, Highland Region (Lochaber District), includes Ariundle, declared 1977, open access (204)

*Reserve has no access roads or paths.

SOUTH-EAST SCOTLAND

The Regional Officer for the South-East, Nature Conservancy Council, Headquarters for Scotland, 12 Hope Terrace, Edinburgh EH9 2AS
Tel. 031 447 4784

Loch Leven, Tayside Region (Perth and Kinross District), is midway between the Firths of Tay and Forth. The loch is world famous for its trout fishing, and the most important freshwater area in Britain for migratory and breeding wildfowl. In autumn thousands of pink-footed geese and hundreds of greylag geese arrive at Loch Leven. Access is confined to Kirkgate Park, Findatie, Burleigh Sands and Loch Leven Castle. (205)

Other NNR in the region are:

Ben Lawers, Tayside Region (Perth & Kinross District), open access (206)

Blawhorn Moss, Lothian Region (West Lothian District), restricted access (207)

Caenlochan, Tayside Region (Angus, Perth & Kinross, Kincardine & Deeside Districts), restricted access (208)

Cragbank Wood, Borders Region (Roxburgh District), restricted access (209)

Flanders Moss, Central Region (Stirling District), restricted access (210)

Isle of May, Fife Region (North-East Fife District), open access (211)

Milton Wood, Tayside Region (Perth & Kinross District), restricted access (212)

Morton Lochs, Fife Region (North-East Fife District), restricted access (213)

Rannoch Moor, Tayside Region (Perth & Kinross District), restricted access (214)

St Abb's Head, Borders Region (Berwickshire District), open access (215)

Tentsmuir Point, Fife Region (North-East Fife District), open access (216)

Whitelaw Mosses, Borders Region (Ettrick & Landerdale District), restricted access (217)

SOUTH-WEST SCOTLAND

The Regional Officer for the South-West, Nature Conservancy Council, The Castle, Balloch Castle Country Park, Balloch, Dumbartonshire G83 8LX
Tel. 0389 58511

Caerlaverock, Dumfries and Galloway Region (Nithsdale District), is eight miles south-east of Dumfries, and extends along six miles of coastline between the estuaries of the River Nith and Lochar Water. The merse is one of the largest unreclaimed saltmarshes in Britain and the most northerly breeding site of the natterjack toad. The foreshore is used as a winter roost by thousands of geese including the entire Spitsbergen population of the barnacle goose. There is a general leaflet on the reserve. (218)

Loch Lomond, Central and Strathclyde Regions (Stirling and Dumbarton Districts), reserve is at the south-east corner of Loch Lomond near Balmaha, and consists of five islands: Inchcailloch, Torrinch, Creinch, Clairinsh and the Aber Isle, with part of the mainland shore and marshy hinterland around the lower reaches of the River Endrick. The four larger islands bear fine examples of deciduous woodland. The area is also noted for several botanical rarities and is of regional importance for the numbers of wintering wildfowl. Access to Inchcailloch, where there is a nature trail, is unrestricted to the casual visitor, but larger organized groups should seek permission from the Regional Office. Visitors to the mainland portion other than Shore Wood should first contact the Reserve Warden at 22 Muirpark Way, Drymen, Glasgow G63 0DX. (219)

Other NNR in the region are:

Ben Lui, Strathclyde Region (Argyll & Bute District); Central Region (Stirling District), open access (220)

Braehead Moss, Strathclyde Region (Clydesdale District), open access (221)

Cairnsmore of Fleet, Dumfries & Galloway Region (Wigtown District), partially open (222)

Clyde Valley Woodlands, Strathclyde Region (Clydesdale District), partially open (223)

Glasdrum Wood, Strathclyde Region (Argyll & Bute District), open access (224)

Glen Diomhan, Strathclyde Region (Cunninghame District), restricted access (225)

Glen Nant, Strathclyde Region (Argyll & Bute District), restricted access (226)

Kirkconnell Flow, Dumfries & Galloway Region (Nithsdale District), restricted access (227)

Mealdarroch, Strathcldye Region (Argyll & Bute District), open access (228)

Moine Mhor, Strathcldye Region (Argyll & Bute District), open access (229)

Silver Flowe, Dumfries & Galloway Region (Stewartry and Wigtown Districts), restricted access (230)

Taynish, Strathclyde Region (Argyll & Bute District), partially open (231)

Tynron Juniper Wood, Dumfries & Galloway Region (Nithsdale District), open access (232)

LOCAL NATURE RESERVES

Under Section 21 of the National Parks and Access to the Countryside Act 1949, various levels of local authority were empowered to establish local nature reserves. The response to such enabling powers has varied immensely. Some authorities have taken the opportunity to create several reserves covering hundreds of acres, others have done nothing at all. A list follows:

ENGLAND

Ainsdale and Birkdale Hills, Merseyside; Sefton BC; 516 acres

Arlington Reservoir, East Sussex; East Sussex CC; 247 acres

Barrow Burn Wood, Northumberland; Northumberland CC; 7 acres

Bedworth Sloughs, Warwickshire; Nuneaton BC; 12 acres

Belfairs, Essex; Southend-on-Sea BC; 91 acres

Berengrave Chalk Pit, Kent; Gillingham BC; 27 acres

Berry Head, Brixham, Devon; Torbay BC; 106 acres

Borough Woods, Northumberland; Castle Morpeth BC; 27 acres

Breadsall Railway Cutting, Derbyshire; Derbyshire CC; 15 acres

Breydon Water, Norfolk; Norfolk CC, Great Yarmouth BC; 1119 acres

Brocton, Staffordshire; Staffordshire CC; 121 acres

Brotherton Park and Dibbinsdale, Merseyside; Wirral BC; 116 acres

Broxhead Common, Hampshire; Hampshire CC; 99 acres

Bude Marshes, Cornwall; North Cornwall DC; 15 acres

Whitethroat feeding young at Chobham Common Local Nature Reserve in Surrey

Burton Pond, West Sussex; West Sussex CC; 175 acres

Calshot Marshes, Hampshire; Hampshire CC; 121 acres

Carlton Marsh, South Yorkshire; Barnsley BC; 35 acres

Catherington Down, Hampshire; Hampshire CC; 32 acres

Chobham Common, Surrey; Surrey CC; 368 acres

Coate Water, Wiltshire; Thamesdown BC; 47 acres

Cooper's Hill, Cranham, Gloucestershire; Gloucestershire CC; 141 acres

Crab Wood, Hampshire; Hampshire CC; 89 acres

Cromford Canal, Derbyshire; Derbyshire CC; 2.25 miles

Daneshill, Nottinghamshire; Nottinghamshire CC; 124 acres

Dawlish Warren, Devon; Teignbridge DC; 534 acres

Drigg Dunes and Gullery, Ravenglass, Cumbria; Cumbria CC; 946 acres

Fairburn Ings, North Yorkshire and West Yorkshire; North Yorkshire CC, West Yorkshire CC; 618 acres

Farlington Marshes, Portsmouth, Hampshire; Portsmouth City Council; 294 acres

Farndale, North Yorkshire; North Yorkshire CC; 2470 acres (approx)

Fen Alder Carr, Suffolk; Suffolk CC; 5 acres

Filsham Reed Bed, East Sussex; Hastings BC; 42 acres

The Firs, Bedfordshire; Bedfordshire CC; 32 acres

Fleet Pond, Hampshire; Hart DC; 119 acres

Frensham, Surrey; Waverley DC; 232 acres

Freshwater Marshes, Isle of Wight; South Wight BC; 40 acres

Gibraltar Point, Lincolnshire; Lincolnshire CC; 1186 acres (approx)

Grasslees Burn Wood, Northumberland; Northumberland CC; 12 acres

Hackhurst Downs, Gomshall, Surrey; Surrey CC; 74 acres

Hangers of the Western Weald, Hampshire; Hampshire CC; 324 acres

Hartlebury Common, Hereford; Hereford & Worcester CC; 215 acres

Healey Dell, Greater Manchester and Lancashire; Rochdale BC, Rossendale BC; 94 acres

Hilbre Island, Merseyside; Wirral BC; 121 acres

Hilfield Park Reservoir, Elstree, Hertfordshire; Hertfordshire CC; 195 acres

Hothfield Common, Kent; Ashford BC; 143 acres

Iping Common, West Sussex; West Sussex CC; 192 acres

Kings Wood, Houghton Conquest, Bedfordshire; Bedfordshire CC; 72 acres

Kingswood, Corby, Northamptonshire; Corby DC; 64 acres

Landguard Common, Felixstowe, Suffolk; Suffolk CC; 40 acres

Litcham Common, Norfolk; Norfolk CC; 69 acres

Longmoor Bog, Berkshire; Wokingham DC; 27 acres

Lytham St Annes, Lancashire; Fylde BC; 37 acres

Marks Hill Woods, Basildon, Essex; Basildon DC; 44 acres

Martins Pond, Nottingham; Nottingham City Council; 10 acres

Mull Wood, Merseyside; Merseyside CC; 52 acres

Newtown Marshes, Isle of Wight; Isle of Wight CC; 297 acres

Nore Hill Chalk Pinnacle, Worms Heath, Chelsham, Surrey; Surrey CC; O.3 acres

Norsey Wood, Basildon, Essex; Basildon DC; 173 acres

North Common, Chailey, East Sussex; East Sussex CC; 430 acres

Nutbourne Marshes, West Sussex; Chichester Harbour Conservancy; 904 acres

Old Lodge, Nutley, East Sussex; East Sussex CC; 618 acres

Oxenbourne Down, Hampshire; Hampshire CC; 158 acres

Pagham Harbour, West Sussex; West Sussex CC; 1280 acres

Pamber Forest, Hampshire; Basingstoke & Deane BC; 477 acres

Parndon Wood, Harlow, Essex; Harlow DC; 52 acres

Perivale Wood, London; London Borough of Ealing; 27 acres

Pleasley Vale, Nottinghamshire; Mansfield DC; 22 acres

Queendown Warren, Kent; Swale DC; 32 acres

Ravenmeols Hills, Merseyside; Sefton DC; 175 acres

Red Hill, Goulceby, Lincolnshire; Lincolnshire CC; 10 acres

Redstone, Hereford & Worcestershire; Wyre Forest DC; 17 acres

Rew Down, Isle of Wight; Isle of Wight CC; 12 acres

Rowhill Copse, Surrey; Waverley BC, Rushmoor BC; 62 acres

Ruislip, London; London Borough of Hillingdon; 12 acres

Rye Harbour, East Sussex; East Sussex CC; 880 acres

Saltwells, West Midlands; Dudley MBC; 109 acres

Sandall Beat, Doncaster, South Yorkshire; Doncaster BC; 170 acres

Scotch Gill Wood, Northumberland; Castle Morpeth BC; 20 acres

Screech Owl, Bridgwater, Somerset; Somerset CC; 30 acres

Seaford Head, East Sussex; Lewes BC; 274 acres

Sellars Wood, Nottinghamshire; Nottingham City Council, Broxtowe BC; 35 acres

Shibdon Pond, Tyne & Wear; Gateshead MBC; 35 acres

Shide Chalk Pit, Isle of Wight; Isle of Wight CC; 1 acre

Siddick Pond, Cumbria; Allerdale DC; 47 acres

Snipe Dales, near Winceby, Lincolnshire; Lincolnshire CC; 124 acres

South Bank of the Swale, Kent; Kent CC; 1038 acres

Staffhurst Wood, Limpsfield, Surrey; Surrey CC; 94 acres

Stanpit Marsh, Christchurch, Dorset; Christchurch BC; 146 acres

Stockers Lake, Hertfordshire; Three Rivers CC; 94 acres

Stockton Railway Cutting, Warwickshire; Warwickshire CC; 2 acres

Street Heath, Somerset; Somerset CC; 20 acres

Sugar Loaf Hill and Saltern Cove, Goodrington, Devon; Torbay BC; 40 acres

Temple Ewell Downs, Kent; Dover DC; 52 acres

Thatcham Reed Beds, Berkshire; Newbury DC; 32 acres

Therfield Heath, Hertfordshire; Hertfordshire CC; 418 acres

Thorpe Wood, Cleveland; Cleveland CC; 42 acres

Titchfield Haven, Fareham, Hampshire; Hampshire CC; 210 acres

Totternhoe Knolls, Bedfordshire; Bedfordshire CC; 32 acres

Ufton Fields, Warwickshire; Warwickshire CC; 79 acres

Vicarage Pit, Stanton Harcourt, Oxfordshire; Oxfordshire CC; 22 acres

Warton Crag, Lancashire; Lancashire CC; 47 acres

Werrar Marshes, Isle of Wight; Isle of Wight CC; 22 acres

Whitbarrow Scar, Witherslack, Cumbria; Lake District SPB; 89 acres

The Wild Grounds, Hampshire; Gosport BC; 52 acres

Willoughby-Farlesthorpe Railway Line, Lincolnshire; Lincolnshire CC; 12 acres

Wilwell Cutting, Nottinghamshire; Rushcliffe BC; 20 acres

Wingate Quarry, Durham; Durham CC; 52 acres

Yantlet Creek, Kent; Rochester-upon-Medway BC; 64 acres

SCOTLAND

Aberlady Bay, Lothian Region; East Lothian DC; 1438 acres

Castle and Hightae Lochs, Lochmaben, Dumfries & Galloway Region; Annan & Eskdale DC; 339 acres

Eden Estuary, Fife Region; NE Fife DC; 1730 acres

Gartmorn Dam, Central Region; Clackmannan DC; 109 acres

Gladhouse Reservoir, Lothian Region; Lothian RC; 497 acres

Montrose Basin, Tayside Region; Angus DC; 2530 acres

Munlochy Bay, Black Isle, Highland Region; Highland RC; 1112 acres (approx)

WALES

Bishop's Wood, West Glamorgan; Swansea City Council; 35 acres

Carreg Cennen Woodlands, Dyfed; Dyfed CC; 40 acres

Cleddon Bog, Gwent; Gwent CC; 37 acres

Cliff Wood, South Glamorgan; Vale of Glamorgan BC; 12 acres

Coed Dinorwic, Gwynedd; Gwynedd CC; 89 acres

Cwm Coed-y-Cerrig, Gwent; Brecon Beacons National Park Authority; 15 acres

Cwmllwyd Wood, West Glamorgan; West Glamorgan CC; 17 acres

Flatholm, South Glamorgan; South Glamorgan CC; 94 acres

Glamorgan Canal, South Glamorgan; Cardiff City Council; 57 acres

Great Orme's Head, Gwynedd; Aberconwy BC; 482 acres

Kenfig Pool and Dunes, Mid Glamorgan; Mid Glamorgan CC; 1421 acres

Taf Fechan, Mid Glamorgan; Merthyr Tydfil BC; 99 acres

Talybont Reservoir, Powys; Powys CC; 489 acres

Traeth Lafan, Gwynedd; Gwynedd CC; 5436 acres

FORESTRY COMMISSION

The Forestry Commission owns large areas of the countryside which it has increasingly opened up to public use and recreation. This does not mean that the public have the right to enter all forests or that they can do what they will in those that are opened. However the Commission is aware of its duties and is taking a more active role in providing information not only about its work but also about the nature of the areas under its care. Information centres and nature trails are the most obvious outward signs, but in many of its forests the Commission has opened up the forest drives and paths for those who care to explore for themselves. Several of the larger and more obvious areas controlled by the Forestry Commission are detailed in this book. The New Forest is, for example, justifiably famous as both a recreation centre and a haunt of wildlife.

With forests at various stages of growth spread throughout the length and breadth of the land, there are few who are not well placed to visit one or more of the Commission's lands. In some parts it has created Forest Parks, large areas where among its woodlands the Commission has established camp sites, picnic places and forest trails and walks. It has offices, study centres and sometimes even a shop. All of its forests are summarized in its publication *Guide Map to Your Forests*, a full and cheap source of information to those who would explore the woodlands of Britain. Each forest is marked and symbols show the kinds of facilities provided. It is staggering just how much of Britain has been opened up to the people in just a few years.

While the map is the key to exploring the Commission's lands, it also publishes guides to major individual forests and to several important ecological aspects of forestry in its relationship with the wild creatures that live there, and a good series of tree identification guides.

All publications are available from the Forestry Commission, 231 Corstorphine Road, Edinburgh EH12 7AT, or from local offices and information centres.

FIELD STUDIES COUNCIL

FIELD CENTRES

30 mls
50 kms

▲ Malham Tarn

▲ Drapers

▲ Preston Montford

Flatford Mill ▲

Dale Fort ◄
Orielton

Epping Forest ▲
Juniper Hall ▲

▲ Leonard Wills

▲ Slapton Ley

The FSC exists to promote a better understanding of our environment and the way we use it. It runs nine residential centres in England and Wales and a day centre in Epping Forest. Residential centres provide accommodation in single, twin and dormitory rooms. Each centre is strategically sited to provide ample opportunities for field research and each is staffed by a warden, a director of studies and teaching staff. Visitors, whether groups or individuals, are free to follow a centre course or pursue their own interest as they will. Facilities for advanced work up to university level are provided, including lecture theatres, laboratories, maps and reference books. Among a wide range of one-week courses are plant and animal ecology, geography, geology, environmental studies, field teaching methods, conservation, land use, meteorology, archaeology, birds, photography and art.

Recognizing that not all of us wish to return to sixth form (or even third form) level, the Council organizes many courses specifically for adults. Many of these are for complete beginners and it is good to know that one's fellow students will not only be just as inept as oneself, but that they will also be about the same age.

The Field Centres are:

Dale Fort Field Centre, Haverfordwest, Dyfed SA62 3RD. Tel. 064 65 205. Dale lies on the old Pembrokeshire coast on a narrow peninsula at the mouth of Milford Haven. It boasts a good list of little-known plants and the cliffs are of great interest in May and June. It is very handy for the bird islands that lie offshore and is particlarly strong on marine biology.

Drapers Field Centre, Rhyd-y-crenau, Betws-y-coed, Gwynedd LL24 OHB. Tel. 069 02 494. The Field Centre is situated in the Conway Valley and is more or less placed over the fault between pre- and post-Silurian rocks. In fact a wide range of geological formations are within easy reach, providing excellent opportunities for study. The effects of glaciation are easy to see and the long history of human occupancy provides further opportunities. Botany and birds are interesting and varied.

Flatford Mill Field Centre, East Bergholt, Colchester, Essex CO7 6UL. Tel. 0206 29 8283. Flatford is perhaps the most attractive of all the field centres in a physical sense – a mellow old watermill and mill house at the head of the Stour estuary in the heart of Constable country. The Stour runs under, through and around Flatford and provides excellent opportunities for aquatic biology both marine and freshwater. The surrounding landscape of east Suffolk is immensely varied and rich.

Juniper Hall Field Centre, Dorking, Surrey RH5 6DA. Tel. 0306 88 3849. Situated in an old mansion on the chalk escarpment of the North Downs over-looking the Mole Gap, Juniper Hall offers a large range of geological phenomena. The corresponding land use is so dependent on the underlying structure that the Centre is well used by geography classes from nearby London. The association with chalk and its rich flora of orchids and other open ground flowers dominates the non-geological interest.

Leonard Wills Field Centre, Nettlecombe Court, Williton, Taunton, Somerset TA4 4HT. Tel. 0984 40320. A house has stood here since the thirteenth century and the Field Centre is only the last in a line of conversions and alterations to this charming old mansion. It lies in the Nettlecombe Valley, which joins the Vale of Stogumber in separating the Quantock from the Brendon Hills. Visitors dine in the Great

Hall – with a log fire in winter. The unspoilt character of the landscape and the nearness of the Brendon Hills and Exmoor make the Centre an excellent site for studying a wide variety of disciplines. Facilities exist for the pursuit of almost every branch of field study, from marine and freshwater biology to human and economic geography.

Malham Tarn Field Centre, Settle, Yorkshire BD24 9PU. Tel. 072 93 331. Malham lies near Malham Tarn at an altitude of 1230 feet on a Carboniferous Limestone plateau in the Pennines. Nearby are the famous Malham Cove and Gordale Scar, the Three Peaks and the varied geology of the Pennines. The 'karst' limestone scenery is unique and the botanical interest rich and diverse. There are a few moorland birds, including numerous curlew, and a long history of human settlement to be investigated.

Orielton Field Centre, Pembroke, Dyfed SA71 5EZ. Tel. 064 681 225. Orielton lies on a peninsula between the gentle mud flats of Milford Haven and the harsh waves of the open Atlantic. Its geology is interesting, showing accordant drainage and inverted relief, and both coastlines show both submergence and emergence. Geologically this is classic ground, but there are woods and grasslands, salt marshes and mud flats, rocks and limestone cliffs all providing a wealth of botanical interest. Nearby the Prescelly Hills are where the bluestones of Stonehenge originated.

Preston Montford Field Centre, Montford Bridge, Shrewsbury SY4 1DX. Tel. 0743 850380. This Field Centre overlooks the River Severn some four miles west of Shrewsbury and is situated among one of the classic grounds of British geology. The highly varied landscape is based on an underlying structure of igneous and volcanic rocks, grits, shales and limestone. The Stiperstones area has old lead mines, and an excellent view from the Long Mynd. Ancient remains litter the landscape and at Coalbrookdale there are monuments to the early industrial revolution, including the iron bridge at Ironbridge.

An ash tree growing from the limestone pavement near Malham in the Pennines. The 'clint and gryke' formations are studied by many of the visitors to the field centre

Slapton Ley Field Centre, Slapton, Kingsbridge, Devon TQ7 2QP. Tel. O548 580466. The Field Centre is housed in a charming and rambling old farmhouse at the eastern end of Slapton village. The 'Ley' is a beach-enclosed lagoon about 2½ miles in length with a rich growth of reeds. The Field Studies Council leases a 460-acre nature reserve which includes the Ley as well as two large areas of deciduous woodland. Outstanding are wild otters (as well as foxes and badgers) and there is a rich avifauna. Bird-watchers search for the rare aquatic warbler in late summer — this is almost its only regular haunt in Britain. The shingle beach is interesting for the succession of coastal plants.

Epping Forest Conservation Centre, High Beech, Loughton, Essex IG10 4AF. Tel. 01 508 7714. Situated on the edge of one of the largest open spaces left near London, and with the varied geology of Epping Forest, this Field Centre is a magnet to the children and educationalists of North London. Once the Royal Forest of Essex, Epping has been a public open space since 1878 under the care of the City of London. Over 400 cattle still graze the Forest, though this is the only right of common that is still maintained. There are fallow deer and a rich avifauna that includes very reliable hawfinches. The Centre has a permanent Conservation Exhibition catering for the casual visitor.

The Field Studies Council is a registered charity dependent on membership, donations and fees charged for the courses it organizes. It welcomes members. Write to Field Studies Council, Preston Montford, Montford Bridge, Shrewsbury SY4 1HW.

ROYAL SOCIETY FOR THE PROTECTION OF BIRDS

The Royal Society for the Protection of Birds (RSPB) is one of the fastest-growing conservation bodies in Britain. It is supported entirely by subscriptions, by appeals and by sales. From its headquarters in Bedfordshire it administers a series of regional offices, a continually growing number of nature reserves and a nationwide organization of members' groups. From its tiny beginnings the RSPB has become a fully professional conservation body with a progressive policy towards conservation.

Most of its reserves are open to visitors by a permit system. These are generally available on site and are often free to members. In fact if you wish to visit an RSPB reserve or two, it quickly becomes cheaper to join the Society. The Society issues a quarterly magazine, *Birds*, which is an excellent production full of pictures, news and interesting articles on birds and the places they live. It is not on public sale, but comes free to members. The local groups, with which new members are put in touch, run regular meetings, film shows and outings in search of birds.

The reserves owned or run by the Society grow in number year by year and many are able to cater for disabled visitors. In all cases it is a good idea to write in advance to the RSPB for their current *Reserves Visiting* leaflet, stating whether or not you are a member.

RSPB HEADQUARTERS

National Headquarters
The Lodge, Sandy, Bedfordshire SG19 2DL
Tel. 0767 80551

Scottish Headquarters
17 Regent Terrace, Edinburgh EH7 5BN
Tel. 031 556 5624

Wales Office
Frolic Street, Newtown, Powys SY16 1AP
Tel. 0686 26678

East Anglia Office
Aldwych House, Bethel Street, Norwich NR2 1NR
Tel. 0603 615920

East Midlands Office
12 Guildhall Street, Lincoln LN1 1TT
Tel. 0522 35596

Midlands Office
44 Friar Street, Droitwich, Worcestershire WR9 8ED
Tel. 0905 770581

North of England Office
'E' Floor, Milburn House, Dean Street, Newcastle upon Tyne NE1 1LE
Tel. 091 232 4148

RSPB RESERVES

Shetland

100 mls
150 kms

Lumbister
Fetlar
Loch of Spiggie

Noup Cliffs
North Hill
Marwick Head
Trumland
The Loons
Birsay/Cottasgarth
North Hoy
Hobbister
Copinsay

Handa

Balranald

Culbin Sands
Loch of Strathbeg

Loch Garten
Insh Marshes
Fowlsheugh

Killiecrankie
Loch of Kinnordy

Inversnaid
Vane Farm

Loch Gruinart
Barons Haugh
Lochwinnoch

Coquet Island

Ken-Dee Marshes
Wood of Crees
Geltsdale

Mull of Galloway
St. Bees Head

Leighton Moss
& Morecambe Bay
Bempton Cliffs
Hornsea Mere

Fairburn Ings
Blacktoft Sands

Point of Air
Eastwood
Tetney Marshes

South Stack
Cliffs
Gayton Sands
Titchwell Marshes

Lake Vyrnwy
Coombes Valley &
Churnet Valley Woods
Titchwell Marsh
Snettisham

Coed Garth Gell
Nene Washes
Strumpshaw Fen &
Surlingham Church Marsh

Ynys-hir
Sandwell Valley
Ouse Washes
Minsmere

Dyffryn Wood
The Lodge
North Warren
Havergate Island

Dinas/Gwenffrwd
Fowlmere
Wolves Wood

Grassholm
Cym Clydach
Nagshead
Rye House Marsh
Stour Wood
Old Hall Marshes

Church Wood
Elmley Marshes

Northward Hill
Chapel Wood
Barfold Copse
Church Wood, Blean

West Sedgemoor
Fore Wood
Dungeness

Langstone Harbour

Aylesbeare Common
Arne
Adur Estuary
Radipole
& Lodmoor

34

North-West England Office
Imperial House, Imperial Arcade,
Huddersfield, West Yorkshire HD1 2BR
Tel. 0484 536331

South-East England Office
Scan House, 4 Church Street, Shoreham-by-Sea,
West Sussex BN4 5DQ
Tel. 0273 463642

South-West England Office
10 Richmond Road, Exeter, Devon EX4 4JA
Tel. 0392 32691

RSPB RESERVES

ENGLAND
Adur Estuary, West Sussex
Arne, Dorset
Aylesbeare Common, Devon
Barfold Copse, Surrey
Bempton Cliffs, Humberside
Blacktoft Sands, Humberside
Chapel Wood, Devon

Church Wood, Buckinghamshire
Church Wood, Blean, Kent
Churnet Valley Woods, Staffordshire
Coombes Valley, Staffordshire
Coquet Island, Northumberland
Dungeness, Kent
Eastwood, Greater Manchester
Elmley Marshes, Kent
Fairburn Ings, West Yorkshire
Fore Wood, East Sussex
Fowlmere, Cambridgeshire
Gayton Sands, Cheshire
Geltsdale, Cumbria
Havergate Island, Suffolk
Hornsea Mere, Humberside
Langstone Harbour, Hampshire
Leighton Moss, Lancashire
The Lodge, Bedfordshire
Lodmoor, Dorset
Minsmere, Suffolk

Fetlar in Shetland is the only site in Britain where snowy owls have bred

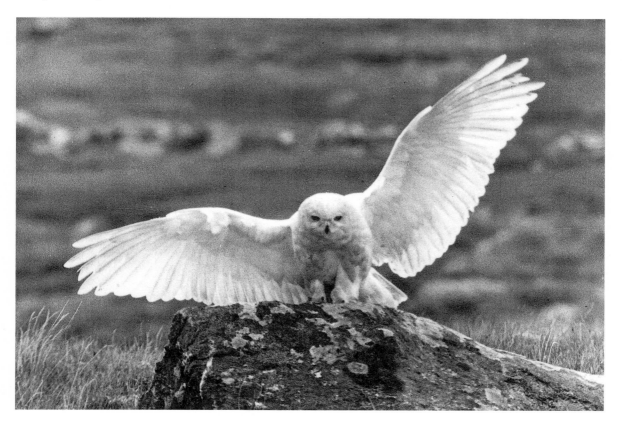

35

Morecambe Bay, Lancashire
Nagshead, Gloucestershire
Nene Washes, Cambridgeshire
Northward Hill, Kent
North Warren, Suffolk
Old Hall Marshes, Essex
Ouse Washes, Cambridgeshire
Radipole Lake, Dorset
Rye House Marsh, Hertfordshire
St Bees Head, Cumbria
Sandwell Valley, West Midlands
Snettisham, Norfolk
Stour Wood and Copperas Bay, Essex
Strumpshaw Fen, Norfolk
Surlingham Church Marsh, Norfolk
Tetney Marshes, Lincolnshire
Titchwell Marsh, Norfolk
West Sedgemoor, Somerset
Wolves Wood, Suffolk

SCOTLAND

Balranald, Western Isles
Barons Haugh, Strathclyde
Birsay Moors and Cottasgarth, Orkney
Copinsay, Orkney
Culbin Sands, Highland/Grampian
Fetlar, Shetland
Fowlsheugh, Grampian
Handa, Highland
Hobbister, Orkney
Insh Marshes, Highland

Inversnaid, Central
Ken-Dee Marshes, Dumfries and Galloway
Killiekrankie, Tayside
Loch Garten, Highland
Loch Gruinart, Islay, Strathclyde
Loch of Kinnordy, Tayside
Loch of Spiggie, Shetland
Loch of Strathbeg, Grampian
Lochwinnoch, Strathclyde
The Loons, Orkney
Lumbister, Shetland
Marwick Head, Orkney
Mull of Galloway, Dumfries and Galloway
North Hill, Papa Westray, Orkney
North Hoy, Orkney
Noup Cliffs, Orkney
Trumland Fen Farm, Rousay, Orkney
Vane Farm, Tayside
Wood of Cree, Dumfries and Galloway

WALES

Coed Garth Gell, Gwynedd
Cwm Clydach, West Glamorgan
Dinas and Gwenffrwd, Dyfed
Dyffryn Wood, Powys
Grassholm, Dyfed
Lake Vyrnwy, Powys
Point of Air, Clwyd
South Stack Cliffs, Gwynedd
Ynys-hir, Dyfed

WILDFOWL TRUST

Established as the Severn Wildfowl Trust by Sir Peter Scott in 1946, the Wildfowl Trust is dedicated to the study and conservation of wildfowl. To this end it has established the most comprehensive collection of wildfowl in the world and opened a number of refuges where wild birds can be seen. Each is dealt with individually, but for convenience all are listed here.

Headquarters: The Wildfowl Trust, Slimbridge, Gloucester GL2 7BT. Tel. 045 389333.

Arundel. The most recent wildfowl refuge, covering fifty-five acres just north of Arundel in West Sussex. Tel. 0903 883355.

Caerlaverock. An exciting refuge on the Solway Firth seven miles from Dumfries. Tel. 038777 200.

Martin Mere. One of the most visited conservation projects in the North-West, only five miles from Southport. Tel. 0704 895181.

Peakirk. These beautiful gardens are a charming combination of woodland and water, blending to form an intimate and peaceful haven five miles from Peterborough. Tel. 0733 252271.

Slimbridge. The world's largest and most varied collection of wildfowl. See above.

Washington. A new centre covering 103 delightfully landscaped acres on the north bank of the River Wear three miles from Sunderland. Tel. 019 4165454.

Welney. The Welney Refuge occupies 850 acres on the famous Ouse Washes, which constitute one of the most important areas for wildfowl in Europe. Tel. 0353 860711.

SCOTTISH WILDLIFE TRUST

The Scottish Wildlife Trust is the national body concerned with the conservation of all forms of wildlife in Scotland – there is no equivalent body in other parts of Britain. By purchase, lease or agreement the Trust has established a chain of nature reserves many of which are open to the public. It is a voluntary charitable organization with a healthy membership and a go-ahead policy towards education and publicity. Though some 30,000 visitors a year flock to the hides at Loch of the Lowes where ospreys can be seen, the Trust makes no charge at this site. The aim is to persuade visitors to become members, and very successful it is too.

As elsewhere, it is advisable before visiting any reserve to inquire from the Trust's headquarters:

The Scottish Wildlife Trust
25 Johnston Terrace,
Edinburgh EH1 2NH
Tel. 031 226 4602.

Reserves

Aberfoyle Bat Cave, near Aberfoyle. OS Map 57–NN5003. Hibernating bats in old mine tunnel now sealed with grille to prevent disturbance. No access.

Addiewell Bing, between Breich Water and the B792 near West Calder. OS Map 65–NT000629. Reshaped and replanted old oil-shale spoil-heap. Many native trees, scrub, heather, bracken and tall herbaceous plants.

One member of the osprey pair calls as its mate approaches

Ardmore Point, near Helensburgh, off the A814 Cardross-Helensburgh road. OS Map 63–NS319786. Promontory on the Clyde Estuary. Heathland, scrub, extensive mudflats and foreshore. Waders and wildfowl. Car park next to reserve near shore.

Auchalton Meadow, five miles south of Maybole, minor road off the B741. OS Map 76–NS335036. Herb-rich calcareous meadow. Car park at roadside adjacent to reserve. Permit needed.

Ayr Gorge Woodland, at Failford, to south of A758 Ayr-Mauchline road. OS Map 70–NS457249. Oak gorge woodland with birch along valley of River Ayr. Car park in lay-by off A758. Path along west bank of river.

Balgavies Loch, four miles east of Forfar off the A932. OS Map 54–NO534508. Eutrophic loch, fen, woodland. Wintering geese and breeding waterfowl. Car park next to hide, also viewing point. Permit needed. Hide (open day, first Sunday each month – otherwise key from Warden on deposit).

Ballachuan Hazel Wood, thirteen miles south of Oban in the south-west corner of Seil Island. OS Map 55–NM763146. Hazel wood, wet grassland, rocky shore. Rich ground flora, important for lichens, heronry, butterflies. Car park off roadside near Ballachuan Farm. Permit needed.

Ballagan Glen, near Strathblane off the A891. OS Map 64–NS572800. Carboniferous rock exposures, ashwood and gorge with waterfall. Car park near Ballagan House. Permit needed.

Ballantrae Shingle Beach, at Ballantrae on the A77 Stranraer-Girvan road. OS Map 76–NX080820. Shingle bank with shore plants and nesting terns at mouth of River Stinchar. Car park in village next to shore. Restricted access in breeding season. Warden in summer with guided walks.

Balnaguard Glen, three miles east of Grandtully on B898 at Balnaguard. OS Map 52–NN941512. Birch wood in glen with waterfall and spectacular landslips. Juniper wood. Car park at farm up first track out of Balnaguard towards Grandtully. Permit needed.

Bankhead Moss, two miles south-east of Pitscottie off the B940. OS Map 59–NO447103. Small raised bog with numerous pools, with fringe of birch and pine. Car park on roadside. Permit needed.

Bawsinch and Duddingston Loch, centre of Edinburgh below Arthur's Seat. OS Map 66–NT284725. Loch with breeding and wintering wildfowl, marsh, ponds, and goose lawn. Car park on Duddingston Road West for Baswinch, or by Holyrood Park gates for views across loch. Permit and hide from Holyrood Lodge Visitor Centre.

Bemersyde Moss, four miles east of Melrose, on minor road between Melrose-Smailholm road. OS Map 74–NT805315. Shallow loch and marsh with large black-headed gull colony and wintering wildfowl. Car park on road edge adjacent to reserve. Permit needed.

Ben Mor Coigach, six miles north of Ullapool, west of A835. OS Map 15–NC075065. Wild open country of Torridonian sandstone hills, coastline and Summer Isles. Eagle, wild cat, red deer, grey seals and upland flora. Car park at various points off road through reserve. Warden.

Brerachan Meadow, seven miles north-east of Pitlochry alongside A924 Pitlochry-Kirkmichael road. OS Map 43-NO015637. Small herb-rich hay meadow. Car park at adjacent roadside. Permit needed.

Cander Moss adjacent to the A74/M74, one mile east of Stonehouse on the east side of the B7078. OS Map 64–NS780464. Heather moor merging with birch/Scots pine.

Carradale Point, half mile south of Carradale, off B842 Campbeltown-Claonig Bay Road. OS Map 68–NR817372. Coastal grassland, low cliffs, good views over Kilbrannan Sound. Car park at end of private road from Carradale.

Carstramon Wood, two miles north of Gatehouse-of-Fleet on a minor road off the B796. OS Map 83–NX592605. Area of ancient, mainly deciduous woodland. Car park opposite lodge.

Coulnacraig Meadow, two miles south of A93 along minor road opposite Slewdrum Forest. OS Map 37–NO623953. Small meadow flushed with spring water. Sedges and early marsh orchids. Car park off roadside. Permit needed.

Dalmellington Moss, on A713 Ayr-New Galloway road, near village of Dalmellington. OS Map 70–NS465063. Raised bog with rich flora, birch and willow carr (boggy woodland), fen. Car park at crossroads near Dalmellington. Permit needed.

Doire Donn, seven miles north of Corran Ferry on A861 on the hill slopes on west side of Loch Linnhe. OS Map 41–NN050703. Oak wood with birch, rich flora with good bird and butterfly populations. Pine marten. Car park on roadside at A861. Permit needed.

Dowalton Marshes, south of Wigtown, minor road off B7052. OS Map 83–NX405467. Mosaic of herb-rich pasture, wet meadow and birch/willow carr on site of a drained loch. Car park at Low Dowalton just off road. Permit needed.

Drummains Reedbed, fourteen miles south of Dumfries off A710 at Drumburn. OS Map 84–NX984610. Reed and merse (close cropped grassland) on Solway estuary. Wildfowl and waders. Car park off main road, short walk along track to reserve.

Drummondreach Oakwood, fourteen miles north of Inverness on B9163 at Drummondreach. OS Map 26–NH581574. Oakwood in small valley, rich in plants and insects. Car park on roadside at reserve entrance. Permit needed.

Duns Castle, just north of the centre of Duns in the Borders. OS Maps 67 and 74–NT778550. Mixed woodland and loch. Pied flycatcher, redstart and wildfowl. Car park at Castle Road, Duns or off B6365 at northern end of reserve. Hide – open entry.

East Lammermuir Deans, six miles south of Dunbar, minor road off A1 from Innerwick road to Wester Aikengall. OS Map 67–NT703700. Consists of four narrow, deep valleys, known locally as deans, cut into north-eastern side of Lammermuir Hills, sections being wooded. Car park off road at Wester Aikengall. No access in lambing season 15th April to 15th May.

Eigg Reserves, part of Small Isles group off the west coast of Scotland reached by ferry from Mallaig. OS Map 39–NM474875. Three reserves on the island, uplands with Alpine plants, hazel wood on steep coastal cliffs, lochans and bog. No cars allowed on island. Permit needed. Warden in summer with guided walks.

Eilean Na Creige Duibhe, island in Loch Carron near Plockton. OS Map 24–NG824335. Small wooded island with heronry. Car park at Plockton. Permit needed. Boat needed for access to island.

Enterkine Wood, between Stair and Annbank, six miles east of Ayr. OS Map 70–NS425241. Mixed woodland with rich plant life, particularly fungi. Car

park in area next to reserve. Permit needed.

Erraid Wood, half mile south of Hillend Ski slopes just outside Edinburgh on the Biggar road A702. OS Map 66–NT2466. Mature woodland developed as an education resource. Car park off road. Permit needed.

Fairy Isles, seven miles west of Lochgilphead along B8025 to Tayvallich. Small islands at head of Loch Sween. OS Map 55–NM766884. Broadleaved woodland on coastal strip and six small islands. Car park off B8025 (at NM784907) and long walk along forest track to reserve.

Falls of Clyde, one mile south of Lanark. OS Maps 71 and 72–NS882425. Ancient gorge woodland, spectacular and famous falls. Dippers. Car park at New Lanark, also limited space at Corehouse (Lodge Gates). Warden. Visitor Centre open every weekend (13.00 – 17.00 hours) and weekdays April to September (11.00 – 17.00 hours).

Farigaig, south-east side of Loch Ness, minor road off the B852 at Inverfarigaig. OS Maps 26 and 35–NH525245. Mixed woodland and scrub on steep slopes. Car park on roadside. Permit needed.

Feoch Meadows, at end of rough track (one mile) to Standard Farm, two miles east of Barrhill on A714. OS Map 76–NX263822. Herb-rich meadow on upland farm with orchids and butterflies. Car park at Standard Farm off track. Permit needed.

Flanders Moss, twelve miles west of Stirling off the B822 at end of rough track past East Polder Farm. OS Map 57–NS645973. Raised valley bog with heather, sphagnum moss and birch scrub close to River Forth. Car park at reserve entrance past East Polder Farm. Permit needed.

Fountainbleau and Ladypark, on edge of Dumfries between A701 and A709. OS Map 84–NX986772. Low lying wet birchwood. Willow tits. Car park at Marchmont Avenue or Dumfries High School. Permit needed.

Glenmuick and Lochnagar, nine miles south of Ballater along minor road off B976. OS Map 44–NO250550. Mountain and lochs. Upland plants and animals. Red deer. Car park at end of minor road. Warden. Visitor Centre open from Easter to end of October.

Gordon Moss, one mile west of Gordon Village, to the south of the Gordon-Earlston road. OS Map 74–

NT635425. Birchwood on peat moss. Rich in plants and insects. Car park at reserve entrance. Permit needed.

Hare and Dunhog Mosses, three miles south of Selkirk on A7. OS Map 73–NT468247 and NT475247. Small loch with wildfowl. Valley bog with wetland plants. Car park in lay-by on A7. Permit needed.

Hermand Birchwood, seventeen miles west of Edinburgh along A71. Take B7008 at West Calder then right at first crossroads, half a mile up minor road. OS Map 65–NT031619. Birchwood on peat with wet grassland. Car park adjoining reserve. Permit needed.

Holyrood Lodge Visitor Centre at Holyrood Road entrance to Holyrood Park near Holyrood Palace. An exhibition of the geology, pre-history, history and wildlife of Holyrood Park. Fulmars on Salisbury Crags. Car park in Holyrood Park. Visitor Centre open Easter to September (10.00 – 17.30 hours), September to Christmas (10.00 – 16.00 hours, weekends only).

Hoselaw Loch/Din Moss, five miles south-east of Kelso, minor road off B6352. OS Map 74–NT805315. Loch with raised bog at southern end. Wildfowl. Car park at end of farm track down to loch. Permit needed.

Keltneyburn, five miles west of Aberfeldy, minor road off B846. OS Maps 52 and 52–NN767508. Rich broadleaved wood in steep-sided gorge. Herb-rich meadow with orchids and scrub. Car park by meadow up rough track from Keltneyburn. Permit need. Warden in summer.

Kilminning Coast, one and a half miles north-east of Crail, turning right past disused airfield to Kilminning Castle. OS Map 59–NO633090. Low coastline with grassland. Migrants. Car park next to coast at NO632088. Coastal footpath.

Knowetop Lochs, five miles east of New Galloway along A712 to Dumfries. OS Maps 77 and 84–NX706786. Small lochs in heather moorland. Car park on roadside. Permit needed.

Loch of Craiglush, two miles north-east of Dunkeld alongside A923. OS Maps 52 and 52–NO043443. Loch fringing marsh and woodland, adjoins Loch of the Lowes. Car park at side of road or at Loch of the Lowes. Permit needed. Warden.

Loch Fleet, two miles south of Golspie on A9. OS Map 21–NH794965. Large tidal basin, sand-dunes, coastal heath and pinewoods. Common seals, terns, waders, wildfowl and rich plant life. Car park at Littleferry or in lay-bys around the basin. Permit only required for access off paths in Ferry Links Wood. Warden in summer with guided walks.

Loch Libo, five miles south-west of Barrhead off A736 at Uplawmoor. OS Map 64–NS435556. Loch with rich flora, waterfowl and deciduous woodland. Car park in lay-by off A736. Permit needed. (Note: access across railway crossing – take care!).

Loch of Lintrathen, seven miles west of Kirriemuir, minor road off B951. OS Map 53–NO278550. Loch with large numbers of wintering wildfowl especially geese. Car park next to reserve (using hide key).

Loch of the Lowes, two miles north-east of Dunkeld, minor road off A923. OS Maps 52, 53–NO050440. Ospreys! Loch with fringing vegetation and woodland. Waterfowl includng great crested grebe. Reserve car park. Warden. Visitor Centre open April to September (April, May and September 10.00 – 19.00 hours, June to August 10.00 – 20.30 hours). Hide open all year.

Longhaven Cliffs, two miles south of Peterhead off A975. OS Map 30–NK114394. Spectacular granite cliffs with breeding seabirds and clifftop plants. Car park at Blackhill Quarry.

Milkhall Pond, three miles south of Penicuik on minor road off A701. OS Maps 66 and 73–NT242573. Disused small reservoir, marsh plants, wildfowl and amphibians. Car park on road edge. Permit needed.

Montrose Basin, west of Montrose. OS Map 54–NO694576. Extensive tidal mudflats, large flocks of wintering wildfowl and waders, especially geese. Car park at various points around basin. Path from Old Montrose Pier to Bridge of Dun along bank of River South Esk. Permit for rest of reserve. Warden. Hide.

Nethan Gorge, six miles north-west of Lanark on A72 at Crossford. OS Map 72–NS820466. Ancient mixed broadleaved woodland on steep slopes of gorge. Car park on roadside adjacent to reserve, or at Tillietudlem Castle. Path through reserve.

Pass of Ryvoan, seven miles east of Aviemore. OS Map 36–NJ998104. Native pinewood, crested tits and crossbills. Car park at forest roadside beyond Glenmore Lodge.

Pepper Wood, on minor road from Carlowrie off A9 to Dalmeny, just south of railway bridge. OS Map 65–

NT142754. Small deciduous wood. Car park on roadside by wood.

Possil Marsh on A879 on the outskirts of Lambhill in north of Glasgow, next to Forth and Clyde Canal. OS Map 64–NS585700. Loch, rich marshland, wintering and breeding waterfowl. Car park in Skirsa Court, off Skirsa Street, Lambhill. Warden in summer.

Rahoy Hills, part of Morvern peninsula, five miles north of Lochaline off the A884. OS Map 49–NM690530. Mountains, loch and upland lochans, oakwood on banks of Loch Arienas. Arctic-alpine plants, upland birds, rich in dragonflies. Car park at entrance of Black Glen on north side of A884 at Acharn. Permit needed. Warden in summer with guided walks.

Red Moss, One and a half miles south of Balerno, eight miles west of Edinburgh on northern side of Pentland Hills. OS Maps 65, 66–NT165638. Raised bog with heather and bog plants, small birchwood. Small car park adjoining reserve. Permit needed.

Roslin Glen, south of Edinburgh on B7003 (off A701) on the south side of River North Esk. OS Map 66–NT275625. Mixed deciduous woodland with a rich woodland flora and breeding birds. Car park in lay-bys on B7003. Permit needed.

St Abb's Head, B6438 to St Abbs off A1. OS Map 67–NT914688. Magnificent seacliffs with guillemot, razorbill and kittiwake. Loch and coastal grassland. Also migrant birds. Car park off B6438. Warden.

Seaton Cliffs, three-quarters of a mile from centre of Arbroath at end of promenade. OS Map 54–NO667416. Red sandstone cliffs, maritime plants, seabirds with cliff-nesting house martins. Car park at Arbroath promenade.

Shewalton Sandpits, one mile south of Irvine off A737 to Troon. OS Map 70–NS327371. Fashioned from worked-out sand and gravel pit. Pools and lagoons, dune grassland, scrub and riverbank. Small car park.

Southwick Coast, nine miles south-east of Dalbeattie on A710. OS Map 84–NX910558. Ancient oakwood on seacliffs, fen, saltmarsh and geological interest, wildfowl on Solway Estuary. Car park on roadside next to reserve. Access on foot down track to Needle's Eye.

Stormont Loch, two miles south of Blairgowrie off the A923 Blairgowrie-Coupar Angus road. OS Map 53–NO193422. Loch and fringing fen, willow scrub and woodland. Wintering wildfowl and geese. Small car park off A923. Hide on south shore, open access.

Tailend Moss, minor road between A89 at Boghall with the A705 Whitburn road. OS Map 65–NT005678. Raised peat bog with many pools. Good range of bog plants, wintering fowl. Car park alongside minor road. Permit needed.

Talich, five miles south-east of Tain, minor road off B9165 (off A9). OS Map 21–NH853787. Alderwood and wet herb rich grassland with orchids. Car park at end of track south of Rhynie Farm. Permit needed.

Thornton Glen, one mile east of Innerwick off the A1 near Torness. OS Map 67–NT735736. Mixed broad-leaf woodland in steep-sided sandstone glen. Car park opposite reserve entrance. Permit needed.

Tummel Shingle Islands, minor road north off A827, islands found on west bank of River Tummel, three miles south of Pitlochry. OS Map 52–NN972534. Shingle, herb-rich grassland and mixed woodland. Very rich plant life and birds typical of open shingle. Car park along roadside of A827 near bridge over river. Access north along path beside river.

Upper Nethan Gorge, off A726 at Blackwood, along minor road northwards to Southfield. OS Map 72–NS801442. Ancient valley woodland with ash, oak, elm, also a variety of small meadows. Park next to old railway track south of Southfield Farm.

Wallacebank Wood, in the centre of Glenbervie Golf Club, off the A9 north of Larbert. OS Map 65–NS847847. Fine lowland oakwood. Permit needed.

Whitlaw Wood, on south edge of Hawick on steep banks above Slitrig Water. OS Map 70–NT500132. Broadleaved woodland of elm and ash with rich ground flora. Car park off Rosebank Road at edge of Hawick Golf Course.

Woodhall Dean, three miles south of Dunbar on the edge of the Lammermuir Hills. OS Map 67–NT680728. Ancient oak woodland. Car park at Weatherly (NT677717). Permit needed.

Yetholm Loch, six miles south-east of Kelso off B6352 to Town Yetholm. OS Map 74–NT803279. Shallow freshwater loch, fen. Breeding and wintering wild-fowl. Car park at loch edge along rough track.

THE COUNTRY CODE

The Country Code was created to help reduce or prevent the unintentional damage that occurs every year, particularly at public holidays. Too many visitors to the countryside are unfamiliar with its ways. They forget that a single careless act – a gate left open, a fence or hedge weakened, a dropped cigarette end – can mean a lot of extra work and expense for farmers, foresters and other country folk.

The Code is a series of ten reminders based on common sense – and common failings. So when in the country remember:

Guard against all risk of fire. Plantations, woodlands and heaths are highly inflammable: every year acres burn because of casually dropped matches, cigarette ends or pipe ash.

Fasten all gates. Even if you found them open. Animals can't be told to stay where they're put. A gate left open invites them to wander, a danger to themselves, to crops and to traffic.

Keep dogs under proper control. Farmers have good reason to regard visiting dogs as pests; in the country a civilized town dog can become a savage. Keep your dog on a lead wherever there is livestock about, also on country roads.

Keep to the paths across farmland. Crops can be ruined by people's feet. Remember that grass is a valuable crop too, sometimes the only one on the farm. Flattened corn or hay is very difficult to harvest.

Avoid damaging fences, hedges and walls. They are expensive items in the farm's economy; repairs are costly and use scarce labour. Keep to the recognized routes, using gates and stiles.

Leave no litter. All litter is unsightly, and some is dangerous as well. Take litter home for disposal; in the country it costs a lot to collect it.

Safeguard water supplies. Your chosen walk may well cross a cachment area for the water supply of millions. Avoid polluting it in any way. Never interfere with cattle troughs.

Protect wildlife, wild plants and trees. Wildlife is best observed, not collected. To pick or uproot flowers, carve trees and rocks or disturb wild animals and birds destroys other people's pleasure as well.

Go carefully on country roads. Country roads have special dangers: blind corners, high banks and hedges, slow-moving tractors and farm machinery or animals. Motorists should reduce their speed and take extra care; walkers should keep to the right, facing oncoming traffic.

Respect the life of the countryside. Set a good example and try to fit in with the life and work of the countryside. This way good relations are preserved, and those who follow are not regarded as enemies.

PART TWO:
REGIONAL
GUIDE

PART TWO
CONTENTS

WEST COUNTRY

AXMOUTH TO LYME REGIS UNDERCLIFFS ✿ ☂

Extending for five miles from Lyme Regis westward to the mouth of the River Axe, this landslip area has created one of the most magnificent stretches of coastal scenery to be found in Britain. It was established as a National Nature Reserve in 1958, and covers 800 acres.

The upper cliffs consist of chalk and these overlay greensand. Both are permeable. But below them lies an impermeable layer of gault clay. It is the action of water seeping through the top layers and running off over the clay that creates the small landslips that occur every year. The whole rests on the older beds of the Jurassic and Triassic periods, which consist of marls, clays and limestones. The exposed beds are all rich in fossils, and it is these glimpses into prehistory that are responsible for the importance of the cliffs.

The most impressive of all modern landslips occurred on Christmas Eve 1839 when twenty acres of land slid toward the sea between Bindon and Dowlands. A chasm opened separating the so-called Goat Island from its original position. Though the most famous fossil to emerge from the Undercliffs is a 25-foot-long

ichthyosaur found in 1809, the most common fossils are molluscs, especially large ammonites and nautiloids. As in other NNRs, collecting without a permit is strictly forbidden.

The Reserve is not open to the public and access is confined to the beach and to the rough and slippery public footpath that leads all the way from Underhill Farm just outside Lyme Regis to Bindon Cliffs. Unfortunately there are no intermediate escape routes, so the visitor is committed to retracing his steps or walking the full tiring five miles. The route is often difficult to find, but the authorities have done their best to mark it.

The natural woodland is interesting because of its regenerative and colonizing qualities, and includes the only naturally developed ash wood to colonize virgin soil over the last half century. Flowers are good in places, and wall-pepper, Carline thistle, rockrose, birdsfoot trefoil and creeping fescue quickly colonize fresh soil. Other good species include bog pimpernel and fen orchid in the damper areas.

Though 120 species of birds have been recorded, this total includes passing seabirds and waders. Those species that actually depend in some way on the

Undercliffs are rather fewer. They include buzzard, sparrowhawk and kestrel, as well as woodpeckers, nightingale, stonechat and jackdaw, herring gull and possibly pure rock doves. Badgers are common and roe deer elusive.

Visiting: by the beach or public footpath out of Lyme Regis. Make a day of it; but do not dig.
Botany: wild madder, everlasting pea, dog's mercury, wood spurge, yellow archangel, slender false-brome, giant horsetail, water-mint, purple loosestrife, fen orchid, bog pimpernel, wall-pepper, Carline thistle, rockrose, birdsfoot trefoil, creeping fescue.
Birds: over 120 species including passing seabirds and waders, buzzard, sparrowhawk, kestrel, herring gull, stock dove, green woodpecker, great spotted woodpecker, long-tailed tit, treecreeper, stonechat, blackcap, lesser whitethroat, chiffchaff, willow warbler, nightingale, goldcrest, rock pipit, jackdaw, carrion crow.
Other: fossils.

BARNSTAPLE BAY 🐦 ❀

Only a few minutes' drive south from the teeming holiday resorts of Ilfracombe and the north Devon coast lies an area of wilderness that is an oasis of life away from the beach and surf. The twin rivers Torridge and Taw form a joint estuary at the head of the Bay enclosed to the north by the massive dunes of Braunton Burrows. The old towns of Barnstaple and Bideford lie nearby and there are views westward to the monolithic Lundy, Isle of Puffins. The estuaries are not easy to view, but those who wish to see waders and wildfowl are seldom disappointed with the views from Appledore in the south.

This is *Tarka the Otter* country and Author Henry Williamson's writing hut can still be seen at Ox's Cross near Georgeham. Braunton Burrows are a National Nature Reserve sublet from the Ministry of Defence. Sometimes military training takes place, and access is not allowed while red flags proclaim their warning. However, at the southern point (Crow Point) there is a car park and excellent views over the estuary. The dune system here is one of the most extensive in the country and botanists will enjoy searching out the colonizing glasswort and sea samphire as well as creeping willow in the slacks. Unfortunately the delicate balance of the dunes is easily upset, and visitors must confine themselves to the boardwalks that funnel them to the beach.

Visiting: free access at Braunton Burrows (but beware of red flags) and at Appledore.
Birds: shelduck, wigeon, brent goose, redshank, dunlin, sanderling, whimbrel, black-tailed godwit, common tern.
Botany: dune colonizers.

BRISTOL ZOO ❀ 🐦 ⚥ ♿

Though covering only twelve acres, Bristol Zoo has earned itself a high place in zoo rankings. It is a charming spot, with well laid out gardens and a number of notable tree specimens surrounding a lake. Its park-like tranquillity is broken by the calls of birds and other exotic animals, a complete contrast to the bustling city of Bristol that surrounds it.

The Zoo exhibits a fine range of species from all parts of the world, and has achieved a considerable degree of fame in its path-finding efforts to breed from stock. Whereas almost anyone can breed lions – so much so that the surplus lion population in the country is something of an embarrassment – many other species prove much more difficult. As one of today's main justifications for the existence of zoos at all is to provide a breeding basis to support the wild stock of endangered animals, the efforts of institutions like Bristol are to be encouraged. Way back in 1934 Bristol bred the first chimpanzee in captivity in Europe. This was followed by the first lowland gorilla in Britain in 1971. There are now breeding groups of both species, as well as orang-utans and other species. A new ape house was completed in 1976. Altogether the collection of apes and monkeys is one of the most representative in the world. A troop of rhesus monkeys is housed in a temple reminiscent of the temples in India and Nepal where, being regarded as sacred, these animals live a privileged semi-domestic life and proliferate. Among the more spectacular species there is a good collection of big cats.

Other significant achievements at Bristol include the breeding of polar bear, okapi, black rhinoceros and peccary, some of which have been passed into zoo commerce and conceivably saved a few animals for the wild. There is an excellent bird collection, including a few rarities like Manchurian crane, peacock pheasant and ocellated turkey – the smaller of the two wild species of turkey found only in central America. There is a good aquarium and a fine reptile house, where this endangered group is well represented.

In addition to the main zoo the Bristol, Clifton and West of England Zoological Society, to give its full name, also owns Hollywood Towers, a secluded retreat where breeding rather than display comes first.

Polar bears are bred at Bristol Zoo

Visiting: Bristol Zoo is located in the Clifton area of Bristol and is served by bus and train (Clifton Down). It is open throughout the year. Tel. 0272 738951. Restaurant, cafeteria, shop, etc.

Mammals: gorilla, chimpanzee, orang-utan and other primates; black rhinoceros, polar bear, okapi, African elephant, Indian elephant, hippopotamus, giraffe, zebra.

Birds: good collection from all parts of the world.

Botany: good plantings around the animal pens. Chilean fire-bush (*Embothrium*) flowers in June.

CHEDDAR GORGE 🐦 ❋ 🦋

Thronged by tourists from an increasing number of countries, it is little surprise that Cheddar, a small sleepy village in the Mendip Hills of Somerset south of Bristol, has been spoilt. If not an actual tourist trap, then at least the 'trappings' are there. It is difficult to get away without paying something, but just down the road is some of the finest scenery in southern England. A vast, rolling, little-inhabited landscape full of attractive villages and woods, downland and copses, dry-stone walls and hedgerows full of flowers.

Two particularly fine areas right next to Cheddar are managed by the Somerset Trust for Nature Conservation. Black Rock Nature Reserve lies along the B3135, the road that runs along the Gorge itself. Over 500 feet up among the hills, its heart is the old Black Rock Quarry. The area is now largely wooded along the scarp, but with open downland with scrub beyond. At Black Rock Gate a track leaves the road eastward to the start of a nature trail that in one way or another covers the whole of the reserve. It leads along the limestone cliffs where the usual rich flora of such areas may be found. Orchids, lady's smock, the fine spleenwort and hosts of other wild flowers can be sought, but not picked. There is a badger sett in the reserve, and a variety of birds.

To the north, and reached by the same track, the Long Wood Nature Reserve also boasts a useful wide-ranging nature trail. *En route* you pass the Velvet Bottom Reserve where the Romans mined lead and silver and where butterflies now abound.

Long Wood boasts a typical limestone community of mature trees including wych elm, ash and yew. It harbours a good collection of mammals, including roe deer, rabbit, badger, fox, grey squirrel, stoat, weasel, hedgehog and wood mouse – though one is fortunate to see more than a couple of these. Birds are generally common species, though there is a good population of summer migrants, including garden warbler and redstart. Buzzard and sparrowhawk may also be seen overhead.

Progressing through the reserve (and according to season) one may see early purple orchid, cuckoo-pint, meadow saffron, broad-leaved garlic, spotted orchid, hemp agrimony, herb Paris and toothwort. There is a plethora of ferns and lichens and a wealth of butterflies including brimstone, comma, small tortoiseshell and peacock. Some areas are locked and others roped off – remember this is limestone country and full of caves and swallowholes.

Continuing by road over the Mendips you drop down to the huge Chew Lake, a reservoir beloved by bird-watchers and anglers alike. Duck, terns, waders and a host of small birds throng this water and its natural banks. It is accessible at several spots, and bird-watchers gather in numbers at some of the best vantage points along the public highway. Anglers can fish for trout from both boat and bank, and the average size is excellent. Just a couple of miles to the west lies the magnificent Blagdon Reservoir, where trout fisherman gather on those balmy summer evenings hoping for the rare 'Blagdon Boil' – a moment of true magic, I am told, when trout appear feeding at the surface in unbelievable numbers.

Visiting: take the B3135 from Cheddar up the Gorge and beyond. Watch for the footpath on the left at Black Rock Gate. Walk up the valley and explore Black Rock Nature Reserve on the right via the marked nature trail. Continue up the track to Long Wood Wildlife Reserve, where another nature trail will be found.
Birds: willow warbler, chiffchaff, garden warbler, redstart, marsh tit, buzzard, sparrowhawk, kestrel, tree sparrow, great spotted woodpecker, lesser spotted woodpecker, green woodpecker.
Botany: wych elm, ash, yew, early purple orchid,

spotted orchid, cuckoo-pint, meadow saffron, broad-leaved garlic, hemp agrimony, herb Paris, toothwort, Cheddar pink.
Insects: brimstone butterfly, comma butterfly, tortoiseshell butterfly, peacock butterfly.

COTSWOLD FARM PARK

This Farm Park is run by the Rare Breeds Survival Trust and forms part of Bemborough Farm between Stow-in-the-Wold and Winchcombe in deepest Cotswold country. There are the usual visitor facilities, including a cafeteria and information centre. The aim of the Park and Trust is to exhibit breeds of domestic animals that disappeared from our countryside as a result of the agrarian revolution of the eighteenth century. By regressive breeding some old breeds have been re-created while others have been brought from elsewhere. Cattle include the longhorn and white; sheep include Portland and Jacob; there are unusual chickens, lop-eared rabbits and much else besides.

Visiting: take the B4077 westwards from Stow to Ford, then turn off southward on to minor roads to the Farm Park. Tel. 045 15 307.
Mammals: rare breeds of domestic stock.

COTSWOLD WATER PARK

Among the headwaters of the River Thames lies an area rich in what the extraction industry calls 'aggregates' – gravel to you and me. As the gravel is removed the pits flood naturally and are becoming one of the largest wetlands in England. Already several areas have been declared reserves and, with easy access, this is fast becoming a very popular outing for anyone living within fifty miles. Birds have already found the waters attractive with garganey, water rail, little ringed plover and over 120 other species. Eventually the Park will include over 12,000 acres, some parts reserved for wildlife: examples already established are Wheelford Pool and Cokes Pit.

Visiting: the area lies south of Cirencester between the A419 and A429. A leaflet can be obtained from both Gloucestershire and Wiltshire County Councils.
Birds and Botany evolving.

DARTMOOR NATIONAL PARK

Amounting in all to 365 square miles, Dartmoor National Park coincides more or less exactly with the

Dartmoor ponies wander over the central area of the Moor

geographically distinct upland area of Dartmoor. Thus it includes HM Prison and a huge and dangerous firing range, as well as some of the finest countryside in the whole of Britain. It also includes several Sites of Special Scientific Interest (SSSIs). The hills do no more than scrape the 2000 foot mark, but can be dangerous for the ill-prepared and inexperienced nevertheless. The high tops, often capped with an igneous pinnacle, are called 'tors' and are generally covered with bracken and rough grasses rather than heather. The green pastures, all neatly hedged, stretch up the hillsides, in many cases almost to the top. Fast-running streams, full of white water and boulders, with dippers, grey wagtails and trout, tumble down the steep-sided valleys in every direction. At the foot of the hills they are crossed by old stone bridges, and there are little villages scattered here and there, all reached by lanes that cut deep into the land they pass through.

In several places these streams have been dammed at a high level among the open moors creating large reservoirs. Judicious planting has created screening coverts of mixed trees that add colour and variety to the scenery. The reservoir of Burrator is a good example; it could almost be in the Lake District. Being at moderate altitude, such waters are poor in wildlife.

In fact Dartmoor really is not too brilliant for wildlife anyway, and what there is can best be searched for in the wooded valleys rather than the high tops. There, on the windswept open areas, meadow pipits and ring ousels may find a living, but even in strong heather areas the native red grouse are very thin on the ground. The odd raven, curlew and wheatear may be encountered, but only occasionally. Things were not always so bleak. There are remnants, at Wistman's Wood and Piles Wood at Black Tor Beare, of the high-level pedunculate oak woodlands that once stretched along many of the valleys, though even they are not prolific in the life they support.

Drop down into the valleys and everything changes. The hanging woods are full of bird song in spring and through the summer. Village gardens are alive with birds, and even the streams cannot drown their songs. Willow warblers, chaffinches, great and blue tits, nuthatch and treecreeper, redstarts and grey wagtails, dippers and common sandpipers, all are numerous, common and easy to find. There are tawny owls occupying almost every old wood, and a barn owl can sometimes be seen drifting over the meadows. There are kestrels, and above all else, there are buzzards – perhaps as numerous among the wooded valleys of Dartmoor as anywhere in the country. Overhead they soar on wings held in a shallow 'V'; at rest they sit on tree or fencepost awaiting their chance to pounce on small prey among the grass.

The valleys are the home of Dartmoor's mammals too. Fox and badger are both numerous and viewable. Otters still play in the streams, but they are becoming more scarce and increasingly nocturnal in habit. They were still hunted in the traditional way, by otter hounds and men on foot, until granted the full protection of the law.

The Dartmoor ponies are hardy little creatures that live on one of the largest unenclosed common lands in England. In the same way as the ponies have the right to wander at will over some 100,000 acres of the central section of the Moor, so too do we. This is the Dartmoor Forest proper, together with the adjacent Commons of Devon. However some 30,000 acres are used for military training, and noticeboards and white posts with two red bands indicate the danger zones. Firing times can be obtained from local police stations and post offices and a red flag indicates firing in progress. This section is mainly in the north-west.

The Dartmoor National Park offers fine countryside with hill walking or valley strolling to naturalist, fisherman and rambler. There are so many superb spots for a day that personal preference is bound to vary. A list of favoured tourist spots would include: Buckland-in-the-Moor, the most photographed village in Devon; Buckland Abbey, once a monastery, later owned by Sir Francis Drake, now leased by the National Trust to Plymouth Corporation as a maritime museum; Buckfast Abbey; Dartmeet, the most famous of all the Moor's beauty spots; Sticklepath, near Okehampton, with its museum of rural industries; Postbridge, for its old drovers' clapper bridge; and Widecombe-in-the-Moor, for its fair held on the second Tuesday of September and made famous by 'Uncle Tom Cobleigh and all'.

For walks through the Park the following is a highly selective bunch:

1. Leave Okehampton westward on the A30 and near Fowley follow the West Okement River upstream to the oak woods at Black Tor Beare. Keep left across the open moor to High Willhays, where the heather may produce red grouse, then on to Yeo Tor and West Mill Tor. Turn north to Okehampton Camp and the road across the railways. Turn left and follow the southern river bank back to Fowley. A good long hard day's walk – map and compass essential.

2. Leave the tourists at Dartmeet and walk downstream along the south bank of the River Dart through delicious oak woods. This soon becomes the National Trust property called Holne Woods. Continue to New Bridge and then walk the A384 to Holne Bridge and cut off southward along the west bank of the Dart to Buckfastleigh. About half a day.

3. Follow the valley of the West Dart northward from Two Bridges to the high-level oaks of Wistman's Wood. Venture no further – this is military country. Also from Two Bridges take the B3212 northward and after passing the pine plantations on the right turn right to Bellever and explore southward along the East Dart River. No permits are required to visit these woods, but visitors are requested to keep to the marked routes and to remain outside the experimental plots. About half a day each.

4. Yarner Wood Nature Trail through the National Nature Reserve of the same name starts above Bovey Tracy at Yarrow Lodge. It leads through some fine old woodland and lasts about a couple of hours. The fortunate might glimpse badgers, but all should see redstart and pied flycatcher in summer.

Visiting: easy access with plentiful accommodation of every type. Information from Dartmoor National Park, Parke, Haytor Road, Bovey Tracey, Devon. TQ13 9JQ.

Birds: buzzard, kestrel, red grouse, raven, common sandpiper, ring ousel, redstart, whinchat, stonechat, grey wagtail, dipper, willow warbler, chaffinch.

Mammals: otter, fox, badger, ponies.

Botany: varied and interesting at all levels. Because of the continued grazing in this area, meadow flowers continue to prosper.

EXMOOR NATIONAL PARK ✿ 🐦 🐝 🦋 ♿

Compared with the starkness of the high tors of Dartmoor, Exmoor is gentle, its appeal less obvious, its landscape less of a contrast to the surrounding countryside. But Exmoor has a beauty all its own, with its little villages all thatch and plaster, tumbling streams lined with thick woodlands alive with bird song, market towns that seem to echo the words of a bygone age –

The River Heddon valley, Exmoor

Withypool, Simonsbath. The highest spot is Dunkery Beacon at a mere 1707 feet above sea level – no more than a hill. This is Lorna Doone country, with a traditional way of life and an intimate social system. The coast has changed. Lynton and Lynmouth were once national headlines when destroyed by floods. They have rebuilt themselves to cope with the tourists, but much is just the same as it was a hundred years ago.

Wildlife is not outstanding, save for the blackcock that here find their southern outpost in Britain, and the red deer which are a local pride and joy. But there are red grouse and merlins on the moors, and dippers and many small birds along the streams.

The National Park authorities have produced three guides to 'Waymarked Walks' within the Park, and these excellent little booklets take the visitor through fine and beautiful countryside some of which has been specially opened to provide continuity away from the rights of way.

Visiting: booklets from Exmoor National Park, Exmoor House, Dulverton, Somerset TA22 9HL.

Mammals: red deer, badger
Birds: black grouse, red grouse, moor and valley species.

LONGLEAT SAFARI PARK ✟ ♿

The 'Lions of Longleat' was the first of the modern safari parks to be opened in the world and has set the style for those which followed this new approach to displaying animals. The vast number of imitators has proved the success of the idea. Large paddocks, simply designed to keep predator and prey (rather than man and animal) apart, can be driven through, giving as genuine a taste of a wild safari as can be had outside Africa. Lions, of course, are the favoured stars of the show, and what a contrast to the old barred and fenced lions they provide. Perhaps unfortunately, the various safari parks that followed the lead of the Marquis of Bath at Longleat felt bound to offer more, with an inevitable increase in the demand for wild animals as stock.

Now at Longleat you can see lions, tigers, giraffes, zebras and baboons, with a special island reserve for chimpanzees and the surrounding lake for sealions and hippo. There are eland, white rhinoceros, ostrich,

Visitors can drive close to watch lions feeding at Longleat

wildebeest, in fact a good cross-section of the great mammal populations of the African savannahs. Of course, many of the animals do breed, but apparently not in sufficient numbers to produce the quantity required by zoos and safari parks, so the capturing goes on.

Nevertheless the grounds of Longleat are a major wildlife attraction, and well worth a visit, especially with children. As elsewhere it is advisable to avoid holiday weekends.

Visiting: Longleat is well signposted off the A362 four miles south-west of Warminster. It is open throughout the year and there are the usual catering facilities and shops. Tel. 09853 551.

Mammals: lion, tiger, giraffe, eland, wildebeest, zebra, chimpanzee, hippo, sealion, baboon, Ankole cattle.

MARLBOROUGH DOWNS ✿ ♿ 🦋

The Marlborough Downs lie at the western end of the chalk to the north and south of the A4 west of Marlborough, which itself follows the River Kennet – one of those famous chalk streams in which trout grow fat and about which anglers dream. Much of the downland is still as empty as ever, for settlements line the valleys and hug the spring line below. But much has also been taken under the plough, destroying the association of sheep and grassland that once made the area rich and prosperous. The Downs are not unknown. Thousands of visitors flock to see the White Horse of Pewsey and take little notice of the wealth of other early human remains. Fewer still appreciate the rich flora typical of the chalk that can be found where agriculture and scrub have not destroyed it. To the south of the A4 between Lockeridge and Alton Barnes lies the Pewsey Downs National Nature Reserve, a farm that has been in the hands of the Stratton family for almost a hundred years and owned by New College Oxford for six hundred years. The area includes the White Horse. The NNR seeks to maintain the character of the area as one of the finest pieces of downland remaining in Britain.

Here one can find an excellent and comprehensive collection of the typical chalk flora. Orchids including the burnt-tip, eyebright, rock rose, chalk milkwort, harebell, round-headed rampion, early gentian, bastard toadflax, snakeshead fritillary and others. Butterflies too proliferate, including the chalk hill blue, which is the subject of experiment regarding the trampling of its habitat by livestock. The reserve is open along many rights of way, but it is not a public open space. Do not pick flowers – it is illegal, and in any case will

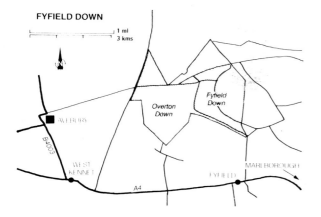

FYFIELD DOWN

is a tropical house designed by Herbert Whitley, the Zoo's founder, to resemble nothing less than a backwater in the Amazon jungle, with epiphytic ferns and orchids clinging to the trees, and creepers weaving their way upward. From time to time animals are displayed in the house. There is also a subtropical house in which flowering plants can be seen throughout the year.

The Zoo has an aquarium, a reptile house, numerous aviaries, and ponds holding cranes, storks and herons and penguins – the latter living in the luxury of a specially created Brooke-Bond Pool. There are lions, tigers, cheetahs, lynx, leopard, serval, ocelot and jaguar, a good collection of primates, and a specialized display of South American rodents, as well as the usual elephant, giraffe, rhinoceros and Barbary sheep. Large paddocks house antelopes and horses, as well as bison and deer. A group of gibbons live on a large island in one of the two lakes, and there are good numbers of birds wandering freely about the grounds.

Facilities include restaurants, a bar, and the Jungle Express miniature railway, which really does get visitors out into the grounds and among the trees and animals. Chusan palms grow luxuriously and there are Katsura trees from Japan, a Mediterranean rockery, Atlas cedars, gunnera and hundreds of other plants.

destroy the attraction of this fine area for others.

To the north across the Kennet and the A4 lies Fyfield Down NNR, another major chalkland site where early gentian, chalk milkwort, frog orchid and other plants may be found. This offers a more variable landscape, and both long-eared and short-eared owls may be found, along with interesting birds like sparrowhawk and wheatear.

Until the 1930s sarsen stones were excavated and cut here for use in all parts of the country. Many thousands remain, particularly at Clatford Bottom, where their tough sandstone quality can be seen.

Visiting: Pewsey Downs is reached from the Lockeridge–Alton Barnes road which leaves the A4 a mile west of Marlbrorough. Access is by marked footpaths on either side of the road. Fyfield Down lies to the north, reached from the hamlet of Fyfield (see map), which is just a little west of Lockeridge, by an unclassified road. For leaflets on both, contact the Nature Conservancy Southern Office.

Botany: burnt-tip orchid, frog orchid, early gentian, chalk milkwort, eyebright, rock rose, harebell, round-headed rampion, bastard toadflax.
Birds: short-eared owl, long-eared owl, sparrowhawk, wheatear, corn bunting.

PAIGNTON ZOO AND BOTANICAL GARDENS ✿ ➤ ❀ 🦋

Paignton can, with some justification, claim to be Britain's most beautiful zoo; certainly it is the only one that combines wildlife with botany with such success. To many the trees and shrubs are just a backdrop for the animals, but the Zoo houses an excellent collection of plants that are of interest in their own right. There

Visiting: the Zoo is open throughout the year and is reached via the A385 inland from the town. There is a large car park.
Mammals: tiger, lion, jaguar, rhinoceros, elephant, giraffe, seals.
Birds: penguins, emu, rhea, macaws, flamingoes.
Botany: outstanding gardens with many interesting specimens.

PORTLAND ❀ ➤

The Isle of Portland is a huge limestone outcrop extending into the Channel near Weymouth. Apart from its obvious attractions to botanists, the stone here is extensively quarried (Portland Stone) and fossil buffs are continually making minor and major finds. Bird-watchers too have major attractions hereabouts, with a bird observatory, two RSPB reserves and the Chesil Beach and Ferrybridge area near Weymouth.

Bird enthusiasts find Portland Bird Observatory one of the best in Britain. Migrants flit around small fields near the Bill, while seabirds are regularly noted offshore, particularly in autumn. All sorts of rarities turn up here.

The Red Panda is a favourite with children at Paignton Zoo

Within Weymouth itself the RSPB's Radipole Reserve is laid out so that even the most casual visitor can enjoy the birds. There are well marked paths, listening posts, hides and an information centre. Radipole is a mixture of reeds and open water offering a wide variety of species. Ring-billed gulls are regular visitors.

To the east of the town is Lodmoor, another RSPB reserve that is for the more serious bird enthusiast, but to the west is the famous Abbotsbury Swanery – where everyone can enjoy the huge nesting colony.

Visiting: free access to all areas and good car parks at Radipole and Lodmoor. A fee is payable at Abbotsbury.
Botany: interesting limestone flora.
Birds: migrants at Portland; little gull, common tern, Cetti's warbler at Radipole; bearded tit at Lodmoor; swans at Abbotsbury.
Other: fossils in limestone quarries (private).

PURBECK AND POOLE ✣ ☘ ✾ 🦋 ♿

Littered with place names like Worth Matravers and Creech Bottom, the Isle of Purbeck is England at its best. From Bournemouth eastwards the coast is built up and boring; westward there is Poole Harbour, a natural playground, and the delightful countryside of the Purbeck Hills. There is Studland Heath, a National Nature Reserve, and Durlston and St Aldhelm's Heads, white chalk cliffs that drop to the sea and which support the most easterly mainland colonies of auks along the south coast. There is Arne, the Royal Society for the Protection of Birds' Reserve, with its nature trail at Shipstal Point, and Poole Harbour itself, with its own nature reserve at Brownsea Island boasting the only strong colony of red squirrels in the deep south. The Island can be visited via a ferry from Poole Quay or Sandbanks Ferry; there is a landing fee and escorted tours can be arranged to see a multitiude of birds as well as the red squirrels.

The main artery is the A351 from Wareham to Swanage through the tourist attraction of Corfe Castle. After half an hour of tourism take the B3351 to Studland and take an optional detour to The Foreland to see the chalk stacks of Old Harry and his Wife. Wild Flowers flourish away from the well-worn paths and are

The coast to St Albans Head, from Warbarrow, Purbeck

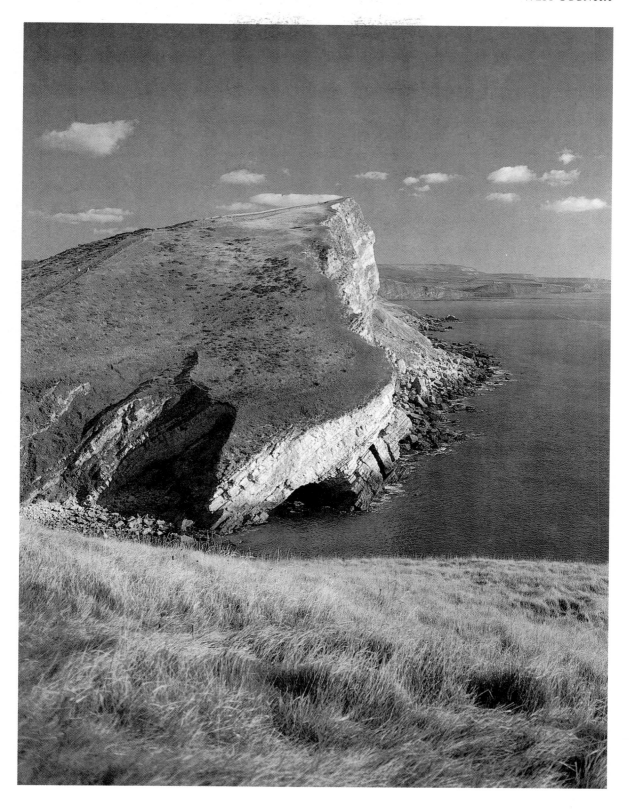

worth an hour in May and June. Continue on the minor road towards the Sandbanks Ferry. A sign shows the headquarters of the Studland NNR with a good display and a hide overlooking the Little Sea.

At Studland there are two well designed nature trails – the Sand-Dune and the Woodland – that enable a good cross-section of the reserve to be enjoyed. It is possible that, in crossing the dunes, you may be fortunate enough to spot some of the reasons for establishing Studland NNR – the fact that all six British reptiles live here. Sand lizard, common lizard, slow-worm, adder, grass snake and smooth snake may all be seen. Insects are interesting and the giant royal fern grows in places. The adjacent Little Sea often holds good numbers of duck.

Durlston Head is excellent territory for birds, and kittiwake, fulmar and guillemot can be seen from the car park of this small Country Park. Tilly Whim caves are an attraction to young and old.

If one animal dominates the Purbeck scene it is the Dartford warbler, a rarity partly because it is highly vulnerable to severe weather. The Arne Reserve is the only spot in the country where this shy and skulking little bird can reasonably be expected to show itself. Visit in early spring and contact the Warden, Syldata, Arne, Wareham BH20 5BJ.

One of the finest cliff walks in Britain extends along the coast from Durlston Head westwards to Winspit, a deep sheltered valley thick with bushes, where a path leads upwards to Worth Matravers. There are orchids among the grasses and some very beautiful scenery. This is the eastern end of the South-West Peninsula Coast Path. Beyond Winspit it borders with Purbeck Marine Reserve, with its information centre at Kimmeridge Bay.

Visiting: Studland Heath National Nature Reserve; Arne Bird Reserve (RSPB); Durlston Head; Brownsea Island.
Birds: kittiwake, fulmar, guillemot, Dartford warbler, stonechat, duck and waders in Poole Harbour.
Botany: heath and dune colonizers.
Other: all six British reptiles: sand lizard, common lizard, slow-worm, adder, grass snake, smooth snake.

ISLES OF SCILLY 🐦 ✿ &

Though they can be visited within the day, the Isles of Scilly deserve a longer stay. They enjoy one of the mildest climates in Britain, are the centre of an early flower industry and have a character very much their own. The group consists of numerous islands and rocks, all but a handful of which are uninhabited. They have some cliffs, but these are generally not very high, and the low-lying nature supports the impression of gentleness. St Mary's, the largest and most densely populated, is the arrival point both for ferry and plane, and has developed something of a tourist industry, but is remarkably unspoilt away from Hugh Town. There are some interesting areas of shoreline and a few marshes which are interesting to botanist and bird-watcher alike.

To the south lies the delightful island of St Agnes, formerly the site of a bird observatory, and its sister island of The Gugh, to which it is connected at low tide. At Horse Point, Manx shearwaters breed.

In the autumn bird-watchers invade the islands *en masse* to search out the rare vagrants that arrive from all points of the compass. Transatlantic waifs are the speciality, but anything may turn up. Accommodation in September and October is virtually unobtainable. Follow bird-watchers for the birds of the day.

Spring in the islands is delightful, with breeding birds arriving and a regular passage of migrants. Generally there are few rarities, but there are advantages in having the islands to oneself, and of course the flowers are marvellous.

Such is the unofficial inter-island communication system that St Mary's may be totally deserted as the seasonal residents head off to some other island in search of a reported rarity. The most likely is Tresco, where the freshwater pool regularly holds transatlantic waders. In fact some bird-watchers make this island their base. Tresco Abbey is the most remarkable subtropical garden in Britain, with palms, mimosas, gum trees, cacti, giant agaves and almost anything that one would expect to see in, say, the Canary Islands.

Annet, just west of St Agnes, is a Bird Reserve with puffins and gulls, but it is difficult to land there and visitors must confine their visit to a cruise offshore. Such trips depart regularly from Hugh Town during the summer and are well worthwhile. Common seals are invariably seen.

Visiting: by ferry or air (helicopter service in summer) from Penzance to Hugh Town. Excellent inter-island ferries connect. Plentiful accommodation on St Mary's, but book in advance, particularly for the autumn bird season. There are nature trails: Higher Moors Trail leads through a marsh with hides for watching birds; and Lower Moors Trail through an old withy plantation; and there is a third trail at Holy Vale, which is a noted rare bird site.

Birds: puffin, razorbill, guillemot, Manx shearwater, fulmar, storm petrel, cormorant, shag, common tern, rock pipit, interesting migrants and autumn rarities.

Botany: cultivated daffodil fields, varied wild flower communities, naturalized agapanthus, mesembry-anthemums, fuchsia.

SOUTH-WEST PENINSULA COAST PATH 🐾 ❀ 🦋

This 515-mile-long path starts at the entrance to Poole Harbour at Studland and runs along the varied coast, over cliff and heath, along beach and marsh until it reaches the Somerset coast at Minehead. The path leads through some of the finest cliff scenery in Britain. It passes close to two national parks, Dartmoor and Exmoor, and through several Areas of Outstanding Natural Beauty: the Dorset coast and heathlands, the east and south Devon coasts, the south Cornwall coast and the Lizard Peninsula and the north-east Cornwall and north Devon coasts. Additionally the path passes through, or close by, several Country Parks.

The path starts at Poole Harbour and immediately heads through Swanage into the Isle of Purbeck. It then continues westward through the geologically interesting and tourist-attracting Lulworth Cove to Weymouth where there is a small group of wildlife haunts (mainly bird). It follows the Chesil Beach past the Swannery and the subtropical garden, on the landward side of the Fleet at Abbotsbury. There is an alternative inland route via Osmington Mills to the White Horse about Sutton Poyntz, the Hardy Monument and over the downs to West Bexington. Both routes pass through the charming village of Burton Bradstock and follow the coast to Lyme Regis, where they pass through the great landslip with its immense wealth of fossils. The path then continues to Exmouth, where a ferry is taken to Dawlish and the footpath that runs just inland of the railway is followed. There then

Lulworth Cove, one of the attractions of the South-West Peninsula Coast Path

follows what is known as the 'Devon Riviera' which leaves Torquay and Paignton to the beach-lovers before the path starts once again, leading to Brixham, Berry Head, and on to Kingswear and the ferry to Dartmouth.

Berry Head is a limestone outcrop rich in flowers and birds. It is something of a tourist attraction, but the environment is nevertheless protected. Fellwort, samphire, Portland spurge, rock sea lavender, pink thrift, white sea campion, autumn squill and wild rock rose can all be found, and there are rarities such as goldilocks, restharrow, hare's ear and honewort. Birds include a good community of seabirds – fulmar, kittiwake, guillemot and the occasional razorbill.

Southward from Dartmouth the beach of Slapton Ley leads onward around the coast to Prawle Point. Thereafter each of the sunken estuaries is crossed in turn to pass into Cornwall beyond Plymouth. All of these estuaries from the Exe to the Tamar are of ornithological interest, and in season and at the right point of the tide each can be full of birds and worthy of a lengthy stop. The Exe is probably the best for waders on a rising tide throughout the year, but the Tamar is the only regular wintering haunt of avocet in Britain. Cargreen is the spot to view.

Within Cornwall the path hugs the coast, giving sections of outstanding beauty and interest and passing through quaint old fishing villages. Looe, for instance, is an attractive little village that now finds itself the centre of the British shark-fishing business. Being sunken, the coast is highly indented, and more and more ferry crossings are necessary, until at the mouth of the Fal there is virtually more ferrying than walking. The path skirts round the Lizard, passes through Penzance and then onward to Land's End, where it turns northward and then north-eastward to St Ives. It then crosses that delightful and bird-rich little estuary, the Hayl, before heading out to Godreavy Point, where guillemots and kittiwakes still breed. Along the north coast to Newquay, across the Camel, through villages that have become resorts, household names that have lost some of their magic, onward through Tintagel, Bude, Clovelly and northward to Appledore, where a gap can be bridged by ferry or bus to Braunton Burrows.

Northward the coast is marked by excellent views toward Lundy and the path continues to Bull Point, where it turns eastward to Ilfracombe, Combe Martin, and then skirts Exmoor to Minehead. What a walk! But better still, what a lovely series of walks for those who would choose the part that they wish and have the time to spend.

Visiting: a number of youth hostels serve the path, and by and large there are no long stretches without a variety of available accommodation. In particular there are many small inns which make the passing walker welcome, and in south Cornwall in the stretch between Looe and St Mawes they are particularly thick on the ground. In comparison the north coast is poorly served: no doubt it is the excellent harbours of the south coast that account for the difference. HMSO publish four guidebooks to various sections of the path that between them

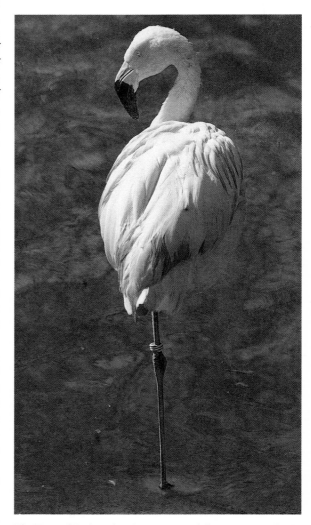

The Tropical Bird Gardens have over 180 different species of birds, including flamingoes

make the whole walk both easier and more interesting. They are available from HMSO and the Youth Hostels Association.

Birds: estuaries in the south and seabird cliffs in the north. Make a point of visiting Slapton Ley, the Exe, the Tamar and the Hayle; and Godreavy Point, St Agnes Head, the Torridge-Taw confluence and Porlock Marsh.

Botany: some really outstanding haunts: slender mullein (*Verbascum virgatum*) is confined to the south-west. The Lizard Peninsula is especially fine – notice the Cornish heather.

Insects: the large blue butterfly is found only in northern Cornwall and the Jersey tiger moth is best spotted between Exeter and Teignmouth.

THE TROPICAL BIRD GARDENS ❦ ᴕ

First opened to the public in spring 1962, the Gardens house an excellent collection of birds of over 180 different species. As far as possible they are kept under 'natural' conditions allowing free flight but relying on the food and shelter provided by the Gardens to pull back would-be wanderers. The result is several hundred birds in large, airy enclosures several of which can be walked through. As elsewhere the macaws of several species are the most obvious of the free fliers, and these colourful additions to the Somerset avifauna are a major attraction.

Pools house the usual waterfowl and flamingoes, and there are pheasants, cassowaries and ibises wandering around as well. Hornbills, owls and vultures are kept in large displays and there is a good collection of smaller birds including parrots, mynahs, toucans and weavers.

This is a good collection and, set in the heart of the Somerset countryside near Trowbridge, is an ideal day out for the people of Bristol.

Visiting: take the A361 between Trowbridge and Frome, or the A36 between Bath and Warminster, and watch for signs to Rode before Beckington. Admission charges are reasonable and there is a cafeteria. Tel. 0373 830326

Birds: macaws, parrots, weavers, wildfowl, flamingoes, pelicans, peafowl.

Other: George Inn at Norton St Philip believed to be the oldest continuously licensed premises in the country.

THAMES

THE LODGE, SANDY 🐦 ♿

The Lodge is a nineteenth-century, Tudor-style house originally built for Robert Peel's son Arthur. It was planted with many exotic shrubs and trees (275 species of flowering plants have been recorded) and the landscaped grounds are typical of their time. In 1961 the Royal Society for the Protection of Birds purchased the house as its headquarters and immediately set to creating a pond. This has added moorhen and little grebe to the breeding list of over eighty species, and the eager eyes of the RSPB staff have built up a total list of 120 species. Within the grounds, species such as nightjar, woodcock, tree pipit and the three wood-peckers all breed, while kingfishers and wood sand-pipers pass through.

Like the good bird gardeners they are, the RSPB have lashed out on nest boxes and bird feeders, and a good number of species can be seen, particularly in winter. There are many fascinating displays, including a nature discovery room, a shop and general publicity about the aims and objectives of the Society. Both school parties and individuals are welcome.

Visiting: by permit, contact the RSPB, The Lodge, Sandy, Beds. Sandy lies just off the A1 between Biggleswade and Grafham Water.

Birds: little grebe, nightjar, tree pipit, green wood-pecker, woodcock.

OXFORD BOTANIC GARDEN ✿ ♿

Established in 1621, the University Botanic Garden at Oxford is Britain's oldest botanic garden and occupies five acres near the city centre. It is noted not only for its pathfinding botanic work, which is intimately tied up with the University and with research, but also for its walls and the famous Danby Gate – both by Inigo Jones. In a city already so well served by fine gardens and open spaces, the Garden is still a major attraction. It has a fine collection of trees, shrubs and flowering plants and good tropical houses through which the visitor can wander.

Visiting: open weekdays throughout the year. Tel. 0865 276920.
Botany: excellent collection.

RIDGEWAY PATH ✿ 🌸 🦋

The Ridgeway extends for some eighty-five miles from Overton Hill near Avebury in Wiltshire to Ivinghoe Beacon in Buckinghamshire. For much of the way it

60

Blackthorn in flower in early May along the Wiltshire section of the Ridgeway Path

runs along the edge of the chalk escarpment that is variously called the Marlborough Downs, the Berkshire Downs and the Chilterns. Throughout its length the Ridgeway is littered with prehistoric remains from the Bronze and Iron Ages. There are fortifications, burial mounds, villages and monuments of a quasi-religious, and often ill-understood, nature. In the west the route is open to cyclists and horse-riders as well as to walkers; beyond the Goring Gap it is for walkers only.

The Ridgeway leaves the chalk from time to time, notably in Oxfordshire, where it passes through fields and woodlands alongside the Thames. Later it joins the ancient Icknield Way, then leaves this where it has become a metalled road, and takes a more attractive route along the Chiltern escarpment. Throughout its length excellent views over the surrounding countryside succeed one another; the Vale of the White Horse, Hackpen Hill and Ivinghoe Beacon were all noted viewpoints before the Ridgeway joined them together.

Chalk landscape is noted above all for its flowers, and visitors in the early part of summer will find a wealth of species everywhere away from the noted beauty spots. Some areas, however, are too important to leave open to free access, and several have been incorporated into nature reserves. Most important of these is Aston Rowant National Nature Reserve, which covers 300 acres of the Chiltern escarpment in Oxfordshire immediately adjacent to the old A40 London–Oxford road. As elsewhere the chalk downland has suffered considerably through ploughing and a lack of sheep and rabbit grazing. Here the natural succession that covers the open downland when grazing ceases can be seen in a more or less 'frozen' state. Sheep, including some primitive Soay sheep from the remote Hebrides of St Kilda, are used to maintain the traditional character of the hills and to protect the rich flora and fauna.

Access to Aston Rowant is restricted to public footpaths and to a nature trail that starts outside the Reserve Centre with the Soay sheep. The trail then follows one of the sunken ways that have been worn into the Chiltern escarpment; along here the yellow flowers are ploughman's spikenard. Continue past the badger sett and rabbit warren among the yews, and beyond the trees you may find spotted orchids in June and July. Though they are scarce there are several other of the thirty species of orchids that flower on the Chilterns. The viewpoint at the end overlooks Oxford, and nearby there may be common lizards and the chalkhill blue in July and August. Hares and kestrels are also frequently seen, and along on the right an enclosure is being used for studying the flora of anthills. Species include germander, speedwell, whitlow grass, forget-me-not and rock rose.

Turning back from the escarpment the path leads to an old flint pit where autumn sees a variety of fungi. Flowers among the woodland here include yellow archangel, sanicle, wood sorrel and, of course, bluebells. As with most woodland flowers, they bloom in early spring.

Visiting: Beacon Hill Escarpment Trail is reached via the old A40 beyond Stokenchurch; Exit 5 of the M40. Please stick to the trail and do not interfere with experiments or fences. Keep dogs on a lead – there are sheep here. HMSO publish a guide called *The Ridgeway Path* by S. Jennett.
Botany: ploughman's spikenard, spotted orchid, germander, speedwell, rock rose, forget-me-not, sanicle, wood sorrel, bluebell, yellow archangel.
Insects: chalkhill blue, peacock and red admiral butterflies.
Mammals: Soay sheep, badger, fallow dear, muntjac, grey squirrel, stoat, weasel, rabbit, hare.
Birds: kestrel, skylark, goldfinch.

Other nature reserves include the Berkshire, Buckinghamshire and Oxfordshire Naturalists' Trust (BBONT) reserve at Grange Sands, Great Kimble, where twenty-five acres of grassland protect adderstongue fern felwort as well as bee and bird's nest orchids and narrow-leaved helleborine. Butterflies include chalkhill blue, small blue and marbled white, and there are fifty species of breeding birds, including whinchat and nightingale.

Pulpit Hill is also nearby, and here a wide variety of botanical habitats in a mere twenty acres include ploughman's spikenard and narrow-lipped helleborine. A larger area is Chinnor Hill to the north, where BBONT has sixty-five acres of Chiltern escarpment overlooking the Vale of Aylesbury. This has the advantage of free public access, save for the sheep enclosures which are part of the management plan to reconvert to 'natural' downland. Here, and in the more open areas, frog orchid can still be found. There is a nature trail and a printed guide.

The Chilterns are rightly famous for their orchids, and BBONT is the custodian of two of the three British spots for military orchid, one of only four spots for monkey orchid, both British stations of the ghost orchid, and the only place outside the Cotswolds for red helleborine. Unfortunately, the areas concerned cannot be made public.

Visiting: The Ridgeway can be joined from the A4 west of Marlborough or from Avebury Circle on the A361. It is crossed in many places by major roads and there are many 'formal' car parks allowing access. One of the best approaches for BBONT reserves is to leave the M40 at Exit 5.
Botany: Chiltern gentian, early gentian, wild candytuft, pasque flower, field fleawort, purple milk-vetch, coralroot, herb Paris, Solomon's seal, columbine, yellow birdsnest, marsh orchid, fragrant orchid, bee orchid, pyramidal orchid, spotted orchid, butterwort, narrow-lipped helleborine, marsh helleborine, viper's bugloss, blue fleabane, chalk eyebright, ploughman's spikenard.
Butterflies: purple emperor, black hairstreak, wood white, marbled white, chalkhill blue, Adonis blue.

THERFIELD HEATH ✺ 🦋

This outstanding area of chalk downland in north Hertfordshire is a local nature reserve of the Hertfordshire County Council, open to the public at all times. While flowers are the main interest, the Heath is also of archaeological importance, with the only long barrow in the county. Outstanding are the pasque flowers, which are magnificent in April, and five species of orchid. There are also spotted cat's-ear and bastard toadflax, as well as an excellent community of other chalk-loving species. Best for all of these is the south-facing slope of Church Hill. To the north at Pen Hills there are abundant butterfly food plants, including horseshoe vetch, beloved of the chalkhill blue.

Visiting: there is a car park near the Pavilion at the Royston end of the Heath. Access is by foot from the A505 and the Therfield Road.
Botany: orchids, pasque flower, spotted cat's-ear, bastard toadflax.
Insects: butterflies, including chalkhill blue.

TRING RESERVOIRS 🦆 ✺ ♿

Tring Reservoirs were built between 1802 and 1839 to service the Grand Junction Canal (now the Grand

Mallard on the Tring Reservoirs

Union) where it cut through the high chalk escarpment of the Chiltern Hills. A series of locks up and down over Tring Summit were filled by pumping water from these four reservoirs, enabling water to flow downhill in either direction with the passing of a barge. An elaborate network of channels and sluices connects the waters, which have become less important with the decline of inland waterways.

Constructed on marshy ground, the four basins quickly built up a significant place in ornithology. It was here that the first colonizing little ringed plovers nested in 1938. Today the basin banks and the surrounding areas of woodland are a National Nature Reserve specifically established to protect birds. Winter brings large flocks of wildfowl, including the graceful goosander, while in spring and summer great crested grebe and grey heron breed among the reeds. A flock of semi-wild greylag geese spend the summer months here, and the surrounding marshes and woodlands are alive with warblers.

The four pools – Wilstone, situated away from the others, and Marsworth, Startopsend and Tringford – are a major bird-watching site and a centre of interest

and attraction throughout the year. Passage migrants often include a number of rarities, and waders in particular are numerous and often exotic. Black tern, osprey and little gull have all been seen in autumn with some degree of regularity.

In comparison, other branches of natural history are poorly served. The edible dormouse was introduced to Tring Park seventy years ago, and there may also be the occasional mink, but both are elusive. The remnants of a marshland flora can still be found, including fen and meadow orchids, as well as the rare orange foxtail and mudwort. Yellow flags, water figwort and amphibious bistort may be easily seen from the north-west bank of Wilstone.

With the exception of Tringford, the reservoirs have a remarkable reputation among anglers. Coarse fishing is allowed every day in season except Sundays, and there are ten-pound bream, three-pound roach and up to twenty-eight pound pike to be taken.

Access is by footpath and via the nature trail that winds between the three contiguous reservoirs. The waters lie north of Tring and are reached via the B489 or B488. Wilstone can be explored along its northern banks from the village of Wilstone Green. The nature trail starts at Startopsend village and runs alongside the Grand Union Canal before cutting along the embankment between Startopsend and Marsworth to the junction with Tringford. It follows the west bank of that water to the pumping station. There is a nicely produced nature trail guide which concentrates (unusually) on birds rather than flowers and there are public hides at Tringford and Wilstone.

Visiting: Tring lies on the A41 where it crosses the Chilterns between Aylesbury and Hemel Hempstead: the reservoirs lie to the north between the B488 and B489. The nature trail, which is the best approach for the three main reservoirs, starts at Startopsend village, but Tringford and the road to New Mill are excellent for branching out in all directions. Approach Wilstone from Wilstone Green.

Birds: great crested grebe, little grebe, grey heron, teal, wigeon, shoveler, pochard, tufted duck, goosander, greylag goose, reed warbler, waders and terns.

Botany: fen orchid, meadow orchid, bog pimpernel, yellow flag, water figwort, amphibious bistort, broadleaved ragwort, round-fruited rush, orange foxtail, mudwort.

WHIPSNADE PARK ZOO 🦌 🦃

Covering over 500 acres of rolling Bedfordshire countryside, Whipsnade is the well-known nursery and safety collection of the Zoological Society of London. But it is also an attraction in its own right, housing over 2000 animals in large 'natural' enclosures. As a result of this revolutionary (in 1931) zoo concept, the animals live at Whipsnade in such ideal surroundings that they breed freely. The Zoo is rightly proud of its achievements in this vital area of conservation: Père David's deer thrive here and animals have been exported back to their native China. It was the first zoo to breed warthog and the first in Britain to breed white-tailed deer, snow leopard, moose and white rhinoceros. It was also the first in Britain to breed cheetah, a notoriously difficult species, but one of crucial importance because of the catastrophic decline of this beautiful plains cat in the wild. The white rhino too was on the verge of extinction when Whipsnade became the first breeding centre outside Africa. Today a large enclosure holds a thriving herd of this, the largest rhino in the world. The North American bison breeds on the downs, musk ox in the grassy meadows, and the Thomson's gazelles have grown thicker coats to cope with the English winter.

Sea World at Windsor Safari Park

One of the features of Whipsnade is the way in which quite disparate species are grouped together in communal pens. Birds, in particular, roam freely among the antelopes and deer, and Manchurian cranes can be found alongside hog deer and nilgai. Perhaps the most remarkable testimony to the success of this beautiful zoo is that over eighty per cent of the mammals on show were born here.

For those who have not experienced the herds of animals that inhabit the plains of Africa and the forests of India, Whipsnade is the next best thing. While the safari parks supply an overlarge population of dramatic species like lions and tigers, Whipsnade is nearer the truth. Predators are few and hidden away; the more numerous and obvious game on which they depend get pride of place in this lovely zoo. There are the usual cafeteria, restaurant and bar facilities.

Visiting: Whipsnade is open every day of the year except Christmas Day and can be reached by leaving the M1 at junctions 9 or 11. It lies just west of the A5 between Dunstable and Markyate and is well signposted. Visitors can tour the Zoo in their own cars, or take the Zoo Motor Train in summer. Tel. 0582 872 171.

Mammals: one of the best collections of breeding mammals in the world, mostly seen wandering freely in large 'natural' paddocks.

Birds: a good collection of the larger species that mix well with the game animals.

WINDSOR SAFARI PARK ✠ &

When the Smart family of circus fame went into the safari business it was inevitable that they would do so with style. At Windsor, only twenty-two miles from London, they have assembled one of the largest collections of large and impressive animals to be found in the country. They have the usual drive-through system in which lions, tigers and baboons can be seen from the safety of one's own car, and the effect is almost natural, save only that some of the tigers are overweight and the lions just will not stop breeding. Baboons climb all over the cars, and there are enough cars on a summer Sunday to cause either traffic jams or frustration at not being allowed to stop.

There are cheetahs, white rhinos, elephants, giraffes, sealions, pelicans and a waterfowl collection, all set in 150 acres of grass and woodland. There are kiddies' rides, boating lakes, a 'Wild-West Fort' and of course licensed restaurants and bars; in fact almost everything that you could want if you were not looking for a day in the country. However, go out of season and all of these empty facilities really do become attractive and the collection of 'star' animal material is really very impressive.

'Sea World' the Dolphinarium is a major attraction, and it is particularly difficult to see killer whales anywhere other than in these places. The fact that they perform tricks in no way makes these magnificent creatures less appealing – in fact the reverse is true.

Visiting: leave the M4 at Exit 6 and proceed to Windsor. On the south side of the town take the B3022 to the well-signposted Windsor Safari Park Tel. 0753 869 841.

Mammals: lion, tiger, cheetah, white rhinoceros, giraffe, Indian elephant. baboon, dolphin.

WOBURN WILD ANIMAL KINGDOM ✠ &

Should there be anyone left in Britain who has not visited a safari park, Woburn Wild Animal Kingdom is included in an attempt to show them what they are in for. When the British aristocracy emerged from the period of post-war austerity they were suddenly faced with the need to earn a living for the first time in many generations. It was a task that was to prove too much for many, but the thirteenth Duke of Bedford quickly rid himself of any hangups he might have had about commerce and threw his home open to the newly-mobile populance. Though the home was the major attraction, the Duke soon found that the Deer Park, and particularly the herd of Père David's deer, a species saved from extinction by his grandfather, the eleventh Duke, had an appeal all of its own. Being both a commercial animal and a born showman, the Duke was one of the first in the safari-drive-through-zoo-park business.

To those who love the countryside the Deer Park is still a restful place of peace and serenity and, because of the eleventh Duke's Père David associations, a place of pilgrimage. As for the rest, there are enclosures that can be driven through that are so full that the normally solitary tiger forms prides, while the lions seem intent on breeding themselves out of house and home. There are plenty of other animals including rhinos, hippos, elephants and unusual species like bongos and timber wolves.

Visiting: Woburn lies between the A50 and the M1 near Exits 12 and 13. The nearest town is Leighton Buzzard. There are restaurants and lots to do and see. Tel. 0525 25 246 or 407.

Mammals: Père David's deer, all the usual big stars including wandering lions, tigers, camel, eland, wildebeest, zebra, black rhinoceros, olive baboon, Canadian black bear and hippopotamus.

Birds: ostrich and not much else.

LONDON AND THE SOUTH-EAST

ARUNDEL WILDFOWL RESERVE ⊛ ㋐

The Arundel Reserve, three-quarters of a mile north of the West Sussex town, was opened by the Wildfowl Trust in 1976 and boasts the usual collection of wildfowl from all corners of the earth. Extending to some sixty-four acres, the marshy pools were already attractive to wild birds before the Trust arrived. Now the collection and feeding routines, and particularly the improvements and extension of the area of open water, makes the area even more attractive. There is an excellent Visitor Centre that includes shop, lecture theatre, refreshment room, interpretative centre and a large viewing gallery overlooking Swan Lake.

One significant difference from other Trust grounds is the special place of seaduck, species that require an inexhaustible supply of clean, fast-flowing water. Here chalk springs meet the requirements of these birds and long-tailed duck, eider and others all prosper. There is also a natural scrape with hides for watching waders and other wild birds.

Visiting: the Arundel Reserve is open every day of the year except Christmas Day. It is well signposted from Arundel, which is on the A27 due east of Chichester.

Birds: excellent wildfowl collection with seaduck a speciality. Wild wigeon, teal, pochard, shoveler, kingfisher, snipe, bearded tit.
Other: Arundel Castle nearby.

BENTLEY WILDFOWL COLLECTION ㋐ ㋑

Ornamental wildfowl have been kept for generations, though it was only quite recently that such collections have been opened to the public and thus gained the revenue by which they could be built up to the extremely high standards of today. The Bentley Collection is openly based on the inspiration of Sir Peter's Scott's Slimbridge. Starting in 1962 it has been continuously expanded, and is now one of the principal collections in Britain.

Of the 147 species of swans, geese and duck in the world, no less than 110 can be seen at Bentley. Mostly they roam at will through the twenty-five acres of grounds, but there are pens for specific birds, each with its own piece of water, as well as larger ponds and islands where a mixture of birds live side by side. The collection is drawn from all over the world. Rarities include trumpeter swan, cereopsis (or Cape Barren) goose and Hawaiian goose (néné).

Looking out from a hide across the water at Arundel Reserve

In addition to the wildfowl there are flamingoes, two species of crane and peafowl. Tea and biscuits can be bought and there is a handy picnic ground and car park. The addition of a motor museum was presumably a matter of necessity in such a highly competitive business.

Visiting: Bentley lies between the A26 and B2191 north of Lewes and is signposted. Admission is reasonably priced and the collection is open daily through spring and summer, except Good Friday.
Birds: Hawaiian, emperor and Cape Barren geese, trumpeter swan, other wildfowl.

BIRDWORLD 🦜 ♿
Situated in five acres just off the A325 between Farnham and Petersfield, Birdworld was opened in 1968 and is now a home to over a thousand birds.

Birdworld is situated right next to Alice Holt Forest, and many of its free-flying macaws evidently find the trees an acceptable substitute for their native South American jungles. They do, however, return to

feed and roost in the comfort and safety of the grounds. There are quite a number of other species that visitors can mix with, including cranes and a good collection of inquisitive geese. Many of these species breed within the grounds and thus add to the stock continuously. One of the most interesting features from the visiting bird-watcher's angle are the uncaged crested seriemas, a fast-walking bird from South America. It is strange the way that birds that are generally poorly housed and ignored in most zoos can suddenly take on stardom given the right circumstances.

The grounds are well laid out, with ponds and paddocks for various species, a café and shop and a good network of paths that wheelchairs can negotiate.

Visiting: Birdworld is well signposted from the southern end of the Farnham bypass and lies just north of the A325 at Holt Pound. It is open throughout the year, and a bus service stops virtually outside. Tel. 0420 22140.

BOX HILL ❀ ♿
Millions of feet have climbed the steep slope upward from Burford Bridge on the A24, the Leatherhead –

Dorking road, and between them they have carved a deep chalk scar along the very crest of the North Downs. At the top awaits one of the very finest of Wealden views southward over the interlocking hill ranges, south-westward over slumbering Dorking to Leith Hill, 965 feet high, with its 35-foot tower to make the 1000 feet. Before the top a precipitous footpath drops away among the box trees to the River Mole below which can be crossed by stepping stones and is a pleasant place to picnic and watch minnows and stone loach. The whole hill is now a Country Park.

Box Hill is not all hard work and hard walking: a turning off the B road between Mickleham and Burford Bridge leads in alpine fashion zigzag up the hill face over well grassed chalk slopes where bee and other orchids can be found in June. Just a little way off the first zig is Juniper Hall, now used by the Field Studies Council as a centre for the children of London's schools. So what was once a breath of Sunday country air for the people of Battersea and Tooting is now a rather more formalized outing for their children and grandchildren.

The Pilgrim's Way skirts along the chalk escarpment at this point on its medieval way between Winchester and Canterbury. On the west side of the River Mole the National Trust (who own Box Hill and its surrounds) also own the remains of the twelfth-century West Humble Chapel, which lies on the Pilgrim's Way.

Visiting: A24 to Burford Bridge between Leatherhead and Dorking.
Botany: orchids on the less frequented chalk slopes.
Other: Wealden views.

BRIGHTON AQUARIUM

Established in 1869 at the height of Brighton's popularity, the Aquarium was designed in the ornate Italian style of the time and, though frequently modernized, still retains an air of times gone by. Today, pride of place goes inevitably to the performing dolphins in their huge modern indoor pool, but they are well handled, immensely entertaining and a major attraction. Sealions perform as well, and together these two mammals bring in the visitors. There are seals and turtles too.

Yet behind the façade of publicity and entertainment the Aquarium houses one of the best collections of predominantly marine fish and other creatures to be found anywhere in the country. Many are familiar and can be purchased outside together with chips, but others are semi-exotic and seldom seen on the fishermonger's slab. It is a fascinating glimpse into the underwater world that most of us still see only in films or at places like this.

Visiting: the Aquarium is on the sea front at the heart of Brighton. Plentiful public transport. Tel. 0273 604233/4.
Mammals: dolphins, seals, sealions.
Fish: excellent collection, principally marine.

CATHERINGTON DOWN AND BUTSER ANCIENT FARM ✿ ❀ 🦋

Situated on the east side of the unclassified Lovedean – Clanfield road north of Portsmouth, Catherington Down is a reserve of the Hampshire County Council, administered by the Hampshire and Isle of Wight Naturalists' Trust. This is a fine example of downland that has been ploughed only once in recent years, as a result it has a good chalk flora on open downland with small belts of woodland at the top and bottom of the slopes. Many typical flowers are present, but there is also round-headed rampion, which is remarkably abundant for so rare a plant. Orchids are not numerous, though fragrant and spotted are regular, and frog orchid and autumn lady's tresses rare. Autumn is a fine time to visit, with the blues of bellflower, small scabious and later felwort giving a splendid effect. Chalkland butterflies and moths are a further source of interest.

To the north, just off the A3, lies Butser Hill, well known as a site of prehistoric settlement and now part of the Queen Elizabeth Country Park. Here the Butser Ancient Farm Research Project is busily putting archaeological theories to the practical test. They have Soay sheep and a cross-bred race of cattle that exhibit many of the qualities of their prehistoric ancestors. They are planting (by hand of course) old strains of cereals such as Emmer and Speit, two primitive strains of wheat that have approximately twice the protein content of modern bread wheat, and have reconstructed various buildings and field systems of the time. No doubt the scheme is of great scientific interest, but it also provides an absorbing way to spend a day.

Visiting: take the main A3 from Portsmouth and turn left on minor roads to Lovedean. Thence northward toward Clanfield, with Catherington Down reserve a mile or so along on the left. OS Ref. 690142. There is no restriction on access. Three footpaths cross the reserve. For Butser Ancient Farm proceed to Rogate House, Rogate, off the A3 watching for signs to Queen Elizabeth Country Park. Tel. 0705 595040.

Botany: bellflower, small scabious, felwort.
Insects: butterflies of the chalk.
Other: prehistoric working farm.

CHESSINGTON ZOO ✷ ☀ ☂

Chessington lies in the outer suburbs of South London, in the Green Belt but with much development nevertheless. The Zoo was first opened in 1931 and continued to operate right through the war. It has, from its earliest days, considered itself an entertainment centre, with circus, kiddies' playground, railway, etc., and in this it was ahead of its time. Today it is more of a fairground and less of a zoo. There is a good collection maintained in predominantly modernized conditions. There are stars like lions and tigers, polar bears and orang-utans, leopards and sealions, but there are many lesser creatures too. A good collection of monkeys includes Assamese macaque, crab-eating monkey, three species of capuchin and two of spider monkeys. A pair of gorillas and a pair of orang-utans are kept more in hope than in belief that they will breed, and unfortunately there are many other 'singles' in the collection.

There are good numbers of antelope and deer, a tapir, elephant, a goodly number of bears and a good collection of the usual zoo-kept birds – for instance, scarlet ibis, white pelican, several pheasants, a waterfowl collection, some free-flying macaws, birds of prey, rock-hopper penguins and three species of cranes. There is an aquarium and a collection of reptiles.

Visiting: admission is reasonable, but the circus, pets' corner and aquarium are all extras, though cheap. The Zoo (not the circus, which is summer only) is open throughout the year. It is easily reached by rail from London to Chessington South, and combined rail-entrance tickets are available. By road it lies on the A243 between Chessington and Leatherhead. There is a cafeteria, two licensed restaurants and two bars.
Mammals: lion, tiger, leopard, polar bear, gorilla, orang-utan, Assamese macaque, Brazilian tapir.

Birds: macaws flying free, scarlet ibis, pheasants, birds of prey and vultures.

CHOBHAM COMMON ☀ ❋ ☂ ✷

The 380 acres of Chobham Common were acquired by Surrey County Council in 1968 and have been maintained as a nature reserve ever since. Though situated right in the heart of the rich commuter belt, only some twenty miles south-west of London, this area of heathland has always been close to the heart of London naturalists. Indeed it is a little special, and the County Council is to be congratulated both on having acquired it and on opening up so many permissive tracks to the public. The underlying sand has created a heath landscape that exhibits a typical community of plant life. Heather, purple moor grass, bristle bent and in some places cotton grass are all to be found. Here and there sundew, marsh gentian and marsh clubmoss grow – all within an essentially suburban area. Even more staggering are the birds, which form as representative a collection of heathland species as you will find for miles. Nightjar, whitethroat, willow warbler, yellowhammer, skylark and perhaps still the declining woodlark may all be sought. There are, of course, badgers and foxes, and a spider found nowhere else in the country.

Visiting: Chobham Common is situated to the north of the B386 and between that road and the Staines and Wokingham Line Railway. Several public footpaths transect the area and many more permissive tracks have been opened to public access.
Birds: a more or less complete heathland fauna.
Botany: sundew, marsh gentian.

FARLINGTON MARSHES AND LANGSTONE HARBOUR ☀ ❋

Langstone Harbour is one of the most important wetlands on the south coast, and home to immense numbers of passage, wintering and breeding birds. Farlington Marshes consist of a walled peninsula extending into the Harbour, giving unrivalled views over the mud banks and estuary and a home to numerous breeding and roosting birds. The northern boundary is the A27, and there is excellent bird-watching from a lay-by near the A2030 flyover. Access to about a third of the reserve is free, but elsewhere visitors must keep to the public footpaths (which give the best views anyway).

The area is much more than a bird reserve. The salt

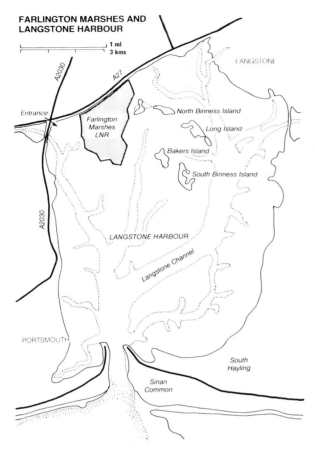

FARLINGTON MARSHES AND
LANGSTONE HARBOUR

Botany: sea aster, sea wormwood, sea milkwort,
seablite, golden samphire, sea lavender, sea pink,
sea clubrush, water crowfoot, slender reedmace,
water plantain, fat duckweed, sea clover, slender
birdsfoot trefoil, grass vetchling, beard grass.

Birds: black-necked grebe, brent goose, shelduck,
goldeneye, red-breasted merganser, teal, wigeon,
pintail, redshank, dunlin, curlew, bar-tailed godwit,
black-tailed godwit, grey plover, turnstone, snipe,
golden plover, short-eared owl, common tern, little
tern, Sandwich tern, wheatear, whinchat.

FRENSHAM

The dry sandy heathlands of south-western Surrey are
both attractive and agriculturally unproductive. Some,
like the Devil's Jumps and Punchbowl, are famous
beauty spots over run by thousands of people every
summer Sunday. Others, like Hankley Common, are
remarkably unfrequented, lonely places where heather,
sand and sky combine to produce a wilderness right in
the very heart of the commuter belt.

This is an area of strange contrasts. At Frensham
Great Pond sailing, water-skiing and all those other
noisy outdoor pursuits convert a rather attractive
water into sheer bedlam. But walk away eastward up
the sand ridge and soon the heather and birches
insulate you from the world. At the top you can look
down onto Frensham Little Pond where birds nest
deep in the reedbeds and where botanists seek out the
elusive plants of oakwood and heath side by side.
Much of the area has been planted with conifers since
the war, but these only serve to insulate areas of
heather and old Scot's pines from disturbance. As a
result the extremely rare hobby can sometimes be seen
sweeping overhead. Reed and sedge warblers croak
away at the lake's edge, and willow warblers and
nightingales sing from the scrub.

Much of the area around the Little Pond is of open
access, though the plantations are private property. It
is possible to walk eastward through to the Tilford –
Hindhead road and then cross over between houses to
Hankley Common, where skylarks and the occasional
deer are the only companions. To the east lies
Thursley Common, offering a wider choice of habitats
and a far richer fauna and flora. This is a noted winter
haunt of great grey shrike and a breeding place for
snipe, redshank and the elusive Dartford warbler. The
whole area is now a Country Park.

To the north, the road that connects Frensham and
Tilford north of the Pond area has the interesting Old

marsh community includes sea aster and sea wormwood as well as golden samphire, sea lavender and sea
pink. The pools on the marshes hold water crowfoot,
water plantain and the localized fat duckweed. Less
usual plants include sea clover and slender birdsfoot
trefoil. Over a third of British grasses have been
identified, and there are beds of eelgrass, beloved of
brent geese. Up to 6000 of these Siberian geese spend
the winter in Langstone Harbour, and there are similar
numbers of shelduck as well as all of the usual marine
duck species. Many thousands of waders fly onto
Farlington Marshes at high tide and the lagoons
invariably hold a rare wader or two each autumn. This
is a top bird-watching site and of interest throughout
the year: the check-list is formidable.

Visiting: an unmade track leads eastward from the
roundabout at the junction of the A27 and the
A2030. There are noticeboards at the main gate
and visitors are requested to adhere to the conditions of entry.

Kiln Museum, housing the Jackson collection of farm implements and machinery of the past that includes a complete wheelwright's shop in working order. It is open during the summer on weekends and Wednesday afternoons. On a Sunday continue to Tilford to sample the ale at the Barley Mow while watching the cricketers trying to beat the ball over the two medieval bridges that guard the green.

Visiting: a good map and sense of direction after reaching Farnham or Hindhead.
Birds: great crested grebe, little grebe, teal, tufted duck, buzzard, hobby, sparrowhawk, stonechat, nightjar, Dartford warbler, reed warbler, sedge warbler, willow warbler, lesser whitethroat, nightingale, redstart, goldcrest.
Botany: dry heathland flowers.

HOWLETTS ZOO PARK ✟ ♿

The brainchild of John Aspinall, professional gambler turned zoo-keeper-conservationist, Howletts is a re-

Seven-year-old Killa-Killa, the gorilla, with her baby daughter

markable extension of one man's ideas. Putting money to use for conservation should be encouraged, and at Howletts Aspinall has certainly created a new attraction in showing animals. His 'friendships' with his animals have been filmed for television and written about in magazines – if he did nothing else he would have brought welcome attention to the cause of conservation. He has, however, managed to achieve much more than that. By gathering endangered mammals to his zoo he has established breeding groups, and if all the tigers in India suddenly disappeared there can be no doubt that John Aspinall would be able to keep the species alive at Howletts. There is, however, a considerable problem in reintroducing zoo-bred animals to the wild and monitoring their successful adaptation to a free existence – a problem that remains to be solved. Howletts has a surplus population of tigers and is now busily supplying other zoos, which is good news for the wild population. There is also a breeding group of Siberian tigers, the only one in Britain.

If the tiger is the star of the show then there are many co-stars. An attempt is being made to breed Indian elephants. Most zoos do not keep males because they are periodically so awkward and indeed dangerous. Though tamed in Asia and put to work, all domesticated elephants are taken from the wild – a continuous drain on an already endangered population. If Howletts can build up a successful breeding herd, then it may show the way to others in Asia. There are breeding chital and nilgai, hog deer and sambar.

The African animals include cheetah, roan, black rhino and, of course, gorilla. At Howletts they vie with the tigers for star billing. The colony numbers over a dozen animals, and the first birth was in 1975. There is some reason to hope that the highly-endangered wild population might be augmented by captive-bred gorillas in the long term. Howletts also has breeding chimpanzees, and other primates including woolly monkeys. There are African wild dogs, snow leopards, leopards, wolves, clouded leopards – in fact one of the finest collections of animal stars to be found in the country. No doubt it is this 'star' quality that brings in the customers. Port Lympne Zoo Park and Gardens is another Aspinall enterprise.

Visiting: leave Canterbury on the A2 Dover road and turn left at Bekesbourne. Howletts is well signposted. Usual facilities include a cafeteria. Tel. 0227 728298.

Mammals: gorilla, tiger, snow leopard, chimpanzee, African elephant, Indian elephant, roan, bongo, nilgai, sambar, chital, black rhino, cheetah, Brazilian tapir.

KEW GARDENS �ib &

First opened to the public in 1841, Kew Gardens extends to some 320 acres including the lake and pond. It is a remarkable institution and a must for anyone interested in the countryside. Among the fabulous collection of plants the trees are perhaps outstanding. From all over the world they have come, offering the visitor the opportunity to gain an impression of a foreign land that he is never likely to see, as well as to 'mug up' the names of trees that he ought to know anyway. Nowhere perhaps is the sense of 'foreign-ness' so apparent as in the heated houses, all glass and Victoriana. Hide away in a dank corner and with a little imagination the smell of the tropics will waft you away to some dark jungle the other side of the world. For the gardener Kew is a delight. It offers inspiration (see it here, buy it elsewhere) and satisfaction in just being somewhere quite beautiful.

Kew is a favourite day out for Londoners. The admission price is one of the great bargains, and there are pleasant glades for picnics, etc. Staggeringly enough, the 'Living Collection' consists of no less than 25,000 individual species of plants. Many of these can be found in the various 'houses'. There are, for instance, an Australian house, a fern house and a Himalayan house as well as the more obscure tropical aroid house, succulent house and the magnificent palm house and temperate house. There are general, reference and wood museums, a refreshment pavilion and a bookstall. There is, of course, a research staff and herbarium collection available to the serious researcher.

By the way, hawfinch and mandarin duck are regular.

Visiting: Kew lies on the south bank of the Thames and can be entered via the gates in Kew Green and Kew Road on the south side of Kew Bridge. From central London leave via Holland Park to the Chiswick Flyover. Buy the handy map on arrival to seek out the areas that interest you.
Botany: 25,000 species to choose from; excellent heated houses.
Birds: hawfinch, mandarin duck.
Other: charming riverside pubs.

KINGLEY VALE ✣

Kingley Vale has been described as the finest yew forest in Europe. The area is a National Nature Reserve covering 351 acres and rising to Bow Hill at 670 feet. It lies to the north-west of Chichester and consists of chalk downland and mixed forest as well as the yew grove, some of whose trees are 500 years old. The steeper slopes of the valley are typical grassland, sheltering a variety of attractive flowers including bee and purple orchids, hawkbit, eyebright, thyme and rock rose. Other plant communities are equally attractive. Birds are not outstanding, though there are nightingales, blackcaps and grasshopper warblers in summer. Both fallow and roe deer are found, though seeing them is never easy.

There is a nature trail and a useful quiz-guide that children will find attractive.

Visiting: the southern part of the reserve is of unrestricted access. Take the B2178 from Chichester to West Stoke. The car park is on the right beyond the village and a footpath leads northward to the Reserve Centre. Follow the nature trail.
Botany: bee orchid, early purple orchid, hawkbit, eyebright, thyme, rock rose, stitchwort, red bartsia, hedge bedstraw, wild parsnip, squinancywort, stonecrop, lady's bedstraw, hoary plantain, hairy violet, salad burnet, St John's wort, dog violet.
Birds: nightingale, blackcap, chiffchaff, grasshopper warbler, marsh tit.
Mammals: fallow deer, roe deer, badger.
Insects: chalkhill and common blue butterflies.
Other: Devils' Humps, Bronze Age burial mounds some 3500 years old and very well preserved.

LONDON ZOO ✣ ✦ &

A day among 'wild' animals is as refreshing as a day spent among the hills and peat bogs, and there is no better place to enjoy them than the grounds of the Zoological Society of London. London Zoo is one of the oldest, most famous, and best in the world. It covers thirty-six acres and is home to some 6800 diverse animals of 1450 species including 200 kinds of mammals, 500 kinds of birds, 200 kinds of reptiles, 42 kinds of amphibians, 270 kinds of fishes and over 100 kinds of invertebrates. It was responsible for bringing the words 'zoo' and 'jumbo' into everyday use. Opened in 1828, there are still three of the original buildings standing, though they do not house animals in the original form. All of the rest is modern, being

Indian elephants, partly responsible for bringing the word 'jumbo' into everyday use

modernized, or about to be. The result is some of the most imaginative displays of animals to be seen anywhere.

The collection, particularly of mammals, is remarkably complete and includes the giant panda. The Moonlight World on the lower floor of the Charles Clore Pavilion simulates nocturnal conditions during the day, so that we can see the host of mammals that normally remain hidden under a cloak of darkness. Loris, echidna, potto, bushbabies – all can be seen to advantage. The bird house echoes to strange tropical calls (particularly bellbirds) and the new display of primates enables these fascinating relatives of ours to be seen in something approaching their natural state.

There are collections of antelope and deer, horses and cattle, rhinos and elephants, lions and tigers, an excellent aquarium, a walk-through aviary, camels, otters, flamingoes, a good collection of birds of prey, goats and ibex, reptiles including snakes and crocodiles and, of course, an excellent children's zoo,

The Snowdon Aviary which houses some of the 500 species of birds at the zoo

73

educational exhibits, two cafeterias and a restaurant. Regent's Park is 'next door' and the Regent's Canal passes through the grounds – both are 'semi-country' in the heart of London.

The London Zoo is an admirable and enjoyable place, but it is not cheap. The overheads in maintaining such a large collection under the ideal conditions in which you and I, the public, want to see them are high, and rebuilding and rehousing are expensive. But the Zoo is well worth supporting for its own sake, as well as being a splendid place for a taste of the wild.

Visiting: the Zoo is open every day of the year except Christmas Day. It lies in the north-east corner of Regent's Park and is within walking distance of Camden Town underground station. Buses stop close by. The Zoo publishes various guides and brochures, with times of feeding, that help you to plan your day to get as much as possible for your money.

Mammals: one of the most comprehensive collections in the world, including the giant panda.

Birds: good collection covering most of the major groups of the world's avifauna.

LYDDEN DOWN ✣

This local Nature Reserve covers fifty-three acres of chalk downland just north of Dover, and is of primary interest to botanists in search of specialities of the chalk. Though there have been considerable inroads by tor grass and by gorse, the continued grazing rights have preserved much of the open landscape that we have grown to think of as typical of the Downs, and many flowers can still be found. Orchids include scented, burnt-tip and early spider as well as autumn lady's tresses later in the year. Other specialities include chalk milkwort, dyer's greenweed, yellow-wort and dropwort. Along with the flowers a variety of butterflies occur, including both chalkhill and common blue and marbled white. Great green grasshoppers occur and among them are the similar, though much rarer, warbiter bush crickets. Birds are generally plentiful, though there are no great rarities or unusual species.

Visiting: leave the A2 between Lydden and Temple Ewell north of Dover, on a track running north-west on the south side of the railway bridge that crosses the road. In 300 yards there is parking space. A footpath leads to the Reserve.

Botany: Burnt-tip orchid, early spider orchid, scented orchid, autumn lady's tresses, dyer's greenweed, chalk milkwort, dropwort, yellow-wort.

Insects: chalkhill blue butterfly, common blue butterfly, marbled white butterfly, great green grasshopper, warbiter bush cricket.

MARWELL ZOOLOGICAL PARK ✣ ♿

Marwell is a Whipsnade-like park in which animals enjoy large enclosures and in which people can either motor or walk the two and a quarter miles round. There are no safari-type gimmicks, and the collection is remarkably good. At present it has herds of scimitar-horned oryx and Przewalski's horse, but these are well-established in captivity. More important are herds of onager and kulan, the wild asses which are under such threats in the wild, as well as various rare subspecies of zebra.

The Zoo is divided into four major parts according to continent. The largest area is devoted to Africa and houses one of the better collections of antelopes to be found in Britain as well as pygmy hippo. Other unusual animals include Asiatic lion. Marwell's aims are well fulfilled and, as it progresses, it could become a zoo of considerable international importance. To do so it will have to specialize and build up herds of animals that its already established relationships with foreign zoos can then most readily benefit.

In addition it has tried to maintain the beauty and feeling of the Hampshire countryside, and the Tree-tops restaurant gives unsurpassed views over this lovely corner of the county.

Visiting: Marwell is signposted from the A33 Winchester bypass. Take the A333 Portsmouth road and watch for signs on the left after its junction with the A3051.

Mammals: onager, kulan, scimitar-horned oryx, Przewalski's horse, Hartmann's mountain zebra, swamp deer, blackbuck, Sumatran tiger. Tel. 096 274406.

Birds: small part of the collection.

NEW FOREST ✣ ♦ ✣ 🦋 ♿

Despite its appropriation as a Royal Forest in the eleventh century the New Forest remains largely common land and the largest tract of unsown, semi-natural vegetation in lowland Britain. Over 48,000 acres of heath and woodland are of free access and another 20,000 acres are enclosed. The whole area has been shaped by man and, in particular, by his animals

A badger emerging from its sett amongst foxgloves

and their grazing and browsing. The soil is largely infertile sands and clays lying in the Hampshire Basin, and the sparse vegetation and grazing make the Forest one of the most important wildlife sites in Britain.

Though the New Forest ponies are the most obvious form of indigenous life, there are in fact red, fallow and roe deer as well as muntjac. There are badgers, and it was in the New Forest that movie-maker Eric Ashby filmed his marvellous badger and deer films. Birds are very important, and the Forest is the headquarters of the Dartford warbler in Britain as well as one of the strongholds of that rare and elusive falcon, the hobby. Buzzards are common and sparrowhawks as numerous as anywhere. There are wood warblers, redstarts, hawfinches, stonechats, crossbills, nightjars and the colonizing firecrests, which were first found breeding in Britain here thirty years ago. Additionally there are birds that bird-watchers tend to go rather quiet about, but which include honey buzzard and goshawk.

The flora of the Forest is exceptionally rich, and the valley bogs are unique in Britain, and even decidedly rare in western Europe. Marsh gentian and bog orchid are two very rare species, and the wild gladiolus occurs nowhere else in the country but along the Forest edges. Heath and marsh orchids are common here.

Among the lesser creatures found in the Forest that are rare or scarce elsewhere, sand lizard and smooth snake are important. Here and there scorpions can be found – almost the only reliable place in England – but they are very rare and unlikely to prove a menace. The large marsh grasshopper, one of the largest of our grasshoppers, is seldom found elsewhere, and the New Forest cicada is never found anywhere else.

Many visitors to the New Forest find wildlife a disappointment, but with such large areas to explore and such varied landscape luck or hard work are necessary. Nevertheless in the New Forest it is quite possible to walk for miles without seeing another person, a remarkable attraction in lowland England. Some areas worth special attention are:

1   Beaulieu Heath, especially in the north between Beaulieu and Dibden.
2   Beaulieu Road, on the Lyndhurst – Beaulieu road, the B3056, north of the railway.
3   Bolderwood Walk, along the minor road between Lyndhurst and the A31.
4   Acres Down, north of the A35 west of Lyndhurst beyond Emley Down.
5   Braemore on the A338 along the Hampshire Avon, which has retained its Tudor style and has a Saxon church and a medieval mizmaze.

Visiting: much of the area is of direct open access from the main A31 and A35. It can be walked along well-marked paths, and many of the woods can be entered, some even driven through. There is good accommodation in a number of Forest villages and camping is allowed by prior permit and at restricted sites: notices lead to permit offices. At all times visitors should respect the Country Code and be particularly careful with fires. Do not pick flowers – for all you know they might be the last of their kind in the country.

Sand lizards are generally rare in Britain, but can sometimes be seen in the New Forest

Mammals: red deer, fallow deer, roe deer, muntjac, fox, badger.
Birds: hobby, Dartford warbler, stonechat, crossbill, firecrest, red-backed shrike, curlew, snipe, wood-lark, wood warbler, redstart, nightjar, nightingale, sparrowhawk, goshawk, honey buzzard, buzzard.
Botany: heather, gorse, marsh gentian, bog orchid, wild gladiolus.
Reptiles: sand lizard, smooth snake.
Insects: silver-studded blue butterfly, fritillaries, emperor hawk moth, bee hawk moth, large marsh grasshopper, New Forest cicada.

NEWTOWN MARSH 🦅 🌸 🦋

Newtown lies on the Solent coast of the Isle of Wight between Cowes and Yarmouth. It is the major inter-tidal zone of the island and rich in birds, plants and other wildlife. The main marsh was formerly wet grazing, but breaches of the sea wall in 1954 allowed the area to revert to the tidal zone. Together with the Newtown River this now forms the major habitat for wildfowl and waders, which congregate in good numbers during passage periods and in winter. Adjacent areas of farmland and woodland are included in the 800-acre local nature reserve.

Perhaps the most attractive feature of Newtown is its size; it is small enough to enable most of its wildlife to be viewed without too much difficulty. Though permits can be obtained on site locally, the average visitor need not depart from the rights of way which have been set out as a quite excellent nature trail.

Along the trail, which starts at an observation post where species of fauna and flora can be studied in advance, most of the specialities can be seen. At the start, for instance, a long-established nest of wild bees is picked out in an old oak. Attention is drawn to the marsh wolf spider, a strange creature that is submerged by the tides twice each day. The flora of the saltings includes sea aster and sea lavender, long-leaved scurvy grass, once used by sailors as a source of Vitamin C, and the hybrid cordgrass that originated in nearby Southampton Water and which now threatens so many of our estuaries. The shingle spits support horned poppy and sea holly.

The route leads beside Clamerkin Lake, still used as a commercial oyster fishery and the site of Britain's first clam fishery. Onward through the Town Copse, a National Trust property, there are interesting plants which include the guelder rose, wood spurge, stinking iris and butcher's broom. Butterflies include white admiral, purple hairstreak and speckled wood, while the orange-tip occurs along the verges. Through Walter's Copse watch for red squirrel and for twayblade, tutsan, betony and saw-wort.

Birds are plentiful and warblers abound in summer. There is even a spot to wait and listen for the nightingale, and cuckoo and green woodpeckers should be heard if not seen. The marshes themselves hold waders, and spotted redshank is regular along with greenshank, ruff, good flocks of black-tailed godwit in winter, snipe and dunlin. Some 170 species of birds have been recorded, of which seventy have bred. This can be compared with the 300 species of plants that can be found.

The Old Town Hall is worth a visit at the end, for the basement contains a summer exhibition of Pleistocene mammalian remains found in the reserve.

Visiting: there is no public transport. Visitors should drive through the village High Street (marked 'No Through Road') to the end and park. There are notices on the footpath to the quay. A leaflet is available.

Birds: cormorant, teal, wigeon, pintail, shelduck, brent goose, Canada goose, oystercatcher, ringed plover, golden plover, snipe, curlew, black-tailed godwit, redshank, spotted redshank, greenshank, dunlin, ruff, common tern, little tern, kingfisher, marsh tit, long-tailed tit, nightingale, willow warbler.

Botany: sea purslane, sea aster, sea lavender, long-leaved scurvy grass, sea arrowgrass, sea plantain, Townsend's cordgrass, guelder rose, wood spurge, stinking iris, butcher's broom, horned poppy, sea holly.

Insects: speckled wood, meadow brown, white admiral, purple hair streak, orange-tip, painted lady, comma, gatekeeper and wall butterflies.

Mammals: red squirrel.

NORTH KENT MARSHES ↟

Between the urban conglomeration and motorways of the Medway towns and the River Thames to the north lies a backwater of mud banks and marshes that have changed little since the days of Dickens. While London extends ever outward, and the country around it becomes an even more ordered and tidy dormitory for its commuters, the marshes that border the Thames between Cliffe and Allhallows retain a breath of true countryside.

Along the river an embankment runs the length of the loneliest walk within thirty miles of London. Here you will meet few others – the occasional bird-watcher, the less occasional gun. On one side, mud banks alive with trips of shorebirds, with the river and the ever-present big ships beyond; on the other, ditches with kingfishers, and meadows with sheep and lapwings. Here primroses still grow among the hedge-rows and poppies among the cereals. In winter the harsh easterly winds can chill a shelterless soul in minutes. Then the wild white-fronted geese honk across the skies while shelduck dabble away over the open flat by courtesy of the Thames Conservancy, which has cleaned up their river in a twenty–year dash for ecological purity.

The quickest approach to the marshes is at Allhallows, where a caravan site and a rash of cafés and pubs with jukeboxes is a reminder that urban 'civilization' is not far away. From here a well-worn path leads northward to the sea wall: turn right for Yantlett Creek, where marsh birds fly against a backdrop of the Isle of Grain refinery, and left for the long walk to Lower Hope Point via St Mary's and Egypt Bays.

At the foot of St Mary's a track leads inland among the sheep walks to Swigshole, Decoy Farm and Northward Hill, the bird reserve where grey herons nest under the watchful eye of the Royal Society for the Protection of Birds. There is a nature trail, and the warden can be contacted at Swigshole Cottage, High Halstow, Rochester ME3 8SR. Visit in summer, when the herons are in the treetops.

Continuing westward along the sea wall there are the Cooling Marshes, scene of *Great Expectations*: indeed the village church still has graves that Dickens wrote about. The open spaces have hares in spring and big skies throughout the year. The pits at Cliffe provide excellent bird-watching, but are somewhat unsalubrious.

Visiting: to Cliffe on B2000 from Rochester, or A228 to Stoke and minor roads to Allhallows.

Birds: white-fronted goose, shelduck, wigeon, teal all winter; grey heron in summer.

OLD WINCHESTER HILL ✿ ⚘ 🦋

Though it apparently has no historical associations with the city of Winchester, over fifteen miles to the west, nevertheless Old Winchester Hill is an ancient site with Iron Age connections. It lies immediately east of the A32 between Alton and Fareham and has been a National Nature Reserve since 1954.

The Hill is part of the South Downs and was fortified to dominate the Meon Valley, which it overlooks. Its importance for natural history stems from its downland chalk geology and from the major factors that have destroyed so much of the Downs during the last thirty years. Ploughing and the lack of grazing by a declining rabbit population have both taken their toll, and it is likely that the typical fauna and flora will survive only in areas like Old Winchester Hill, where they are carefully maintained. From most of the reserve scrub is eradicated, and the cropped grass of the traditional downland landscape is maintained by a rotational system of grazing within enclosures. This is one of the few National Nature Reserves where the visitor may wander at will, but the excellent nature trail is recommended.

Though Mesolithic and Neolithic remains have been discovered, the most impressive remains are those dating from the time of the second Iron Age invasion from the Continent in 250 BC. The fort dominates the southern part of the reserve.

The chalk slopes are excellent for plants, and no less than fourteen different species of orchids can be found. These include fragrant, spotted and autumn lady's tresses. Cowslips, now so rare, are found spring, and the aromatic thyme and marjoram are common. Lady's bedstraw, kidney and horseshoe vetch, and Carline and stemless thistles are also found. The beech and ash woods were planted about 1800 and enchanter's nightshade and dog's mercury can be found on the forest floor.

Mammals are scarce, though badger, fox, rabbit, hare and grey squirrel – or at least signs of their presence – can all be found. Though ninety species of birds have been observed there is nothing special. Butterflies are more important. Chalkhill and common blues, meadow brown, small skipper, small heath, speckled wood, as well as the migrant clouded yellow, are all found. In spring there are brimstones and small tortoiseshells and in early summer green hairstreak and Duke of Burgundy fritillaries can be seen, and there are some good moths.

Willow warblers are found in numerous sites in South-East England

Visiting: turn eastward on a minor road at Warnford on the A32. The car park, information centre and nature trail are well signposted on the right. Take the longer version, which includes visits to a badger sett and a butterfly-rich combe.

Botany: cowslip, violet, thyme, marjoram, restharrow, rampion, fragrant orchid, wild parsnip, Carline thistle, stemless thistle, lady's bedstraw, kidney vetch, horseshoe vetch, early purple orchid, spotted orchid, twayblade, autumn lady's tresses, felwort, enchanter's nightshade, dog's mercury.

Insects: green hairstreak, Duke of Burgundy fritillary, clouded yellow, chalkhill blue, common blue, meadow brown, small skipper, small heath, speckled wood, green-veined white, small tortoiseshell, and brimstone butterflies.

Mammals: badger, fox, grey squirrel.

Birds: yellowhammer, turtle dove, stock dove, tree-creeper, green woodpecker, willow warbler, chiff-chaff, kestrel.

QUEENDOWN WARREN ✿

Though it covers only eighteen acres of chalk down-land and has access only by two rights of way, this is a popular open space where picnics are a favourite summer pastime. It is, in fact, a local nature reserve of the Swale District Council administered by the Kent Trust for Nature Conservation, and a leaflet is available giving details of the flora. This is a dry valley heavily grazed by rabbits, and the short turf holds a wealth of chalk plants. No less than twelve orchids can be found, including early spider, bee and fly, with man and green-winged near the lower part of the slope. There are also milkwort, thyme, autumn lady's tresses and meadow sage. There is an area of woodland where traveller's joy (old man's beard), lords and ladies and dog's mercury grow. Both common and chalkhill blue butterflies are found. Just over the entrance stile there is a toadstool 'Fairy Ring' fifteen yards in diameter, indicating an age of several hundreds of years.

Visiting: leave the M2 on the A249 Maidstone road and turn right for Stockbury. Minor roads lead to the Reserve, which is entered from the north next to Potter's Wood, where there is parking space.

Botany: Early spider orchid, bee orchid, fly orchid, man orchid, green-winged orchid, milkwort, autumn lady's tresses, meadow sage, traveller's joy, dog's mercury.

RYE HARBOUR AND PETT POOLS ✦ ✿

The old Cinque Port of Rye attracts thousands of holiday-makers every year. After a few hours of cobbled streets and 'ye olde tea shoppes' most visitors need a breath of air and there is nowhere better than Rye Harbour. This local nature reserve consists of well-managed gravel diggings with well positioned hides giving fine views of nesting terns, gulls and grebes, plus an excellent collection of high tide waders and migrants. Oystercatchers and turnstones are often abundant and, in season, there are brent geese and a good selection of duck. Garganey are usually present in late summer.

Colonising plants of shingle are noteworthy and sea kale, horned poppy and so on are well worth more than a passing glance. There is also a strong colony of the introduced marsh frog.

A little to the west the sea wall between Winchelsea Beach and Pett is backed by a road giving good access to a group of pools. These 'borrow' pits are a home to duck in winter, but in late summer a local bird group pumps one of the pools dry to attract passing waders to feed. This artificial management is highly successful and through August and September there is a constant stream of interesting waders viewable from the car window. At weekends there is always a member of the local group on hand to offer advice and information.

Visiting: Rye Harbour is found by leaving the town westwards on the A259 and turning left 100 yards after the major roundabout. It is well signposted. Park at the car park, visit the information centre and walk the private track running southwards parallel with the river. This leads to a hide and may be followed for the extended walk to Pett Pools. Alternatively, return to the A259 and turn west-ward toward Winchelsea. Below the town turn left signposted 'Winchelsea Beach'. Follow this road and watch for the pools on the right after a couple of miles. If you visit at a weekend, support the group with a donation or by purchasing a report.

Birds: Sandwich tern, common tern, little tern, oystercatcher, turnstone, curlew, little stint, spotted redshank, curlew sandpiper, brent goose.

Botany: horned poppy, sea kale and marine colonizers.

Other: marsh frog.

SELBORNE ✦ ✿ ♿

A small, rather nondescript village in northern Hampshire that rests its claim to fame on being the

Looking west along the sea wall by Pett Levels, towards Cliff End. The sea is to the left and the 'borrow' pits to the right

home of Gilbert White, the founder of modern British natural history. His book *The Natural History of Selborne* has passed through so many editions that its sales must be bettered only by the modern genus of field guides. It is still an essential read and companion to those who would get the best out of this typical piece of rural England. Gilbert White's home is now the Wakes Museum, open to the public. Behind it lies the beech hanger with its famous zigzag path created by Gilbert and his brother. The woods still echo to the same bird calls as in his day, though we now know that swallows do not spend their winters in the bottoms of ponds – a view current in White's time. There is a Selborne Nature Trail created by the Alton Natural History Society that leads up the path to the hanger for flowers, deer (if lucky) and birds.

Visiting: Selborne lies on the B3006 south of Alton. Visit the Wakes Museum, the Church and the hanger.

Birds: wood warbler, willow warbler, great spotted woodpecker, marsh tit, rook.
Botany: good collection of chalk woodland species.
Other: Gilbert White associations.

SOUTH DOWNS WAY ✾

Opened in 1972, this was Britain's first Long Distance Bridleway. From Eastbourne it stretches westward as far as Harting in Hampshire, with plans to extend to Winchester. As the name implies, you can ride a horse the whole way, or walk if you prefer. Alternatively you can break journey at a number of points where the pathway dips down to road or river level, or walk between two such points over the open Downs.

From Eastbourne, for instance, the path leads southward along the cliff edge to Beachy Head, where there are stupendous views over the Channel below. Continue on to Birling Gap and the Seven Sisters Country Park in an Area of Outstanding Natural Beauty. Here the path follows the switchback nature of the cliffs and hollows of this fine chalk landscape. Here too there are typical chalkland plant communities rich in species. By the meandering Cuckmere

The Wakes, Selbourne, home of the naturalist, Gilbert White

River the path turns inland to Exceat with masses of cowslips on your right. Here Sussex CC have a fine visitors' centre with the excellent 'Living World' exhibition. The river is well reeded, and sedge warblers croak from their fastnesses. The main A259 leads back to Eastbourne, or you can continue northward to Alfriston before climbing back up to the Downs and follow the northern escarpment to Firle Beacon. Throughout this section and onward to the Ouse the views are open over predominantly ploughed land. The small birds are meadow pipits, the large ones lapwings. The wild flowers are few, but the odd humps and bumps indicate a human tenancy that extends back thousands of years to Neolithic times. Leaving the Way at the River Ouse, the A275 leads to Lewes or Newhaven.

Almost every viewpoint along the Way was a fortress in some far distant time. Chanctonbury Ring, east of the A24 Worthing Road, is perhaps the best example. Even the strong growth of mature trees cannot hide its fortification foundations. This is the section of South Downs that is for everyman. A path leads southward from the A283 up a wooded defile to the open Downs above. It is a fine walk, and Chanctonbury lies a mile or so away to the west. For even easier downland access take the minor road to Worthing southward out of Steyning. Ploughed downland stretches away in each direction and the South Downs Way can be joined eastward or westward.

After Chanctonbury the Downs are more overgrown and less dramatic from above and below. Those who continue toward Harting are rewarded by branching off southward on the A286 Midhurst – Chichester road to Singleton where half a mile south of the village is the Weald and Downland Open Air Museum Country Park. Here there is a lake, historic buildings reconstructed to form an open air museum, and woods and meadowland.

Whether you dip in or walk the whole way, the South Downs Way is a fine area for botanizing, for archaeology, and for superb scenery.

Visiting: see *The South Downs Way* by S. Jennett, published by HMSO.

81

Botany: excellent flowers of the chalk in unploughed areas.

STODMARSH 🦅 ❀ 🦋

Created by mining subsidence in the valley of the Great Stour north-east of Canterbury, Stodmarsh was declared a National Nature Reserve in 1968 to protect the community of breeding birds. Though considerable areas of open water remain, by far the largest part of Stodmarsh is covered by the common reed, *Phragmites communis*. Here the rare birds for which the area has long been famous can be found. They include bittern, bearded tit and, with luck, the two colonizing warblers Cetti's and Savi's. The strident notes of the former are unmistakable, while the reeling of Savi's warbler can only be confused with that of the grasshopper warbler, which has a different pitch. Harriers are regularly present during passage periods and there is always an early spring influx of garganey. Indeed this is probably the best place to see this attractive little migrant duck. Winter brings many northern duck, and waders are always a feature.

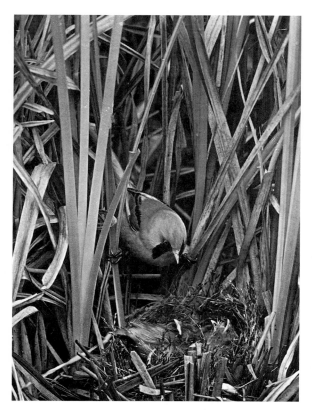

Bearded tits build their nests among the reeds of Stodmarsh

The interesting plants of the area include great spearwort and great water dock, and there is a small area of dittander.

Access is along the Lampen Wall and along the footpath which leads from Stodmarsh to Grove Ferry via the marsh and along the banks of the Stour. This is an excellent walk, full of interest the whole way.

Visiting: take the lane past the Red Lion to the NCC car park and walk out to the Reserve and the Lampen Wall. The best areas for birds lie between the start of the Wall and the River Stour. Continue to Grove Ferry.

Botany: great spearwort, great bladderwort, marsh stitchwort, bog-bean, great water dock, blunt flowered rush, frogbit, water dropwort, hornwort, hairy buttercup, marsh arrow grass, marestail, sea club-rush, dittander.

Birds: bittern, bearded tit, Savi's warbler, Cetti's warbler, sedge warbler, reed warbler, garganey, harriers, wigeon, teal, ruff, waders.

VENTNOR BOTANIC GARDEN ❀ ♿

The Ventnor Botanic Garden at Steephill, Isle of Wight, was established only in 1970, on the site of the defunct Royal National Hospital. In the face of pressure to turn the site to a multitude of other uses, it is a testimony to the local authorities that they settled on a botanic garden. At the time the garden was an overgrown wilderness, but several botanic features survived, including a huge *Cypressus macrocarpa* planted in 1897 by Princess Henry of Battenberg. As clearance progressed each vacant spot was planted so that the overall pattern present in most botanic gardens is lacking. However, this does not detract from its appeal.

Because of its remarkable position and the underlying geology, Ventnor has a remarkable opportunity to develop a fascinating collection. Already this development has been rapid. There is a 'pop' rose garden whose lushness appeals to the non-botanist, as well as many attractive plants of more specialist interest. Outstanding, perhaps, is the fact that many plants more familiar in mainland greenhouses can survive in the open in this mild climate, and that others grow in such lush abandon. A temperate house was opened in 1987.

Visiting: Steephill is 1½ miles west of Ventnor on the A3055 road. Tel. 0983 852501.

Botany: lush subtropical growth on a highly accommodating soil.

WYE AND CRUNDALE DOWNS ✿

This National Nature Reserve covers 250 acres of the easternmost part of the chalk. Almost due east of Ashford in Kent, it encompasses the steep scarp of the North Downs and allows public access over a considerable area to the Devil's Kneading Trough, a deep chalk gully, with excellent views to the south over Romney Marsh and the Channel, and occasionally to France.

Further exploration of the reserve is facilitated by a good nature trail that leads down the scarp and then traverses into Pickersdane Scrubs, an area of ash and hazel coppice with whitebeam and yew. The birds and mammals are no more than one would expect, with willow warbler, blackcap, whitethroat and night-ingale, fox, badger, weasel and the occasional fallow deer. In contrast the flora is particularly rich, and a considerable attraction to botanists, who will be pushed to find some species elsewhere in Britain. No doubt this is in no small measure due to the reserve's proximity to the Continent. Orchids, for instance, number no less than seventeen species including the rare late spider orchid. There is a small information centre on the north-west side of Broad Down, the area available to the public, which is open most weekends during the summer.

Even on the open downland there are interesting flowers to be found. Wild thyme, salad burnet, rock rose and stemless thistle mix with early purple, common spotted and pyramidal orchids. Among the thick tor grass species such as knapweed, marjoram and St John's wort manage to survive. Where the grass is grazed there is birdsfoot trefoil. Among the experimental fields where a staggered system of cutting is operated you may find fragrant and pyramidal orchids as well as marbled white butterflies. The coppiced areas hold wild strawberries, ground ivy and hemp agrimony as well as woodpeckers, nuthatches and grey squirrel.

Visiting: leave Ashford eastward on the A20 and turn left into the village of Willesborough. Continue through Hinxhill toward Hastingleigh. Broad Down is easily found.

Birds: nightingale, great spotted woodpecker, willow warbler, blackcap, whitethroat.

Mammals: badger, fox, weasel.

Botany: pyramidal orchid, spotted orchid, early spider orchid, late spider orchid, birdsfoot trefoil, marjoram, St John's wort.

EAST ANGLIA

North Norfolk Marshes

Peakirk Wildfowl Reserve

Roydon Common

KING'S LYNN

A47

A47

Norfolk Wildlife Park

NORWICH Norfolk Broads

GREAT YARMOUTH

Breydon Water

PETERBOROUGH

Breckland

A11

Banham Zoo and Monkey Sanctuary

Ouse Washes

Kilverstone Wildlife Park

Otter Trust

A12

Wicken Fen

Rex Graham NR

CAMBRIDGE

Grafham Water

A45

Devil's Dyke

Mickfield meadow

Cambridge Botanic Garden

A11

Benacre to Sizewell

Havergate Island

IPSWICH

M11

Colchester Zoo

COLCHESTER

Fingringhoe Wick

A12

ROMFORD

A127

SOUTHEND

50 mls

50 kms

BANHAM ZOO AND MONKEY SANCTUARY ✝ ➤ ♿

Banham Zoo is a comparatively small affair, but with an enviable reputation. It has always specialized in monkeys, and has one of the finest collections of these species to be found in the country. Though the collection is varied there is considerable emphasis placed on natural colonies, with the result that Banham has achieved a considerable degree of breeding success. There are spider monkeys, the howlers whose calls echo through the surrounding countryside, vervets, gibbons, langurs and the strange crab-eating macaques. There is also a chimpanzee colony, which is inevitably a major attraction. The boldly-marked black and white colobus monkey, which leaps from tree to tree in the forests of Ethiopia and West Africa, can be seen and there are also the only red colobus monkeys in Europe. For a zoo of only twenty acres this is indeed a remarkable collection, and Banham is worth visiting for the monkeys alone.

There are, however, other attractions, including porcupines, coypus, pelicans, penguins, flamingoes, egrets, sealions, several birds of prey, hummingbirds, parrots and a museum of bygone country crafts. The fact that there are no lions, tigers or elephants can only help to concentrate attention on these equally interesting though less spectacular animals.

Visiting: the Zoo is open throughout the year and lies on the B1113, eighteen miles south-west of Norwich. There is the usual shop and cafeteria. Tel. 095 387 476.

Mammals: red colobus monkey, black and white colobus monkey, vervet monkey, lar gibbon, spectacled langur, grey langur, black ape, crab-eating macaque, chimpanzee, wallabies, porcupines, deer, sealions.

Birds: varied assortment, including birds of prey and owls.

BENACRE TO SIZEWELL ☘ ⚙ ♿

The north-east corner of Suffolk is one of the richest wildlife sites in the whole of Britain. The underlying geology, in part at least, accounts for the variety of the landscape, but man's history shows as well. Huge, empty and mostly decaying churches testify to more prosperous days, and the thick reed marshes (intentionally flooded in 1940) to the fear of invasion during the last war. There are coverts where pheasants breed and heaths where nightjars and woodcock can be found.

This corner of Suffolk is becoming a virtually continuous strip of nature reserves, with birds as the most important object. But there are plentiful rights of way and it is possible to walk for miles and miles in and out of the sanctuaries. Southwold is the natural centre, and the River Blyth to the south of the town is the only break in the otherwise continuous beach walk from Benacre Ness to Sizewell.

This is a long, hard walk, but varied and rich. The coastal broads of Benacre (now a National Nature Reserve), Covehithe and Easton are well-reeded homes of waterbirds and after six miles of beach the excellent Adnams Ales of Southwold come as a welcome relief. Continuing southward there is a rowboat ferry across the Blyth to Walberswick in summer (said to be haunted). The Anchor Hotel at Walberswick provides an alternative base. The marshes here are part of the Walberswick National Nature Reserve and maps show footpaths and other access details. Hosts of shorebirds frequent the pools in spring and autumn, and the bittern may be heard in early spring booming from the reedbeds. The beach itself is one of the finest hunting grounds for amber and other semi-precious stones, and the flowers are worth a journey on their own account.

Dunwich, one of the rotten boroughs that elected two members of Parliament until the Reform Act of 1832, has disappeared into the sea so many times, the bells of the sixteen drowned churches are said to be heard on stormy nights. Do not dig in the cliffs: they regularly collapse and kill people and, besides, it disturbs the sand martins.

Southward past the old Coastguard Cottages the beautiful Minsmere Bird Reserve extends inland to Eastbridge. Hides along the inner bank are open to the public and give excellent views over feeding pools where avocets and other waders feed and rest. Here there are Sandwich, common and little terns, though these latter still try to nest on the beach itself. Ask the bird-watchers who swarm along here to help pick out the different species – they are quite human when spoken to politely. Permits to penetrate the reserve may be obtained from the Royal Society for the Protection of Birds.

On to the south lies Sizewell with its monument to nuclear power: when you reach here you know you have come to the very end of the road and that it is time to return to everyday life.

Birds: avocet, marsh harrier, bittern, bearded tit, redshank, common tern, Sandwich tern, little tern, passage shorebirds.

Botany: reedbeds, shoreline salt plant community, orchids in woods.

Other: amber, cornelian and other semi-precious stones along the beach.

BRECKLAND ✿ ☘ ⚙ ♿

This once vast sandy wasteland in East Anglia has been changed out of all recognition over the past hundred years. Where once a few sheep and shepherds roamed the lonely wastes, now over half of the Brecks have been turned into forestry plantations. Another wilderness has been converted to the service of man. Originally heather and gorse dominated the landscape, broken here and there by belts of old Scots pine. The area held a unique fauna and flora that once included the great bustard. Now only isolated pockets remain, and the bustard has disappeared for ever.

Fortunately some areas have been retained, usually by conservation bodies. There are National Nature Reserves at Cavenham, Thetford and Weeting Heaths and the Norfolk Naturalists' Trust has East Wretham Heath. Some of these reserves are, for various reasons, closed to the public, but Cavenham Heath is generally accessible along the River Lark, and East Wretham has a hide overlooking the interesting water of

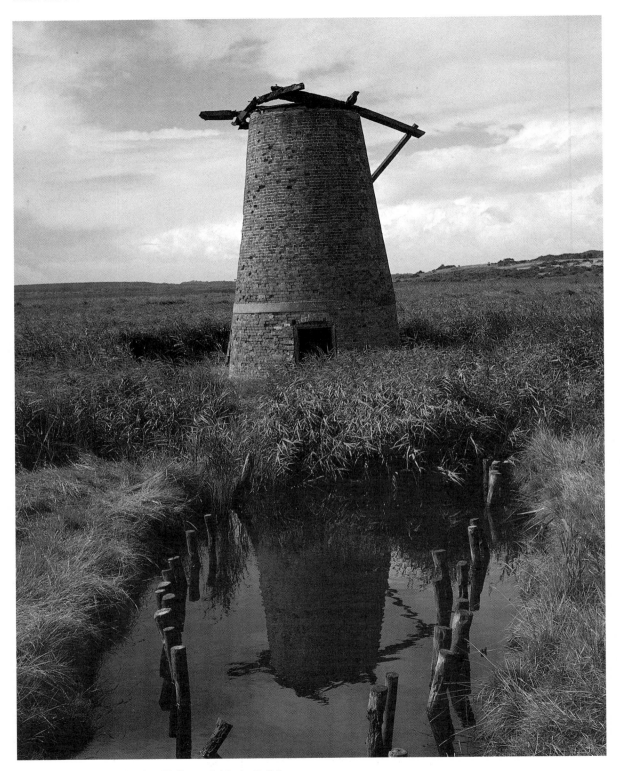

Bittern are frequently sighted at Walberswick Marsh, Suffolk

Langmere, and a nature trail. Because of the facilities it offers, a visit to East Wretham is recommended. Here there is a good chance of seeing the native red squirrel and both red and roe deer are possibilities. Stone-curlews frequent the sandy wastes, although, as elsewhere, they are as likely to be found on ploughed fields as anywhere. Weeting Heath has two hides offering the most viewable stone-curlews in Britain. Crossbills frequent the pines and there is still a chance of seeing the fast-declining woodlark. Botanists will enjoy searching out the rarer heathland plants, though the decline of the rabbit has, as elsewhere, led to considerable growth of scrub.

Visiting: the whole of Breckland between Mildenhall, Bury St Edmunds and Methwold is worth exploring, though visitors usually start at Thetford or Brandon. East Wretham Heath lies four miles north of Thetford on the A1075. Visitors should contact the Warden at East Wretham Heath Nature Reserve, Thetford, Norfolk, IP24 1RU. Tel. 095 382 339. The office lies at the north-east corner of the reserve. There is a small charge for entry and use of the Langmere hide. Weeting Reserve lies on the minor road between Weeting and Hockwold. Permits from the warden's caravan. The Furze Hills at Hildersham offer an isolated area which is well known botanically for typical Breckland plants.

Botany: shepherd's cress, maiden pink, biting stone-crop, hoary cinquefoil, spring vetch, Spanish catchfly.

Birds: gadwall, shoveler, Canada goose, snipe, red-shank, stone-curlew, crossbill, woodlark, willow tit, whinchat, redstart.

Other: Grime's Graves at Brandon is a Neolithic flint mine.

BREYDON WATER

Breydon Water is the estuary of the River Yare and the boundary between Suffolk and Norfolk. It is also effectively the estuary of the whole Norfolk Broads

The stone-curlew lays its eggs on the open ground; their only protection is their camouflage pattern system as well as of the River Waveney, which for most of its length is the actual boundary between the two counties. Though its exit to the sea lies southward beyond Gorleston, the estuary is fronted by the great holiday agglomeration of Great Yarmouth, and it is this Borough in association with the Norfolk County Council that owns and administers the reserve.

The estuary, which is about a mile wide and four and half miles long, empties out at low tide to reveal the enormous mudbanks that are then thronged with birds throughout the year. If the quietest time is midsummer then at every other season there are thousands of waders and wildfowl present. Today, after almost a hundred years of active protection, it is easy to see why Breydon Water had such a hold on the minds of those nineteenth-century path-finding protectionists. Wildfowl, including small flocks of wild geese and swans, are numerous throughout the winter, especially in the new year. Most species of wader on the British list have popped in from time to time and there are good concentrations of the more common

species in season. Rarities like avocet and spoonbill are regular and bitterns invariably turn up and may breed from time to time. Short-eared owls are legend here, and hen harriers visit regularly every winter. There are many small birds, including bearded tit at some times of the year.

With such a huge holiday population Great Yarmouth is to be congratulated on establishing this significant reserve on its doorstep. Let's hope that the trippers enjoy it for what it is.

Visiting: access is restricted to the walls along both north and south banks of the estuary. Both sides of Breydon are easily reached from Yarmouth; the south by crossing the Yare by the Haven Bridge and following the river bank on the right; the north by going to the railway station and following the

Bewick's swans are found on many waters of East Anglia including the Ouse Washes and Grafham Water, and are occasionally seen at wildfowl refuges footpath along the river bank. There are hides here, but access is not necessary.

Birds: Bewick's swan, shelduck, wigeon, pintail, goldeneye, cormorant, bar-tailed godwit, dunlin, redshank, avocet, bittern, bearded tit.

CAMBRIDGE BOTANIC GARDEN 🕸 ♿

The Cambridge University Botanic Garden was founded in 1760 in the centre of Cambridge on a five-acre plot on Free School Lane. In 1831 a larger site of forty acres was acquired some three-quarters of a mile south, and it is this area (developed in two distinct halves) that is the present home of the collection. At first only the western half was laid out; later, in the present century, the eastern half was developed.

As with all such institutions the Garden's purposes are a mixture of research, education and amenity. There is a long tradition of research (early genetic work for example), and it is now a fully-fledged educational institution offering a variety of courses in botany and gardening. It is, however, so near the city centre that it inevitably acts as a park for local people.

The nineteenth-century garden was laid out by John Stevens Henslow, then Professor of Botany, and consists of a fine collection of trees native to Europe, though because of the light calcareous soils of the area and its 'continental'-type climate, conifers do not grow well. A walk around the outer path leads one naturally through the various groups of trees, though being now some 130 years old, many are mature while others are in decline. Systematic replanting has maintained the representative quality of the collection.

There is a stream and lake, and the natural chalk-spring feeders did not dry up until the remarkable drought of 1976. Trees and shrubs dependent on water flourish, and visitors should note the parasitic (on willow) *Lathraea clandestina* with its large purple flowers. This is an idyllic spot and nearby the Water Garden holds a fine collection of native wetland flowers. There are specialist collections of tulips and cranesbills and of European saxifrages.

The twentieth-century garden was originally developed in 1925, but from 1950 onward the research collections were established, followed by the development of representative collections of native British plants on an ecological basis. Of particular interest are the artificial limestone beds and the juniper natural variation collection. There is even a scented garden with a special seat for the blind.

The Winter Garden is a fine concept, consisting as it does of plants that are at their best between November and April. And since 1974 the Gardens have had a contract with the Nature Conservancy to build up a collection of the rarer plants of East Anglia.

No garden would be complete without its glass-houses, and over the years Cambridge University has established a full and attractive range of such exhibits. There is a temperate house, a cool fern house, a stove house, a palm house and aquarium with a central 'lantern' reaching 43 feet in height, an orchid house, a tropical fern house and so on. This is a fine garden and worthy of a visit.

Visiting: There are entrances in Trumpington Road, Bateman Street and Hills Road. There is a car park in Brookside and a nice little guidebook.
Botany: first-rate collection in fine surroundings.
Other: small but interesting aquarium.

COLCHESTER ZOO ⅄ 🐪 ♿

Based on Stanway Hall, Colchester Zoo is a zoo with its heart in the right place. Its large grounds enable animals to be kept in good conditions, in light and airy paddocks rather than cramped cages, and as a result a large number have bred. In fact there is no greater compliment to the zoo manager than having his charges breed themselves out of house and home.

Where possible, animals can be seen against something like a natural background. Brown bears and the white rhinoceros enjoy the freedom of large paddocks, and zebra look almost natural, though against a backdrop of English trees and shrubs. Others, for obvious reasons, must be more carefully confined. Lions and tigers, puma and cheetah, leopard and caracal are kept well caged, but not over-confined. Smaller predators include leopard cat, lynx and genet. There is a modern 'Moonlight World' where mongoose, bushbaby, kinkajou, armadillo and chinchilla are on display during the day (their night).

Primates include orang-utan, and there are squirrel and spider monkeys. There is an aquarium with many tropical and larger fish and a good collection of reptiles. Birds are well represented, and apart from the usual flamingoes and penguins there are macaws, parrots, trumpeters, owls, waterfowl and crowned pigeons.

Visiting: the Zoo is easily reached on the B1022 between Colchester and Tiptree. Entrance fees are a bargain and include all the exhibits including aquarium, Moonlight World and reptile house. The Zoo is open throughout the year and there are adequate cafeterias.

Mammals: tiger, lion, cheetah, caracal, bushbaby, armadillo, zebra, black and brown bears.

Birds: penguins, macaws, owls, trumpeters.

DEVIL'S DYKE ✿

The Cambridgeshire Devil's Dyke runs across the heathlands south of Newmarket between Reach and Ditton Green, and extends for seven miles. Though one of the most impressive monuments of its kind, and despite extensive excavation in 1973, the exact purpose of this earthwork remains a mystery. It dates from some time between AD350 and 700, and may well be a defence of the Anglians against the Mercians to the west. It is a splendid walk, and scheduled as a Site of Special Scientific Interest.

Part of the Dyke is leased to the Cambridgeshire and Isle of Ely Naturalists' Trust as a nature reserve, mainly for its botanical interest. The geology is chalk and several unusual plants can be found. Indeed the Trust (CAMBIENT) has adopted one such, the pasque flower, as its emblem. At the Dullingham Road, bloody cranesbill is plentiful. Wild thyme is common and the bastard toadflax rare.

Visiting: to east and west from the A11 south of Newmarket.

Botany: excellent chalk flora with pasque flower and bloody cranesbill.

Other: perhaps the most northern spot in Britain for sand lizard.

FINGRINGHOE WICK ✿ ✿ ♿

All along the Essex coast, marshes and creeks, mud flats and sand banks stretch virtually without interruption. Deep estuaries carve into the landscape and small areas of saltings become estuarine islands. From Southend in the south to Harwich in the north the bird-watching is excellent. Some place names are virtually synonymous with bird-watching: Foulness, impenetrable military fortress and almost London's third airport; Dengie Flats; Bradwell, site of a bird observatory; the Blackwater estuary; Tollesbury marshes; Mersea, a strange mixture of birds and sailing with, inland, the magnificent Abberton Reservoir; the Naze at Walton, a prime bird place and one of the less difficult to visit; and the Stour, one of the best spots.

Much of this vast coastline is, for one reason or another, difficult to visit. Lookout places require long walks, or permission from landowners, or the blessing of the Ministry of Defence. One major exception is the delightful 125 acres of Fingringhoe Wick on the west bank of the River Colne only four miles south of Colchester. Based on some old gravel workings the reserve is an important area for breeding, wintering and migrating birds. The vegetation is varied and includes horsetails, spiked water milfoil and celery-leaved buttercup. Over the sea wall there are sea thrift, sea aster, sea purslane and sea plantain.

But the major attraction of Fingringhoe is its development as an educational and interpretive centre and the headquarters of the Essex Naturalists' Trust. The reserve and the centre are open to the public and attract many visitors. There are displays, several well-sited bird hides and a full-time warden. A bunkhouse provides accommodation for four enthusiasts at a time, and a well laid out nature trail picks out the more interesting features of the reserve.

Visiting: contact the Warden, Arch Hall, Fingringhoe, Colchester, for permit (donation expected). The Wick is reached via the B1025 southward from Colchester and then on minor roads to the village of Fingringhoe. Turn southward at the crossroads (church) to the reserve.

Birds: little grebe, tufted duck, mallard, wigeon, teal, redshank, common sandpiper, curlew, ruff, wood sandpiper, twite.

Botany: reedmace, spiked water milfoil, celery-leaved buttercup, sea lavender, thrift, sea aster, sea purslane, glasswort, sea plantain.

GRAFHAM WATER ✿ ♿

Once the largest man-made water in England (nearby Rutland Water has now taken over that mantle), Grafham is an outstanding and surprisingly beautiful area. It offers recreational facilities on a remarkably large scale to fishermen and sailors, and a refuge to thousands of birds at different times of the year.

The lake lies in Bedfordshire, just west of the A1 at Buckden. It is easily approached from north and south, though it is the latter side that holds the angling and sailing headquarters, which are well signposted with large car parks. The western, 'shallow' end of the reservoir is a nature reserve administered by the Bedfordshire and Huntingdonshire Naturalists' Trust with a land area of 370 acres. Here among the shallows really good numbers of birds occur, including thousands of gulls and duck in winter. At passage periods, in spring and autumn, virtually anything can turn up, and waders and terns are faithful visitors. Black terns in particular are regular here, resplendent in their full nuptial plumage in mid-May (try the twelfth of that month) or in larger numbers throughout the autumn. A public right of way runs along the southern edge of the reserve and another on the north shore between Hill Farm and Savages Creek. There is a hide available free to members and for a small fee to the public on Sundays between October and March.

Visiting: access at several well signposted parking
    areas including fishing centre, off A1 at Buckden.
Birds: Bewick's swan, pintail, wigeon, teal, common
    tern, black tern, common sandpiper.

Havergate is an RSPB reserve and breeding ground for avocet

HAVERGATE ISLAND 🐦

Here, at one of the more remote parts of the lonely Suffolk coast, the sea dominates the land and has, by creating a shingle bar, diverted the mouth of the River Alde almost ten miles southward. Instead of emerging into the North Sea at Slaughden the river now turns southward along the coast between grazing marshes and the sweep of Orford Ness to emerge at Shingle Street. The main roads pass well inland and even minor roads are few. In summer people come to play on the Deben to the south, but the Ore estuary (as the Alde becomes) is a lovely peaceful place. After the last war the graceful avocet was found breeding on a large flooded island in the estuary, Havergate Island, and to the north at Minsmere. Thirty years later these are still the two major colonies where this pied wader with the upward curving bill breeds regularly.

Havergate is a reserve of the Royal Society for the Protection of Birds, and now boasts some hundred pairs of avocets every year. By systems of sluices and dykes virtually the whole island has been turned into a marsh, and visitors can watch the birds at close quarters from well constructed and strategically sited hides. As well as avocets there is a ternery and many waders pass through in spring and autumn. There are short-eared owls breeding and harriers are frequently present.

Havergate is reached by a pleasant twenty- to thirty-minute boat trip down the narrow estuary, leaving from Orford Quay, the small, attractive town frequented by small boat enthusiasts in summer. With its eighteen-sided Castle Keep and old world charm, Orford is worth an hour or two itself.

SUFFOLK COAST

Visiting: write to the RSPB for details of the current season's arrangements for issuing permits which are very reasonably priced. The reserve is open to members and non-members alike.

Birds: avocet, common tern, short-eared owl, waders on passage.

Botany: some emergent salt-marsh plants flourish around the edges of the pools.

KILVERSTONE WILDLIFE PARK ✢ ✦ ♿

Kilverstone, near Thetford in Norfolk, boasts a remarkably representative collection of animals that, in the main, have their origins in the Americas. At a time when zoos are progressively breaking away from the wide spectrum of animal stars, and beginning to specialize, it was perhaps inevitable that someone would choose the remarkably rich New World areas of North, South and Central America. At Kilverstone this specialization has worked, and within a small area all of the large and more obvious mammals and birds can be seen. The elusive jaguar of South America, a predator seldom seen in the wild and only just beginning to be seriously studied, is on view along with the puma or mountain lion of further north. There are bobcats, Arctic foxes and the extraordinary long-legged maned wolf of the pampas, which looks more like a fox on stilts than a wolf.

There are good colonies of the smaller mammals, including those ground squirrels romantically named 'prairie dogs' by the early pioneer settlers of North America, and a fair collection of South American monkeys including the woolly monkey and the tiny titi monkey. The two-toed sloth is an unlikely animal star, but there are also Brazilian tapirs, capybaras, skunks, agoutis, and a collection of birds that includes quite a few neotropical specialities like oropendolas, guans and king vultures which are not on display in many zoos.

Kilverstone is a fine little zoo and one that deserves to be visited. Do not forget the nocturnal house where night is turned to day.

Visiting: watch for signs two miles north of Thetford on the A11. Usual facilities include cafeteria. Tel. 0842 5369.

Mammals: jaguar, puma, bison, maned wolf, prairie dog, capuchin monkey, spider monkey, squirrel monkey, woolly monkey, titi monkey, skunk, agouti, guanaco, alpaca, llama, capybara, collared peccary, Brazilian tapir, two-toed sloth.

Birds: oropendolas, guans, toucans, flamingoes, military macaw, Quaker parakeet.

MICKFIELD MEADOW ✿

This is a four and a half acre reserve of the Suffolk Trust for Nature Conservation, lying east of the main Norwich-to-Ipswich road. It consists of nothing more than an undrained field, where the dominant plant is meadowsweet with a selection of others including wild angelica, pepper saxifrage and yellow meadow vetch-ling. However, its prime attraction and the reason why it has been a reserve for over forty years is the presence of the fritillary *Fritillaria meleagris*. Over the years birds have destroyed much of the population, but a conservation programme is in hand to allow the seedlings to mature rather than be destroyed.

Visiting: by permit only. Leave the A140 to Mickfield north of the A1120 junction. The reserve is one mile north of the village on the Wetherup Street road and lies to the east adjacent to a watercourse. Best time April – May.
Botany: *Fritillaria meleagris*.

NORFOLK BROADS 🐦 🌸 🦋

The low-lying land east of Norwich is drained by a network of rivers, spotted here and there with large lakes – the Broads. Though they look so natural they are in fact ancient, worked-out peat diggings. Looked at on a map they form strange shapes, and it is the huge length of their shorelines and the general inaccessibility of their banks that has turned these intricate waterways into one of the most important areas for wildlife in Britain.

A week on the Broads on a hired craft is a popular traditional holiday for town and city dwellers from both London and the Midlands. With little danger the inexperienced set out to explore the Bure, the Ant and the Thurne. Horning, Acle, Potter Heigham, Wroxham – the names have almost the same familiar ring as Southend, Blackpool and Torquay. Yet these masses of would-be mariners hardly touch the Broads at all. The reedbeds and sedges keep them at bay and the willow carrs and alders block their way. A few coots, mallards and Canada geese may get disturbed, but masses of people enjoy themselves alongside.

The Broads are noted as a home, in many cases the last home, of many rare animals and plants. Marsh harriers breed, one of the rarest of British birds of prey. Bearded tits and bitterns hide away among the dense reed beds, and in a couple of places the splendid swallowtail butterfly can be found feeding on milk parsley and confined to where this plant can grow. There are otters still, but the uninitiated might well confuse them with the far more numerous coypus. Introduced for their fur (nutria), these South American rodents are increasing again following the population slump caused by the severe winter of 1962–3. Many plants that are rare in most of Britain are quite common in some parts of the Broads. Royal fern, marsh fern, greater spearwort, cowbane, water parsnip, marsh pea, water soldier, frogbit and bladderwort can all be found.

Almost every stretch of water is worth a day's investigation, but several nature reserves are worthy of particular attention.

Bure Marshes National Nature Reserve

This area of over 1000 acres lies in the Bure Valley between Ranworth and Wroxham. The surface is typical fen with four large open waters, the most important of which are Hoveton Great Broad and Ranworth Broad. It is in the open fen areas that milk parsley grows and swallowtail butterflies are found. Adults can be seen in June and, in some seasons, in late August. Plants include bladderwort, frogbit, water soldier (rare) and the deadly cowbane, marsh fern, royal fern and water parsnip.

A typical Broadland bird community includes bearded tit, water rail, reed and sedge warblers, woodcock and duck. There are several heronries and the largest inland roost of cormorants is at Ranworth Broad. Here too common terns have been persuaded to nest on specially constructed rafts. Otters and coypu are present most of the year.

Visiting: access is virtually impossible due to the character of the terrain, but the Nature Conservancy Council has established a nature trail at Hoveton Great Broad where a half-mile-long path winds through fen and woodland, and where there is also an observation hide. In places logs are laid over eight feet of liquid mud, so take care and do not leave the walkway at any point. The nature trail is open from May to September every day except Saturday, though on Sundays only in the afternoon. It starts on the north bank of the River Bure just upstream of the entrance to Salhouse Broad. This is two and a half miles from Wroxham and visitors can moor their boats free of charge. There is no access by land. Boats can be hired at Horning or Wroxham. Along the trail there are spots for royal fern and the swallowtail butterfly.

Hickling Broad National Nature Reserve

Hickling is part NNR and part a reserve of the Norfolk Naturalists' Trust and has always been considered a

A bittern and chick hide away on their nest deep in the reed bed

Visiting: the reserve is open from April through October every day except Tuesday. The 'Water Trail' is a half-day with transportation by boat and visits to seven hides. There is also a half-day without boat and visiting fewer hides at roughly half price. Bookings (and details) from the Warden, Stubb Road, Hickling, Norwich NR12 0BW, Tel. 069 261 276. The Warden's House and Office are reached by following Stubb Road from the Greyhound Inn, Hickling Green. Take the third turning on the right at a small crossroads. Hickling lies east of the A149 north of Yarmouth.

Horsey Mere

The Mere lies east of Hickling Broad and just a short distance from the coast, and is owned by the National Trust. Its 120 acres together with the surrounding Hall, grounds, farmlands and marrams amount to 2300 acres in all. The Mere is a famous bird haunt, but it is also noted for rare plants and insects including, of course, the swallowtail butterfly. The huge reedbeds hold numbers of bearded tits, bitterns and water rails, though the harriers that once counted Horsey as a major stronghold now only pass through. Winter wildfowl are impressive, and garganey arrive in spring. Autumn waders can be very good.

Visiting: there is access to the Mere by boat, but otherwise access is restricted to a track starting at the Windmill. This is usually open free during the summer. Horsey Hall is definitely not open to the public.

Birds: grey heron, bittern, wigeon, shoveler, pochard, garganey, gadwall, goldeneye, pintail, mute swan, Bewick's swan, Canada goose, greylag goose, marsh harrier, black tern, common tern, water rail, black-tailed godwit, ruff, greenshank, redshank, wood sandpiper, green sandpiper, spotted redshank, short-eared owl, bearded tit, sedge warbler, reed warbler.

Insects: swallowtail butterfly.

Botany: royal fern, marsh fern, greater spearwort, cowbane, water parsnip, marsh pea, water soldier, frogbit, bladderwort.

NORFOLK WILDLIFE PARK ♈ 🐦 ♿

The Norfolk Wildlife Park was created at Great Witchingham by Philip Wayre, and is now home to the largest single collection of European mammals and birds in the world. This in itself is a considerable

fabulous place for birds. The enlightened attitude of the NNT ensures that this jewel is seen by as many interested people as possible. The reserve covers 1204 acres of Broad, woodland, fen and surrounding land. Huge areas are thickly covered with reeds and it is these that provide a home (and a major stronghold) for bearded tit and bittern. Marsh harriers are now quite sporadic here, and the Montagu's harriers that once cruised over the reed tops are a thing of the past. There is a good collection of wildfowl, including garganey and gadwall, and an outstanding assortment of passage waders. While black-tailed godwit and ruff are regular there is also a scattering of black terns, ospreys and spoonbills.

There are swallowtail butterflies in June and this Broad, together with nearby Horsey, is the species' stronghold in this country. Botanically the reserve is similar to the Bure Marshes, but with a greater preponderance of semi-brackish species.

Arnold's Marsh, one of the best wader marshes along the north Norfolk coast

achievement, but the Park is also a net producer of wildlife, and its admirable breeding record is studded with outstanding achievements. These include the first European otters to be bred in captivity in Britain since 1881, the first European lynx for over thirty years and the first European beavers, ibex and brown hare to be bred in captivity in Britain. The seven species of deer to be found wild in Britain are on view, and there are European bison, brown bear, seals, wolf, Barbary ape, badger, moufflon and so on.

The Park is also the home of the Pheasant Trust and houses the largest collection of rare and beautiful pheasants in the world. Breeding these birds has proved highly successful, and in Swinhoe's pheasant, a very rare and highly threatened bird from the island of Taiwan, the work of the Trust has been instrumental in safeguarding the species. The even rarer mikado pheasant, only a few hundred individuals of which survive in the wild, is another species which the Trust

hopes to benefit. At present exactly half of the sixteen rarest pheasants in the world are being bred at Great Witchingham, which is worth visiting on that account alone.

Refreshments, lunches, a gift shop and free car parking complete the usual facilities in this quite excellent zoo-collection.

Visiting: the Park lies just north of the A1067 between Norwich and Fakenham. Watch for signposts to Great Witchingham and then for the Park. Reasonable entrance fees. Tel. 060 544 274.

Mammals: European otter, bison, lynx, beaver, ibex, wolf, red deer, roe deer, fallow deer, sika deer, muntjac, reindeer, Chinese water deer, grey seal, common seal, Barbary ape, moufflon.

Birds: cranes, flamingoes, herons, eagle owl, pheasants.

NORTH NORFOLK COAST 🐪 🕸 ♿

From Holme in the west to Salthouse in the east the coastline of north Norfolk is one of the wilder and

95

NORTH NORFOLK COAST
(East and West)

3 mls
5 kms

most interesting parts of lowland Britain. There are beautiful beaches but, protected behind a barrier of intertidal mud, they have not been developed as other British coastlines. Here and there a small village has become a resort of boat enthusiasts or a caravan site attempts to hide discretely in a field, but the main occupations are still agriculture and the sea, with tourism at best a poor third.

Above all this is a bird-watcher's coast, and reserves follow one after another. In the east are the marshes at Cley, where the Norfolk Naturalists' Trust have one of the country's finest bird marshes – an all-year-round resort of bird-watchers galore. Next is Blakeney Point, run by the National Trust, a fine breeding site for terns and an admirable education centre. Next westward is the National Nature Reserve at Holkham, near Wells, where the mudflats and the birds they attract can be viewed and where the pines behind the beach are ideal for picnics and watching small bird migrants. Scolt Head is separated from the mainland by a marshy channel and is a huge dune system of interest to botanists as well as ornithologists. Further west still, the Royal Society for the Protection of Birds has a reserve at Titchwell, where careful manipulation of water levels has turned a 1963 flood disaster into a fine reserve of varied bird-rich habitats. At the end, on the corner of the Wash, lies Holme, another reserve of the Norfolk Naturalists' Trust. Here a reed-fringed lagoon attracts many marshside water birds.

Throughout the area nature is of paramount importance and even the villages, with their flint houses and rust-coloured tiles, fit into our image of the country life. The local people have fine accents and a countryman's sense of humour. There are huge walls enclosing the meadows and walking them can (thank heaven) still be a lonely business: try the eastern bank out of Overy Staithe, or walk the beach from Cley Harbour to Blakeney Point. Accommodation is plentiful and it is a pity to stay for a day when there is so much to see. Those short on summer time should visit Blakeney Point as a priority.

The birds along this coast are remarkably varied, often rare, always interesting. Check lists, encompassing over 300 species, can be obtained at local shops, with marsh harrier, bittern, bearded tit, black-tailed godwit and ruff the summer stars.

Visiting: Cley: permits may be obtained from the visitor centre east of the village of Cley after 10.00 hours. Much can be seen from the A149 and from the 'East Bank' which lies east of Cley and is marked by a small car park. Arnold's Marsh on the right side of the East Bank belongs to the National Trust.
Blakeney Point: reached by boat from Morston Quay: contact Eales and Bean. There is a refreshment room, information centre and hides and the warden will show you round the terneries.
Holkham: public footpaths facilitate exploration. Car park at Holkham Pines reached directly northward from Wells Harbour: brent geese in winter. At Holkham Gap there is further access to pines and shore, plus a good gathering of 'grey' geese.
Scolt Head: reached by boat from Brancaster Staithe signposted from the A149. Beware disturbing the terns in summer.
Titchwell: access from the A149 about half a mile west of Titchwell. Several hides and a visitor centre facilitate viewing.
Holme: follow signposts from A149 north-east of Hunstanton. The NNT reserve is open every day except Tuesday and permits can be obtained on site.
Birds: bittern, marsh harrier, bearded tit, black-tailed godwit, ruff, duck, brent goose, white-fronted goose, snow bunting, Sandwich tern, common tern, little tern.

96

Botany: rich marshland flora at Salthouse and dune flora at Blakeney and Scolt Head. Excellent Scots pines at Holkham with associated fungi in autumn. At Holme, sea buckthorn is spectacular in fruit in September, though its growth is reducing areas for rarer species such as marsh helleborine.

Other: rich deposits of mud and sand alive with intertidal creatures if you dig fast enough. Many excellent pubs and, at Cley, the famous 'Nancy's Cafe' – centre for bird information countrywide.

OTTER TRUST ⚥

Established in the 1970s the Otter Trust has the aim of presenting the otter's case for conservation to the public, acting as a clearing house for information and actively trying to conserve these highly threatened animals. In Britain the European otter is now an endangered species, generations of legal and illegal hunting having brought the population down to the level of a few hundred. Now the species is fully protected, but the otter remains a rare sight on our rivers. With the aid of the Trust its recovery will be considerably speeded up.

Elsewhere in the world otters – and there are a large number of different species in this cosmopolitan

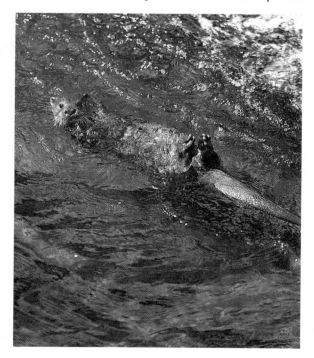

An otter rolls playfully in the water, a rare sight even though the species is now fully protected

family – are suffering from the same pressures. Here too the Trust seeks to help by establishing healthy breeding stocks which can supply zoos and wildlife parks with the animals they need thus taking pressure off wild populations.

Otters are superb swimmers and remarkably appealing mammals in general. The Trust offers views of the best single collection in the country with a variety of otters from many lands.

Visiting: take the A143 westward for a couple of miles from Bungay: inquiries, The Otter Trust, River Farm, Earsham, Bungay, Suffolk.

Mammals: otters.

OUSE WASHES 🐦 ✿ ♿

In that vast flat landscape, famous to schoolchildren as the home of Hereward the Wake and the place where King John lost his baggage, there is not so much as a hill to break the skyline. It is artificial scenery, a land that man has dragged from the marshy wastes that once made it the largest wasteland in all of lowland Britain. Its landmarks are ditches and banks with crude names like Middle Level Drain and Nene Outfall Cut, Emneth Hungate and Friday Bridge. These are instant eighteenth-century names, not names that evolved along with the place itself. So man created the Fens, and although there are many who do not like what he has done here, fishermen intent on thirty-pound pike from a drain do, and so do bird-watchers for, as a byproduct of draining these tangled fens, the engineers had to create fail-safe overflows where they could put excess water when the rains of winter brought more water than their narrow cuts could deal with.

The largest and most important of all these is the Bedford Level or, as it is known now, the Ouse Washes. From Earith to Denver stretches a fenland overflow a mile wide by twenty miles long. Every late winter the sluices are opened at Earith and excess water is allowed to run over the grassy meadows. At such times the splashes instantly come alive with birds, including the most important concentration of wild Bewick's swans from Siberia to be found in Britain. There are duck here too – pintail and shoveler, mallard and teal. Late winter bird-watching is magnificent, but as the waters subside and the wildfowl leave two specialities move in to breed. Both require damp meadows that have been recently under water and both are very rare: the black-tailed godwit and the gregarious ruff.

So important had these wet pastures become that by the late 1960s three conservation organizations were actively engaged in their acquisition. Today the three are by far the largest landowners in the area. The Royal Society for the Protection of Birds owns a central section: access by signposts from Welches Dam where there is a car park and a footpath to public hides or from Purls Bridge to the north. No permits required, but do walk below the banks to minimize disturbance. The Cambridge and Isle of Ely Naturalists' Trust also has hides in this stretch.

The Wildfowl Trust owns a section north of Delph Bridge, itself one of the finest vantage points for seeing birds in winter, which holds huge numbers of wildfowl. There is a hyper-modern observatory and a network of more traditional (and draughty) hides. Floodlights pick out the Bewick's swans after dark as well as the sixty other species numbering perhaps over 40,000 birds that may be seen. The feeding programme here brings the wild birds close enough to make binoculars redundant.

The hosts of birds and immense richness of this area can only be appreciated by those who are prepared to give the big fenland skies a chance to show their best at daybreak or dusk. Then the effect as you walk one of their lonely embankments can be a truly moving countryside experience. The actual Washes are open for botanical studies from 1 July – 30 September each year.

Visiting: the Washes lie north and south of Welney, which is on the A1101 south of Wisbech. The Wildfowl Trust Observatory is open every day, except Christmas Day, from 10.00 to 17.00 hours and all visitors should report to the Warden at Pintail House, which is one and a quarter miles north-east of the Suspension Bridge opposite Welney and 200 yards south of the footbridge which gives access to the Reserve. There is a shop and information centre that issues permits.

Birds: Bewick's and whooper swans, pintail, shoveler, gadwall, teal, golden plover, all in winter; in summer, black-tailed godwit and ruff along with redshank and snipe.

Botany: osier beds still cut commercially and many water-loving plants such as yellow flag, frogbit, fringed water-lily, greater water parsnip. Total of 260 flowering plants.

PEAKIRK WILDFOWL RESERVE ♥ &

The collection of wildfowl at Peakirk near Peterborough was created as a safety stand-by for the main Wildfowl Trust collection at Slimbridge in Gloucestershire. With so many birds crowded together, disease is an ever-present risk, and though every conceivable precaution against epidemics is taken the idea of a reserve collection was common sense. Over the years Peakirk has developed into a collection in its own right. There are now over 600 individual ducks, geese and swans of over eighty different species housed in fine, natural-looking surroundings. The Hawaiian goose, the Trust's greatest success story, wanders at will through the grounds and there are flamingoes as well.

The usual Wildfowl Trust gift shop, exhibition and refreshment rooms are available, and admission prices are really a bargain. As elsewhere, the grounds are open throughout the year except Christmas Day.

Nearby is the Borough Fen Decoy, an old commercial duck decoy that is still worked regularly and which now provides up to 2000 dabbling duck a year to be ringed. Strange as it might seem, no one has yet invented a better method of catching duck, and so this medieval technique persists today. As absolutely nil disturbance is essential, the decoy is open to visitors for only two days in late May or early June – details from the Warden. Tel. 0733 252271.

The Welney Wildfowl Reserve lies to the east at Welney (see Ouse Washes) and there is much to be said for visiting the two areas on the same day. Note, however, that Welney is essentially a winter place while Peakirk is interesting throughout the year.

Hawaiian geese or Néné, wander through the grounds at Peakirk Wildfowl Reserve

Visiting: the reserve lies just off the A15 some six miles north of Peterborough, and is well signposted. There is a free car park and no prior booking is necessary, except for large parties. The A1 passes nearby to the west.

Birds: duck, geese, swans and flamingoes plus collared doves galore.

REX GRAHAM NATURE RESERVE ✵

Named after a botanist-conservationist, Rex Graham Nature reserve is unique in being open for only four and a half hours each year. At this time, usually the first Saturday in June, visitors can walk the board-walk erected with the aid of the World Wildlife Fund within feet of a whole bed of the rare military orchid. There is no other attraction and no other times to get in to see them. If a day in the country needs to be different then this is surely it – try finding them elsewhere.

The rare military orchid, on show for only a few hours each year at the Rex Graham Nature Reserve

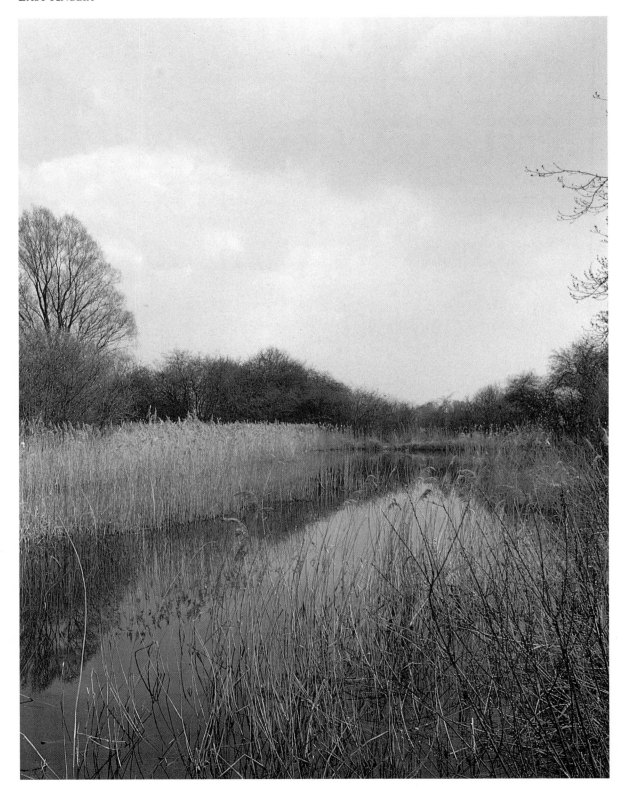

This tiny reserve is owned by the Suffolk Trust for Nature Conservation. The site was discovered in 1955 by Mrs M. Southwell and is now recognized as a Site of Special Scientific Interest.

Visiting: access from the Icklingham–Barton Mills road, the A1101. Details should be sought from the Trust at St Peter's House, Cutler Street, Ipswich IP1 1UU, enclosing a s.a.e. and, if you feel so moved, why not a small donation? Access to see the military orchids is free, but a small charge is made for photography.

Botany: military orchid, twayblade, ploughman's spikenard.

ROYDON COMMON ✿

Lying immediately off the A148 King's Lynn–Fakenham road, Roydon Common is on the greensand and has a very low rainfall. As a result it is of exceptional interest to botanists, because these circumstances combine to produce a growth of ling on the drier parts, often with the parasitic dodder, while the wetter parts have a fine peat bog flora. Here bog asphodel, bog myrtle and cranberry can be found, and there are three distinct species of sundew. In winter the area is known for hen harrier and merlin.

Visiting: open access off the A148 near Roydon.

Botany: dodder, bog asphodel, bog myrtle, cranberry, sphagnum moss, sundews.

WICKEN FEN ✿ ✿ 🦋

Following the Dissolution the estates of Thorney and Whittlesey were given to the Earl of Bedford, and it was the fourth Earl who was given the right by Royal Charter to drain the Fenlands. Together with his 'Adventurers' (thus Adventurers' Fen) he employed the great Dutch engineer Vermuyden to divert the rivers and turn swamp-ridden sedges into summer grazing. The result was a dismal failure at first, but eventually new rivers were cut and wind (later steam and diesel) pumps drained the vast marshlands. The one sizeable wetland section remaining is Wicken Fen north of Newmarket. As a direct result of the almost universal drainage, the Fen stands higher than its surroundings, and its character can only be maintained artificially.

Today Wicken Fen, together with its neighbouring Adventurers' Fen, cover 730 acres and is the property of the National Trust. It is heavily overgrown with bushes, sedges and reeds and together with cleared areas, including an artificial pool (the Mere), is a fair sample of what the Fens must have been before drainage.

The area is rich in life and a magnet for botanists, entomologists and ornithologists. The Fen is best known as the haunt of rare butterflies, but there are orchids and unusual birds as well. Many of the latter can be viewed on the Mere from the comfort of hides. A labelled collection of the wild plants of the Fens grows by the Education Centre.

Visiting: Wicken is reached from the A10 at Stretham by turning eastward between Cambridge and Ely on the B1085. At the western edge of the village turn southward where a signpost reads 'Wicken Fen'. Permits can be obtained from the centre – free for National Trust members. There is also a permit dispensing machine.

Botany: orchids, marsh hog's fennel, and many other fenland plants in profusion.

Birds: great crested grebe, long-eared owl, grasshopper warbler.

Insects: swallowtail butterfly.

Wicken Fen, with its reeds and bushes, shows what the Fens must have looked like before they were drained

EAST MIDLANDS

GIBRALTAR POINT 🐦 ✿ 🦋

Situated at the northern corner of the Wash, Gibraltar
Point Bird Observatory and Field Station has an
enviable reputation in the field of education and
public relations. Throughout the year courses as varied
as marine ecology and bird ringing are taking place,
and there are school visits during term-time weekdays
that bring children out into the countryside to learn
for themselves.

Gibraltar Point is interesting from a variety of
angles, and the simple facts of its geographical existence are quite fascinating. The mudbanks, saltings,
dunes and 'real land' all depend on a complex inter-
relationship of the forces of the sea. The colonization
of plants and the vast feeding grounds for birds that
open up at every low tide are part of the same balance
of forces. Every spring and autumn bird-watchers are
attracted by the migrant waders and seabirds, and
often vast numbers of waders congregate here in
winter. Occasionally a rare land bird may appear, but
it is the varied shorebirds that are the main attraction.
To those who prefer to understand the countryside
they walk, Gibraltar Point is an ideal spot, with plenty
of information and explanatory displays.

Visiting: Gibraltar Point is free of access, but visitors
   should report to the Field Centre on arrival. There
   are overnight facilities for serious students.
Birds: knot, dunlin, oystercatcher, bar-tailed godwit,
   terns, Arctic skua.
Mammals: grey seal, common seal.
Botany: very interesting colonizing flora with some
   unusual species.
Insects: excellent spot to watch migrant butterflies in
   late summer.

LINCOLNSHIRE COAST ✿ ⚘

Tetney lies on the east coast five miles south of
Grimsby and consists of grazing marshes intersected
by dykes and creeks and separated from the sea by a
seawall. The shallow saltmarsh and the intertidal area
beyond extend for up to a mile at low tide with a
continuing growth of annual glasswort and sea purslane
pushing out over the sandy banks. Here the Royal
Society for the Protection of Birds established a
reserve to protect the excellent population of the little
tern. There are other breeding birds as well, including
ringed plover, oystercatcher and short-eared owl.
However, during migration shorebirds and terns are

numerous and varied and there is always something of interest. Winter high tide roosts can be very dramatic.

Further to the south lies the area of Saltfleetby-Theddlethorpe Dunes, which consists of nearly five miles of coastline owned or leased by the Nature Conservancy Council and the Lincolnshire Trust for Nature Conservation. This fine area is of considerable interest, with the older dunes, dating from at least the fourteenth century, showing a distinct plant community from the more recent ones. There is a freshwater marsh as well as a good salt marsh and, of course, an open shoreline. Though the area is good for passage waders as well as birds such as short-eared owl and harriers, the botanist will find a good variety of flowering plants. Among others there are pyramidal, bee and marsh orchids, autumnal hawkbit, birdsfoot trefoil, common century, viper's bugloss, fairy flax, yellow flag, kingcup, lesser spearwort, bog pimpernel and skullcap. Butterflies include green hairstreak, and this is the only locality in the county for natterjack toad.

Visiting: Saltfleetby-Theddlethorpe is of open access (but beware RAF bombing offshore) from the coastal A1031 at Seaview, Sea Lane, Rimac, Sea Bank, Brickyard and Crook Bank. There is parking space at each access point. For Tetney follow signs to Tetney Lock. Park and walk seawards along the northern bank of the Louth Canal to the RSPB summer caravan. Cross the bridge and follow footpaths to the shore.
Botany: pyramidal orchid, bee orchid, marsh orchid, birdsfoot trefoil, viper's bugloss, lesser spearwort, bog pimpernel, annual glasswort, sea purslane.
Birds: little tern, common tern, ringed plover, oyster-catcher, short-eared owl, harriers, waders on the shore in season.
Other: natterjack toad.

PEAK NATIONAL PARK ✔ ♟ ֍ &

Though it is a decidedly upland area, the Peak District is one of the most populous of our National Parks. It includes the high massif of The Peak, reaching 2088 feet at Kinder Scout, and Bleaklow Hill further to the north at 2061 feet, but much of the Park consists of gently rolling country with densely settled (in a rural sense) valleys and many market towns. At its heart but excluded from it lies Buxton, and the Park extends from Lack and Ashbourne in the south to beyond Crowden in the north.

A glance at a map suffices to show the strategic significance of the Park as a breath of air to the industrial cities of the region. To the south-west lie Stoke and the potteries, to the west the conurbation of Manchester, to the east Sheffield, and to the south Derby and Nottingham. Yet despite such a huge potential population intake, the District retains its rural charm and agricultural economy. Above all it is the hills, with their strange 'Edges', stone outcrops beloved of athletic rock climbers, that dominate the scenery and provide the major attractions. At Castleton, north of Buxton, Peveril Castle rises in ruins above the village. Underneath is Peak Cavern, reached along a wooded stream. Here the famous caves and the flowing water that created them can be visited without potholing equipment. Nearby is Treak Cliff Cavern, the only place in the world where Blue John stone is quarried, to be turned into ornaments.

Immediately west of Buxton is the delightful Goyt Valley, running down to the reservoirs in the valley floor. This beauty spot is so popular that it has been made a no-traffic zone at weekends. A walk down (or up) the valley passes from gritstone moorland through deciduous woodland to farmland. The valley is rich in bird-life and flowers.

In the south, Dovedale is another noted beauty spot set in the limestone district north of Ashbourne. The stream is lined by fine ash woods alive with small birds in spring and summer. Part of the valley belongs to the National Trust and there is a convenient car park off the A515. Lathkill Dale south of Bakewell is another typical wooded Peak District valley, and has the advantage of being less frequented than Dovedale.

The Pennine Way starts at Edale just south of The Peak and slogs upward to Kinder Scout as a prelude to what is to follow.

Visiting: the area is crisscrossed with roads, and access to the valleys is generally straightforward. Contact Peak National Park, Aldern House, Beslow Road, Bakewell, Derbyshire DE4 1AE.
Birds: moorland species with excellent woodland birds in the valleys.
Botany: wide range of flowering plants.

RIBER CASTLE WILDLIFE PARK ✔ ♟ &

The idea of specializing in a representative collection of European animals with the intention of breeding to return to the wild is not new. But this effective Park is

Edale in the Peak District with its typical dry stone walls

doing very well in its attempt to cope with the difficulties involved in breeding, say, polecats; so much so that these animals have been reintroduced in the Lake District, where they had long been extinct. Its ongoing plans for whooper swan and European quail are perhaps less likely to succeed. The Park has lynx and pine marten as well, and will be doing a considerable service to conservation when these animals are bred in sufficient quantity to release.

Among a good collection of animals, mention must be made of reindeer, beaver, wild cat, otter, European genet, Arctic fox and porcupine. Equally interesting is the collection of rare breeds of domestic stock, many of which were on the verge of disappearing altogether. The varieties of sheep, for instance, were formerly very numerous, but modern husbandry has turned out a 'universal sheep' to replace many of them. The same applies to cattle, goats, pigs, poultry and so on. The Park is ensuring that many of these forms will now survive – economic or not.

There is also a collection of models of prehistoric animals (some life-sized) as well as a model railway, a car museum and a farm cart collection.

Visiting: leave the A6 at Matlock eastward to Tansley then turn right (southward) on Alders Lane to Riber Castle. Beware the apparent short-cut via Starkholmes Road – it includes a 1 in 4 hill and some fraught hairpins. Large car park, reasonable entrance fees, nice countryside.

Mammals: lynx, pine marten, polecat, reindeer.

Birds: golden eagle, flamingoes and waterfowl, storks and cranes.

TWYCROSS ZOO PARK 🐦 🦌

Situated roughly equidistant between the Midlands conurbation and Derby, Twycross Zoo is a model of what can be achieved within narrow confines. It is also a true breath of air for the large cities that surround it, and shows wild animals to advantage. The stated aim of the Zoo is 'to educate and interest the public in wild animals and to breed those species in danger of extinction'. As a result it has one of the finest collections of primates, including the great lowland gorilla, orang-utan, chimpanzee and a wealth of monkeys, including the only group of proboscis monkeys in the country. Breeding is well established in the colobus, De Grazza, langur and capuchin monkeys and white-handed gibbon. While these are

Riber Castle specializes in European animals such as this lynx

the conservation stars, visitors naturally swarm to see lion, tiger, cheetah and leopard.

Those other large and appealing animals – elephant, camel, giraffe – can be seen, and most of the exhibits are housed in large enclosures where they have room to move about. Many birds are housed in a walk-through aviary and there are flamingoes and waterfowl in large pools. Special performances include the ever-popular Chimps' Tea Party and Elephant Bathtime. The enclosures are well laid out and there are good facilities for eating and refreshments.

Visiting: the Zoo lies on the A444 Nuneaton to Burton-upon-Trent road just north of Twycross. It has large car parks and is set in open countryside. Moderate entrance fees.

Mammals: lowland gorilla, orang-utan, breeding monkeys including proboscis and capuchin monkeys.

Birds: good collection including tropical species.

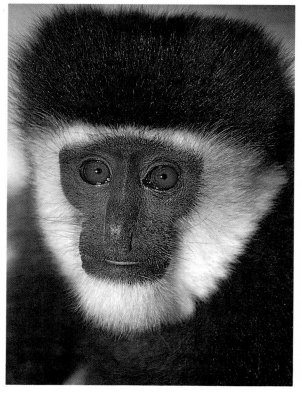

The Colobus monkey is one of several species bred successfully at Twycross Zoo Park

HEART OF ENGLAND

BIRDLAND 🦜 ♿

Covering a mere three acres of the pretty Cotswold village of Bourton-on-the-Water, Birdland has an enviable reputation. Throughout the summer visitors come by the thousand to see a collection of birds in one of Britain's most attractive settings. Neatly trimmed lawns border the trout stream and the stone houses have that Cotswold charm. As the visitor approaches he is quite liable to get a free view as a flight of macaws skim swiftly overhead. Indeed so many of Birdland's inmates are free-flying that there is a free bird show for the taking by just walking around the village itself.

Birdland really got free-flying collections going. Zoos and conservation 'must walk hand in hand' says the guidebook, and to prove the point many of Birdland's inhabitants have been born there.

If the free-flying macaws and parrots are the stars of the Zoo show, the more discerning visitor will be watching for Lear's macaw and drawn to the tropical houses where hummingbirds fly around as you pass. Small cages house touracos of various species, hornbills, including the magnificent great Indian hornbill, and many smaller species whose names must be searched out on the cages themselves. Then there are the penguins, viewable through a glass-sided pool.

There is an excellent education centre featuring a modern lecture hall and a huge Peter Scott mural, a shop and good facilities for dining nearby.

Visiting: Bourton-on-the-Water is on the A429 where it crosses the River Windrush. Birdland is easy to find from the village centre, though parking is a problem on summer Sundays. Admission is reasonably priced.

Birds: hyacinth macaw, red and gold macaw, green-winged macaw, Lear's macaw, purple-capped lory, lorikeet, great palm cockatoo, flamingoes, penguins, great Indian hornbill, jacobean hummingbird, coquet hummingbird, sunbittern, bee-eaters, Victoria crowned pigeon.

BIRMINGHAM NATURE CENTRE ✚ ☙ &

The Nature Centre is another go-ahead idea developed by the progressive Birmingham Corporation. It was opened in 1975 on the site previously occupied by an old zoo, and into its four and a half acres the designers have managed to cram one of the most sensible and enlightening wildlife exhibits in Britain, complemented by museum material and educational back-up. The collections include fox, badger and small mammals; fish; reptiles and amphibians; and, of course, British birds. The Centre has an exhibit built around live bees, and a walk-through living butterfly collection. The tiny grounds show the variety of British habitats, and there is a farm collection which includes old breeds of domestic stock as well as antique machinery.

Visiting: Cannon Hill Park, Pershore Road, Birmingham, which is in the Edgbaston district opposite the BBC's Pebble Mill. Tel. 021 472 7775. It is open all year round except Tuesdays and is easily reached by bus.

Botany: recreations of major British habitat types.
Birds: collection of various species.
Mammals: badger, fox, etc.
Other: walk-through butterfly collection.

BROCKHAMPTON WOOD ☙ ☙

Lying roughly halfway between Hereford and Worcester, this fine woodland area is a property of the National Trust. It has extensive plantations of larch and Douglas fir, with some old beeches and both pedunculate and sessile oakwoods. There are also stands of the exotic wellingtonia and giant redwood. Birds are plentiful, with buzzard, raven, woodcock and abundant summer visitors including pied flycatcher. There is also a small lake that supports little grebe among other aquatic bird species. The fine nature trail takes about an hour, or a little longer if the lake is included.

Visiting: the Wood lies off the A44 some two miles east of Bromyard. The National Trust runs a car park, and guides are available for the nature trail there or at the local post office.

Botany: good variety of woodland flowers, stitchworth, dog's mercury, self-heal.
Birds: buzzard, raven, woodcock, pied flycatcher, redstart, wood warbler, willow warbler, little grebe, moorhen.

COOPER'S HILL ☙

Lying in the Cotswolds east of Gloucester on the A46, this area is a fine example of limestone beechwood. Some 137 acres are included in a nature reserve of Gloucestershire County Council, though this is only a part of a larger area scheduled as a Site of Special Scientific Interest. Though occupied since at least the Iron Age, there is little trace of early settlement left to

see today. The Romans too found Cooper's Hill an advantageous place, and medieval times have bequeathed the traditional habit of rolling cheeses from the 'Maypole' site every Whit Monday. The Hill also offers a fine panorama over the surrounding countryside from the Malvern Hills to the Black Mountains of Wales.

Apart from the obvious signs of human activity which are pointed out by the nature trail guide, there is considerable botanical and ornithological interest. Golden saxifrage, wood sanicle, violet and yellow archangel can be seen, and birds include willow warbler, chaffinch, chiffchaff, yellowhammer and others. The whole takes about an hour and a half to walk, but make a day of it to enjoy the views.

Visiting: car park on the A46 north of Cranham about five miles south-east of Gloucester.

Botany: golden saxifrage, yellow archangel, wood sanicle.

Birds: varied beechwood species.

DUDLEY ZOO ∀ ☝ ♿

Situated in the heart of the Black Country, Dudley is an old market town with a character of its own. Nearby is the old Dudley Castle and around the Castle are the forty acres of Dudley Zoo. Though a private zoo that only just survived in 1977, Dudley has a remarkable reputation for breeding rare and often difficult animals, perhaps due to the large enclosures and enterprising attitude of the management. The Zoo is particularly proud of its breeding orang-utans, Arabian gazelles, tigers and polar bears. What is achieved at Dudley and at places like it must become standard at all zoos if they are to serve their major purpose.

Among an impressive array of other animals a lowland gorilla takes pride of place, though chimpanzee and gibbon, together with the orang-utan, ensure that all visitors can see the five great apes at one place: the fifth ape is you yourself. Pumas and polar bears, lions and leopards, antelope, deer, giraffe, tapirs, birds, sheep and, of course, sealions are all to be found, all kept in ideal conditions and displayed to an exceedingly high standard.

As with all good zoos, the smaller creatures are not ignored, so that small birds, small mammals and reptiles are all catered for. They may not be the stars of the show, but they are an important part of any zoo!

The special Land of the Dinosaurs exhibition re-creates the monsters that walked the earth in the Mesozoic era 65–225 million years ago. And there are also an aquarium, a pets' corner and a children's farm.

Nearby is Wren's Nest National Nature Reserve covering seventy-four acres of disused limestone quarries. There is a nature trail which starts and finishes by the Caves Inn on Wren's Hill Road, and nowhere in the country can the connection between geology and human land use be better observed. The rocks are rich in fossils and as you wander along the trail you will see specimens of a wildlife that has long since disappeared. Though many famous specimens have been found here collecting is positively discouraged. Nevertheless it is a remarkable area as the museum in James Road, 200 yards north of the town market place, testifies.

Visiting: Dudley is extremely convenient to visit. It lies near the M5/M6 junction and is easiest to reach via Exit 2 of the M5. Just follow signs to Dudley and then to the Zoo. The Zoo is open every day except Christmas Day.

Mammals: orang-utan, gorilla, chimpanzee, gibbon, tiger, Arabian gazelle, polar bear.

Birds: good collection.

EARLS HILL ☝ ✿

The Shropshire Conservation Trust has made a real point of encouraging the public to visit many of its reserves by establishing well-designed nature trails and publishing quite excellent leaflets that lead the visitor along them. Earls Hill is a fine example. It lies just off the A488 some seven miles south of Shrewsbury and rises through a mixture of landforms to the peak of Earls Hill at 1049 feet. Though the trail is three quarters of a mile from the road, even that walk is full of interest. There are nuthatches, treecreepers and warblers in summer, along with cowslip, lady's smock, greater stitchwort, heath speedwell, the changing forget-me-not, greater celandine, a plant whose juice was formerly used for curing warts, and the rare rock stonecrop.

The trail itself can be as long or as short as you like, with several 'escape' routes, though the climb to the top is rewarded by superb views in all directions. Overhead, buzzard, kestrel and jackdaw soar, while dippers frequent the streams and pied flycatchers the specially-erected nest boxes. Botanists will enjoy the flowers and there are masses of wild garlic.

Visiting: take the A488 south-westward out of Shrewsbury and stop at the Shell filling station near Pontesford. Park at the rear of the garage. Walk eastward along the metalled road and then turn left onto a footpath to the reserve and information centre.

Botany: shining cranesbill, greater stitchwort, greater celandine, common figwort, wild garlic, lady's smock, cowslip, heath speedwell, mouse-eared hawkweed, changing forget-me-not, rock stonecrop, wall pennywort, lesser celandine, dog's mercury, spearwort, meadowsweet, creeping buttercup, alternate-leaved golden saxifrage, heath bedstraw.

Birds: buzzard, kestrel, dipper, pied flycatcher, grasshopper warbler, green woodpecker, raven, nuthatch, treecreeper.

THE FALCONRY CENTRE ✦ ♿

Established by Philip Glasier at Newent in Gloucestershire in 1967, the centre holds a remarkably fine collection of birds of prey from many parts of the world. The emphasis is on the noble and ancient art of falconry, but a quite amazing variety of birds have been trained to come to the hand by the traditional techniques. Whereas most birds of prey exhibited in Britain are (of necessity) housed in cages each isolated from the other, at the Centre many birds can be seen in their true glory in flight. Actually birds of prey are generally rather dull in colour and tend to sit lethargically for long periods. They thus have comparatively little appeal to the non-specialist visitor. In flight, however, they are fast and dramatic, among the most exciting of all birds.

Naturally it is the traditional falconers' birds that are usually flown, and peregrine, saker and lanner can all be seen to advantage flying to the lure. But there are goshawks, eagles and even exotics that are seldom if ever flown elsewhere.

One of the aims of the Centre is to breed birds, thus aiding the conservation movement at a time when falcons, in particular, are under great pressure. The Centre has an incubator and is successfully producing young birds to add to its stocks. Another aim is to act as an information centre for falconry, and special courses are arranged during the year.

Visiting: Newent is eleven miles from Gloucester and is open throughout the year; inquiries to The Falconry Centre, Newent, Gloucester, GL18 1JJ. Tel. 0531 820286.
Birds: flying falcons, peregrine, lanner, saker, goshawk, eagle owl, barn owl.
Others: falconry courses.

FOREST OF DEAN ✦ ✦ ✱ 🦋

The Forest of Dean is a National Forest Park covering 35,000 acres of old mature woodland. It is managed by the Forestry Commission, who have done much in recent years to improve its appeal to the visitor, whether bird-watcher, botanist or rambler. The Forest

A nightjar in the Forest of Dean, an extensive ancient woodland managed by the Forestry Commission is bounded to the south by the Severn and to the west by the delicious Wye Valley. Monmouth and Chepstow are the obvious starting points.

The Forest of Dean is the most complete hardwood woodland community to be found in Britain, and of obvious attraction to anyone interested in our countryside. Here deer, badger and fox, along with many less obvious mammals, find their ideal niche. Birds are plentiful, with pied flycatcher something of a local speciality. The Forestry Commission has erected masses of nest boxes for this species. Buzzard, sparrow-hawk, crossbill, nightjar and warblers galore can all be found, and the forest streams are a haunt of dipper.

To the botanist the very age of the Forest is of immense attraction and there are plant communities that are as perfect as any.

Visiting: there are several very good nature trails, details of which can be obtained from The Warden, Forestry Commission, Crown Office, Bank Street, Coleford, Gloucestershire GL16 8BA. Trail start-ing points are given by grid reference: Biblins Adventure Trail about 6 miles (SO/540153); Cannop Ponds Forest Walk, 1¼ miles (SO/608105), ¾ miles south of Cannop; Christchurch Trail, 1½ miles to 3 miles (SO/569179); Churchill Trail, 1½ miles to 2½ miles (SO/621081), ¼ mile from Parkend/Yorkley Road; Speech House Trail 1½ to 2½ miles begins 3 miles from Cinderford and Coleford off the B4226 (SO/620121); Symonds Yat Forest Walk is 1 mile to 2½ miles long and starts at the Log Cabin Refreshment Hut near Symonds Yat Rock (SO/562160), where peregrines breed.

For those who would explore the Wye Valley there is the Wyndcliffe Nature Trail from St Arvans above Chepstow (ST/523973), which has excellent flowers and views.

Mammals: red deer, roe deer, badger, fox.

Botany: classic hardwood community with associated flowers.

Birds: buzzard, sparrowhawk, peregrine, pied fly-catcher, dipper, crossbill, warblers.

Insects: butterflies including brown argus, wood white and white admiral.

SLIMBRIDGE WILDFOWL TRUST 🐦 ♿

Home of Sir Peter Scott, its founder and Honorary Director, and of 2500 birds of 170 species, Slimbridge is the finest collection of ducks, geese and swans in the world. As the visitor wanders among the pens and pools he can see more species of wildfowl than anywhere else. The rare Hawaiian goose, or néné, whose world population was once down to the last few birds, is now one of the most common of the Trust's guests – be careful not to trip over one. Along with greylags and pinkfeet, snow and Ross's geese, the nénés have the freedom of the park.

To be fair, even ducks and geese can become a bit of a bore after a couple of hours, but the Wildfowl Trust has already anticipated your needs with a collection of

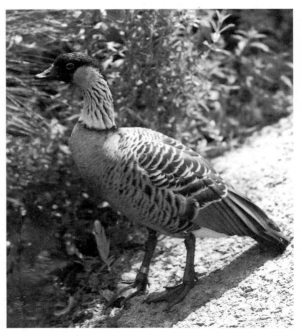

The Hawaiian goose was once nearly extinct, but it is now one of the most common birds at Slimbridge

Red deer, badger and fox are to be seen in the Forest of Dean

Many swans and ducks have made Slimbridge pools their home

graceful flamingoes from various parts of the world. among them you may find a screamer, while in the tropical house there are hummingbirds and tanagers from America. On a cold day the tropical house is particularly popular, but your binoculars and cameras will fog up instantly and can only be cleared by holding them in front of one of the electric fan heaters. Walking through this house a wonderful impression of a South American forest can be enjoyed – unfortunately it's an inaccurate one, for birds are never so common in the wild.

Slimbridge is not just a bird garden. Peter Scott chose this place primarily because of the thousands of wild white-fronted geese that spend the early part of the year on the New Grounds bordering the Severn. Up to 5000 birds have wintered here (Christmas to March) for generations, and the visitor at this time can see wild geese, often at close quarters, from one of the tower hides. Keen bird-watchers search through the flocks for hours looking for the rare lesser white-front or the red-breasted goose, often with some success.

With a little encouragement from the Trust the grounds have become the winter home of wild Bewick's swans, and several hundred now grace the Rushy pool where they are fed. In spring (March) their calls are a remarkable reminder of the wild places toward which they are about to depart. Less welcome are the collared doves that find the grounds a virtual pigeon paradise, with spilt grain everywhere and nice people to feed it to them.

Visiting: Slimbridge lies north of Bristol to the west of the M5 between junctions 13 and 14. It is well signposted from the A38, which runs parallel with the motorway. Admission charges are reasonable and there is a restaurant, a gift shop and educational displays and exhibits.

Birds: largest wildfowl collection in the world; wild geese and Bewick's swans.

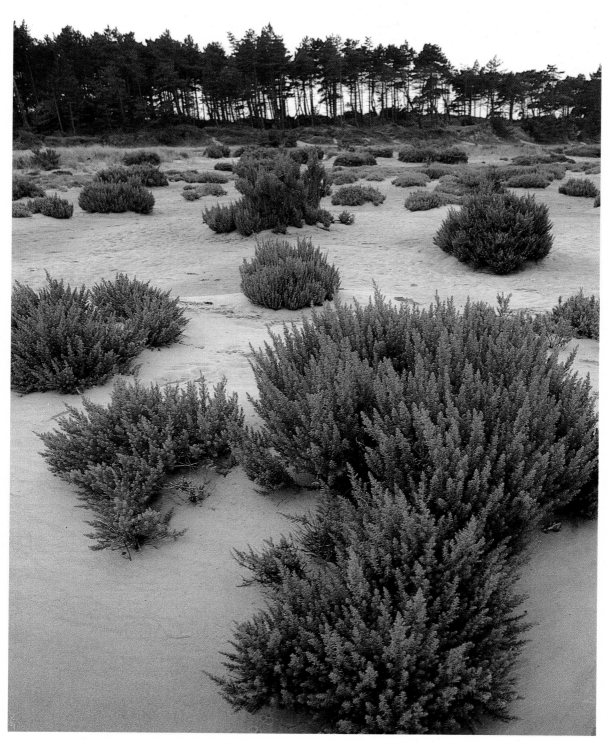

Holkham flats in Norfolk is the largest coastal nature reserve in England

Above: Greylag goose on a breeding islet. Every autumn hundreds of them arrive at Loch Leven

Below: Merrivale Standing Stone, a reminder of Dartmoor's rich history

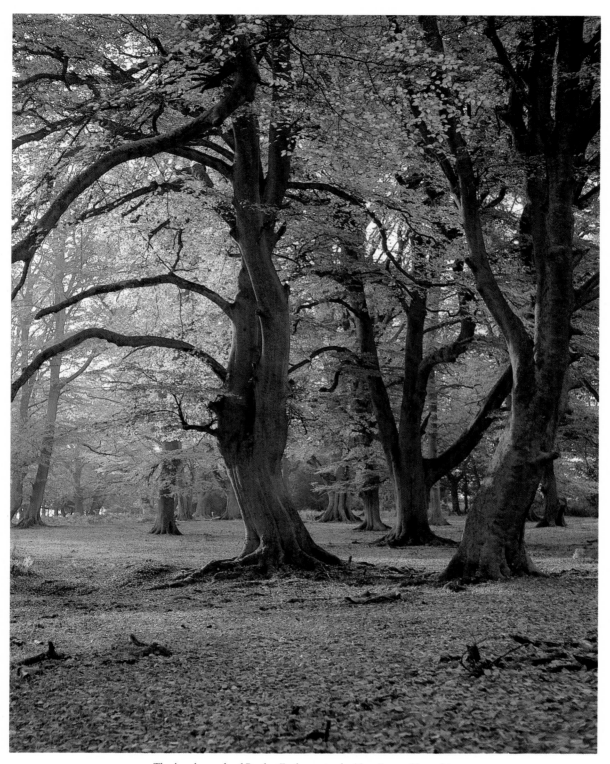

The beech woods of Bartley Enclosure in the New Forest, Hampshire

Left:
One of the brightly coloured macaws
at Paignton Zoo

Opposite:
The Alpine Garden in Oxford
University's Botanic Garden

Below:
Dartford warblers can sometimes be
seen at the RSPB Arne reserve

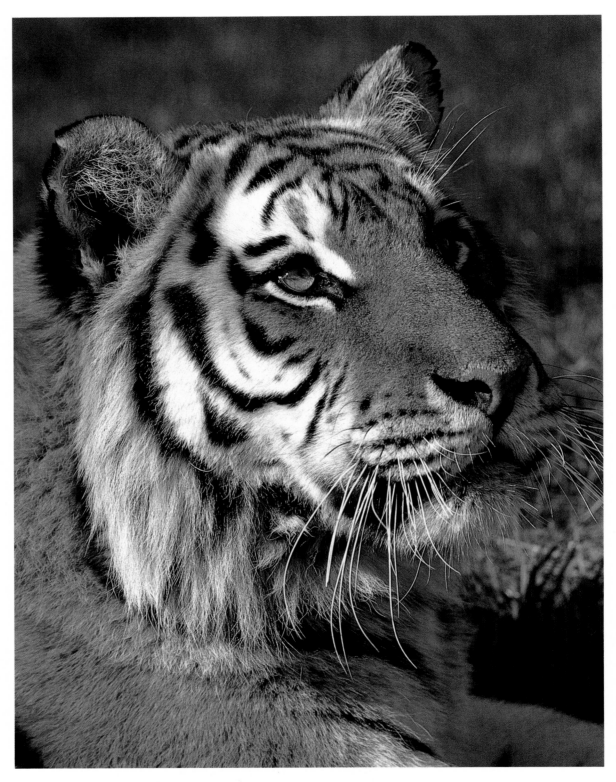

A female Siberian tiger from North-East Asia, one of a breeding group at Howletts Zoo Park

The new temperate house at Kew Gardens

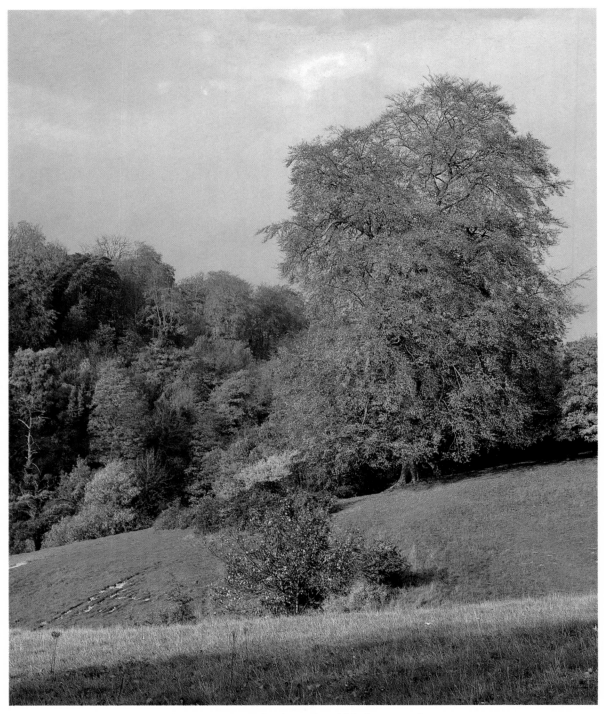

Above: In autumn the beeches in Arundel Park are magnificent

Opposite above: Chanctonbury Ring, Sussex, once a fortress, is an excellent viewpoint for walkers on the South Downs Way

Opposite below: Giraffes and zebras occupy the same enclosure at London Zoo

Polecats bred at Riber Castle have been re-introduced to the Lake District

There are seventeen species of orchid at the Wye and Crundale Downs NNR, including this rare late spider orchid

Opposite:
There is a good chance of seeing red squirrels at East Wretham Heath

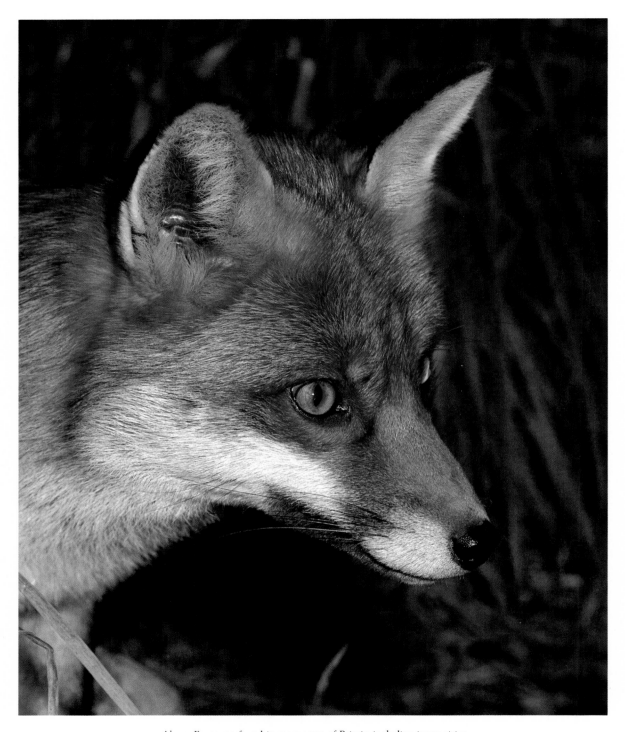

Above: Foxes are found in most areas of Britain including inner cities

Opposite above: Cley Nature Reserve, one of the finest bird marshes

Opposite below: The River Senni valley in the Brecon Beacons National Park. The Park covers over 500 square miles

125

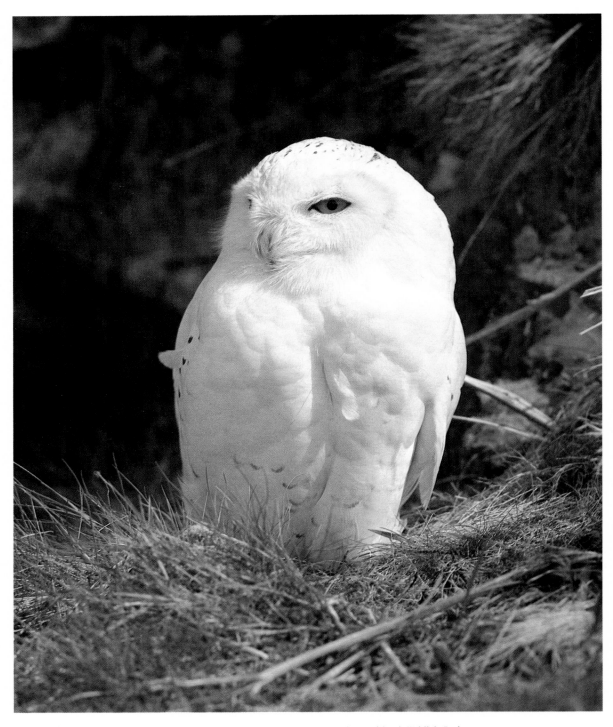

Above: Snowy owls can be seen close up at the Highland Wildlife Park

Opposite above: An Arctic tern lands on a fence post on Inner Farne

Opposite below: Manx shearwater after landing near its breeding burrow at night

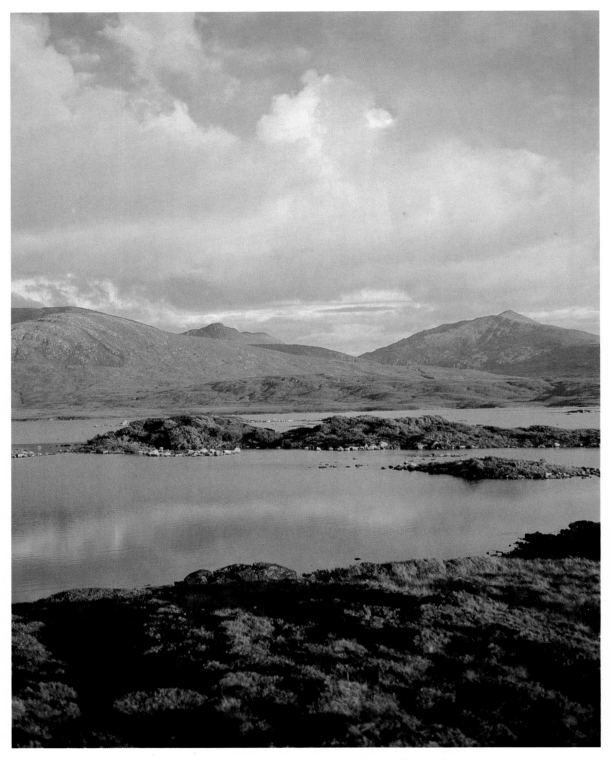

Loch Druidibeg Nature Reserve on South Uist where greylag geese breed

WALES

HOLYHEAD
South Stack
Newborough Warren
ANGELSEY
BANGOR
CAERNARVON
COLWYN BAY
Welsh Mountain Zoo
A5
A55
LLANGOLLEN
Snowdonia National Park
A494
Cadair Idris
WELSHPOOL
A470
A487
ABERYSTWYTH
Offa's Dyke Path
A470
Dinas and Gwenffrwd
A487
CARDIGAN
Pembrokeshire Coast National Park
HAVERFORD WEST
A40
BRECON
Brecon Beacons National Park
A40
MONMOUTH
Skomer and the Welsh Islands
Gower
SWANSEA
A48
M4
NEWPORT
CARDIFF

50 mls
50 kms
N

BRECON BEACONS NATIONAL PARK ✦ ❀ ♿

Because they are not as high as the mountains of North Wales, and perhaps also because their name makes them sound more like hills than the all but 3000 foot peaks that they are, the Brecon Beacons are often passed by. They call back those who know them, but tempt few newcomers. The Beacons are named from their use for signal fires, for from their summits one can see across the Bristol Channel and as far as the Malvern Hills. Highest of all is Pen y Fan, just a bare 93 feet under 3000 feet. From its summit, reached via a gentle path from the main A470 at Storey Arms in not much more than an hour, the sheer face falls an awe-inspiring 600 feet before it gradually levels out. Layers of rock can be picked out with ease, all weathered by

frost and water. This central section of the Park, some 8192 acres in all, is owned by the National Trust and there is free public access.

The National Park, which covers 519 square miles, extends from the Black Mountain in the west, through the Beacons to the Black Mountains (beware confusion) and the Welsh border. The drainage pattern flows north and south (mainly south) and the walker who decides to go from east to west is due for a tough ordeal. Only the River Usk has really cut a way through between Brecon and Abergavenny, and it is interesting to note that the only large lowland water of the region, Llangorse Lake, flows northward to join the Wye, though its feeder streams rise no more than a couple of miles from the fast maturing Usk. Llangorse is something of a gem. The largest natural lake in south Wales, its reedbeds shelter a first-class collection of wildfowl (including wild swans) in winter; and an increasingly disturbed number of breeding birds including reed warbler and yellow wagtail, both of which are here nearing the edge of their summer range.

Birds are also interesting among the mountains themselves. Here red grouse, merlin and even the occasional peregrine can be found. There are golden plover and dunlin, curlew and, along the streams, common sandpipers, dippers and grey wagtails. Botanists will find much of interest. There are trout in the Usk, and at the national nature reserve at Craig y Cilan near Taf-fechan Reservoir the cliffs shelter whitebeam.

The wooded valleys and sheep pastures of the lowlands are a delight, and the banks of the streams in spring can be carpeted with anemones, primroses and violets.

Visiting: the Park is within easy reach of the Welsh Valleys (indeed Merthyr Tydfil is just outside the boundary) and the industrial cities of South Wales. There are plenty of tracks and footpaths, and a variety of accommodation. For more information contact Brecon Beacons National Park, 7 Glamorgan Street, Brecon, Powys LD3 7DP.
Birds: great crested grebe, buzzard, merlin, kestrel, red grouse, dipper, grey wagtail, common sandpiper, dunlin, golden plover, reed warbler, yellow wagtail.
Botany: interesting cross-section of plants.

CADAIR IDRIS 🐦 ❀
Cadair Idris rises to less than 3000 feet and seems a lot higher. From almost every side it is approached from low ground and from the west it is only a very few miles from the sea. This isolated position never fails to create an impression of majesty on anyone who looks upon it. Indeed it often seems a very remote and hostile place. It is, in fact, not difficult to climb and the rewards on a clear day are fabulous, with views out over the sea, northward to Snowdonia over the Mawddach Estuary, and eastward to the borders.

Nearly a thousand acres are a National Nature Reserve dedicated to the study and conservation of the Arctic-Alpine flora to be found here. There are no restrictions on access. Other attractions are mainly confined to the lower slopes, where buzzard, sparrow-hawk, hosts of wood and willow warblers, grey wagtail,

dipper, common sandpiper and others may be found. To the north is the excellent shallow estuary of the Mawddach, with waders and wildfowl in season, while to the south-west is the tiny Broad Water backed by some really excellent grazing marshes.

Visiting: free access over Cadair Idris, which can be traversed from both north and south. Nearest towns are Dolgellau and Machynlleth to north and south respectively.
Botany: purple saxifrage, mossy saxifrage, spring sandwort, globeflower, moss campion.
Birds: buzzard, grey wagtail, dipper, common sandpiper, warblers.
Other: superb country walking.

DINAS AND GWENFFRWD ⚥ 🐦 ❀
The remote hills of central Wales have always had a pull on the lowlanders who live to the east. Now many of the reservoirs that serve the Midlands are situated among the valleys, and many Midlanders look westward for their recreation. The hills are fine without being too high, the valleys green with rich sheep pastures, and between the two are the old, lichen-strewn oak woods that cling tenaciously to the rocky and often precipitous hillsides. Together they constitute the charm of this part of Wales.

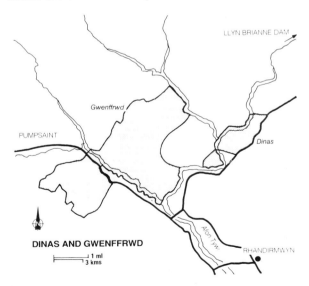

DINAS AND GWENFFRWD

The woods themselves are richest in wildlife, for while the hills above may shelter merlin and red grouse, ring ouzel and wheatear, the woods are full of warblers and pied flycatchers, finches and redstarts.

There are large badger setts among the rocky woods, and fox earths too. There may still be polecats, for this is their last British stronghold, and there are still the last red kites among the hills above Llandovery.

Dinas and Gwenffrwd woods are an RSPB reserve and typical of this part of Wales. Red kite is a possibility here, though it does not breed. Though it is the major attraction there are plenty more, like the buzzards that soar on still wings over the steep valley sides, the whinchat on the hedges and the stonechats on the heaths. Curlews bubble over the moors in spring and snipe bleat on stiffly-held tails, while over all the kite hangs motionless on the rising air.

Visiting: leave Llandovery north-westward on minor roads along the upper Towy valley to Rhandirmwyn and then turn northward to Gwenffrwd to the west and Dinas to the east. Map Ref. SN/788472. Public nature trail and information centre at Dinas.
Birds: red kite, buzzard, merlin, red grouse, pied flycatcher, wood warbler, redstart, ring ouzel, wheatear.
Mammals: polecat, red fox, badger.
Botany: interesting communities on the unploughed meadows and particularly in the old hillside woodlands.

GOWER ✦ ❀

The Gower peninsula is one of those beauty spots that is so well known that it is almost impossible to visit during summer weekends. It is straightforwardly beautiful and is thronged with traffic during the peak season. At other times its beauty and particularly its birds and flowers are available to those in search of wildlife.

Bird-watchers concentrate at the Burry Inlet for waders and wildfowl; at Worms Head for breeding and passage seabirds; and Oxwich Bay for a wide range of species and habitats. The botanist need look no further than the latter area, for Oxwich Bay has a truly outstanding flora. The surrounding limestone hills and cliffs have thrift, rock-rose, bloody cranesbill and some rather rare plants such as horseshoe vetch. The marshy hinterland of the Bay itself has a typical fen vegetation with bullrush and yellow flag, while the enclosing dunes have sea-holly and sea-spurge with a variety of orchids in the slacks. The latter include fen, green-winged and autumn lady's tresses.

There are sedge and reed warblers among the reeds along with bearded tit and Cetti's warblers. Water rail, sparrowhawk, buzzard and numerous migrants put in appearances and marsh harrier is often present. The shoreline has turnstone, oystercatcher, purple sandpiper and this is an excellent area for exploring a variety of rich habitats in a comparatively small area.

Visiting: Oxwich lies on the south coast of Gower off the A418. There is a reserve centre in the village and a nature trail that leads through most of the habitats. The fresh marsh is probably best seen from the road north of the village. There is a hide, permits for which can be obtained at the centre except during the school summer holiday.
Birds: fulmar, shag, razorbill, guillemot, kittiwake, sparrowhawk, buzzard, turnstone, oystercatcher, purple sandpiper, water rail, bearded tit, sedge warbler, reed warbler, Cetti's warbler.
Botany: fen orchid, green-winged orchid, pyramid orchid, autumn lady's tresses, sea-holly, sea-spurge, yellow flag, thrift, rock rose, bloody cranesbill, horseshoe vetch.

NEWBOROUGH WARREN ✦ ❀ ♿

The south-west corner of Anglesey from the Menai Straits to the Cefni Estuary near Malltraeth is a land dominated by sand. Nearest the sea are mobile dunes where marram grass is continually being swamped and continually recolonizing. Further inland the dunes have been fixed, allowing a more luxuriant growth of vegetation. Here there are dune slacks, places between the high heaps of sand where damp conditions allow a different flora to prosper. This is the simple progression of a growing coastline, but Newborough has a sandy heart that is a vast forest created by the Forestry Commission and covering some 2000 acres. There is a huge estuary exposing large sand banks at low tide, where hosts of migrant shorebirds gather in season. There is a fresh marsh created by the building of a sea wall by Thomas Telford, builder of the Menai Bridge and other miracles, in the last century. Called 'The Cob', it is a remarkable bird-watching edifice. And there is also a rocky promontory called Ynys Llanddwyn that juts out into Caernarvon Bay and which is composed of Pre-Cambrian rocks more than 600 million years old – some of the oldest in the country.

The Newborough Warren National Nature Reserve covers the coastal zone from Malltraeth to Abermenai

Oxwich Bay contains a variety of different wildlife habitats

Point, and surrounds Newborough Forest on three sides. Its 1565 acres include all of the most interesting life zones, and a number of routes lead to several parts of the reserve. For visitors to North Wales this offers a complete contrast to the mountains and resorts.

The flora of the reserve is rich, but the decline of rabbits and consequent growth of scrub has turned what were once open sandy areas into thick embryonic forests. The result has been a disaster for flowers of open areas. The mobile dunes remain uncolonized and dune pansy, sea spurge and sand catstail can be found. Naturally enough the fixed dunes are richer, and plants like birdsfoot trefoil, lady's smock, lady's bed-straw, meadow saxifrage, tormentil and marsh and other orchids can all be found. The slacks between the dunes hold butterwort and grass of Parnassus as well as creeping willow and buckshorn plantain.

The salt marsh along the Cefni is being colonized by the inevitable cord grass, though more slowly perhaps than elsewhere. Sea rush too has become well established since it first appeared in 1956–7. Neverthe-

less sea aster, seablite and thrift can all be found. The rocky landscape of Ynys Llanddwyn provides niches for the spleenworts, and the grassy areas are one of the few homes of spring squill in Britain.

One cannot visit Newborough without being conscious of the birds, and each season brings its own interest. In summer there are colonies of herring gulls, cormorants and shags, oystercatchers, lapwings and curlews. The estuary invariably holds shelduck and redshank, but visitors include wild whooper swans, duck such as goldeneye and pintail, godwits, ruff and a host of dunlin and other waders.

Visiting: there is a nice drive through Newborough Forest south-westward from Newborough, passing the church, that leads to a car park near the sea. Otherwise access is confined to public footpaths leaving the A4080 at various points between Penlon and the Forestry Commission Office south of Malltraeth Cob. A leaflet describing the reserve and access can be obtained from the car park in the summer, and there are two nature trail booklets as well. Malltraeth Pool can be seen from the A4080, and there is a hide overlooking Llyn Rhos Ddu.

Botany: dune pansy, sea-spurge, catstail, lady's smock, meadow saxifrage, tormentil, lady's bedstraw, birds-foot trefoil, wild thyme, marsh orchid, creeping willow, creeping bentgrass, sand sedge, jointed rush, wintergreen, butterwort, grass of Parnassus, spleenworts, spring squill, sea aster, seablite, sea arrowgrass.

Birds: whooper swan, shelduck, goldeneye, pintail, wigeon, teal, ruddy duck, cormorant, shag, herring gull, oystercatcher, lapwing, redshank, greenshank, wood sandpiper, green sandpiper, ruff, dunlin, curlew, black-tailed godwit, bar-tailed godwit.

OFFA'S DYKE PATH ✝ ✸

King Offa of Mercia constructed the Dyke that bears his name in the late eighth century to keep the Celts at bay and prevent invasion of the plains by marauding hillmen. Border towns grew up around the major forts in the Middle Ages and the Dyke then became a routeway. Today the Dyke marks the start and end of Offa's Dyke Path, and for some sixty miles the path coincides with this ancient bank and ditch. It runs from north to south through the Welsh border country, crosses the Shropshire Hills, an Area of Outstanding Natural Beauty, fringes the Brecon Beacons National Park and runs along the beautiful valley of the Wye.

For much of its length it is fine country walking suitable for anyone in a reasonably fit state, but the Denbigh Moors and the Black Mountains at the northern and southern ends of the trail respectively are severe tests and should not be attempted by those without experience in navigating by map and compass. Good boots, protective clothing and adequate food are essentials in these areas.

Starting from Prestatyn in the north, the path scales the Clwydian Range and continues over the moorland and hills to Llangollen (try not to arrive during the festival if you plan on overnighting). The Vale of Llangollen is crossed by way of the Pont Cysyllte aqueduct and the path continues past Chirk Castle and coincides with lengthy parts of the original Offa's Dyke along the foothills of the Berwyn Mountains. It then drops down to the Severn flood banks and climbs the Long Mountain to Beacon Ring. The best of the ancient earthworks is then followed across Clun Forest on to Knighton and Kington. Leaving the old wall, the path leads to Hay-on-Wye before climbing the Black Mountains and heading off over moorland to Monmouth. The path then drops down through the fine woods of the Wye, keeping to the Dyke or to the bank of the river itself.

Visiting: there are plenty of roads crossing Offa's Dyke giving access to various sections of the path. Youth Hostels are handy, though few are actually along the route itself. Clun Forest is the most typical stretch that coincides with the ancient wall. Read *Offa's Dyke Path* by J. B. Jones, published by HMSO.

Birds: a good cross-section of border birds including moorland, woodland and streamside species. Red grouse, pied flycatcher, wood warbler, ring ouzel, merlin, buzzard, wheatear, whinchat, redstart, dipper and common sandpiper should all be seen.

Mammals: scant.

Botany: highly varied with the landscape and underlying geology.

PEMBROKESHIRE COAST NATIONAL PARK ✶ ✝ ✸ ♿

Covering 225 square miles, this is at once the smallest and arguably the most beautiful and interesting of our national parks. It is predominantly coastal, but also includes the uplands of the Prescelly Mountains and the deep sea inlet of upper Milford Haven. There are some spectacular cliffs, some fine beaches, a few quaint villages and some of the most impressive seabird colonies to be found in the North Atlantic. Additionally the Pembrokeshire Coast Path was the third long distance footpath to be opened and, in the words of the pathways' brochure: 'It runs for 180 miles . . . through scenery as beautiful and impressive as any in Europe'.

The National Park is not a wilderness devoid of life. The people here are engaged in agriculture and fishing, as well as in the more recent industries of oil and tourism. But the landscape is truly and refreshingly rural. There are many days' enjoyment to be had walking the Coast Path in various sections, or exploring the convenient Mynydd Prescelly, where you may have sheep and little other company. There are the birds of St Ann's Head in the south and Strumble and Dinas Heads to the north, some of the very best on the British mainland. And, of course, the fabulous seabird islands of Skokholm, Skomer and Grassholm.

The motorway network brings this once remote corner of the country much closer than you had imagined; a weekend is quite certainly more than just a possibility.

Botanically and geologically the area is a true feast,

with the unique Tenby daffodil hidden away in a few meadows near the south coast town. There are otters, a dying breed, along the streams, as well as badgers and foxes.

Visiting: the National Park is as open as any other area of the countryside, no more and no less. In general hill farmers are tolerant of walkers, but visitors do not have special rights because of National Park status.

Coastal Path: the path runs from St Dogmaels in the north to Amroth in the south, and is continuous apart from a ferry crossing of Milford Haven and a couple of detours to avoid military firing ranges. By and large it clings tenaciously to the coast itself. For information contact Pembrokeshire Coast National Park, County Offices, Haverfordwest, Dyfed JA61 1QZ. Read *Pembrokeshire Coast Path* by J. H. Barrett, published by HMSO.

Mammals: otter, badger, fox.

Botany: Tenby daffodil.

Razorbill on Skomer Island. There are thousands of seabirds on the island

Birds: guillemot, razorbill, puffin, fulmar, Manx shear-water, kittiwake.

SKOMER AND THE WELSH ISLANDS

Of all the seabird islands that surround the coast of Britain, those off what used to be Pembrokeshire, now Dyfed, are among the most famous. Certainly they are rich in both numbers and species, and the ease with which they may be visited has made them a popular day out for both naturalist and tripper alike. Most frequently visited, and also the best for birds, is Skomer Island, the site of the first Welsh nature trail. From the sheer clifftops visitors can look down (and across – important for photographers) on one of the most spectacular assemblies of seabirds. Puffin, guillemot, razorbill, fulmar and kittiwake are present in their thousands, and it is a soulless person who is not moved by the experience. There is a unique mammal, the Skomer vole, to be searched for, as well as seals, and a good sea-cliff flora. Day trips are easily arranged from Martins Haven and a boat leaves regularly at 10.00 hours each day from April to late September. Details from the Lockley Lodge Information Centre, Martins Haven. A landing fee is payable by non-

Wild flowers on Skomer in May

members of the West Wales Naturalists' Trust. For enthusiasts, simple overnight accommodation is available: details from the Trust at 4 Victoria Place, Haverfordwest.

Skokholm is a smaller island with a similar collection of birds, but is really for the enthusiast and migration student. Accommodation is available for weekly or longer periods by arrangement with the Trust. Organized parties may be catered for, and the island offers opportunities for group study.

Grassholm is smaller still, and further out in the Atlantic. It is a flat-topped mound that has been half taken over by one of the North Atlantic's largest colonies of gannets. Though these birds can be seen on the surrounding seas a visit to the gannetry itself is a unique experience. The reserve is administered by the RSPB and landings, after mid-June only, and then only in really calm weather, can be arranged via the Dale Sailing Company at Martins Haven.

Visiting: Skomer by local boatmen out of Martins Haven between April and September. Skokholm for serious students. Grassholm by arrangement with Dale Sailing Company.

Mammals: Skomer vole, rabbit.
Birds: guillemot, razorbill, puffin, kittiwake, fulmar, cormorant, gannet.
Botany: sea-cliff flora: thrift, rock samphire, tree mallow, and a surprising display of bluebells before the bracken grows up.

SNOWDONIA NATIONAL PARK

Snowdonia National Park includes the Snowdon massif, as well as the adjacent mountains that are frequently referred to as 'North Wales'. But it also includes a lot more besides. In the north it borders Conway Bay at Aber near Bangor. In the south it reaches Aberdovey at the mouth of the Dovey estuary not too far from Aberystwyth. On a map it looks as if a quarter of Wales lies inside the Park; in reality it is only 845 square miles, making it the second largest National Park in Britain.

Within the Park there is a great variety of landscape, and considerable variety of fauna and flora. In altitude it encompasses Snowdon, at 3560 feet the highest British mountain outside Scotland, while the deep estuaries of the south coast have huge intertidal areas of sand and mud. There is open rugged country walked by sheep and hikers, there are deep open valleys, wooded valleys with tinkling streams, and low

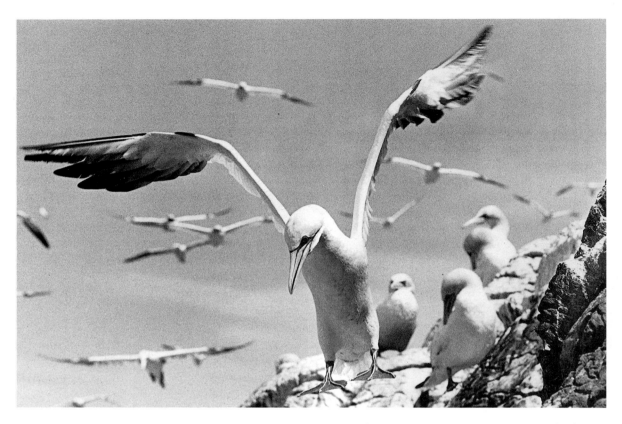

A gannet steadies itself to land on the cliffs

bog-filled moors where meadow pipits are almost the only companions. There are cwms and lakes, forest plantations and sweet green grazing farms.

The whole area is well populated with cars through the summer, and there are caravan and camping sites, cottages to let, bed and breakfast places, and a variety of hotels. Throughout the year serious climbers come to test their skill on the sheer drops of the Snowdon crags. 'Very Severes' are two a penny here, and you can watch from the comfort of Llanberis Pass as young brightly-clad youngsters seek to come to terms with routes pioneered in the 1960s by Joe Brown. Drop down the valley a little and seek out the choughs that soar so effortlessly among the slate quarries. They are a rare bird now.

One constant factor in all hill districts is water, and here there always seems to be plenty. The streams are the centres of life – our roads follow their courses, we live in the valleys they have created and, as far as wildlife is concerned, they are much richer than the surrounding hills. Along the streams, full of small

trout and the occasional salmon, grey wagtails, dippers and common sandpipers stake out their territories, while in the woods alongside there are more wood warblers than in any other part of the country. There are pied and spotted flycatchers too, and willow warblers and redstarts. These woods are more typical

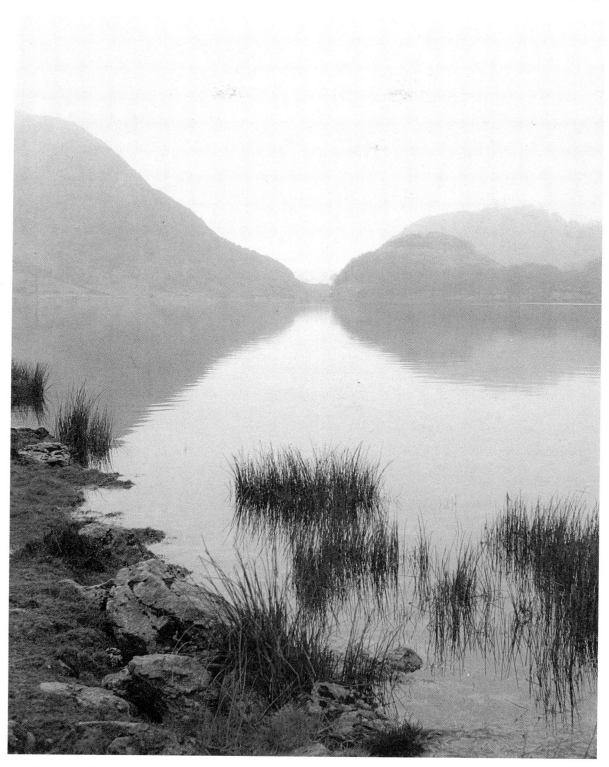

Llyn Cwellyn is still home to the rare Welsh Charr

of the southern part of the Park, away from Snowdonia proper. They are predominantly oak and hung with green trailing lichens. They grow among the rocks that hug the hillsides over which buzzards mew endlessly. In the southern part of the Park the buzzard is almost as common as in Devon, some think it even more so.

High up on the open grassy moors, beyond the range of even the hardy hill cows, a revolution is taking place. Grass and heather are giving place to young conifer plantations built on a terrace structure that follows the contours. This new crop displaces the ring ouzel, the red grouse and the few merlins that remain.

The torgoch or Welsh charr (a subspecies) has been isolated at Llyn Padarn and Llyn Peris near Llanberis for 10,000 years. Recently a hydro-electric scheme eliminated this little fish from Peris, and it is found now only at Padarn and Llyn Cwellyn to the south. It reacts well to maggot bait and is said to be delicious if you fancy eating a piece of rare evolution in action.

Dominating the south is one of the most impressive mountains in Britain, Cadair Idris, all dark and menacing. Its buttresses are severe enough to attract rock climbers, though it is said that anyone who overnights will awake mad, blind or a poet.

This then is the Snowdonia National Park. Over most of the moors visitors can walk without let or hindrance, even the grazing meadows can usually be trodden, and there are well-marked footpaths everywhere. Watch for the path to 'hwyr Cyhoeddus' – it's Welsh for 'Footpath', and of course there is always the Snowdon railway for the elderly or weak of leg.

Within the Park there are no less than fifteen National Nature Reserves varying in size from the huge Snowdon NNR at over 4000 acres to the tiny thirty-three acres of Coed Gorswen. Though all of these are of interest, four have created nature trails specifically for the visitor.

Coedydd Aber

Leave the A55 southward between Bangor and Conway on a minor road through Aber. Park just before the bridge as signposted. A trail leads along the Afon Rhaedr Fawr and a booklet is available. The woods here are oaks with hazel and birch near the tops. The open area near the bridge where the trail begins has wych elm, alder, ash, blackthorn and sallow. Early spring produces primrose, bluebell, wood sorrel and wood anemone, and there is navelwort to be found as well. At Nant Farmstead there is a ruined sheep dip,

and as well as the Welsh mountain sheep, there are Welsh mountain ponies. At the end of the trail the falls tumble 120 feet down Creigian Rheadr Fawr, where the rocks, foind nowhere else in Snowdonia, are igneous granophyre. There are several liverworts associated with the falls. Birds along the way may include buzzard, grey wagtail and dipper.

Cwm Idwal

Park at Ogwen Cottage Mountain School and follow the footpath southward up the hill to Llyn Idwal. The trail starts here and immediately crosses the outlet stream to proceed along the western bank of the lake. The reserve covers 984 acres, and it is the geology and the dependent botanical communities that are the primary interest. From Point 2, excellent glaciated scenery includes the U-shaped valley of Nant Francon, hanging valleys and moraines. At the enclosures note the strong growth of heather when protected from sheep, and watch out for feral goats from here onward. The lake has trout, but birds are few; fossils can be found among the pebbles, they are 450 million years old. At Point 4 look for bogbean and marsh cinquefoil among the boggy areas around the lake. The enclosures at Point 8 are richer than those encountered earlier, and around the head of the lake there are more flowers to be found. At Point 9 there are the remains of a plant community that was common at the end of the Ice Age. Species include purple saxifrage, mountain sorrel, alpine meadow-rue, green spleenwort and greater woodrush. Move on to the Idwal Slabs and then back along the lake shore. Flowers are a major interest all the way.

Snowdon

The Miners' Track leaves the A4086 at Pen-y-pass – the top of Llanberis Pass. It leads directly southward to Llyn Teyrn and then to Llyn Llydaw, where it ends at the lake. The ongoing path eventually leads up through Glaslyn to Snowdon Summit. Point 2 is rich in calcium and the plant growth attracts sheep to the grazing; plants include wild thyme and heath bedstraw. Point 3 is wet peat, and here cotton grass, bog asphodel and butterwort are found. Point 5 is on dolerite, and this is rich and conducive to flowers. Point 6 overlooks Llyn Teyrn (Tyrant Lake) with some trout and plants like quillwort and water lobelia. Point 7 is on peat, with wheatear, ring ousel, raven, perhaps chough. At Llyn Llydaw the causeway and buildings are remains of the old copper industry.

On the walk up Snowdon the Miners' Track ends at the lake, Llyn Llydaw

Coedydd Maentwrog

This reserve covers 169 acres north of the Vale of Ffestiniog around Llyn Mair, and protects some of the original old oak woods in this part of the country. The nature trail can be started at Tan y Bwlch Station or from the car park near Llyn Mair. From the station from Point A to Point B the trail passes through meadows thick with primroses, violets and celandines and butterflies like meadow brown, hairstreaks and fritillaries. At Point C there is a display of nest boxes. Point D offers whooper swan and goldeneye on the lake in winter, and now you are at the car park where you may start or finish.

Cross the stream and walk northward along the eastern bank where mosses grow in profusion. The valley is beautiful, but interesting botanically after crossing the bridge to a small marsh (Point 6) where marsh thistle and meadowsweet can be found.

These nature trails only scratch the surface of this rich and varied national park. Their advantage is that, step by step, the landscape is explained.

Visiting: Contact Snowdonia National Park, Penrhyndendraeth, Gwynedd LL48 6LS.
Mammals: polecat, fox, otter, feral goat.
Birds: chough, buzzard, raven, merlin, curlew, redstart, wheatear, stonechat, whinchat, wood warbler, grey wagtail, dipper, ring ousel, red grouse, pied flycatcher.

Botany: navelwort, marsh cinquefoil, purple saxifrage, mountain sorrel, Alpine meadow-rue, green spleenwort, bog asphodel, quillwort, water lobelia, marsh thistle.

Other: Butterflies including fritillaries, hairstreaks and meadow brown; the dwarf grayling lives on the nearby cliffs of Great Ormes Head.

SOUTH STACK ⌁ ✤

These excellent seabird cliffs lie at the western corner of Anglesey on Holy Island. The RSPB has 780 acres of reserve here featuring most of the birds that one could reasonably expect to see: razorbill, guillemot, puffin, shag, fulmar, kittiwake, plus chough and peregrine. There is an information and viewing centre at Ellin's Tower, which is open throughout the summer, and access is otherwise free. Another good viewpoint is the steps that lead to the lighthouse. Flowers are also interesting here with heath-spotted orchid abundant in June. A real rarity is the spotted rock rose and spatulate fleawort.

Visiting: from Holyhead follow signs to South Stack and park in the RSPB car park.

Birds: fulmar, peregrine, chough, guillemot, razorbill, puffin, kittiwake.

Botany: orchids including heath-spotted, spotted rock rose, devil's-bit-scabious, pale heath violet.

Puffins are comical birds and easily identified by their bills

WELSH MOUNTAIN ZOO ✶ ✶ ♿

This claims to be the only mountain zoo in Britain, though it is difficult to see why a hillside situation outside the bustling resort of Colwyn Bay should count as 'mountain', and it is certainly not the only 'mountain' zoo in the country. Indeed if a mountain situation and a mountain fauna are the prerequisites of a mountain zoo, then there are no such institutions in Britain.

Nevertheless this is an interesting place, with a reasonable collection of animals from a variety of lands housed in large enclosures. Some of the area is left natural to encourage local wildlife including fox, badger, weasel and (claimed) polecat. The usual woodland birds are present, and the whole makes a nice background for the collection.

Indian elephant, lion, puma, leopard, chimpanzee and gibbons as well as spider, woolly and capuchin monkeys are the stars of the show – though they have little to do with mountains. There are sealions, llamas, wallabies, and black and brown bears as well as many smaller mammals and birds. All this is fine, and pretty standard stuff, but the Zoo has one speciality – birds of prey. Gathered here is one of the best collections of these birds in Europe, and there are eagles, condors, vultures, falcons, hawks and buzzards all to be seen. The outstanding feature is the daily flight of trained eagles and falcons, trained that is in the methods of falconry. Here free-flying birds of prey can be seen as they would be in the wild. Suddenly a rather dull-coloured hawk sweeps into the air and impresses everyone with its power; a great piece of conservation propaganda were it not for the fact that these already scarce birds are in great demand by falconers. It is not the falconers who have made them rare, but it might be they who put the last nail in the coffin. There is a Tree Tops Safari Restaurant overlooking the lion enclosure, a zoo shop, a children's zoo and a Lookout Cafe.

Visiting: leave the A55 as it passes through Colwyn Bay on Kings Road, which is well signposted to the Zoo. Frequent buses operate from the pier. The Zoo is open every day throughout the year: Tel. 0492 532938 or 531660.

Mammals: lion, puma, leopard, elephant, llama, sealion, wallabies, chimpanzee, spider monkey, woolly monkey, capuchin monkey, lar gibbon.

Birds: free-flying displays by eagles and falcons.

Lake District National Park

A69

CARLISLE

A595

M6

A590

Morecambe Bay and Leighton Moss

A65

BARROW

MORECAMBE

South Walney

Blackpool Zoo and the Tower Aquarium

M55

BLACKPOOL

M6

A646

PRESTON

M61

BOLTON

M62

Martin Mere

A59

LIVERPOOL

MANCHESTER

BIRKENHEAD

A6

Gayton Sands

M56

Cheshire Meres

CHESTER

Chester Zoo

A41

A49

M6

50 mls

50 kms

BLACKPOOL ZOO AND THE TOWER AQUARIUM ☘ ☙ ♿

Though quite distinct and separate institutions, the would-be visitor to the wildlife attractions of Blackpool should not miss either of these. The Aquarium is the older of the two by ninety-nine years, and indeed pre-dates the famous Blackpool Tower that now stands (literally) over it by twenty years. Throughout its history it has been a famed home of fish, particularly local marine species, but with more recent additions of a tropical collection and a British freshwater section. Now some 2000 fish representing over 225 species are on show – a marvellous place for anglers to brush up their identification and for students young and old to see many otherwise elusive fish.

The Zoological Gardens is one of Britain's newest zoos. It was opened in 1973 and is owned by Blackpool Corporation, which no doubt saw it as another attraction to be set alongside Blackpool Tower, Blackpool Rock and the illuminations, but it is much more than that. The collection is full of quality, with lion, tiger, elephant, lowland gorilla, orang-utan, and the highly-endangered Arabian gazelle. There are camels, gazelles, antelopes, and a Bird Hall where the visitor can walk among the birds as they fly about the exotic vegetation of their large home. There are over 300 species of birds to be found.

There have been some notable successes. The Arabian gazelles are breeding quite freely and a good herd is in the making. There is some hope that the siamang might also breed. An unusual zoo animal is the all-but-exterminated white-tailed wildebeest, with its handlebar-type horns. The species is now confined to a few South African parks and cannot be found in very many zoos. From the same general area comes Chapman's zebra, another vanishing animal, while Grevy's zebra is from further north in East Africa.

One of the features of Blackpool's Zoo is the zoogeographic approach to the layout of the enclosures. This enables a cross-section of the animals of a particular region to be seen one after another and, perhaps, contrasted with an adjacent region nearby. Thus one area of the Zoo is devoted to American species, and puma, bison, llama, tapir, peccary and monkeys can be seen. In another area the fauna of Australia is on show, with kangaroos and wallabies in a variety of different forms. There is, of course, a European section as well as a children's zoo.

Visiting: Blackpool Tower Aquarium is under the Tower – it's difficult to miss. Having paid the entry fee to the Tower the Aquarium, as well as a tiny zoo at the top, is free. The Zoological Gardens are on East Drive, but are signposted as you enter the town. The Corporation would not want visitors to miss them. They can be reached by bus and train and are open throughout the year. There is a

licensed restaurant, a cafeteria, snack bar and shop.
Mammals: white-tailed wildebeest, Arabian gazelle, lowland gorilla, orang-utan, tiger, lion, elephant, Bactrian camel, chamois, llama, sealion, puma, plains bison, Chapman's zebra, Grevy's zebra.
Birds: walk-through aviary with over 300 species.

CHESHIRE MERES ☙ ☙

Lying just off the M6 at Exit 19, Rostherne and Tatton Meres are the most famous of the lowland meres of Cheshire. They are handily situated for the inhabitants of the Manchester conurbation and are popular resorts at summer weekends. Tatton Mere is part of the 2086 acre Tatton Park estate, which was acquired by the National Trust in 1960. Its surrounding deer park and gardens are open to pedestrians through most of the year (except Mondays and Christmas Day) and the house is open at various times in summer. When it comes to opening times the National Trust is a law entirely to itself, so always check with them before visiting any of their properties. Though considerably disturbed, Tatton Mere is a good haunt of wild birds, including goodly numbers of duck in winter. Summer sees great crested grebes displaying, and there are a few wild flowers in the less frequented corners. For picnics, swimming and fishing Tatton Park is the place; for more serious bird-watching the larger lake to the north, Rostherne Mere, is better.

Rostherne Mere was declared a National Nature Reserve in 1961 and the 118-acre lake is now enclosed by some 250 acres of protective woodland and farmland. It is a deep lake and offers little food to the hordes of wildfowl to which it is a winter resort. Its main function is to protect these birds from disturbance, and access is thus limited to permit holders and to a few observation points from public highways and rights of way. Duck, particularly mallard, and teal, are often present in their thousands, along with wigeon, shoveler, tufted duck and pochard. There are occasional goldeneye and goosander to be found. Several thousand gulls come to roost in winter evenings and a few great crested grebes and Canada geese breed. There is a regular migration of black terns.

The A. W. Boyd Memorial Observatory was opened as a testimony to the man who was primarily responsible for saving Rostherne Mere. Permits, valid for a calendar year, can be obtained from the Manchester Ornithological Society, 13 Kingston Drive, Sale, Cheshire M33 2FS. These are available only to bird-watchers who live in the area and can watch regularly.

Visiting: A. W. Boyd Observatory. Also view from Manor Lane and Rostherne Churchyard off the A556; and from Dirty Lane at the north-eastern corner near the A556. The Nature Conservancy Council has produced a leaflet. The A556 joins the M6 to the M56.
Birds: great crested grebe, mallard, teal, shoveler, wigeon, tufted duck, pochard, Canada goose, woodcock, reed warbler, hawfinch.

CHESTER ZOO ☙ ☙ ☙

Though no more than a couple of miles from the city centre, Chester Zoo has an enviable reputation as a haunt of outstanding wildlife displayed in a modern and thoughtful environment. Its full name, 'The North of England Zoological Society Gardens', gives a hint that entrance fees paid here will buy a little more than the razzamatazz provided by the safari parks. The brochures and guides are so cheap and so full of information that they must have been produced by a non-commercial outfit. Nevertheless the Zoo attracts over a million visitors a year and spends almost all of its income on the animals and their greater comfort. The majority are housed in large outdoor enclosures, but with ample covered quarters for all during bad weather.

The outstanding attractions are orang-utan, rhino, hippo, antelope of great variety, collections of waterfowl, birds of prey, the big cats and so on. There are tropical houses where flowers are as attractive as the animals, and there are even Arabian gazelles, Amur leopards and tuataras. In the nocturnal house, secretive forest animals can be seen in their own twilight world.

Most of the animals are kept in decent-sized family groupings, and because of the continuous year-round care that is lavished upon them they respond by breeding. In fact it is the open quality of the enclosures plus the caring of the staff and the Society that has made Chester one of the great zoos of the world.

Visiting: the Zoo is well signposted within Chester and is situated just off the A41 Chester by-pass at Upton, to the north-west of the city. Entrance fees are not cheap, but they are good value for money, and you are contributing to a really worthwhile cause. Tel. 0244 380280
Mammals: orang-utan, elephant, rhino, lion, tiger, cheetah, leopard, zebra, deer, antelope, wallabies, bison.
Birds: huge variety including Andean condor, birds of prey, flamingoes, waterfowl.

Pink-footed goose

GAYTON SANDS 🐦

Although thronged with birds, estuaries are often difficult to enjoy, particularly by those without powerful telescopes. At the famous Cheshire Dee, the RSPB has established a reserve of over 5000 acres at Gayton Sands where the visitor stands a real chance of enjoying waders and wildfowl in large numbers. In winter there are large numbers of pintail here, along with other duck and the occasional flock of geese. Black-tailed godwit are regular and there may be water rail, twite and snipe. In summer several 'marshy' warblers can be found among the reeds.

Visiting: take the A540 and turn off on to the B5135 to Parkgate. The reserve is open throughout the year.

Birds: pintail, teal, wigeon, pink-footed goose, hen harrier, merlin, peregrine, black-tailed godwit, knot, whimbrel, curlew sandpiper, spotted redshank.

LAKE DISTRICT NATIONAL PARK ✝ ♦ ❀ ⚐

The Lake District was the second National Park to be created and covering 880 square miles is still the largest of them all. It covers the vast majority of the hills and fells of the Lake District roughly westward of the Kendall-Penrith road and includes Scafell Pike, Helvellyn and Skiddaw together with seventeen of the major lakes. This is one of the backwaters of Britain, and the hills and valleys, farms and towns have changed but little over the past hundred years. The only new development has been the influx of visitors seeking the beauty and relaxation that such a fine and unspoilt area can offer. Inevitably this influx has had an effect on the very attractions that brought visitors in the first place.

Initially it was the poets (artists and writers are inevitably the first to discover attractive backwaters) Wordsworth, Coleridge and their set that put the Lake District on the tourist map. Later it was the motorcar that enabled everyman to penetrate the wilderness, and latterly the passion for boating has turned some of the larger lakes, Windermere in particular, into teeming pleasure grounds. Yet despite the masses of people who pour into the area during the summer, the fells of the Lake District remain one of the last unspoilt wilderness areas of Britain. The Pennine Hills may be more lonely, but the Lakes have a majesty and grandeur that outstrip everything else to be found this side of the Scottish border.

In geographer's terms the Lake District is an excellent example of radial drainage. Look at a map and almost every lake and river stems from a central point – the great massif of Great Gable and Scafell Pike. This is the heart of Lakeland, and those who would penetrate the great hills need to start from here. There are two major routes inward. In the north the road southward from Keswick along the eastern shore of Derwent Water leads to Seatoller, where a lane leads, in turn, southward through Borrowdale. At the

The Langdale Pikes provide tough terrain for walkers

Little Langdale and Tilberthwaite Fells, Cumbria

end of the road a shepherd's farm may offer a cup of tea and a cake in the parlour to the walker as he sets out along the footpath that leads up to Sty Head Pass, a wonderful spot from which Scafell can be climbed or the route across the enormous screes of Great Gable can be walked. Beyond is the loneliness of Wasdale, where the hills dip down to Wast Water. This is wonderful country and is within a day's exploration of much of the industrial north. The routes are not very long, but the terrain is tough and the explorer should not step lightly onto these fells without map, compass and the experience to use them. A companion is also essential – break a leg with a silly slip, and you may die.

Another route into this central section is via Langdale, where the Old Dungeon Ghyll Hotel has been a mecca for climbers since climbing was invented. From here famous paths lead up to the Pikes of Stickle, to Bow Fell, and over into Borrowdale itself.

The valleys are flat bottomed with green meadows full of sheep, and streams full of trout. Mostly the hillsides have been grazed clean, but here and there birch woods cling tenaciously to their toe-hold sites and willow warblers sing. Along the streams grey wagtails, dippers and common sandpipers can be found, and high above there are a few golden plover, ring ouzel and the occasional buzzard. In the late 1960s the golden eagle returned to breed in England for the first time this century (do not ask where) and they still do so each year.

If villages attract you, then Grasmere is one of the best, and a good centre for starting a tour. Ambleside is nice, but a bit busy, Windermere is full of boats and nineteenth-century hotels, and Keswick is a town. Borrowdale is delicious, with expensive hotels and cheap picturesque places for tea. There are numerous guides to the Lake District, but Wainwright's seven guides to the Lakeland Fells (available in all shops or

146

from the publishers, The Westmorland Gazette, Kendal) are in a class of their own. To walk the area without the appropriate 'Wainwright' is to miss everything and even to take a chance on getting lost. They are unique, superb and essential – no hill walker should miss an opportunity to follow in the footsteps of the master.

The Lake District is so immense that visitors must purchase a guide and seek out what they want for themselves. Nevertheless there are some nice hill walks that can be accomplished (round trip) in a day provided you do not consider hill walking a countryside stroll.

Easedale

From Grasmere take the road to Easedale House and cross the river through nice woodland. A footpath is well marked along Sourmilk Gill to Easedale Tarn. There and back is a nice day's walk in fine weather.

Stickle Tarn

Take the footpath behind the Hotel up Dungeon Ghyll in Langdale – steep at first, easier later. Keep to the left of Stickle Tarn and climb Pavey Ark if you have a head for heights. It's a good scramble, but dangerous for those with shaky knees. Cross to Pike of Stickle, enjoy the view and descend once more to Langdale. Compass, map, protective clothing, experience essential.

Sty Head

Take the B5289 through beautiful Borrowdale, all woodside streams and singing birds – watch for common buzzard. Turn left to Seathwaite (not Stonethwaite) and park at the end of the road. Walk up the valley and turn right over Stockly Bridge before climbing up to Styhead Tarn and on to Styhead Pass. A wonderful place if you are prepared for nasty weather. If not, do not take a chance.

Helvellyn

Take the A591 to the southern end of Thirlmere and then the footpath eastward from Wythburn. Follow the well-worn path to Helvellyn and then out and back along Striding Edge. You cannot miss it! If footloose and free, continue to Patterdale and one of the least spoilt parts of the Lakes.

Visiting: there is accommodation and food to suit all tastes in the Lake District from farm house to international luxury. The scenery is beautiful, but the wildlife pleasantly unspectacular. Go to walk, to fish or just to wander. For information contact Lake District National Park, Barclays Bank Chamber, Cresent Road, Windermere, Cumbria LA23 1EA.

Birds: buzzard, raven, sparrowhawk, dipper, grey wagtail, common sandpiper, willow warbler, pied flycatcher.

Botany: varied communities at different altitudes.

MARTIN MERE ♟ ❀ ♿

Once the site of the largest stretch of inland water in England, the Wildfowl Trust acquired Martin Mere for its usual double-pronged development. Here, over the last few years, it has created a wildfowl collection that contains close to a hundred bird species and where the visitor can wander and watch in comfort.

There are excellent amenities, including a shop and refreshment facilities as well as a lecture theatre, laboratory and classrooms for educational purposes. Martin Mere is probably visited by more schoolchildren than any other wildlife site in Britain. While all of this development attracts visitors throughout the year, it is winter, when the wild geese come, that brings the naturalist here.

For generations thousands of pink-footed geese have roosted on the open flats of the River Ribble and flighted inland to feed on the marshes of Martin Mere. The Southport Sanctuary established the foreshore itself as a National Nature Reserve and controlled access and shooting. Now the Wildfowl Trust has taken care of the other end of the pink-feet's daily commuting and opened up the sight of 15,000 wild geese to public view. At few other places in Europe can

Bewick's swans can be seen flying over the open water of Martin Mere

such a wildlife spectacle be enjoyed by the ordinary public. The geese are present throughout the winter and this is the peak period for a visit.

Visiting: The grounds are open every day except Christmas Day, and are best in winter for the wild geese flocks. They are reached from the A59 north of Ormskirk, which is south-east of Southport, and the nearby M6 brings them within reach of the whole of industrial Lancashire. Follow signs from the village of Rufford.

Birds: pink-footed geese, whooper swan, Bewick's swan, plus thousands of ducks; wildfowl collection.

MORECAMBE BAY AND LEIGHTON MOSS �废 ✦ ✿ ♿

Morecambe Bay is one of those places where the tide comes in faster than a man can run. It's a bleak, dangerous, lonely sort of place, but it is also one of the most important wildlife sites in Britain, so important that the Royal Society for the Protection of Birds acquired 3600 acres of it in 1974. All they got for their money were some pretty worthless saltings, a lot of sand covered by the tides twice a day and a collection of up to a half of the 200,000 waders that feed on the rich marine life that shelters among the sand.

For long only the cockle fishermen and a few wildfowlers penetrated the fastnesses of Morecambe Bay; now the birds have it to themselves. The best roosts of birds at high tide can be seen from Hest Bank. Thousands of waders congregate there, including huge

Morecambe Bay is one of the most important wildlife sites in Britain

MORECAMBE BAY
AND
LEIGHTON MOSS

2 mls
5 kms

banks of knot, dunlin, oystercatcher and curlew. At various times of the year, except June and July, almost all of the shorebirds of Europe pass through.

Duck and geese are regular visitors, and those who time their visits to coincide with a rising tide (two hours before high water) are in for a staggering treat. A great variety of other birds frequent the general area, and another RSPB reserve at nearby Leighton Moss offers the chance of different birds in different surroundings. The Moss, which is adjacent to the village of Silverdale (you'll find out why when you get there), is a large reedbed and fresh marsh reserve that echoes to the sound of the bittern every spring. Harriers,

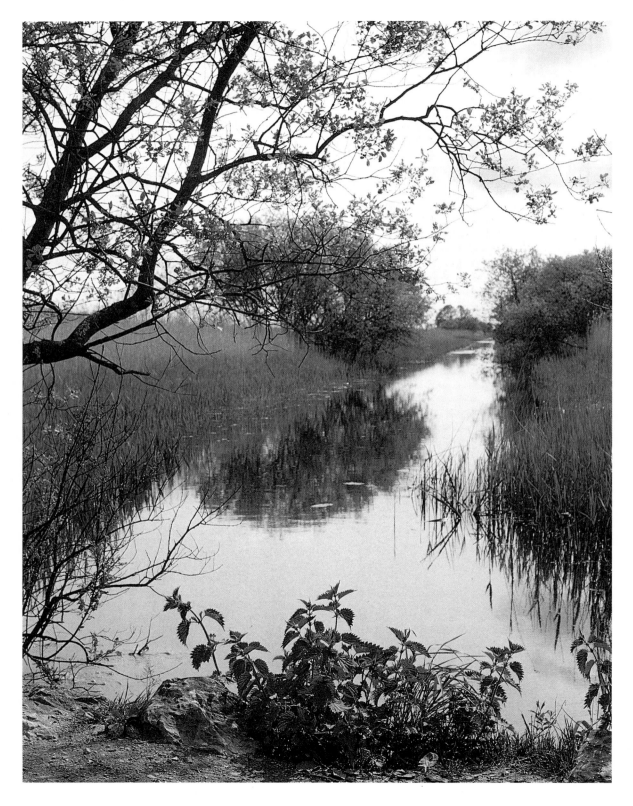

duck, waders and warblers are among the attractions, and there are hides to facilitate viewing.

Visiting: Leighton Moss can be visited every day except Tuesday. Morecambe Bay is a vast area, and those who would see the birds well should take the A5105 north of Morecambe to Hest Bank and cross the railway over the level crossing. There is parking space and visitors should arrive before high water and watch the birds come in to roost. A walk northward along the shoreline from the end of Morecambe promenade will suffice on the lower tides.

Birds: knot, dunlin, oystercatcher, curlew, redshank: and at Leighton Moss, bittern, greenshank, common sandpiper, little stint, common tern, reed warbler, bearded tit.

SOUTH WALNEY ✦ ❀ ♿

Walney Island is a low-lying strip of land at the southern end of the Lake District off Barrow-in-Furness. The southern part is a Nature Reserve administered by the Cumbria Naturalists' Trust and is best known as the largest ground-nesting colony of lesser black-backed and herring gulls in Europe, as well as the southernmost colony of eiders in Britain. It is also the site of a bird observatory and is a noted haunt of waders and wildfowl in winter. In fact the area is one of the major wader roosts of the huge Morecambe Bay complex, and at high tide these birds number many thousands. Being created by the sea the area is interesting in showing colonization by successive plant communities.

Visiting: the Reserve is open daily except Mondays and there is cottage accommodation to be booked in advance. Contact The Warden, Coastguard Cottages, South Walney Nature Reserve, Barrow-in-Furness, LA14 3YQ (but enclose s.a.e.).

Birds: lesser black-backed gull, herring gull, eider, oystercatcher, knot, dunlin, shelduck, wigeon, teal.

Botany: colonizing plants including silverweed, sea holly, sea campion, corn salad, sea sandwort, mouse-eared hawkweed.

A channel between the reed beds of Leighton Moss

NORTH-EAST ENGLAND

BEMPTON CLIFFS 🐦 ❀

Bempton, which lies just north of Flamborough Head and Bridlington on the Yorkshire coast, has long been known as a major seabird breeding site. For a good number of years it was the only gannetry on the British mainland, but the birds stubbornly refused to increase from the handful of pairs present before the war. Finally in the 1960s they took off, and now a good population (about 650 pairs) of these spectacular birds can be seen. Around them are 80,000 other cliff-

nesting seabirds, and come spring and summer the cliffs are alive with their calls. The spectacle from the clifftops is exhilarating, moving and remarkable for being so freely available. There is no entry charge, no fees to pay, simply a lovely walk along the white chalk cliffs, watching the birds wheel over the sea below. Being chalk, the clifftop flowers are worthy of investigation, though at all times be wary of the drop below. Sometimes binocular botany is the better part of valour.

Over 80,000 seabirds nest at Bempton Cliffs every spring

Visiting: leave Bridlington northward on the B1255 to Flamborough, turn left and then right continuing on the B1255 to the coast. Walk northward along the cliffs for miles. Alternatively, take Cliff Lane in Bempton to the RSPB car park.

Birds: gannet, guillemot, razorbill, puffin, kittiwake, fulmar, shag.

Botany: chalk-loving species.

BLACKTOFT SANDS 🐦 ✿

This wetland reserve of the Royal Society for the Protection of Birds lies at the confluence of the Rivers Trent and Ouse where they combine to form the Humber. The area, which was originally created by the Dutch engineer Vermuyden before he embarked on his most noteworthy British project, the draining of the Fens, is partly submerged by the tide. It also includes much 'dry' land and some huge reedbeds, and is a habitat of numerous breeding birds. The flat landscape echoes to the calls of redshank and reed and sedge warblers through the summer, but in winter it is a well-established resort of the wild geese that have found refuge in this part of the Humber for generations. In early autumn up to 5000 pink-footed geese are regularly present. Most roost on Whitton Sands nearby. The geese also resort to Read's Island downstream, where thousands of wigeon and mallard can be found. Other birds, especially passage waders, are even more numerous, with large flocks of dunlin together with oystercatchers, redshank, etc.

As elsewhere, the RSPB has created even better conditions for birds by managing the water level and by creating lagoons where birds can feed in peace and people watch without disturbance. Among the specialities are bearded tit, water rail, little ringed plover and short-eared owl.

Visiting: the Reserve is open every day except Tuesday. There is a car park, reception and a series of strategically sited hides immediately east of Ouse-fleet. Goole is the nearest large town.

Birds: bearded tit, short-eared owl, grasshopper warbler, reed warbler, tree sparrow, redshank, dunlin, oyster-catcher, pink-footed goose, wigeon.

Botany: interesting colonization by 'salting' species.

CASTLE EDEN DENE ✝ ❀ 🦋

Owned and developed as a local nature reserve by Peterlee Development Corporation, this local authority is justly proud of Castle Eden Dene. Comparatively few local authorities have taken advantage of their powers to create nature reserves, and fewer still have achieved such an important contribution to wildlife and recreation. Situated in the heart of the coastal colliery land of Durham, Castle Eden Dene is the largest of the densely-wooded ravines that cut through this coast. To the north, Hawthorn Dene is a private nature reserve of the Durham County Conservation Trust, but Castle Eden is a larger and richer site.

The Dene extends to 500 acres and stretches four miles inland. It is densely wooded with oak, ash and conifers, a small area of beech and some magnificent yews. The geology is varied, and this in turn creates a variety of soils supporting a richness of life. In spring the woods are carpeted with anemone, bluebell, wild garlic, primrose, violet, wood sorrel and lesser celandine. Summer brings a show of early purple and spotted orchids, wood cranesbill and pink campions.

Butterflies are sometimes quite numerous, including the Eden argus, a race of the brown argus. Other species regularly observed are orange tip, large skipper and common blue. Fifty-six species of birds have bred and the excellent geographical position attracts a regular variety of passage migrants. The nuthatch is here approaching its northward limit, and both tree-creeper and great spotted woodpecker breed. There are goldcrests, and in winter snow buntings haunt the beach. Mammals are rather thin on the ground, but both badger and fox are regular.

Visiting: the reserve lies immediately south of Peterlee, extending from the A19 to the coast. There are access points at the A19, at A1086 in the east, and just off the B1281 in the south. Three footpaths leave the suburbs of Peterlee southward to penetrate the reserve. There are several footpaths and more (not less!) are planned to facilitate access and the enjoyment of this fine wooded valley.

Botany: wood anemone, bluebell, wild garlic, primrose, violet, wood sorrel, lesser celandine, golden saxifrage, wood avens, water avens, pink campion, wood cranesbill, meadow cranesbill, early purple orchid, fly orchid, spotted orchid, bird's-nest orchid (rare), sweet woodruff, hawkweed, burdock, toadflax, enchanter's nightshade, grass of Parnassus, harts-tongue fern, great horsetail.

Birds: nuthatch, treecreeper, great spotted wood-pecker, marsh tit, coal tit, long-tailed tit, tree sparrow, bullfinch, garden warbler, blackcap, gold-crest, spotted flycatcher, grey wagtail, yellow wagtail.

Insects: Castle Eden argus butterfly, green-veined white, large white, orange tip, common blue, meadow brown, small tortoiseshell, dingy skipper, large skipper.

CLEVELAND WAY ✝ ❀

Virtually encircling the North York Moors National Park, the Cleveland Way extends nearly 100 miles over the Cleveland Hills and North York Moors. It offers the walker some of the finest and least-used hill walking in the country, as well as a lengthy stretch of some of the best coastal scenery to be found in northern England.

From the attractive market town of Helmsley, with its twelfth-century castle, the route strikes westward to Rievaulx Abbey, founded in 1131 but now a majestic ruin. It continues along Whitestone Cliff to pick up the scarp of Hambleton Hills leading northward to Osmotherley before climbing to Mt Grace Priory and thence on over Whorlton Moor, Carlton Moor and Cringle Moor to Hasty Bank. On across Ingleby Moor to the village of Kildale, then northward out of the valley to Captain Cook's monument on Easby Moor and on to Roseberry Topping, Cleveland's best-known monument. Across Gisborough Moor, and the Way slowly descends to reach the coast at Saltburn.

Turning southward, the National Park is re-entered beyond Skinningrove, and the Way then heads over Boulby Cliffs to Staithes, Runswick Bay, Sandsend and Whitby. A bird's-eye view of this charming fishing town can be obtained by climbing the 199 stairs of the church. Whitby was formerly the site of a small jet industry, and pieces of this fossilized wood can occasionally be found along the shoreline. Past Whitby Abbey the Way continues to Robin Hood's Bay, Ravenscar and Filey, where the path ends. This latter stretch is generally good for seabirds, but lacks the cliffs and stacks that are such a feature of the coastline further north. Indeed birds and mammals are of no great interest throughout the walk, or in the adjacent National Park come to that. Botanically there is considerable variety to be found, with areas that have not been disturbed by man for generations alongside more recent quarries and constructions. Archaeologists will find the marks of man over most of the route; some remains date back to the Bronze and Iron Age, especially around Danby and on Shooting House Moor.

Visiting: the walk is well signposted, and there are Youth Hostels at Helmsley, Saltburn, Whitby, Boggle Hole and Scarborough. Cleveland Way joins with Ebor Way at Helmsley and Wolds Way at Filey to make up part of a huge inter-linking system of footpaths that extends from the north midlands to the Scottish border country.

Botany: good and varied flower communities including stinking hellebore.

Birds: usual moorland species with passing seabirds offshore during the latter parts of the walk.

COWPEN MARSH ᶻ

Lying adjacent to Teesmouth and surrounded on virtually all sides by the teeming industrialism of Middlesbrough and Tees-side, Cowpen Marsh is really a remarkable place. First it belonged to a chemical giant, then a local enthusiast persuaded the giant to make it a reserve, and now it is a reserve of the Cleveland Nature Conservation Trust. Large, open but shallow waters are surrounded by grazing marshes and, with effective wardening, the birds have prospered. Duck and waders in winter and on passage in spring and autumn are the major attractions, along with a gasp of (almost) fresh air in the overdeveloped little world of Tees-side. There are shelduck, godwits, curlew, oystercatcher, dunlin and plovers as well as the terns that frequently gather to feed in the estuary in vast numbers in August.

Visiting: there are signposts and a car park on the A178 between Middlesbrough and Hartlepool and hides nearby from which many of the birds can be seen. The reserve is open from February to August, but members of the Trust, the Teesmouth Bird Club and RSPB have access at all times. The warden will be happy to direct enthusiasts to several other good bird spots nearby.

Birds: dunlin, curlew, oystercatcher, shelduck, teal,

bar-tailed godwit, grey plover, golden plover, ringed plover.

FARNE ISLANDS ᶻ ᶻ

Thirty-odd islands constitute the Farnes, some two to five miles off the rugged Northumberland coast. These are romantic islands brimful of history, stories of the seventh-century St Cuthbert – eider duck are still called 'cuddy-ducks' to this day – and of Grace Darling's heroic deeds. St Cuthbert was, of course, a patron saint of animals, and it is the tameness of the birds and seals that still inhabit these low-slung islands that most captivates the visitor. For many, a trip to the Farnes may just be a day in the country, but their fame has stretched so far that visitors arrive from all over Europe. Mixed with the trippers there are the bird-watching enthusiasts of a continent.

Surprisingly enough, both groups, layman and devotee, come for the same purpose – to soak up the atmosphere of one of the most accessible genuine seabird colonies in Europe. Here guillemots crowd together on the offshore stacks, terns by the thousand nest over the flat grasslands and scream overhead. The enthusiast's eyes search for the rare roseate tern, others are more easily satisfied with the spectacle itself. Eiders, the most confiding of duck, will allow themselves to be stroked on the nest, and common and grey seals bask in the sun. Puffins, razorbills and cormorants all nest and can often be approached close enough for photography, and fulmars are abundant.

Visiting: only two islands, the Inner Farne and Staple, are open during the summer months. The Inner Farne, which has a nature trail, is best. Boats can be obtained at Seahouses Harbour, where landing tickets can be obtained from the Information Centre. They can also be purchased (quite easily) from the watchers (wardens) on landing. The Warden/Naturalist can be contacted in advance at The Shieling, 8 St Aidan's, Seahouses, Northumberland.

Birds: cormorant, shag, fulmar, eider, common tern, Arctic tern, Sandwich tern, roseate tern, guillemot, razorbill, puffin, oystercatcher, ringed plover, kittiwake.

HAREWOOD BIRD GARDENS ᶻ ᶻ

Situated five miles north of Leeds, Harewood Park and its house have been open to the public for some years.

In 1970 Lord Harewood opened the Bird Gardens and today they represent one of the best collections in this part of the country. There is a walk-through aviary, a tropical house, enclosures, and cages housing many different species. As an added attraction there is a lake in the grounds that is a noted haunt of a large flock of Canada geese together with various wild ducks in winter. There are also breeding great crested grebes.

Among the many attractions there are penguins, flamingoes, a goose and duck collection and free-flying macaws. But for those in search of the less usual species the tropical house is alive with hummingbirds from the New World and sunbirds from the Old, while the walk-through aviary houses the delightful touracos and no less than half a dozen species of mynah. There are rare pheasants, many starlings including Rothchild's, and the magnificent red-billed blue magpie, which is difficult to see in its natural habitat. A good bird library may be consulted by appointment.

Visiting: the Park and Bird Gardens are open throughout the year and there is a restaurant, snack bar, shop, etc. It is reached on the A61 roughly halfway between Leeds and Harrogate. Tel. 0532 886238.
Birds: Andean flamingo, crowned crane, black-necked swan, macaws, Rothschild's starling, red-billed blue magpie, pheasants, hummingbirds, sunbirds, plus wild Canada geese, great crested grebe and duck.
Other: grounds by Capability Brown.

JOE'S POND NATURE RESERVE ✦

Deep in industrial Durham this nature reserve covers only eleven acres and is the primary creation of Joe Wilson, who leased it from the National Coal Board and has now handed it over to the Durham County Conservation Trust. It is no more than a freshwater pond carefully maintained by Joe against pollution and vandals. It is stocked with a self-maintaining population of trout and has been modified to attract a variety of birds. There are tufted duck, coot, little grebe and moorhen and many small birds in the shrubbery. The emergent vegetation is rich and varied. But what really counts is that Joe Wilson cared enough to create this little bit of nature in such hostile surroundings.

Above: Guillemots crowd together on cliffs and offshore stacks

Below: A puffin colony in the Farne Islands

Visiting: a leaflet is available from the Trust: DCCT, 52 Old Elvet, Durham, DH1 3HN.
Birds: little grebe, tufted duck.

LINDISFARNE ✦ ✦ ❀

Lindisfarne lies on the Northumberland coast just south of the Scottish border. It is a considerable tourist attraction with its old cathedral and historical connections and the romance of access only at low tide. At such times a car can drive across the causeway that separates Fenham Flats to the south from Goswick Sands to the north, between the village of Beal and the island. Visitors should plan their retreat, or be prepared to await the turn of the tide. This is a fine open area with marram-clad dunes, huge open flats alive with birds and a wildness that has an atmosphere of its own. While birds are the major attraction, and these include brent, pink-footed and greylag geese in winter along with hordes of wildfowl and waders, there is much to interest other lovers of the countryside. In particular the dune system of the Snook shows the colonization and succession from open shore to the grassland of the dunes.

Though much of the area is a National Nature Reserve it is of free access everywhere. Visitors to

Lindisfarne should not trespass on farmland; there are several tracks that facilitate full exploration.

Visiting: access by several minor roads directly from the A1 trunk road between Alnwick and Berwick.
Mammals: seals, hare.
Birds: passage and winter wildfowl and waders including brent goose, pink-footed goose, greylag goose, and all the British grebes in season.
Botany: excellent salt marsh and dune flora.

MOOR HOUSE AND UPPER TEESDALE ☙ ✲

Moor House National Nature Reserve, covering nearly 10,000 acres, lies high in the North Pennines and is as lonely an area as any could wish. It was once a grouse moor, and red grouse are still characteristic birds of the heather-clad hills. Much of the ground is wet, and in places the underlying peat is ten feet thick. Here the typical sounds of spring are curlew 'bubbling' and meadow pipit 'tweeting' before dropping to the ground like miniature parachutists. Botanically the area holds the normal upland plants of wet peatland. The old shooting lodge has been converted into a field station and is the centre of experimental research.

A little way to the south lies Upper Teesdale, scene of a heated environmental conflict between the giant ICI and local conservationists in the 1960s. The plan to build a reservoir here involved the destruction of much of the unique flora, and the price paid was the establishment of this National Nature Reserve, which is full of unusual species of an Arctic-Alpine nature. At Moor House there are a number of rights of way that facilitate casual exploration, though permits are required to leave them.

Visiting: Moor House and Upper Teesdale are reached via the B6277 between Middleton-in-Teesdale and Alston taking a minor road north of Newbiggin.
Birds: curlew, lapwing, meadow pipit, wheatear.
Botany: unique flora with several species otherwise decidedly rare in Britain.

NORTHUMBERLAND NATIONAL PARK ☙ ✲

Northumberland National Park covers 398 square miles of some of the most remote land in Britain. It lies in England, but like so much of the border country it is ignored by the Sassenachs heading northward to the more obvious beauties of Scotland, and by the Scots because of its 'Englishness'. It lies astride the Pennine Way, but along one of that path's least frequented sections; and yet it is truly a beautiful region full of interest to the outsider. It includes the area north and east of the A68 at Byrness, a mere five miles from the border, from the River Rede to include the upper reaches of the River Coquet above Harbottle. It extends south-westward to include much of the upper Tyne and Wark Forest.

Much of the landscape is bleak and boggy, but there are no great hills and much is simply sheep country.

Here it is possible to walk for a day in spring and see only the occasional shepherd's cottage among the hills. There are curlew calling, wheatears flitting and the ever-present meadow pipit. Dippers and grey wagtails frequent the streams and there are wild flowers of a variety of different species. Like so much of upland Britain there is nothing special, nothing outstanding or rare; just beautiful countryside largely devoid of people save only for fellow searchers after solitude. The Romans, of course, were not seeking solitude so they built the fort at Housesteads to house a thousand soldiers and the temple of Mithras at Carrawburgh.

Visiting: use the access points of the Pennine Way or start walking north or south from the River Tyne above Bellingham. Further information is available from Northumberland National Park, Eastburn, South Park, Hexham, Northumberland NE46 1BS.
Botany: good general upland botanizing.
Birds: short-eared owl, curlew, wheatear, meadow pipit.
Other: Roman connections.

NORTH YORK MOORS NATIONAL PARK ✲

Covering 553 square miles, the North York Moors is one of the less frequented of our National Parks. If it is less spectacular than some, less open than others, it makes up for this in its immense beauty and variety of landscape. It includes a goodly chunk of the coast, with spectacular fishing villages like Staithes and Runswick. It has high moors dissected with deep beautiful valleys. It is almost encircled by the Cleveland Way and has the unique attraction of the Farndale Local Nature Reserve. An estimate found that 56,000 people visited this valley during the brief daffodil season, for Farndale is the Vale of the Daffodils.

The colonies of wild daffodils (were they planted by medieval monks?) stretch for seven miles along the banks of the River Dove and were regularly picked by visitors until 1955. By then it was obvious that the increasingly mobile population of Tees-side was going to destroy this unique site and picking was prohibited. Now the local nature reserve covers 2500 acres of the lower valley north of Lowna. In April and early May a one-way traffic system comes into operation and visitors may tour the fields (almost in convoys at peak weekends) to enjoy the magnificent sight of so many

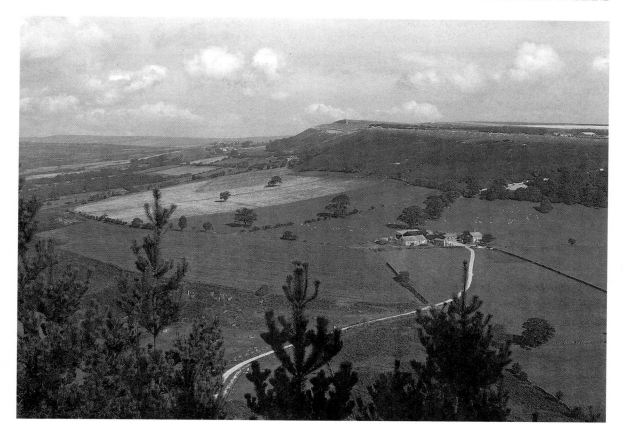

North York Moors National Park, near Helmsley

wild flowers. Visitors are handed a plan (yellow naturally) that will enable them to get the best out of Farndale's daffodils.

Visiting: Hutton-le-Hole, the starting point for exploring Farndale, lies north of the A170 north of Kirkbymoorside; for the National Park see Cleveland Way. Further information from North York Moors National Park, The Old Vicarage, Bondgate, Helmsley, York YO6 5BP.

Botany: daffodils in April and early May.

PENNINE WAY ♟ ✿

Opened in 1965, the Pennine Way was the first of the long-distance footpaths and, covering 250 miles, is still the toughest of them all. Its route runs from the Peak District in Derbyshire northward along the backbone of England switching first this way then that to take in points of interest *en route*. Along the way it scales high peaks, visits outstanding natural scenery, uses old drove roads and miners' tracks and crosses some peat-sodden moors that only the fit and experienced should attempt. The scenery is beautiful, the landscape often remote, and there are people to be met who live a life that seems quite remarkably isolated in late twentieth-century Britain.

The Way starts at Edale in Derbyshire, immediately climbs the great inhospitable moor of Kinder Scout, and continues over uplands until it reaches the moors of the Brontë country by way of the Calder Valley. It continues to the limestone and dry stone wall area around Malham, skirts the eastern side of Malham Tarn, and climbs Fountains Fell and Pen-y-ghent. Those who wish to can stay overnight in upper Ribblesdale and take in Ingleborough with its huge limestone caves at Gaping Gill, or even the peaks of Ingleborough, Whernside and Pen-y-ghent (again!) to complete the Three Peaks in a day. An old packhorse trail leads to Wensleydale.

Onward the path leads to Tan Hill and Britain's highest inn before crossing Teesdale. The waterfall at High Force should not be missed and the Way continues to its highest point at Cross Fell (2930 feet). It then drops down to the Tyne and joins Hadrian's Wall eastward and at its best part. It passes between the high-level loughs at Broomlee, Greenlee and Grindon, best known as a winter haunt of whooper swans. The Way then winds over the border moors, past the Cheviot, to finish at Kirk Yetholm in Roxburgh. This last stretch, between Byrness and Kirk Yetholm, is twenty-seven miles which must be covered in a day or with an overnight stay at a shepherd's cottage in Upper Coquetdale.

Throughout its length the Pennine Way has been planned with stopovers in mind. Youth Hostels are quite well supplied and there are a number of old inns where accommodation can be had. It's a long hard walk, and many will be content with walking even a short section of it. It also passes through some of the loneliest parts of Britain, and offers a true opportunity to think and refresh oneself. Wainwright, the guide to generations of Lakeland walkers, has produced a guidebook to the Pennine Way throughout its length.

Wildlife among the hills is generally rather scant. Meadow pipits accompany the walker all the way and wheatears and curlews are quite common. Short-eared owls haunt the younger plantations in the border country, and ring ouzel and merlin should be seen. The streams hold dipper and grey wagtail and the heather is the haunt of the native red grouse. Botanically the Pennine Way is of interest because of the variety of geological structures over which it passes. From the plant-rich limestone outcrops to the bare and uniform peat hags there is much to see, much to identify.

Visiting: the Pennine Way is dangerous and should not be attempted by anyone not experienced in finding their way with the aid of map and compass and nothing else. Walks average twelve or fifteen miles daily over heavy and rough going, and protective clothing, good boots, emergency protection and food are still not enough if suddenly you are confronted with rain or mist, snow or gale. See *The Pennine Way* by T. Stephenson, published by HMSO.
Birds: red grouse, meadow pipit, wheatear, curlew.
Botany: rich and varied communities on the limestone, poor collections on the peat.

SANDALL BEAT WOOD ✝ ⁂
To most, Sandall Beat Wood is barely worth a trip, but to the people of Doncaster it is a lungful of fresh air on their doorstep. It is small, notable for the absence of rarities, but a delight all the same. The wood was planted by the Town Council in 1810 in response to the need for wood for ships to fight Napoleon. Fortunately wooden ships disappeared from the naval scene before the plantations were ready for use. Larch, oak and ash are the dominant species, with chestnut, elm and beech close behind. For the botanist such a mixed wood with such a definite date of origin is particularly interesting. A nature trail has been laid out from the entrance to the reserve in Sandall Beat Road and the visitor is guided along to the major points of interest. In late spring the rhododendron bushes are in full flower and visitors are numerous; at other times the woods may be completely empty.

In addition to the woodland there is a small fen where the succession from open water, through reed marsh to willow carr, can be seen. Here the birds of the woodland are replaced by marsh-loving species such as snipe, reed and grasshopper warblers and willow tit. In the woods themselves a good variety of birds reflects the variety of habitats. There are woodcock, great spotted woodpecker, willow warbler, blackcap, long-tailed tit, tree pipit, treecreeper and so on.

For the botanist too there is much to find, aided by the excellent checklist published by the Doncaster Museum.

Visiting: access from Doncaster via Sandall Beat Road.
Birds: woodcock, snipe, grasshopper warbler, long-eared owl, great spotted woodpecker, moorhen, goldcrest, willow tit.
Botany: purple small reed, reedmace, fungi.

WASHINGTON WILDFOWL REFUGE ✝ ♿
The people of Tyneside have always been favoured by open countryside on their doorstep, so it is not perhaps surprising that Washington New Town should act as hosts to the Wildfowl Trust in their first venture in the north-east. The refuge covers 103 acres along the northern bank of the River Wear just west of Sunderland, and houses the usual excellent wildfowl collection. In keeping with Washington's obvious transatlantic connections there is a definite transatlantic bias. Thus hooded merganser, Carolina duck, black brant, emperor goose and other American species are the centrepieces of the collection. This does not mean that Washington will be free of

Washington Wildfowl Refuge

Visiting: Washington lies immediately east of the A1(M) and north of the River Wear due west of Sunderland. Follow signs to Washington District 15. The Wildfowl Trust is then well signposted. The refuge is open every day except Christmas Day. The address is The Wildfowl Trust, Middle Barmston Farm, Pattinson, District 15, Washington, Tyne and Wear.

Birds: wildfowl collection, waders.

YORKSHIRE DALES NATIONAL PARK ✦ ✾

The Yorkshire Dales National Park covers 680 square miles of some of the finest upland scenery in Britain. It lies in the heart of the Pennines and is roughly bounded by the towns of Reeth in the north-east, Grassington in the south, and Kirkby Stephen in the north-west. In the south it includes the 'Three Peaks'

Hawaiian geese, black swans or Laysan teal.

As is usual with the Wildfowl Trust, a part of the refuge is given over to wild birds, and there are ponds alongside the river where waders come to feed and roost along with small numbers of wild duck.

There is an exhibition building, a gift shop, and vending machines offering hot drinks.

district and the Malham area, and in the west the beautiful upper part of Dentdale.

This is a rolling landscape with moors and wooded dales typical of the Pennines. It is a gentle land, though the peak hags and bogs of the poorly-drained tops are as bleak as any could wish. The small towns are all market places for the local sheep rearing industry, and while many sheep have the freedom of the hills others are confined by the dry-stone walls that are such a feature of the landscape.

The Pennine Way runs through the Park from Gargrave to Tan Hill, opening up the landscape to the long or short distance walker. There is no better method of exploration for those seeking a day or more in the superb countryside of the Yorkshire Dales. But to those who wish to branch out on their own, the appropriate Ordnance Survey map, a compass, protective clothing and some experience can lead across fells and sheep paths where the sight of another walker is cause for surprise.

To the botanist the Park offers excellent opportunities to examine a typical upland flora, and plants associated with peat proliferate. The peculiar formation known as 'Limestone Pavement' occurs in several areas, notably around Ingleborough. This is limestone that has been worn into deep fissures by weathering. A typical flora exists including several ferns and the beautiful bloody cranesbill. To the bird-watcher there are opportunities to find breeding dunlin, golden plover, red grouse, curlew and other typical upland species. To the potholer the area is full of magnificent opportunities – the very best part of England. And to the walker the Park is simply a joy.

Visiting: several well-used roads cross the area. The A684 from Sedbergh to Aysgarth (note the Falls) is the major route, but the B6259 leads northward to Kirkby Stephen and the B6255 southward to Burton in Lonsdale giving access to more remote areas. The B6479 from Settle leads to Horton-in-Ribblesdale and the B6160 from Bolton Abbey to Kettlewell and the remote Langstrothdale. In the north the B6270 runs along Swaledale. Contact Yorkshire Dales National Park, Colvend, Hebden Road, Grassington, Skipton BD23 5LB.

Birds: red grouse, merlin, raven, curlew, wheatear, meadow pipit, cuckoo.

Botany: varied upland flora, but explore limestone pavements around Ingleborough for bloody cranesbill and various ferns.

SOUTH SCOTLAND

BEN LAWERS ❀

Covering 8000 acres, Ben Lawers is owned by the National Trust for Scotland and administered as a nature reserve. The mountain of the same name is the highest in Perthshire at just under 4000 feet, and for those with the energy to climb, it offers views from the North Sea to the Atlantic with the massive Cairngorms to the north. The reserve lies immediately north of Loch Tay. From the excellent visitor centre and car park, much of the area can be explored on foot, but visitors would be well advised to follow one of the nature trails that winds its way up toward the top of the peak, armed with an inexpensive little guide. Though there are birds on Ben Lawers – wheatear, dipper, red grouse and curlew – it is the remarkable flora that attracts the visitor. Even from the trail a few Alpine flowers can be seen, but the high cliffs offer protection from sheep grazing to the most significant Alpine flora to be found in these islands.

It is a strange series of coinciding factors that has

created the unique flora of Ben Lawers. The same (or similar) flowers flourish only among the mountains of central Europe and in the high Arctic. Left behind by the last ice age the plants died out on most other British mountains. Here on Ben Lawers the rich minerals of weathered schist enabled them to survive. So among the cliffs, where the ubiquitous sheep cannot graze them, there are Alpine golden rod, devil's bit scabious, viviparous fescue, northern bedstraw, purple saxifrage and harebell. Other and more widespread plants that survive despite grazing are Alpine ladies' mantle, Alpine meadow rue, gentians and wild thyme. Apart from such specialities Ben Lawers offers many of the other typical highland flowers, flowers that have survived the onslaught of man and sheep alike.

Visiting: leave the A827 along the shore of Loch Tay and follow signs to Ben Lawers Visitor Centre. Park, explore the centre, buy something to help the work continue and follow the nature trail to the foot of the cliffs.

Botany: the most remarkable Alpine flora in Britain.

CAERLAVEROCK ✦

For generations Caerlaverock has attracted wild-fowlers to try their hand with the wild geese over the merse – the close-cropped grassland on the seaward side of the sea wall. Later, bird-watchers turned the area into a place of wintery pilgrimage. Today the merse grasslands are a National Nature Reserve with access strictly limited and shooting carefully controlled, and the adjacent agricultural land, Eastpark Farm, is owned by the Wildfowl Trust. Thus the true wilderness of this fine spot on the Scottish Solway can be visited and enjoyed in comfort by thousands of people every year.

Two ponds and a regular feeding programme have attracted wild whooper swans to make this their Solway base. They can be watched at close quarters from a splendid hide and watch-tower. Many other hides, including another tower, facilitate views of the wild geese on the merse.

The main attraction of the area is its status as the traditional home of the Siberian barnacle geese. The birds, up to 10,000 of them, arrive in early October and stay to early April. Throughout this period they are viewable every day from the numerous hides positioned at strategic intervals along the surrounding embankments. Other geese are to be seen here as well as the occasional wild swan. Hen harriers are regular in

CAERLAVEROCK NNR

winter and there are always duck and waders to be seen.

Visiting: Caerlaverock is reached from Dumfries via the B725 and from Annan via the B724. There is an admission charge with reductions for children and parties during the season, which lasts from 1 September to 15 May. Visitors are escorted by the warden starting at 11.00 and 14.00 hours daily except Christmas Day.

Birds: barnacle goose, pink-footed goose, whooper swan.

CALDERPARK ZOO ✦ ✦ ♿

Calderpark Zoo is owned by the Zoological Society of Glasgow and the West of Scotland and covers forty-five acres near Uddingston on the A74, the main Glasgow-Hamilton road. From elsewhere, the junction with the A74 and M74 is the most straightforward approach.

This reasonably-priced zoo has a commendably strong educational side to its activities, catering as it does for the youngsters of Glasgow. It offers most of the usual zoo animals including all of the big stars – elephant, white rhino, lion, tiger, leopard, cheetah, etc. It has Przewalski's horse, some black leopards, Père David's deer and a motley array of smaller attractions. Though many of the animals breed (a good thing) the *raison d'être* of the Zoo is its exploitation of the immense educational opportunities provided by a collection of wild animals. Such exploitation, in fact, compensates for the taking of animals from the wild which is still such a characteristic of all zoos.

Caerlaverock is known as the home of the Siberian barnacle geese

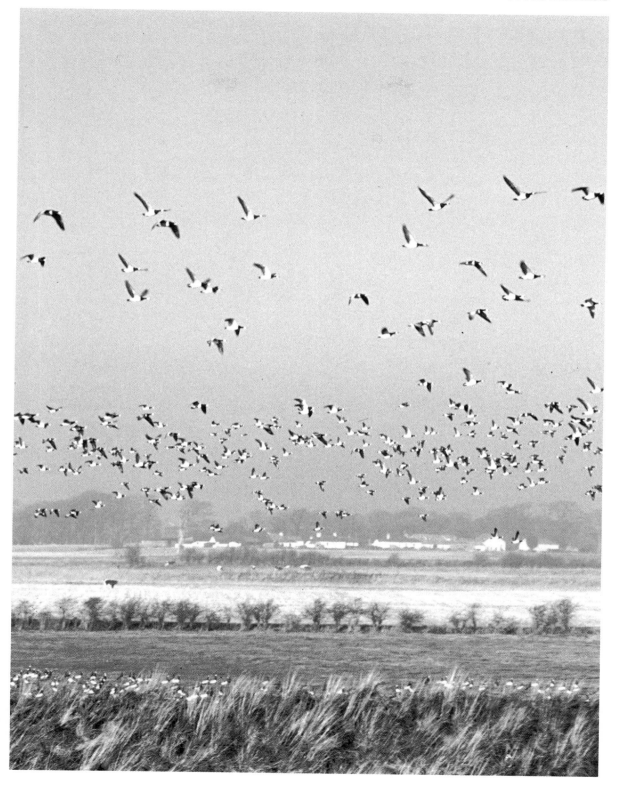

There are lecture tours for primary schoolchildren and special tours for those taking examinations. The Society publishes an excellent magazine, *Zoolife*, which is well written and illustrated, and it also provides lectures for schools free of charge. It is refreshing to see a zoo make such a point of good and informative labelling of its exhibits.

Visiting: A74 and M74 junction, thence signposts. Uddingston Station is two miles away and buses leave both Anderston and Buchanan bus stations regularly. There is parking for 1500 cars. The Zoo is open throughout the year from 09.30 to 17.00 or 19.00 hours according to season. Tel. 041 771 1185/6.

Mammals: white rhino, elephant, camel, llama, zebra, Przewalski's horse, Père David's deer, polar bear, tiger, leopard, cheetah, porcupine, racoon, ring-tailed lemur.

DEESIDE ✌ ➤ ⚹

It has always proved a difficult decision for the naturalist wondering which side of the massive Cairngorms he should visit. To the north this mountain massif is bounded by the Spey Valley, well known, touristy, but full of interest none the less. To the south lies Deeside, unfrequented and with a distinctive charm all its own. Between the two, and an excellent mountain walk for the fit and well prepared, lies the Lairig Ghru, the high-level pass that cuts deep between the mountains. Further north is Glen Feshie, less austere, with pines and meadows offering the best chance of seeing both red and roe deer.

On Deeside itself there are some quite excellent wildlife areas, outstanding among which is the Balmoral Estate, part of which Her Majesty the Queen has allowed to become a Scottish Wildlife Trust reserve. This is easily reached by a minor road leading southward along Glenmuick out of Ballater. To the west the craggy Lochnager is worth a climb from Spittal – here all the specialities of the Highlands can be found, including golden eagle, ptarmigan and blue hare.

To the north of Ballater too the hill of Morven is another fine moorland area, full of red grouse and blue hare.

Visiting: Glenmuick and Lochnagar are reached via a minor road off the B976. There is a visitor centre and nature trail.

Mammals: red deer, roe deer, blue hare.
Birds: golden eagle, ptarmigan, red grouse, black grouse, greenshank, golden plover.
Botany: good Alpine-type flora.
Other: Balmoral Castle.

EDINBURGH BOTANIC GARDEN ✿ ⚹

The Royal Botanic Garden at Edinburgh had its origins, as did so many other gardens, in the physic or medicinal gardens of earlier times. Its origins date back to 1670, making it second only to Oxford among British botanical gardens. It has been in its present site at Inverleith since 1820. The Garden is exceptionally beautiful and attracts many visitors, though the authorities are quick to point out that its real purpose is botanical research, especially taxonomy – the classification of plants. Today the Himalayan region and south-west China are its specialities and the herbarium, occupied since 1964, houses a remarkable one and a half million specimens mostly from that region. It has one of the finest botanical libraries in the world.

In 1967 the exhibition houses were opened to replace a series of ancient and outdated structures and house a remarkable collection of plants in mostly systematical sequence. Thus there is a cactus house, a warm temperate aquatic house, a temperate plant house, a fern house, an orchid house and so on. Additionally there are Victorian palm houses and an exhibition hall opened in 1970.

The visitor could easily be utterly confused faced with such a superabundance, but a sound guide draws the attention to specific plants and their biology and relationships one to another, a vast improvement over the 'plastic label search for it yourself' approach to plant displays.

With their excellent guidebook, and the series of well-laid-out paths that enable much to be seen even on a short visit, the Gardens are rather like a tamed nature trail with the Tea Room and Modern Art Gallery as the ultimate reward. Though the plant houses are of interest throughout the year, the seasonal nature of flowering plants indicates a visit between April and July; earlier for azaleas, later for lilies.

Visiting: the Garden is open to the public throughout the year (except Christmas Day) and can be entered from the West Gate on Arboretum Road or the East Gate on Inverleith Row. Tel. 031 552 7171.
Botany: huge collection in beautiful surroundings.

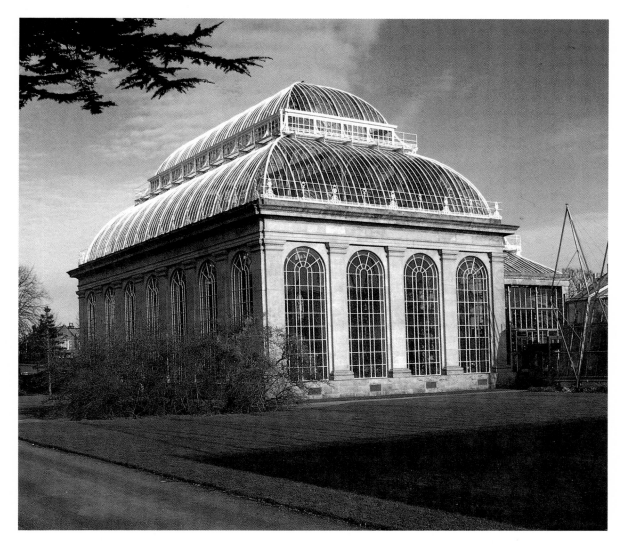

The old glasshouse in the Royal Botanic Garden in Edinburgh

EDINBURGH ZOO ✌ ♟ ♿

This is one of Britain's senior zoos and one of the best. Its animals, which include many breeding pairs or groups, are well housed in modern, light and airy enclosures. The Zoo is situated on the north side of the main Edinburgh–Glasgow road between Murrayfield and Corstorphine. Because of its urban situation it has been appointed suitable for quarantine purposes, so it houses a floating population of other zoos' and collections' animals.

Starting at the entrance there is the Carnegie Aquarium, which houses a couple of the world's turtle species as well as numerous fishes. A series of adjacent ponds are home to sealions, waterfowl and polar bear, while the Bramton Aviaries have a good collection of pheasants. Further north there is a monkey house, penguin and seal colonies, elephant and giraffe flanking the Education Centre, and various animals such as Père David's deer, capybara, beaver, pygmy hippopotamus and a flamingo lake. In the north-east are the tiger enclosures, the lion house, a very large orangutan enclosure and clouded leopard. There is an ape house, a tropical house and a house for nectar-eating birds. In 1939 three pairs of night herons escaped, and these birds formed the basis of the free-flying flock that feed in the local ponds and return to the Zoo each morning to roost away the daylight hours.

167

In the far north-west, on ground rising to Corstorphine Hill, there are Soay sheep, Highland cattle and yet more tigers. This stress on tigers is due to the success of the Zoo in breeding this species. One tigress bore twenty-six cubs and brought the Zoo £10,000 from sales. If zoos are to continue to show rare animals, then, like Edinburgh, they must breed them themselves.

The Edinburgh Zoo is an admirable institution. Its educational facilities are as excellent as its exhibits. It has lectures, guided tours, audio-guides and project sheets, interlinked with radio and TV broadcasts. It produces a ZooEd Services brochure and the thrice-yearly *Gannet* for its junior members' society. Its guidebook is full of accurate facts and marvellously useful information.

Visiting: well signposted on the Edinburgh–Glasgow road at Murrayfield, the Zoo is open throughout the year and there is a large car park. Tel. 031 334 9171.
Mammals: tiger, clouded leopard, orang-utan, polar bear.
Birds: very good and representative collection including night heron.

GALLOWAY ⵤ ⵑ ⵘ ⵕ

For those who enjoy their Scotland, but who have become rather fed up with the tourist developments in the Highlands, there is always Galloway, a place too often rushed past on the way north. Here, west of the geese grounds of Dumfries, are moors and mountains, streams and lakes and a superb bonus in the form of outstanding estuarine habitat nearby. Three major areas attract the visitor. Wigtown Bay is a major haunt of greylag geese, joined by pink-feet in March prior to departure. There is a huge flock of summer scoter, and duck are numerous in winter, as are waders virtually throughout the year. Walk the estuary on the minor road running northward from Wigtown.

Northward, immediately east of Newton Stewart, the ideal centre of exploration, rises Cairnsmore of Fleet, a superb area best explored via the B796 between Creetown and Gatehouse of Fleet. Further north still is the Galloway Forest Park on the slopes of Merrick, the highest hill in the region. Here golden eagle and red deer can be found along with other interesting birds including hen harrier. There is Loch Trool with its old oak woods as well as vast areas of spruce, larch and pine. Access is from the A714 north of Bargrennan and there are nature trails, marked walks, picnic spots, camp sites, etc.

Other attractions that may persuade the visitor to rest longer are the cliffs of the Mull of Galloway, where seabirds nest, and Scar Rocks offshore from Luce Bay, where gannets breed. At Logan south of Stranraer is the Edinburgh Botanic Garden's subtropical out-station; what are perhaps the finest tree ferns in the British Isles flourish in an extraordinarily mild climate.

Visiting: Wigtown Bay can be viewed from the A75 along the eastern shore, but is best in the west from an unclassified road north of Wigtown. Explore Cairnsmore of Fleet from the B796, but be prepared to walk for superb views from the top. The Galloway Forest Park is reached via the A714 north of Newton Stewart. The bird cliffs of the Mull of Galloway are approached on the B7041 to the lighthouse. Ask the keepers for permission to view. Scar Rocks can be approached by boat from Drummore or Port William.
Mammals: red deer, roe deer, wild goat.
Birds: golden eagle, buzzard, sparrowhawk, hen harrier, curlew, snipe, golden plover, dunlin, short-eared owl, crossbill, willow tit, greylag goose, duck.
Botany: plants of all Scottish habitats except the true Alpine.

LOCH LEVEN ⵑ ⵕ

Covering nearly 4000 acres, Loch Leven is one of the richest lowland lakes in the country. It is the most famous trout lake in Scotland, with anglers virtually queuing up for the privilege of dapping a fly over its surface, and it is also the main point of arrival for huge numbers of geese that later spread through Scotland to winter. But such bare facts do not do justice to this magnificent water. Beautifully situated in a shallow depression, and virtually ringed by hills, Loch Leven is remarkably easy to get to. Cross the Forth Road Bridge near Edinburgh and a few minutes' motoring leads directly to Kinross, the major access point. From the main A90 hordes of birds can be seen, especially in autumn when the geese arrive. The geese fly out to feed on the surrounding fields and are, therefore, most spectacular at dawn and dusk.

Despite its size the Loch is of restricted access and visitors may approach via three points only. Best access is at Vane Farm, where the Royal Society for the Protection of Birds has its 300-acre reserve and Loch Leven Nature Centre. Vane is farmed commercially, but this does not interfere with the main activity of showing people geese. A nature trail leads from the

observation post up the Benarty Hills through woodland with redstart and redpoll to the rivers above with
their panoramic views over the Loch and with curlew
and red grouse nearby. Several thousand geese arrive
at the end of September to feed on the barley stubbles,
and about 14,000 pink-footed have been counted on
the Loch as a whole. Duck are often present in their
thousands, and there are several hundred whooper
swans in winter. Numerous duck breed on St Serf's
Island, but this is out of bounds to visitors. Up to
80,000 brown trout are caught annually, with an
average weight over a pound.

Visiting: access at Kinross Pier and Kirkgate Park; at
    Findalrie next to Vane Farm; and at Burleigh Sands
    two miles north-east of Kinross on the A911. There
    is also access to Castle Island, with its associations
    with Mary Queen of Scots. For the visitor intent on
    geese, Vane Farm is the best bet. The Centre is
    open throughout the year, except on Fridays, and
    offers excellent views of birds plus interesting
    natural history displays.
Birds: pink-footed goose, greylag goose, whooper
    swan, wigeon, pochard, tufted duck, shoveler,
    goldeneye, goosander, gadwall, mallard.

LOCH LOMOND 👤 🦆 ♿

Loch Lomond has always held a special place in the
minds and hearts of Scots and Sassenachs alike.
Heading northward it offers a first taste of the

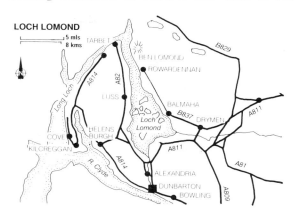

Highlands, and to the millions who live in the
Glasgow conurbation it is wilderness on the doorstep,
an ideal day's run to freshen the body and spirit. Even
along the resort-strewn western shore there are fields

Loch Lomond, a wilderness on Glasgow's doorstep

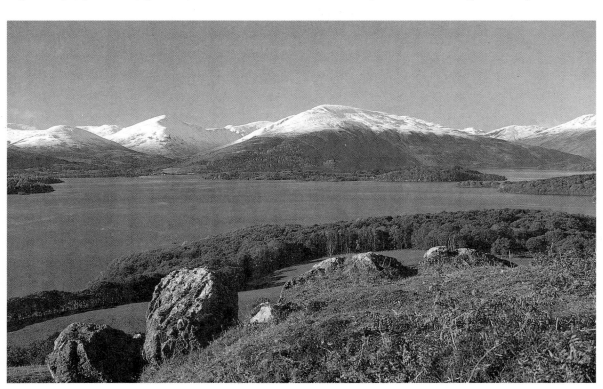

of flowers, farms and superb scenery along with camp sites, bed and breakfasts, boats and jetties, cafés and all the other industries that follow people to the countryside. In contrast the eastern shore is unspoilt. There is a road, but it does not go anywhere. Beyond Rowardennan there are only tracks, with goosander, buzzard and common sandpiper, red deer and wild goat. Loch Lomond National Nature Reserve at the mouth of the Endrick is a place where wildfowl flock in winter and where mink have become established since the 1960s. From Balmaha, a little further north, boats can be taken to Inchcailloch Island. Out of season this can be a very pleasant way to enjoy the countryside, and there is a nature trail through oakwoods full of warblers, including wood warbler. The main bird attractions are the greylag geese and whooper swans in winter, along with wigeon, pochard, red-breasted merganser and goldeneye, and in summer the typical Highland birds. The Queen Elizabeth Forest Park beyond Balmaha has good nature trails, but this is best approached from the east via Aberfoyle.

Visiting: Loch Lomond lies east of the A82 out of Glasgow. The National Nature Reserve at Endrick is approached on the A811 toward Drymen, turning northward on a loop road west of Gartocharn.
Birds:whooper swan, greylag goose, wigeon, pochard, tufted duck, red-breasted merganser, goldeneye.

LOCH OF THE LOWES 🐦 🦌 ♿
Situated in Perthshire just east of Dunkeld, Loch of the Lowes is a reserve of the Scottish Wildlife Trust and is splendidly set against a woodland background. Its main attraction to the general public is the pair of ospreys that nest every summer and which, apart from the famous pair at Loch Garten in Speyside, are the only viewable ospreys in Britain. There is an informa- tion centre and observation hide, but there is much else here besides these avian stars. A good population

LOCH OF THE LOWES

of ducks in winter includes both goldeneye and goosander, and greylag geese are regular in small numbers. In summer duck are also present, along with grebes and a variety of woodland birds.

Other interests are less prominent, though the keen botanist will find the ferns and fungi of interest.

Visiting: leave Dunkeld on the A923 to Blairgowrie, forking right after a couple of miles onto unclassified roads. Much can be seen from the lay-bys. Access to the information centre by following signs: The Warden, SWT Loch of the Lowes Centre, Dunkeld, Perthshire, Tel. 035 02 337.
Birds: osprey, duck, geese, woodland species.
Botany: ferns, fungi.

SAFARI PARK ⋔ ♿
This safari park offers good fare to those who enjoy the drive-through-Africa type of zoo. The animals are the usual species, with large areas devoted to lions and little else, but there is a unique drive-through cheetah enclosure and another with elephant, zebra, eland and a 'monkey jungle'. There are giraffe, camels, a dolphinarium and tigers, together with the usual pets' corner, a garden centre, refreshments, shops, etc.

It is all very commercial, of course, but nevertheless good value for those whose ambitions do not reach to the hills to north and south. The park lies to the west of Stirling at Blair Drummond and is conveniently placed on the A84. The nearest city is Glasgow, though Edinburgh is connected via the M9 motorway and is probably quicker to reach.

Visiting: by road on the A84 near Stirling. Usual car entrance fee includes all passengers, but there are also minibus trips.
Mammals: tiger, cheetah, lion, eland, elephant, zebra, dolphin.

TENTSMUIR 🐦
Tentsmuir Point and the adjacent Morton Lochs are both National Nature Reserves in Fifeshire, lying between the Firths of Forth and Tay. Tentsmuir itself is a huge dune system stretching from the famous Eden estuary northward for some five miles. The sandy foreshore is a noted haunt of waders, terns and gulls, perhaps outshone by the richer estuaries to north and south. There are regular 'grey' geese and seals present. Morton Lochs are small, lie a mile south of Tayport and are being restored to provide improved habitats for

birds. Winter is perhaps most appealing, with large numbers of duck, while passage periods bring many waders.

The Eden estuary, flanked in the south by the famous greens of St Andrews, is a splendid place frequented by hordes of wildfowl and waders. Being little more than a mile across at its widest point, it is eminently viewable, and a contrast to the huge Firths nearby. There are always scoter and eider present, along with many terns, and little gulls are a springtime speciality.

Visiting: approach Morton Lochs first on the B945, turning left two miles south of Tayport on a track that runs between the lochs. Much can be seen from the road and there is a public hide. Permits to use two other hides can be obtained from the Nature Conservancy Scottish Office. Continue on to Morton and Fetterdale, where forest tracks lead to Tentsmuir Point. Cars cannot enter the Reserve. For the Eden estuary, approach along the foreshore from St Andrews Golf Course, or view from the A91 at various points and especially at Guardbridge.

Birds: tufted duck, gadwall, shelduck, goldeneye, greylag goose, pink-footed goose, wigeon, long-tailed duck, scoter, eider, redshank, sanderling, common tern, Arctic tern.

Mammals: seals.

YTHAN ESTUARY AND SANDS OF FORVIE ✦

Few areas in the country can be so famed for both angling and birding as this fine little estuary north of Aberdeen on Scotland's east coast. That splendid hotel the Udny Arms not only offers the finest sea trout fishing in the country, but also publishes a guide to *Bird-Watching in the Newburgh Area*. If you want to catch summer running sea trout, fish from a boat after dark; if it is birds you are after, there is something of interest throughout the year.

The estuary is no more than a few hundred yards across, and so the waders, terns, gulls and wildfowl are all brought within easy binocular view. At high tide the birds flock to the island of Inch Creek, just north of the village of Newburgh, and they are easily viewed from the road. Redshank, oystercatcher, dunlin and curlew are invariably present, but in autumn their numbers build up and they are joined by hordes of migrants from further north: greenshank, ruff, whimbrel, spotted redshank. At this time the local

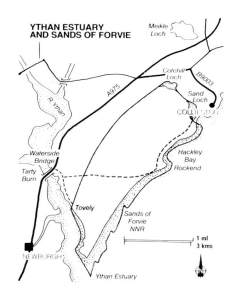

breeding terns are joined by migrants and huge numbers of kittiwakes. Naturally the pirates follow and a concentration of Arctic skuas regularly harass the terns and gulls. All four British skuas can sometimes be seen.

Winter sees concentrations of wildfowl including a build-up of shelducks together with wigeon, goldeneye and red-breasted merganser. Geese are regularly to be seen feeding on adjacent fields and roosting on Meikle Loch across the river on the way to Peterhead. Pink-foot and greylag are the dominant species, but others occur from time to time. Whooper swans regularly winter here.

Breeding terns hold their territories at the southern-most tip of the Sands of Forvie, a National Nature Reserve that covers 1774 acres between the Ythan and Collieston. A public footpath leaves the Waterside Bridge via the southward track on the eastern bank. The track is a right of way southward along the Ythan east bank as far as Tovely and the Nature Reserve boundary, but then continues to a fenced off area where the terns breed and where there is a convenient hide. Sandwich terns are the dominant breeders, but there are also numbers of common and Arctic terns, and a few little terns. Eiders nest among the dunes with over 2000 pairs in a good year, the largest concentration in Britain. In winter they are joined by wigeon, merganser, goldeneye, scaup and scoter.

Visiting: Newburgh is reached via the A92 from Aberdeen turning off on the A975. Most of the

Long-tailed duck can be seen on the Ythan estuary, north of Aberdeen

birds can be seen from the highway and from footpaths on the eastern shore through the Sands of Forvie. The Forvie Centre lies just inland of Collieston and has information and a car park. From there a path leads southwards past Sand Loch to Rockend and back to Waterside Bridge.

Birds: black-headed gull, Sandwich tern, common tern, Arctic tern, little tern, kittiwake, Arctic skua, eider, shelduck, wigeon, goldeneye, long-tailed duck, scaup, common scoter, velvet scoter, pink-footed goose, greylag goose, whooper swan, oyster-catcher, redshank, turnstone, greenshank.

HIGHLANDS AND ISLANDS

ISLE OF BARRA ✟ 🐾 ❀ ♿

The southernmost major island of the Outer Hebrides, the Isle of Barra is one of the most beautiful. In the west its long shell-sand beaches are backed by the sweet grass machair (pronounced 'macha') where fat sheep graze. Inland the hills rise green only to fall away into the more rugged and austere country of the peat in the east. Yet it is along this barren eastern coast that the larger part of the population lives. This apparent contradiction is explained by the lifestyle of the people, who live predominantly by fishing with a little subsistence crofting thrown in for good measure.

The island was formerly owned by the clan MacNeil, and it was the forty-fifth chief of the clan, Robert Lister MacNeil, an American architect, who returned to restore the family seat – the castle in Castlebay. His son is now the chief, and he returns most years from America to holiday in the austere castle surroundings.

Barra is small enough to manage a complete walk-around in a day, but there is more to see and explore, and even a week is insufficient to see it all and soak up the unique atmosphere. The hills – Heavel at 1260 feet is the highest – offer superb views southward over the last outliers of the Hebridean chain. To the east the Cuillins of Skye stand out on a clear day. To the north lies a huge beach called the Cockle Strand, where the island air service lands on a schedule dictated by the tides. The alternative to air travel is Caledonian MacBrayne's steamer out of Oban, which in summer sails into the setting sun with the islands before it. Transportation is thin on the ground, though the school bus may take a party out when not on official business, but there are bicycles for hire and walking (even on the fourteen miles of road) is a pleasure.

Birds are a major attraction, with most British seabirds seen offshore in the west. There are small breeding colonies in the north-west at Greian Head.

Immediately to the south lies Seal Bay, where singing may encourage the grey and common seals that loaf on the offshore rocks to come in close to the beach. The only other mammals of note are the rabbits, which are everywhere. For an outstanding wildlife experience the visitor must take the regular Sunday excursion from Castlebay to the island of Mingulay, where he can walk among the puffins and watch the spectacle of a massive seabird colony. At other times a charter may be arranged locally. There are buzzards on Barra, but no eagles, and small birds include wheatear and rock pipit.

The island boasts over a thousand species of flowers, though it is perhaps best known for the largest banks of primroses in the country. There are also some attractive orchids.

A variety of accommodation can be obtained, from crofts to the delightful, though modern, Isle of Barra Hotel, overlooking the beach at Halaman Bay. This is

A razorbill and two guillemots, common sights on the Isle of Barra a splendid place, well run and offering excellent accommodation and service. Saturday night in the bar is Gaelic (and occasionally English) singing time – and very good it is too.

The steamer continues from Barra northward to Lochboisdale on South Uist. Aircraft land on the Cockle Strand.

Visiting: by Loganair from Glasgow with connections to other southern cities by British Airways. Or by Caledonian MacBrayne ferry from Oban via Lochaline, an experience in itself.
Botany: 1000 species including gigantic primrose beds and orchids.
Mammals: grey seal, common seal, rabbit galore.
Birds: gannet, puffin, razorbill, guillemot, black guillemot, shag, fulmar, kittiwake, great black-backed gull, buzzard, wheatear, rock pipit.
Other: history, Gaelic, atmosphere, scenery, hospitality.

COPINSAY ✦

A small dot of 210 acres surrounded by sea and with some pretty fearful cliffs is the memorial to James Fisher, first of the modern bird popularists. To James seabirds were a passion, perhaps even more so than his love of islands, and it is appropriate that his memorial should be a seabird island in the Orkneys, a place where he would have felt very much at home. From the top of the 210 feet high north-western cliffs one can look down on row upon row of guillemots and razorbills, fulmars and kittiwakes – it is a great seabird island. James Fisher was much more than a popularist, he was the man who counted the gannets of the North Atlantic and wrote the best monograph on a single species of bird ever published, *The Fulmar*. Copinsay is a great little island, and if you get there for a day remember James Fisher.

Visiting: boat out of Skaill in Deerness, Tel: 085674 252.
Birds: guillemot, black guillemot, puffin, razorbill, kittiwake, fulmar, cormorant, shag, great black-backed gull, lesser black-backed gull, Arctic tern, rock dove, rock pipit.

FAIR ISLE ✦ ✦ ✿

Politically part of Shetland, Fair Isle is now easily reached by regular Loganair air services from Tingwall and, in summer, Edinburgh and Kirkwall. Though the

hard-working could explore its cliffs in a day, it would be better to overnight at the Bird Observatory and devote a couple of days or more to exploring what is an exceptionally attractive island. In few other similar-sized islands is the naturalist so well looked after and cared for. The buildings are modern, well equipped and inexpensive; but they are also crowded in autumn, when the island has a reputation for attracting the rarest of rare birds. In summer, however, you may share with only a few other fellow seekers after solitude. Armed with a packed lunch you can trek up Ward Hill and explore the western cliffs where the best seabird colonies are. Walk southward into the crofting area, or explore the cliffs around Sheep Craig, where puffins will stand and stare. Everywhere there are Arctic and great skuas as well.

Visiting: fly via Loganair to Fair Isle airstrip, a short walk from the Fair Isle Bird Observatory, where accommodation may be had by booking in advance: Fair Isle Bird Observatory, Fair Isle, Shetland ZE2 9JU. There is also a regular service of the Good Shepherd mail-boat from Grutness, Shetland every Tuesday and, in summer, every Saturday as well.
Mammals: grey seal, common seal.
Botany: well catalogued by the Observatory.
Birds: Arctic skua, great skua, puffin, razorbill, guillemot, kittiwake, fulmar, and vagrants in autumn.

HANDA ✦

Though small islands have been largely excluded from this guide, Handa, a reserve of the Royal Society for the Protection of Birds, is so attractive and so accessible that it deserves a place in any book on British wildlife. Extending in all to 766 acres, Handa is one of the primary seabird resorts along the bird-rich north-west coast, in Sutherland. Its magnificent cliffs hold all of the species that make Britain so rightly famous for its seabirds, and truly monumental numbers can be seen and photographed without risk. Guillemot, razorbill, kittiwake, shag and fulmar are all numbered by the thousand, and there are several hundred puffins and black guillemots. Both Arctic and great skuas breed, and there are Arctic terns, truly wild rock doves, eider and the occasional visiting golden eagle. The nearby mainland is rich in other species typical of the Scottish Highlands, giving the area a strong pull on those interested in birds. There is a reconditioned bothy available for overnighting to members of the

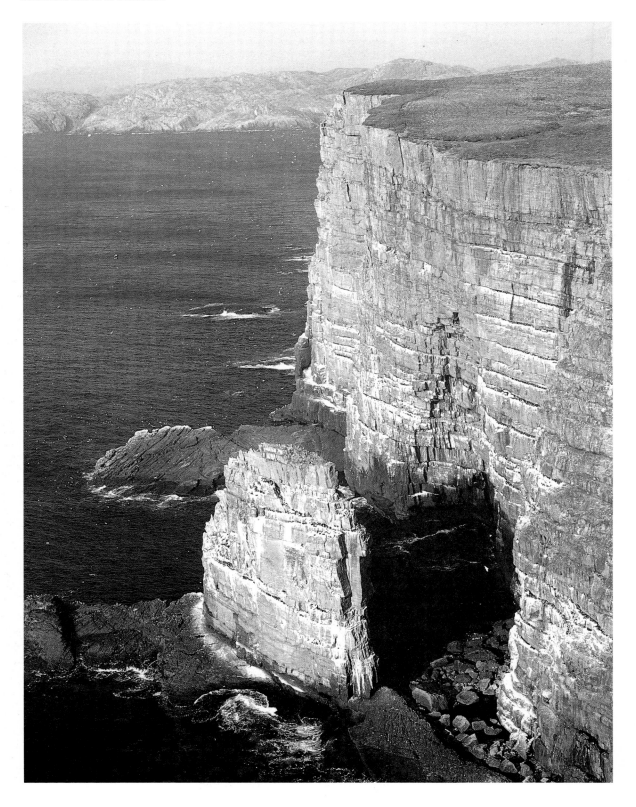

RSPB – details from their Scottish Office, 17 Regent Terrace, Edinburgh EH7 5BN.

Visiting: day visitors can obtain boats at Tarbet, which is north of Scourie, every day from 10.00 hours onwards, except Sundays. No landing permits are required, though the Society appreciates donations or, better still, membership.

Birds: razorbill, guillemot, puffin, black guillemot, fulmar, kittiwake, eider, Arctic tern, Arctic skua, great skua, rock dove, twite.

HIGHLAND WILDLIFE PARK ¥ ➤ ♿

Situated halfway between Aviemore and Kingussie in the beautiful Spey Valley, few zoos or wildlife collections can rival the majestic backdrop enjoyed by this excellent establishment. With 250 acres to drive through, it is the nearest thing to a real wildlife safari that most people are ever likely to enjoy – but it is a remarkably authentic experience. The major difference is that this beautiful park has made a point of specializing in Scottish wildlife as it was ten thousand years ago. There are perhaps rather more animals than at that time, but the species are more or less right.

European bison wander over the vast landscape, across streams and into the woodland. They breed freely and are approachable as well. Alongside them gallop Przewalski's horses, not truly Scottish, but representatives of the wild horses that did extend from Britain across Eurasia to the China Sea. They delight in the huge enclosures, romp, chase, even fight, and of course breed. Red deer wander in herds, all taken from the stock of the surrounding hills. Feral goats, Soay sheep and Highland cattle are all found in the huge grounds, and among them the discerning visitor will be able to pick out wild birds breeding. Curlew and wheatear, snipe and lapwing, red and black grouse all nest in the enclosure, and some nests of wild birds near the road are signposted so that visitors can find them easily.

As well as animals in the large drive-through enclosures, there is a central section of the park where visitors can leave their cars and wander freely among the collection of animals that cannot be left to roam. Wild cat, golden eagle, snowy owl, polecat, pine marten, beaver, wolf, lynx, eagle owl, brown bear and

The cliffs of Handa Island provide nesting sites for many of Britain's seabird species

reindeer can all be seen in close-up, but displayed in pens and cages that are large enough not to make the animals feel cramped. As a result they too breed freely. Set in magnificent country, this is truly a splendid park.

Visiting: the park is well signposted on the A9 south of Aviemore. Entrance is by car or coachload only, and there are binoculars for hire and free kennels for visitors' dogs. Open every day from March till October. Tel. 054 04 270.

Mammals: European bison, Przewalski's horse, red deer, Highland cattle, wild goat, Soay sheep, saiga, polecat, roe deer, lynx, reindeer, wolf, brown bear, Arctic fox, wild cat.

Birds: snowy owl, golden eagle, white-tailed eagle, capercaillie, black grouse, dotterel.

Other: Lynwilg Hotel north of Kincraig is very homely and Coylumbridge Hotel near Aviemore is modern and excellent.

INVERPOLLY ¥ ➤ ❀

Inverpolly, covering 26,827 acres, is second only to the Cairngorms Reserve in size, but second to none in wildness. Here, between the sea and the high sandstone peaks, is a true British wilderness, a place of immense diversity frequented only by those who would stalk the red deer, fish for trout and salmon, or watch wildlife. There is good access from a series of minor narrow roads, but the whole area is crisscrossed by an intricate network of streams, rivers and lakes. By and large access is unrestricted, save only in the stalking season from 15 July to 15 October, but visitors who intend to leave the roads or nature trail paths should contact the Warden in advance.

This wild country offers perhaps the best opportunities in the whole of Britain to those who seek wild cat, pine marten, otter, golden eagle, greenshank, black-throated diver and ptarmigan. There are also treats for the botanist at the base of the cliff at the Knockan nature trail where a strip of limestone is found, with moss campion, glove flower, mountain avens and yellow mountain saxifrage. Above all, this is deer country, and both red and roe occur in good numbers and are not difficult to see if you are prepared to penetrate the mountain fastnesses. The easiest route to higher ground is to climb Stac Polly from a lay-by on the Achiltibuie road next to Loch Lurgain. Here, on the sandstone, Alpine flowers can be found, and red deer and golden eagle are possibilities.

Bird-watchers will wish to penetrate the more remote areas of western Loch Sionascaig and the high peak of Cul Mor. The best way to reach this area is from Lochinver southward to Inverkirkaig and then follow the River Kirkaig eastward.

All visitors would be well advised to start at the Knockan Reserve Centre and Nature Trail, which is open every day except Sunday during the summer. It is situated on the A835 adjacent to Lochan an Ais, where there is a convenient car park. The geological features indicate a considerable degree of folding and overlaying, and by studying the evidence here geologists were able to find the key to the understanding of the origin of mountain chains throughout the world. Plant life is interesting too, with the juxtaposition of lime-rich and lime-poor soils giving rise to a diverse flora. The inaccessible cliffs have protected the plant communities from damage.

After a viewpoint and a geological section that asserts a staggering indication of time, the trail seeks to show brown trout, greenshank, common sandpiper, water lobelia and lesser spearwort before moving upward toward the cliffs, with their spleenworts, wood sorrel and polypody. Higher still the trail encounters red grouse, golden plover and then ptarmigan and perhaps snow bunting. At Point 12, red deer may be seen by those with binoculars. Among the heather, emperor moths may be found.

Visiting: despite its remoteness Inverpolly is not without facilities. Lochinver is a good centre, but the pleasant Inchnadamph Hotel by Loch Assynt is a favourite haunt of anglers. Cam Loch by Elphin is rich in birds and trout, and the visitor centre is just to the south. You can find the Warden at Knockan Cottage, Elphin, by Lairg.

Mammals: red deer, polecat.

Birds: black-throated diver, red-throated diver, grey heron, red-breasted merganser, wigeon, golden eagle, buzzard, peregrine, red grouse, golden plover, common sandpiper, greenshank, raven, hooded crow, ring ouzel, wheatear, stonechat, whinchat, twite, redpoll, snow bunting.

Botany: aspen, creeping willow, dwarf willow, crowberry, wild thyme, wood sage, Alpine bistort, wild angelica, self heal, English stonecrop, common birdsfoot trefoil, bog asphodel, heath bedstraw, speedwell, heath spotted orchid, herb Robert, wood sorrel, Alpine lady's mantle, green spleenwort, common spleenwort, common polypody, yellow mountain saxifrage, golden saxifrage, autumn gentian, mountain avens.

Other: there is a geological trail at Knockan with a special leaflet available.

ISLAY ✠ 🐦 ✾ &

In general, the Inner Hebrides are not a great attraction to the naturalist, which is a pity, for they contain some of the most superb scenery in Britain. For those who want seabirds the Outer Island stacks are far better, while for those seeking flowers or mammals the mainland holds far more interest. Nevertheless the island of Islay (pronounced 'I'll a') is an exception, and a magnificent one at that. It is a rich land with good grazing, is large enough to support a fair-sized town and, being open to the Atlantic, has some excellent cliffs. Unlike the Outer Isles there are some decent-sized woods as well as substantial moorland hills. It is this variety and lushness perhaps more than anything else that make the island such an excellent place both for birds and other wildlife.

For the bird-watcher Islay offers a variety of interesting species. There are good cliffs with colonies of guillemots, razorbills, puffins, black guillemots and kittiwakes. In particular the cliffs at Portnahaven and in the extreme west of the island hold a variety of species. There are rock doves and choughs too, some of the last left in Scotland, though the visitor seldom has to travel far to see these acrobatic crows as there are often a few at the airport. Also on Islay are peregrines, while the moors support a good population of merlins, red grouse are found on all of the hills, and black grouse are widespread. Even hen harriers breed in some numbers.

However, while Islay has its summer attractions, in winter it becomes one of the most significant wildfowl haunts in the country. Up to 20,000 barnacle geese — that's about a third of the world population — winter here. The grazing is ideally suited to their needs, and they fly out from their two main roosts at the heads of the two sea lochs that form a 'waist' between the eastern and western parts of Islay, Loch Gruinart and Loch Indaal. The RSPB reserve is centred on this area and should be visited. White-fronted geese, of the Greenland race, are also numerous, and up to 5000 spend the winter here. There are also a few greylags and a host of duck and waders to be seen off the flats at Bridgend.

Both native seals, the common and the grey, can be found around the coasts, and the hares are of the Irish

Barnacle geese taking off by a small loch on Islay. Up to 20,000 barnacle geese winter on the island

race. There are roe deer too, one of their few strongholds in the islands, and there is also much of interest for the botanist. Though so far to the north, pale butterwort occurs here, and otherwise only in the south-west and again in Iberia. There is an excellent flora associated with the machair, the sweet grassland that grows on the shellsand on the western coast.

Visiting: Islay is served by steamer from West Loch Tarbert to Port Ellen, and by air from Glasgow. There is a good variety of accommodation and cars can be hired.
Mammals: common seal, grey seal, roe deer, blue hare.
Birds: chough, peregrine, merlin, barnacle goose, white-fronted goose, wigeon, guillemot, razorbill, puffin, black guillemot, shag, red grouse, black grouse, hen harrier, Arctic tern, common tern.

Botany: frog orchid, lady's bedstraw, birdsfoot trefoil, wild pansy.

JOHN O'GROATS 🦅 ❀

For reasons best sought by psychologists, thousands of visitors flock to John o'Groats every year. It is a strange pilgrimage, for there is nothing there but a small village and the usual array of tourist mementoes. The views northward over the Pentland Firth to Orkney are pleasant enough, but this is neither the northernmost nor easternmost point of Britain, though it is the 'far right hand top corner' as Land's End is the 'far left hand bottom corner'. Those who make the pilgrimage are often startled by the similarity between these two outer points of our island. After the long drive over rough peat moors and craggy hills the green mellowness of Caithness comes as a pleasant surprise. The area enclosed by the Wick–Thurso road is fine grazing land with some of the finest cliff scenery in Britain. Just out of Wick, across the airport runway, lies Noss Head, a seabird cliff with approachable puffins, fulmars and kittiwakes. From Duncansby Head (near John o'Groats) the cliffs stretch southward, covered with birds for mile after mile. Just stop by the coastal road and walk over the fields near Auckingill.

To the west lies Dunnet Head, actually the northernmost point of the mainland, where the cliffs are more spectacular. Ask the lighthouse keepers to let you through a 'No Entrance' gate for superb views of thousands of birds.

Away from the coast, birds are interesting too. There are short-eared owls and hen harriers as well as curlews galore and a few pairs of Arctic skuas.

Visiting: Wick has a well served airport and there is a variety of accommodation there and at Thurso.
Birds: gannet (offshore), razorbill, puffin, guillemot, black guillemot, kittiwake, shag, fulmar, red-throated diver, curlew, Arctic skua, great skua, short-eared owl, hen harrier.
Botany: species that prefer more fertile soils.
Other: castles here and there, including one that is the home of the Queen Mother.

ISLE OF LEWIS ❦ ☙ ✿

Largest of the Outer Hebrides, the Isle of Lewis is joined by a narrow isthmus to Harris to the south, but the road is a tough climb and the two are to all intents and purposes separate. Harris is a bleak and austere place, the scene of Lord Leverhulme's attempt to industrialize island life and home of the world-famous tweed, although any tweed made in the Outer Hebrides bears the same name. Lewis in contrast is magnificent. It has vast open hills and moors where roads are non-existent and people seldom seen. There are red deer here, and much of the landscape is devoted to 'sport' in one way or another. Huge lakes dissect the region into separate mountain massifs, and rivers run their short courses to the sea. Yet despite its emptiness in the north and west this island is the centre and in parts the most densely populated area of the Outer Hebrides, and the standing stones at Callanish, second in stature only to Stonehenge, testify that man has lived here for thousands of years. Stornoway is the only sizeable town.

The rivers, especially the Grimersta River, have some of the best salmon fishing in Europe, and the red grouse attract hunters from the south. But it is the lakes with their breeding waders and divers, and the moors with greenshank, hen harrier and Arctic skua that are the main attractions. This is golden eagle

country and several pairs can be seen by those with an eye for them.

Students of bird migration have found the Butt of Lewis an exciting place, particularly in autumn, when flocks of geese arrive from the north. Barnacle geese even winter along the beaches and grasslands of the west coast. The woods at Stornoway Castle, now an educational institution and of free access, were planted by Lady Leverhulme and are the only significant area of trees on the whole of the 'Long Island'. As a result they have a host of birds such as blue and great tits, woodpigeon, jay, etc., that, while common enough on the mainland, are decidedly rare out here. For the west though a stay at Carloway enables exploration of a fine coastline and access via motorized transport to the excellent Loch Roag area. From the road toward Gisla one can branch off southward into magnificent wild country.

Visiting: by air to Stornoway from Glasgow, and by Caledonian MacBrayne steamer to Stornoway from Ullapool. Access also to Tarbert in Harris from Uig in Skye. At present there is no steamer service from island to island up the full length of the Outer Hebrides – a pity.
Botany: varied flora of sweet grassland in the west and peatland in the east. Some interesting remnants on the higher hills that escaped glaciation during the last ice age.
Mammals: red deer, grey seal, common seal.
Birds: golden eagle, red-throated diver, Arctic skua, great skua, hen harrier, buzzard, red grouse, greenshank, redshank, lapwing, barnacle goose.
Other: standing stones at Callanish, 'Black Houses', Harris tweed woven in crofters' homes, Gaelic.

ORKNEY ISLANDS ❦ ☙ ✿ ♿

A large group of islands off the north coast of Scotland, the Orkneys, like the coast of Caithness to the south, are lush and green in comparison with the stark beauty with which we frequently associate Scotland. In particular they can be contrasted with the bleak Shetlands to the north, though each in its different way has an irresistible appeal. Though a mass of islands constitutes the group, Mainland is dominant, and it takes more than a day or two to explore it thoroughly.

Almost inevitably the visitor arrives at Kirkwall, a grey stone place with a few quaint corners, an old red cathedral and not much else. The alternative is

The Italian chapel was built from Nissen huts, concrete and waste materials by Italian prisoners of war

Stromness, where the ferry from Scrabster berths, and that at least is smaller. For the general visitor Mainland offers some excellent scenery – the historic 'Churchill Walls' built between the southern islands to protect the naval base on Scapa Flow, and incidentally facilitating inter-island exploration; the Italian Chapel, a masterpiece of *trompe l'oeil* created by the Italian prisoners of war who constructed the 'Walls'; Skara Brae, a Celtic settlement of great beauty set among the dunes of the west coast, and some interesting and excavated burial chambers. The outer islands – Hoy, Westray and Papa Westray, Sanday, Stromsay, etc. – offer a sample of island life, for there are no hotels and the visitor must stay in crofts or on farms.

For the naturalist there is much else besides. The 'Moors' road between Dounby and Georth climbs high over the major hills of the island where great and Arctic skuas chase all summer. There are hen harriers here too, for this is their British headquarters, though they may also be seen at the excellent little marsh near Dounby. Here there is a good collection of waterbirds among the reeds, though Loch of Harray and Loch of Stenness to the south are generally better for duck.

Around the coasts there are shelduck, oyster-catcher, eider, Arctic tern and redshank in good numbers. Both grey and common seals can be found. But Orkney has one truly outstanding sight – the seabird cliffs at Marwick Head. There are larger seabird colonies, and some with a greater variety of seabirds, but few are so easily watched over and give such spectacular views as these. Marwick lies on the west coast and is easily approached along narrow lanes. A monument stands high on the clifftops marking the nearest point to where Lord Kitchener was killed at sea: it is also a very convenient check-

A Stone Age house at Skara Brae on Orkney mainland

point for seabird watchers. Approaching across the fields, the best cliffs lie to the left, a place to sit and wonder. Marwick is a reserve of the Royal Society for the Protection of Birds, but there are no limitations on access. Enjoy the thrill of masses of seabirds and then join the RSPB to support its work.

The other great seabird site of Orkney is Papa Westray, which together with nearby Westray is the richest by number of species in Britain. No less than nineteen species breed here, but the logistics of viewing pose far more problems. The RSPB has a reserve at North Hill with a huge colony of Arctic terns and Arctic skuas.

Visiting: by air to Kirkwall from Edinburgh, Inverness or Wick via Loganair or British Airways. Car ferry from Scrabstern to Stromness daily except Sunday.
Mammals: grey seal, common seal.
Botany: rich and varied.
Birds: puffin, razorbill, guillemot, black guillemot, shag, fulmar, kittiwake, hen harrier, short-eared owl, great skua, Arctic skua, Arctic tern, shelduck.
Other: Kirkwall Cathedral, Skara Brae, Italian Chapel.

RANNOCH MOOR ✿ ✦ ✤

Rannoch Moor, though only about eighty kilometres north of Glasgow, is one of the loneliest places in Britain. Roads and a railway skirt along its edges, but its heartland is a wilderness of moors, hills, lochs and peat bogs. To cross the Moor on foot is a considerable journey and not one to be undertaken lightly. The mileage may not be over-long, but the going is as tough as any. Here, for those who would go prepared, are red deer, with greenshank, snipe, golden plover, dunlin, black-throated diver and golden eagle. Part of the area in the north-east is a National Nature Reserve covering nearly 4000 acres. It is the only such reserve to include high-altitude (1000 feet) blanket bog, and is of considerable botanical interest. It is easily reached from the east via Rannoch Station.

In the west the main A82 crosses the edge of the

Rannoch Moor and Clack Leathad under their winter coat of snow

Moor between Lochan na Achlaise and Loch Ba. This is an excellent area, with several typical birds on Loch Ba and the possibility of golden eagle overhead. Continuing northward the magnificent Glen Coe is a bonus of unusual quality.

Yet another good area lies to the south and is not properly part of Rannoch Moor at all. Loch Tulla can be seen from the A82, but for excellent wildlife opportunities take the A8005 to Inveroran, where the shoreline is backed by a remnant of the old Caledonian Forest of Scots pine which once covered so much of the Highlands. Here red and roe deer may be found, along with capercaillie, and there are goosander and divers on the Loch. Waders on the marshes are an added attraction. The hills have otter and wild cat, though they are difficult to see.

Visiting: Rannoch Moor can be approached from the east on the B846 along Loch Rannoch to Rannoch Station, where the National Nature Reserve can be explored. In the west the A82 near Loch Ba is easily found, and southward the A8005 to Victoria Bridge is excellent.

Botany: bog flora, Rannoch rush, bladderworts.

Mammals: roe deer, red deer, wild cat, otter, fox, badger.

Birds: golden eagle, black-throated diver, goosander, greenshank, golden plover, dunlin, snipe, capercaillie, ring ouzel, wheatear.

Other: the loneliest country in Britain.

RHUM ❦ 🐦 ✿

Until 1957 Rhum, in the Inner Hebrides, was a private, forbidden island. No one could land there without permission – which was seldom granted. Even today it is difficult to enjoy the Island's delights – though for different reasons. Since 1957 Rhum has been a National Nature Reserve and an open-air laboratory of the Nature Conservancy Council. Day visitors may land at Loch Scresort and explore a considerable area without formality. Though there is no catering there are toilets and a picnic spot. As you

183

sail up the Loch there are cliffs with breeding seabirds to the south, and eiders and mergansers on the water itself. Red deer may be seen on the slopes of Hallival. After landing, a walk along the bank of the Kinloch River to the waterfall at Balach Mhic Neill is worthwhile; and the NCC have set up a nature trail along the south side of Loch Scresort from the jetty to a deserted village. There is a booklet available from the White House.

Botanists may well be frustrated by the Alpine flowers that they cannot get to in the short time available, and bird-watchers that they cannot get among the Manx shearwaters that nest by the thousand among the mountains – the largest British colony. But there is a chance of golden eagle, peregrine and merlin, and visitors will see the shearwaters offshore in the evening. A good herd of red deer inhabit the island.

From 1975 to 1985 a programme of reintroductory white-tailed eagles here culminated in final successful breeding. Despite the number released there is no guarantee that a visit will produce a sighting.

Visiting: by charter from Mallaig or Eigg to Loch Scresort. Free access over immediate area. There is a camp site (midge infested from July to September), but visitors can now stay at Kinloch Castle. Contact Hebridean Holidays Ltd. Tel. 0687 2026.

Mammals: red deer, grey seal, common seal, Rhum pony.

Birds: guillemot, razorbill, puffin, kittiwake, fulmar, eider, golden eagle, peregrine, merlin, Manx shearwater.

Botany: ling, bell heather, bilberry, bearberry, crowberry, little heath milkwort, lesser butterfly orchid, bog myrtle, bog asphodel, grass of Parnassus, moss campion, and various saxifrages and ferns.

SHETLAND ⵚ ⵟ ⵯ ⵬

The furthest north of the British Isles, Shetland is a rugged landscape that has developed at a remarkable rate since the discovery of oil in the North Sea. New villages, construction works and a new road system have all taken their toll on the landscape, but it is not difficult to get away to isolation and peace in these wildlife-rich islands. Oil business or wildlife – there are few other reasons for coming as close to the Arctic Circle as this. Yet Shetland has a mysterious beauty, a positive charm, that is most evident on the offshore islands of Hoy, Unst and Fetlar. Of course there are

wild places on the mainland, but not with the atmosphere of these more manageable smaller places. Fetlar has always been favoured. Known as the 'Green Island' because its underlying geology makes it fertile, it can be walked and explored virtually without let or hindrance. There are excellent seabird cliffs in the north of the island, where fulmars, kittiwakes, shags and puffins abound and where both seals can be seen. To get to them you must walk the shore the long way round rather than over the top of Vord Hill. This is a reserve of the Royal Society for the Protection of Birds, and the site of Britain's only snowy owls, a pair of which formerly bred. Odd individuals are still present, though males are lacking. Merlin, red-necked phalarope, whimbrel and other waders are to be seen.

On one occasion, at a small and intentionally nameless pool, a screaming mass of Arctic terns was wheeling over a pair of otters playing in the surface. As soon as they saw they were being watched they disappeared, only to be replaced by three diminutive red-necked phalaropes that swam by within arm's length.

To the north the more austere hulk of Unst sticks out of the sea. Bird-watchers flock to Hermaness, a National Nature Reserve and, with the exception of Muckle Flugga, the most northern point of Britain. Along the way they pass pools with red-throated and black-throated divers and marshes with redshank and black-tailed godwits, all to get at some of the finest seabird cliffs in Britain. Those with nerves of steel may descend among the birds themselves and get face to face with puffin, guillemot, razorbill and gannet, but it is not to be recommended without a guide. Arctic and great skuas are numerous and there are whimbrel, golden plover and dunlin as well. Since 1972 a black-browed albatross has returned each summer to the cliffs above Saito. Accommodation is at Baltasound, which can be reached by Loganair and by car ferry from Yell.

Yell is perhaps the most neglected of islands, yet in that lies its charm. There are plenty of birds, including breeding scoter, and some splendid wild country. The new ferry system connects Brough and Copister, making motorized access straightforward. The far north is worth anyone's time, especially if they wish to be alone.

Visiting: easily reached from the south by air to Sumburgh with onward connections via Loganair to all the other main islands. Also a regular steamer

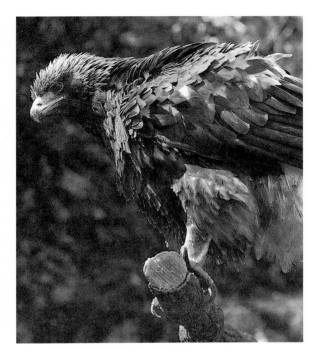

A golden eagle shakes out its feathers

service from Aberdeen to Lerwick. Accommodation is available on all of the main islands, though hotels are confined to Mainland. Contact: Shetland Tourist Organization, Market Cross, Lerwick ZE1 0LU. Tel. 0595 3434.

Mammals: grey seal, common seal, otter.

Botany: interesting and varied.

Birds: gannet, Arctic skua, great skua, puffin, guillemot, razorbill, black guillemot, shag, fulmar, kittiwake, red-necked phalarope, whimbrel.

SPEYSIDE ✌ 🐦 ✾ ♿

The Spey Valley, for long a haunt of the discerning and dedicated, has had tourism thrust upon it. The Scottish charm of Aviemore has disappeared under a forest of glass and concrete, and what were once lonely hillsides are now flocked by skiers in winter and tourists in summer. For many the area has been spoilt beyond repair, and if they seek the feel of a former age they must seek it further north at Grantown, Boat of Garten or Nethybridge.

Things are not really as bad as they sound. Most of the modern hotels are grouped west of Aviemore's main street and, with all the so-called contemporary amenities there as well, the development is confined.

Of course there are plenty of people, but they are concentrated by season and anyway tend to stick to the better-known spots. Loch Morlich is virtually overrun with campers, picnickers, canoeists, sailing dinghies and so on. The road onward to Cairngorm is full of cars, and the ski-lift enjoys a booming business. Even the very top of Cairngorm is littered with people on a hot summer day. But take an anorak, a map and a compass and walk in any direction away from modern transport and you are on your own in some of the finest countryside to be found anywhere. The traditional walk up the Lairig Ghru is as empty as ever, and if Cairngorm itself is avoided, the hills are occupied only by dotterel, snow buntings and golden eagles.

Even the lowlands are empty away from a few well-beaten paths. Take the nature trail from Loch Morlich itself and you quickly leave people behind. Instead you will find black grouse, crested tit (a rarity that is difficult to find anywhere else in Britain), siskin and perhaps the odd buzzard. In winter you might find wildfowl including whooper swans on the lakes, and the countryside is alive with fieldfares and redwings.

Different forests offer different birds. To reach Craigellachie you must pass through modern Aviemore, but soon you are among the birches and the air is full of willow warbler song. From the top of the hill the whole of Speyside lies before you, the bowl of Glen More Forest Park with the Cairngorms behind, and Rothiemurchus Forest, scattered pines that have survived the onslaught of generations. Away to the north lies Abernethy Forest and the Spey below, full of salmon for those who can afford the right beats.

Speyside offers a variety of landscape to explore; the areas that follow are highly selective.

Cairngorms National Nature Reserve

The Reserve covers 64,118 acres and is the largest NNR in Britain and one of the largest reserves in Europe. It includes most of the huge range of mountains that lie to the south of the Spey valley, though not the summit of Cairngorm itself. For the toughened hill walker it is the only place in the country where he can walk all day around the 4000 feet mark, but – perhaps more important – here he can walk vast areas of wilderness with a great chance of seeing red deer. Over 2000 acres are wooded, and a considerable proportion of this is made up of the old Caledonian Forest of Scots pines. Higher up pines give way to birches, and in the high screes and corries there is an interesting Arctic-Alpine flora. Wild cat, red deer and roe deer are widespread, and golden eagles are quite numerous.

Access is virtually unrestricted save only in Mar and Glenfeshie in August, September and October, when the red deer are in rut. The nature trail at Loch an Eilein is reached from the B970 a mile south of Inverdruie and it wanders round the Loch concentrating mainly on the botany of the area. The trail at Achlean is reached by leaving the B970 further south at Feshiebridge and following the track along the eastern side of the Feshie River. It enters the reserve at a higher level and there is a good chance of seeing red deer from an observation tower.

Cairngorm and Ben Macdui are a reserve of the RSPB covering 5300 acres of high top. The area abuts the NNR and adds extra protection to the special birds found at this altitude.

Craigellachie National Nature Reserve

This covers 642 acres, of which 250 acres are woodland on the steep slopes west of Aviemore. The nature trail leads from the modern Aviemore Centre through the birch woods, which are full of flowers in early summer. Views over the Spey can be obtained, but even better views are attainable by those who penetrate the open moorlands above the woods and the trail to the summit at 1700 feet. Though alive with willow warblers, the reserve is mainly known for its insect life, and in particular for its moths, which include Rannoch sprawler, Kentish glory and great brocade. Peregrines are regularly seen here.

Glen More Forest Park

Over 3000 of the Park's 12,000 acres are woodland, and though much of this is planted foreign trees there is still a substantial area of Scots pine around Loch Morlich. Unfortunately this area has now become a trippers' paradise and lost most of its appeal, but a good nature trail starts from the Loch, as noted earlier. Surrounding the Park the open moors are empty save only for the area around the ski-run and the roads. Thus wild mammals such as red and roe deer are often to be seen, along with blue hare and, more rarely, wild cat. A feature of Cairngorm slopes here is the introduced herd of reindeer, which have prospered and now number about a hundred animals. Visits are arranged every morning, leaving Reindeer House, Glen More, at 11.00 hours. Contact Mikel Utsi, Reindeer Company Ltd, Aviemore, Inverness PH22 1QU.

Loch Garten

After twenty years of regular osprey breeding, during which time over half a million people were able to see the recolonizing pair of 'fish-hawks', the Royal Society for the Protection of Birds finally purchased the Loch Garten area of Abernethy Forest. Now 1500 acres and another part of the old Caledonian Forest has been protected. Ospreys, well signposted and reasonably reliable, are the main attraction, but the visitor may well come across crested tit and crossbill, capercaillie and blackcock, buzzard and sparrowhawk. In winter the lochs are a roost for whooper swans and greylag geese, and up on the moors above the forest in summer there are curlew and wheatear, merlin and passing hen harrier.

Mammals, best seen in the early morning, include red deer and roe deer, fox, stoat and weasel. There are even otters in the Loch.

Visiting: there are excellent road connections both north and south and, via motorways, London–Aviemore is just a long day's drive. There are regular air services to Inverness, as well as overnight trains and car-train ferries from various parts of the south. Accommodation is plentiful and varied: write to the Aviemore Tourist Development Board, Aviemore, Inverness. The Coylumbridge Hotel is modern and excellent, and the Nethybridge Hotel traditional and comfortable. Small inns are rather scarce, but the Lynwilg south of Aviemore is good. There are camping and caravan sites and some good

Scots Pine forest of the Loch Garten area. There are red deer, roe deer, stoat, weasel and a variety of birds including ospreys

restaurants and fish and chip shops. As elsewhere in Scotland the beer is served in hotels.

Mammals: wild cat, red and roe deer, reindeer, otter, fox, badger, stoat, weasel, wild goat.

Birds: osprey, golden eagle, hen harrier, merlin, buzzard, sparrowhawk, capercaillie, black grouse, red grouse, ptarmigan, curlew, common sandpiper, golden plover, dunlin, dotterel, snow bunting, redstart, dipper, wheatear, willow warbler, crested tit, crossbill, siskin.

Botany: crowberry, blaeberry, wavy hair grass, stiff sedge, heath bedstraw, starry saxifrage, dwarf cudweed, purple saxifrage. Alpine saxifrage, Alpine forget-me-not, rock speedwell, mountain bladder fern, club moss, Alpine meadow rue, Alpine cinquefoil.

TORRIDON AND BEINN EIGHE ✟ ☘ ✿

Torridon, owned by the National Trust for Scotland, and Beinn Eighe (pronounced 'Ben-ay'), a National Nature Reserve, lie in the north-west Highlands immediately west of Kinlochewe. They have been described as the best mountain scenery in Britain: certainly their heights are among the most impressive. The Torridon sandstone has been eroded to reveal the layers of sediment previously laid down by rivers running off the hard Lewisian gneiss. The effect is startlingly beautiful. In contrast, the steep flanks of Beinn Eighe are a stark, hostile-looking grey. Between them the two massifs extend over an area twelve miles by four miles, much of it open to access by walkers. A number of routes have been established and are described in a guide-book called *Torridon*, available from the National Trust for Scotland or at their visitor centre at the head of Loch Torridon. Many of the walks are long and hard, but anyone can enjoy a few steps away from the road into these mountain fastnesses.

Though not as rich as the famous Ben Lawers in Perthshire, Torridon has an excellent Arctic-Alpine flora, particularly on the cliffs that are out of reach of the grazing sheep. Streams produce Alpine meadow rue, Alpine bistort, Alpine willowherb, and starry and mossy saxifrage. Drier areas have Alpine ladies' mantle and Alpine clubmoss. High screes boast some of the rarer plants, including northern rock cress and Arctic mouse-ear, while on the tops there are least willow thrift and the rarest plant of all, the curved woodrush.

Deer are rather thin on the ground, and the other mammals are generally nocturnal and difficult to observe. But wild cat and pine marten (watch litter bins at dusk) occur, as do otters along the wilder streams and coast. Birds are more numerous, but it needs many hours and much hard walking to find great northern diver, golden eagle (try the mouth of the Kinlochewe River), peregrine, merlin, ptarmigan, corncrake and greenshank, all of which have bred. Redwings frequent the alder woods along Loch Maree.

Beinn Eighe is, perhaps, a more impenetrable place, but the main purpose in its establishment as a reserve was to protect the remnants of the old Caledonian Forest that lines the southern shores of Loch Maree. Here, signposted on the A832, is the Glas-Leitire Nature Trail ('Coille na Glas-Leitire' means 'Wood on the Grey Slopes' in Gaelic). There is a car park, and the trail leads up into the woodland picking out various features of the landscape, its fauna and flora. It is possible to see the golden eagle, wild cat and pine marten, but most visitors will have to make do with wood anemone, wood sorrel, tormentil, woodruff and enchanter's nightshade. There are sundews, lousewort and bog asphodel all picked out with the aid of an excellent little trail guide.

Also starting from the Loch Maree car park is the much longer mountain trail. This follows the Glas-Leitire Trail up the hill but then continues southward into the interior of the reserve. Though the route is easy to follow and marked with cairns, it is four miles long and rises to 1800 feet. The track is rough and, in places, steep, but allowing four or five hours should be sufficient. The major climb is up the gorge that has been created along the Allt na h-Airidhe fault between 1000 feet and 1500 feet. Here pines cling to the precipitous slope, out of reach of browsing. Higher still the landscape becomes virtually lunar, with scant vegetation, and from the Conservation Cairn at the top of the trail, thirty-one peaks over 3000 feet may be seen. Watch for golden eagle, ptarmigan and red deer. On the way down watch for pine marten, moonwort, gloveflower and dwarf cornel. To the south is the NCC Visitor Centre.

Loch Maree also boasts some of the finest early sea trout fishing in the country. See the Fishing Record Books at the Loch Maree Hotel.

Visiting: the A896 and A832 out of Kinlochewe give access to the area. There is good accommodation in crofts at Alligin and Lower Diabaig, on Loch Torridon, and a delightful remote Youth Hostel at Craig. (But watch out for arriving, departing or

BEINN EIGHE MOUNTAIN
NATURE TRAIL

fishing, etc., on the Sabbath.) There is a camp site for single nights at Taagan Farm, just off the A832 at Beinn Eighe, and a private longer-term site in Kinlochewe. Loch Maree Hotel is typically highland, built like a fortress and very hospitable.

Birds: black-throated diver, red-throated diver, fulmar, grey heron, eider, red-breasted merganser, goosander, golden eagle, common buzzard, peregrine, merlin, red grouse, ptarmigan, corncrake, ringed plover, golden plover, curlew, common sandpiper, redshank, greenshank, herring gull, common tern, Arctic tern, great spotted woodpecker, redwing.

Botany: cotton grass, crowberry, bearberry, dwarf juniper, lousewort, milkwort, bog asphodel, heath violet, royal fern, mountain sorrel, Alpine sawwort, water avens, starry saxifrage, mossy saxifrage, Alpine meadow rue, Alpine bistort, Alpine willowherb, Alpine ladies' mantle, bog whortleberry, dwarf cornel, Arctic mouse-ear, spiked woodrush, least willow thrift, curved woodrush.

NORTH AND SOUTH UIST AND BENBECULA ✤ ➤ ✤

This central section of the Outer Hebrides, or 'Long Island' as it is often called, is by far the richest part in terms of natural history. Like the other islands it is a strange contrast of rich shell-sand grassland (machair) in the west and tough peat-clad hills in the east. While the west coast is smooth, with headlands only here and there breaking up the run of golden beaches, the east is indented with deep fjords cutting into the heart of the islands. Naturally the road runs nearer the west coast, and as it goes it flirts here and there with the divide between fertile sheep-grazed slopes and rugged heather moors. In the east the nature of the land has created a maze of lochs and lochans the largest of which are the

primary natural history attraction of the islands.

At Loch Druidibeg on South Uist, for instance, the largest flock of the native greylag geese breed and gather with their young. The area is a National Nature Reserve with a handy watchtower, but it is quite unnecessary to go through the formalities, for the geese can be seen from the roads. Just to the north is Loch Bee, which is really an inlet of the sea that all but cuts off the northern part of South Uist. Here swans galore loaf and feed – most are mute swans, but it's worth a scan for whoopers. Northward still runs the causeway across the straits that separate the island from Benbecula, notable for its airport and not much else. Continue to North Uist which, for the birdwatcher at least, is the most attractive of all. The shellsand beaches are alive with waders in season, and in summer eiders, Arctic terns, redshank and, if you look in the right place, even the rare red-necked phalarope may be found. The best place to look is the Royal Society for the Protection of Birds' reserve at Balranald – ask the Warden.

To the east the hinterland with its bogs, hills and lochs is wild territory indeed. Here there are golden eagles, red-throated divers, some duck, buzzards and many other hill birds. It is perhaps the contrast that is so exciting in these outer islands, a contrast within such a small and manageable area.

To the north lies the Sound of Harris, one of the most treacherous stretches of sea in Britain. The tide races here have seen the demise of many who have risked the crossing. The small islands and rocks are a major haunt of seals, and they can be seen to advantage from the ferry that regularly plies between Newton and Leverburgh.

There are three ways to the islands: by air to Benbecula, by boat from Oban via Barra to Lochboisdale, or from Uig in Skye to Lochmaddy. There are several hotels and considerable less formal accommodation. Contact: Outer Hebrides Tourist Board, 4 South Beach St, Stornoway, Lewis. Tel. 0851 3088.

Visiting: by air from Glasgow to Benbecula. By Caledonian MacBraynes steamer from Oban via Barra to Lochboisdale, or from Uig to Lochmaddy.
Botany: varied, with orchids in the west.
Mammals: grey seal, common seal.
Birds: greylag goose, red-necked phalarope, golden eagle, buzzard, Arctic tern, shelduck, oystercatcher, redshank, mute swan.

INDEX OF PLACES

Places in bold type are those with main entries in the text; those in normal type are other wildlife areas mentioned in Part Two.